DADDY SERIES BOX SET

ELOUISE EAST

Contents

SPOIL ME, DADDY

LOVE ME, DADDY

LOREN & NATHAN

Chapter One

NATHAN

Nathan Sanderson strode down the street, hands fisted deep in his bomber jacket as he headed for his usual destination. He was glad for the thick coat that kept the chill from sinking into his bones, although he wished he had something to stop it from freezing his nostrils. Focusing on the positive, he scented the freshness of the air; spring had arrived.

He veered left down an alley, cutting between businesses and homes to reach the exit on the other end. Glancing left and right, he crossed the road, avoiding the potholes which were more extensive the closer he came to his target. This run-down area of Cambridge was not the most lucrative for some people, but, it provided much-needed resources for him. Entering another alley, he slowed his steps, unzipped his jacket despite the weather and added a sway to his walk.

This alley was busier than others, and he nodded to several men he knew as acquaintances before switching his gaze to the other types of men. The buyers. Running his gaze over several of them, he chose the most likely of them: a guy with a balding head who was hunched into his padded winter coat and glancing furtively around.

"Hello, handsome." Nathan stepped closer to the guy, running a finger down the front of his coat with a coy smile on his face. "What can I do for *you*?"

"Um…oh…a…I want a blowjob." Apart from the initial stumbling, the words were exhaled in a rush, and the guy's onion breath bathed Nathan in eye-watering fumes.

Fucker must have just eaten. Inwardly, Nathan gritted his teeth and rolled his eyes. Outwardly, he pursed his lips and leaned closer to the guy's ear. "Would you like me to help with that?" He made sure to blow gently across the guy's ear as he spoke, providing stimulus to an already eager countenance.

The guy said nothing but bobbed his head vigorously.

Nathan leered at him, tugging gently on his coat as he stepped back towards *his* space. When he reached a six-foot gap between two wheelie bins, he paused, stepping closer once more.

"It's twenty for a blowjob. You okay with that?" Nathan never sold himself short, regardless of the degrading aspect of the position. The guy nodded once. "Shall I get down to business?"

The guy nodded once more and fumbled for the money, pressing it into Nathan's hand. Nathan blew him a kiss and sank to his knees, making sure they were on the softer cushion of folded cardboard boxes instead of the bare ground. He didn't want any more stains on his clothes; he'd learned the hard way the first time.

Nathan tucked the money into his pocket and ran his hands up the guy's legs, feeling the tell-tale tremble of either nerves or excitement. Or both. He hoped the guy managed to finish and didn't let his nerves take over, leading him to run. He could do without having to find another source of income today.

Reaching for the guy's button, Nathan popped it open and unzipped, finding the cock behind held back by briefs. A slightly stale smell greeted Nathan, and he twitched his nose in response, lifting his gaze to the guy's face. The balding guy had his eyes tightly shut, sweat dotting his brow and his mouth wide open, panting as though he had run a mile. And that was before anything had happened.

Running his palm up the underside of the guy's cock, he felt the trembling increase and knew the guy wasn't going to last long. He pulled the briefs down, revealing a nice-sized dick with a slight curve in it.

Nathan wrapped his hand around the guy's shaft, fingers meeting, but only just. He stroked the guy a couple of times to get him used to the feeling and leaned forward to lick at the tip. The guy groaned emphatically; Nathan was sure the guy would blow his load before he had a chance to do anymore, but the guy managed to hold on. Not wanting to disappoint and potentially have the money taken back, he sucked the cock into his mouth, making sure to take him as far back as possible.

The guy thrust his hips and moaned. Nathan lifted his gaze and watched the guy's head drop back, and his hands clench by his sides. He was grateful the guy didn't fist his hair. Feeling restrained wasn't Nathan's favourite scenario. Now, give him a Daddy who took control over his life and cared for him, and Nathan would be more than content.

Concentrating he pressed his tongue on the underside nerves on every lift, Nathan put his all into the task. The guy's trembling increased tenfold, then he shouted and curled in on himself, thrusting his hips sporadically into Nathan's mouth.

Pulling back, Nathan wiped his mouth, shooting another coy glance up at his client. "Was it okay for you, handsome?" He ached for a favourable response; good results created return customers.

"Perfect." The guy began buttoning his trousers quickly.

"You know where I am should you need more relief, alright?"

The guy dipped his head, turned and shuffled away. Nathan rose and dusted off his knees, double-checking the money was still in his pocket. He sauntered out of his space, a sway on his hips as he left the alley. He had to keep in character as much as he could. It was the only way to get and retain clients.

As soon as he turned the corner, he sagged against the wall, exhaling loudly. As most homeless people did, Nathan wished his life hadn't come to this. His *work* was a necessary evil. Getting food on the table—or rather on his lap—was more important than his dignity.

Inhaling a deep breath, he pushed away from the wall

and hustled down the street towards the supermarket. Entering the shop was one of Nathan's favourite moments of all: the smell of fresh bread and fruit, the feeling of being anonymous amongst everyone else, the sounds of normalcy. All the aspects of an ordinary life that Nathan craved.

He picked up a basket and, knowing he had twenty pounds to spend, chose his food wisely. He grabbed a couple of tins of fruit, a loaf of bread, a jar of jam, a block of cheese, some crisps, a bottle of squash and some chocolate bars, and, as a treat, chose two small cartons of custard and three bananas, mentally calculating the cost as he went.

Bagging his items, he pocketed the change, which would allow him some leeway if he needed anything else over the next day or two.

The afternoon got darker, and Nathan hurried to reach his destination before the rain fell; there was nothing worse than sleeping in wet clothes.

Ducking down yet another alley, he squeezed his way through a hole in a wire fence and skirted the edge of the boundary line until he reached a small shack. Nathan glanced around to make sure there were no witnesses and knocked twice, opening the door and shutting it quickly behind him.

"There he is." Robbie was a bit younger than he was, as was Daisy, but they all got along well enough to squat in the shack together. Each took turns in bringing some-thing to the group. Last night, Robbie managed to get a blanket for each of them, which was an amazing feat. "Everything okay?"

Nathan nodded at the blond-haired man and threw a wink at Daisy. "Yep. I got us a little treat for later."

Daisy sat upright, her fingerless-gloved hands meeting with a muted double clap. "What is it?"

"Ah, ah, ah. That would be telling. I got some things for sandwiches. We should be able to keep most of it fairly fresh for a few days." Nathan grinned as he crouched on his side of the small torchlit area. He rustled through the carrier bag and produced the sandwich items, hiding the custard and bananas for later that evening.

Lowering himself to sit on his pillow—another remarkable find one evening—Nathan rested his head back against the cold brick wall and watched Robbie and Daisy make a sandwich each. He hadn't recovered from his *work*. He would eat a little later, but he reached for the water they had and opened the squash; the water had a metallic taste, which the squash overrode. Taking a deep drink, Nathan felt his body relax. He knew he had no other option, but it left a bitter taste—pun intended—in his mouth. He wished he'd bought a toothbrush and toothpaste because he didn't want to tarnish his meal with this horrid taste in his mouth.

One day, he would see a better way out of the position he was currently in. One day, he would be able to use his brain to earn money instead of his body. One day, he would have what Robbie and Daisy had. He flicked his gaze over to the lovebirds, currently snuggled underneath their blankets, wrapped around each other, talking quietly and kissing. One day.

Chapter Two

Sitting in the café, sipping his lukewarm coffee, the lull of the conversations going on around him comforting rather than annoying, Loren Moore checked over the figures he'd input into the spreadsheet, saving the document. He clicked on his next project as someone dropped into the seat opposite him.

"It would be a miracle if Karen could get herself ready in time to be here." Ben grinned, rubbing a hand over his rugged, lined face.

Loren raised an eyebrow. "Well, if you waited for your wife instead of telling her to make her own way here, you would both be here."

Loren rolled his eyes at his two best friends. Ben and Karen had been married for fifteen years, and Loren was sure they would be married forever. Sometimes, he prayed for Ben's life, because every time he left his wife behind when she took too long to get ready, she threatened him with divorce, and Ben ended up sleeping on his sofa for the night. And Loren could do without it. Especially that night.

"Nah, she doesn't mind." Ben threw a wink at him and diverted his gaze outside to the car park. Loren knew he was scanning for his wife despite what he said. Ben had no patience whatsoever, but he loved the woman with every fibre of his being.

"That's not what my sofa says," Loren deadpanned.

Ben glared at him and returned his gaze to the view. "Anyway, how are things? Any luck finding your kink partner?"

"Ben!" Loren hissed at him, checking around them for people being close enough to have heard.

"What? You're looking, aren't you?"

"Yes, but I'm not advertising it to the whole city. Jesus, Ben." Loren picked up his now cold coffee, grimacing as he swallowed the remainder, hoping for another hit of caffeine.

"Well…" Ben shrugged, brushing off the fact that Loren tried to keep his Daddy issues quiet. "And you never answered my question."

He sighed. "No, I've not had any luck yet." He tried to keep his voice from sounding as melancholic as he felt. Finding a boy when Loren hated socialising was not an easy feat. He'd tried, time and again, the clubs catering for his type of kink, to no avail. Any other members he found with the same needs were either already attached or searching for boys, same as he was.

Loren could get his rocks off as well as the next male, but it was always a disappointment when he realised he couldn't do *everything* he wanted to: tucking his boy into bed, caring for him, cooking for him, being what his boy needed as much as his boy being what he needed.

His last boy had lasted less than a year. Evan had told him he needed something less controlling and less twenty-four-seven, which was a bit of a shock when that was what they had agreed upon at the beginning of their relationship. Loren understood tastes could change, but it had thrown him when Evan had done a one-eighty about his requirements. Everyone is entitled to change their minds.

Even if it had made Loren camera shy now.

"You need to go further afield. I know——" Ben's words were cut off.

"I hope you're looking to have company tonight, Loren, because this asshole is pissing me right off." Karen's voice penetrated Loren's thought process, and he quickly switched his gaze to see her storming towards their table.

"Karen, sweetheart, you know how antsy I get when we're going to be late. I needed to get here, honey. You look beautiful, by the way, my sweet."

Karen slapped at Ben's shoulder when he tried to reach for her. "Don't you 'my sweet' me, you shithead. For once, I would love for you to consider that I want to arrive at the same time as you, not chasing after your coattails. When are you going to learn?"

Loren watched as Ben grabbed her and planted a kiss on her lips, witnessing Karen pretty much swoon into him. Ben pulled back, and Karen followed, blinking rapidly. Guiding her into the seat, Ben wrapped his arm around her shoulders with a smirk on his face directed at Loren.

That smirk meant Ben had won this round. Chuckling and shaking his head, Loren switched off his laptop and packed everything away.

"You're not heading home already, are you?" Karen's soft, melodic tone always calmed him for some reason.

"Yes. I need to get a few things sorted for the next lot of work I have arriving. I've recently taken on a few new clients, so I need to get them all set up properly before I can start them off." Loren exhaled wearily, his gaze focused on his packing. If only he had someone to relax with at home. Instead, he headed towards an empty, silent house. Maybe he should go out tonight and find someone to help him take the edge off.

Loren shook his head. No, it wouldn't work. He knew exactly what he needed, and he could find it nowhere around here.

"See you soon, you two." Loren dragged his coat on, shouldered his laptop bag and leaned down to kiss Karen on the cheek before striding to the exit. He didn't want to be accompanied tonight. He would bring the others' jubilant mood down.

Buttoning his coat as high as it would go and lifting the collar to cover his neck, Loren drifted towards home. Despite his assurances to his friends, he had nothing waiting for him, not even work.

By the time he'd made the twenty-minute walk, Loren had lost the feeling in his fingers. His gloves had been misplaced at some point in the last week, and he had yet to replace them. He struggled to unlock his front door, and, once he'd entered, struggled to lock it again.

He pivoted but stayed frozen in the hallway, surveying his home. It was in a prestigious area, not extremely wealthy, but not bad either. He had bought it when property prices were low and had reaped the benefits of the choice now the market had risen. His bedroom was to the left off the main hallway, and he headed there first to drop off his laptop and paperwork; he'd sort everything out later.

Returning to the hallway, he removed his coat and shoes and trailed to the kitchen. More coffee was needed. It was only five-fifteen, but Loren felt like he'd been awake for days.

As the drink brewed, Loren thought back to Ben's words: he needed to go further afield. It wouldn't hurt, but Loren wasn't sure he had the energy. Not tonight, anyway. He was too tired of the emotional toll it took.

Taking his doctored coffee to the sofa, he sat, sipping the brew, waiting for the heat to warm his bones. He wrapped both hands around his mug as he sat in the corner and tucked his legs up underneath him. Staring at the blank TV, he tried to figure out what he was doing wrong. There must be something about him different from the other Daddies around; otherwise, one of the boys would have stayed.

Evan had been the latest of four boys Loren tried having relationships with. The first two had not wanted an all the time Daddy and boy situation, and Loren had agreed to try. Both went wrong because it wasn't who Loren was. Hugo had been a delight; he was a boy through and through. Loren had thought they would be together forever because they seemed to mesh so well into each other's lives. They hardly needed to change anything. Unfortunately, Hugo hadn't understood the monogamy of the situation, and as soon as Loren found out, he had ended things with Hugo. That had devastated Loren.

By that point, he had lost his "mojo," as Ben said. He hadn't wanted to risk trying again with anyone, but one night, several months later, Ben had convinced Loren to accompany him to a Daddy and boy night at the club. Loren had gone, under protest, and had found Evan. Evan had been new to the city and finding his feet as a boy. Loren had happily taken him under his wing and explained everything he could about the lifestyle. Evan agreed to Loren's terms and added a couple of his own, and their relationship began.

Everything had been going swimmingly until eleven months later, Evan told Loren he was too overbearing, too much, too there all the time. When Loren had asked what had changed from the beginning of their relationship to then, Evan had avoided the question.

Loren knew he could be overwhelming at times, but he couldn't change who he was. He had tried previously, and it hadn't worked either.

He exhaled, gripping his mug tighter. Loren knew himself. He needed a twenty-four-seven Daddy and boy relationship, or nothing. He'd have to live with being alone.

Chapter Three

NATHAN

The coughing woke him. He pushed up onto his elbow and squinted across the moonlit room to where Robbie and Daisy were laid. "You okay, Daisy?"

He heard rustling. "She's not doing so good, Nathan. She's burning up." Robbie's voice trembled.

Nathan sat upright, rubbing the sleep from his eyes then from his whole face. He cleared his throat and tried to wake himself properly. "Have we got any antibiotics left?"

"No. We used them when I was down a few weeks back if you remember."

"Shit, yeah. I forgot about that." He exhaled. "Okay, let me get sorted, and I'll go see if I can find something."

"It's okay, I'll go." Nathan could see shadows moving and knew Robbie was getting up. "No, Robbie. I'll go. You stay and comfort her." He stood up, shivering in the chilled air. "You know the rules. If I'm not—"

"Back by six, you're not coming back. Yes, I get it."

Robbie's voice was harsh. "You wouldn't have to give me those warnings if you didn't do what you did."

"Robbie…there's not much else I can do to get the kind of money we need to keep going out here."

Robbie sighed. "Sorry. I know. I'm worried about you. There are too many creeps out there."

"I'll be fine. I say it as a precaution, that's all." Nathan passed over his share of the remaining food and drink from the shopping two days ago. "See if you can get her to drink something. I'll grab some more on the way back."

"Thanks, man."

"No problem."

Zipping up his jacket and pulling the collar up as far as he could, Nathan braced for the cold, slipping out the door and closing it solidly behind him. The shack was drafty as all hell, but it sheltered them from the worst of it. Quickening his footsteps in the shadowy night, he hustled through the streets to his usual workplace. Stopping at a public toilet, he spent a few minutes preparing himself—some men were too impatient to be kind—then carried on his way. Inhaling deeply before turning into the alley, he altered his stroll and opened his jacket, pasting a serene smile on his face, masking his real feelings.

Antibiotics were not easily found on the streets, and he knew he would have to pay over-the-odds for them. Because of the price issue, his work would have to be the kind he refused for the most part—he had a little dignity after all was said and done.

Scanning the clients, he chose his target, sauntering

over with an enhanced sway to his hips. "Hey, handsome. You seem like someone who could rock my world." He paused in front of the guy, licking his lips suggestively and stroking his arm.

The guy's pupils blew wide, and his breathing increased. "Hell, yes."

"What can I be for you tonight, gorgeous?" Nathan could see the lust for control take over the guy's expression: the slight narrowing of his gaze, the licking of his lips, the extension of his spine, making him taller.

The guy leaned forward. "You can be the bitch who stands there and takes it while I pound into you."

Nathan bit his lip, a little turned on despite the surroundings. He loved a man who took control. He loved it more when they looked after him as well as themselves. This would be the former rather than the latter but still. Mmm. He lowered his voice to a whisper. "I am that bitch."

"How much?" The guy closed the gap and rested his hands at Nathan's hips, grinding his hard cock against Nathan's stomach. He reminded Nathan of a bear. He was tall, wide—be it from muscles or fat, Nathan had no idea—a full beard and moustache and shoulder-length hair.

"Sixty and you use a condom," Nathan replied.

"Forty."

Nathan pretended to think about it. "Fifty."

"Done." The guy shoved a hand into his pocket and fanned out some bills. Nathan raised his eyebrows at the amount he had but said nothing. "Half now, half after."

The bear shoved twenty-five pounds into Nathan's hands and shoved the rest into his pocket.

Pursing his lips, Nathan took the money. He usually made sure they paid upfront, but he needed the money too much to argue. "Follow me."

Turning on his heel, Nathan sauntered further through the alley towards the other end, which exited onto the main nightclub-and-bar-lined street. It was a lot darker there, but they'd have the semblance of privacy. Halting at a semi-comfortable perch, Nathan wheeled to face the bear.

Hands immediately grabbed his hips and pulled him close, a hard cock thrusting against Nathan. Those hands fumbled for Nathan's jeans. "Come on, baby. Let's see what you have for me."

Cold fingers pulled open his jeans and down his boxers, exposing him to the freezing air. "Fuck."

"Yeah, tell me about it. You feel amazing."

Nathan hadn't meant about the fucking. He spoke about the cold, but he carried on as if it was what he meant all along. "I'm ready for you."

The guy exhaled roughly, twisting Nathan to face away from him and pushing on his back.

Impatient, impatient. Nathan rolled his eyes but stuck his ass out further, humming in pretend delight. Well, kind of pretend. He enjoyed being manhandled sometimes.

A palm caressed his bare ass cheeks, massaging intermittently and pulling them apart. "Look at you," the bear whispered reverently.

Nathan preened under the compliment. He felt the

guy move closer, rubbing his fabric-covered cock against his crack. Nathan pressed back, moaning.

"Yesss." Hands left his body, and Nathan heard the familiar sounds of a belt, zip and wrapper. "This will be cold." Bear's voice was soothing.

Nathan's brow puckered. Why...? Oh. He was pleasantly surprised when the guy rubbed lube against his hole with a finger, preparing him. "Oh!" Pleasure, more from the care the guy took than from the situation, filled his body, and he found himself responding. He licked his dry lips as the man carefully stretched him. The tenderness in his ministrations had Nathan's emotions opening, his mind wishing for a different scenario.

"Right, bitch. Take it." The guy's tone had taken a different edge, and before Nathan could ready himself, the condom-covered shaft pushed in forcefully, taking Nathan's breath.

He slammed his hands further forward to halt his body's movement, pressing back against the guy.

"That's it, bitch. You take what I give you." The guy exhaled roughly in time with his thrusts.

"Fuck, yes." Nathan breathed erratically. If only this were real. If only this was his Daddy giving him what he needed in both ways—preparing and fucking him.

"Oh, yeah. Yes. You're so tight. Made just for me."

"Yes, I am. Just for you." Getting lost in the fantasy wasn't his usual routine. But Nathan couldn't help it as the feelings of loneliness abated for a short time. The guy knew what he was doing and changed his angle. "Oh, fuck!"

"There we go. Let me feel your ass strangling my cock, baby."

The words pierced Nathan's brain, and he felt himself careen closer to his orgasm. He was surprised—not about climaxing with a client, but that he was there so fast. "Yes. Yes, please!

"Ah, fuck. Yes!"

Nathan was manhandled backwards once more, and, with a groan of satisfaction, the guy emptied himself into the condom. Trying to move, Nathan growled, his impending orgasm slowly losing steam as he was restrained.

"Fuck. That was fantastic." A hand slapped his ass after the guy pulled out of him, Nathan flinching away in surprise and annoyance.

Standing, Nathan pulled his underwear and jeans back into place. He clenched his jaw against the words he wanted to say and smirked at the bear. "Glad you were satisfied." The undercurrent of which was 'why the hell wouldn't you let me be satisfied, too?'

"Here." The guy held out some notes, and Nathan took it, squinting down to see thirty-five pounds. He glanced up, confused. "Worth it." The guy winked, pivoted and strode away, Nathan's annoyance going with him.

Frustrated and horny as he now was, Nathan decided he may as well find another client to make some money for food and drink. If Daisy was extremely ill, they needed to make sure they had enough for her to get through it.

Nathan tucked the money deep into his pocket and

returned to the alley, sizing up the remaining customers. It was getting late, so he didn't have as much choice but saw one who resembled someone nice. Sashaying over, Nathan studied him up and down. Under normal circumstances, the guy would be his usual type. Maybe he could help Nathan *finish*.

"You look like someone who could help me." Nathan cocked his hip and tilted his head.

The guy's peak cap shadowed his face as he examined Nathan, revealing it again when he glanced up, nodding. He held out his hand. "Gray."

Eyebrows raising at the formality, Nathan shook Gray's hand. "Nathan."

"Nice to meet you, Nathan."

Narrowing his eyes, he stepped forward. "What can I do for you tonight?"

"I need to take the edge off." Gray's tone was melancholic, and Nathan wondered what he was going through to sound sad.

"I can do that." Not even discussing the price, Nathan led him back to his previous tryst's position.

"How much?" Gray asked.

"Fifty."

Gray nodded.

Nathan wasn't sure if it was easier or harder knowing the guy's name, but he continued, feeling the need to help the guy. He reached to undo his jeans, but Gray halted him. Eyes connected with Gray's, Nathan dropped his hands, allowing Gray to release his cock from its confines. The cool air was welcomed this time with Nathan feeling a lot warmer.

Warm, calloused hands gripped Nathan's hips and turned him around, brushing across his ass, making Nathan inhale briskly. He automatically leaned forward, presenting his ass in his usual position.

He heard a shaky inhale and felt overwhelmingly aroused by the sound. Nathan closed his eyes, the feeling of being wanted, cared for, overpowering his usual distance from the activity.

Familiar sounds once more reached his ears, and Nathan prepared for the intrusion. Gray pressed his cock against Nathan's hole, fingers gripping his hips as Gray pushed forward slowly. Nathan was already on the edge, especially after being left high and dry last time, but this felt…more. It felt like he was being cared for.

He bit his lip against the words wanting to escape but groaned as Gray bottomed out.

"You okay?" Gray asked, voice husky and deep.

"Uh-huh," was all Nathan could manage.

Gray withdrew then pushed in again, a slow rhythm starting, and Nathan kept his mouth tightly closed, not wanting to break the unspoken rule of quiet. Gray's hands travelled the length of Nathan's spine underneath his jacket and t-shirt, and Nathan shivered.

If he ignored their surroundings, eyes closed as they were, Nathan could pretend he was bent over a table in a nice house, being fucked by his Daddy. The dream hardened his cock further until he could feel precome dripping from the tip. He wasn't going to last long.

"Yeah," he breathed, hardly making a sound.

Gray picked up his speed, the slap of skin against skin

loud in their silence, and Nathan couldn't withhold his groans any longer.

"Fuck, yes."

Hands moved to his shoulders, pulling him back against Gray as he thrust his hips forwards but still no words.

"Yes. I'm gonna come. Yes, please, Daddy!" Nathan vocalised.

Seconds later, he felt himself falling forward and hitting his head.

Chapter Four

LOREN

Trudging down the street after having been harassed during dinner at Ben's house, Loren jumped as a guy ran out in front of him, exiting from an alley. He watched as the guy crossed the road and kept running. Shrugging and shaking his head, Loren drifted away again, only to hesitate when he heard a pain-filled groan coming from the same alley the guy had come from. Loren paused, not knowing what he could be getting himself into, but he didn't want to leave someone in pain if he could help them.

He squinted into the semi-darkness and fumbled to retrieve his phone, using the torch to light his way. Panning it from side to side, he followed the sounds until he reached a guy lying on his side on the concrete, hand to his head and trousers and underwear around his knees.

Loren was no prude. He knew the sex trade was alive and well in Cambridge but had never come this close to it. If that was what this was. It could have been a mutual hook-up.

"Hey. Are you alright?" he asked the guy on the ground.

No answer apart from more groans.

Loren stepped closer, making sure to scratch his shoes across the gravel to indicate his presence.

"Are you okay?" he repeated.

"Fuck, my head." The response was quiet, he could only just hear it.

"Sir? I'm going to help you, okay? Let's get your clothes on so you don't freeze." Loren rested his phone against his bag on the floor in a way that the light could shine on them. He tentatively reached forward, ensuring he didn't touch the guy in any way except the waistband of his underwear and jeans as he pulled them up awkwardly. He managed to get them higher but not all the way, accompanied by the groans of the guy as it was, over his ass and cock, but couldn't lift the jeans far. Loren rested back on his heels. The guy hadn't flinched at the touch of Loren's hands, which pointed him closer to the sex trade theory.

"Sir? What happened? Do you need to go to the hospital?"

"No!" The voice was adamant, regardless of how quiet the sound.

"Does your head hurt?"

"Yes. Fell."

Yeah, right. "Can I take a look?" Loren had first aid experience, but it was from over ten years ago. He didn't think things had changed too drastically.

More groans followed his question, and Loren didn't think the guy would let him check him over. But the guy shakily peeled his hands away.

Loren leaned closer after reaching for his phone. "Sorry, this might be a bit bright, but I need to see." He aimed the light to the man's forehead, finding a cut on the edge of his hairline where a lump was forming already. Loren winced, knowing the guy would undoubtedly have a pounding headache, if not already, the next day. "Okay. You've cut your head. You need to go to the hospital to get it checked out."

"No!" Dark eyes blinked up at him. "I'll be fine. I just need…" The guy trailed off as he attempted to sit up, groaned and laid back down.

"Let me help you to sit." Loren replaced his phone on his bag and shifted his position, sliding his hands under the guy's armpits and taking most of his weight. After a couple of stumbles, they managed to get the guy leaned against the alley wall. Loren fished out a handkerchief from his pocket and offered it to the guy.

"Thanks," the guy whispered.

"Care to tell me what happened?" Loren wasn't sure why he was so interested.

"I couldn't keep my mouth shut." He pressed the fabric to his head, grimacing and closing his eyes again.

"What do you mean?"

"It doesn't matter." The guy didn't elaborate.

Loren didn't know what to do. The guy was coherent, but Loren knew concussion was a possibility and didn't want to leave the guy alone. "What's your name?"

The dark-haired man tensed and flicked a frown his

way, inspecting Loren up and down, then relaxing his shoulders once more. "Nathan."

"Nice to meet you, Nathan. I'm Loren."

"Loren? Where's that name from?"

Loren chuckled. "No idea, in all honesty. My parents were never vocal as to why they chose this particular unusual name." He observed Nathan grimace again. "We need to get your head checked. I'm not happy leaving you alone when you've bashed your head pretty badly."

"I'll be fine. You don't need to worry about me. I'll head back to my friends; they'll keep an eye on me." Nathan attempted to stand, but only managed to lean forward before he groaned and grabbed his head.

"Yeah, you'll be fine," Loren deadpanned. He was not letting the guy stay by himself. He could call a taxi and get Nathan to his friends. "Where do your friends live?"

"Um…in the city centre."

Loren hesitated, waiting for more information, but none was forthcoming. "Whereabouts in the city centre?"

"Why would I give you my address? I don't know you." Nathan glowered up at him.

Loren tilted his head, acknowledging the answer. "True. But I would've thought the fact I didn't take advantage of how I found you would speak for itself."

They locked gazes, a world of information passing between them in the silence. Finally, Nathan spoke, "I share a small…space with two of my friends, not far from here."

Loren narrowed his eyes. Turning over what he knew

about Nathan so far, he presumed Nathan skirted the fact he was homeless. "Would you be willing to come home with me and have use of my spare room?"

Whipping his gaze toward him fast enough to have Loren wincing with the potential whiplash, Nathan stared at him open-mouthed. Loren waited for him to finish impersonating a fish and find his words.

"Why would you do that?"

"Do what?"

"Offer your house to a stranger?"

The heavily puckered brow made him look cute, Loren noted. He shrugged. "If I can help someone, why not do it? You don't need to worry about probing questions or me expecting 'benefits' from it. Just a place to go where you can recuperate, and I can ease my mind knowing I've not left you to die from concussion complications."

The silence surrounding them was tense, and Loren needed to move, the cold in the air making his muscles ache, but he didn't want to startle Nathan. He waited him out.

A throat cleared. "If you don't mind—" Nathan's voice cut off.

"I don't." Loren exhaled slowly, his shoulders relaxing under his thick coat. He had something he could now do to help…get Nathan to his house. Loren picked up his phone, opened an app and booked a taxi. As it was before midnight, most people were still in the pubs and clubs, so they had spare cars available quickly. "Okay. Let's get you on your feet and see how steady you are." Loren pocketed his phone and crouched in front of Nathan once more.

Sliding his hands behind Nathan's back, Loren tucked his hands under his arms and took most of Nathan's weight. He refused to acknowledge the sweet scent tickling his nose apart from a brief closure of his eyes. Then he was back to work. Nathan used one hand on the wall to help lever his body upright, and his other had hold of his jeans, luckily.

Or unluckily.

Loren shook his head to wipe the thought away, concentrating on steadying Nathan as he finally found his feet. "How are you doing?" Audible exhales and inhales were the reply. "Do you feel sick?"

Another exhale. "A little."

"Okay, rest back on the wall for a moment and breathe deeply." Loren manoeuvred Nathan until he was propped against the brick. He noticed Nathan still had hold of his jeans. Clearing his throat, he asked, "Would you like me to refasten your jeans?"

He watched as twin splashes of red appeared on each cheek, spreading down Nathan's neck as he tightly rolled his lips together. He nodded once, sharply.

Not wanting to make a fuss and show his embarrassment, Loren grabbed the waistband of the jeans, pulling them up and fastening the button and zipper. He tried to be mechanical about it all, but he loved that Nathan allowed him to take care of him.

And that right there was one reason he should not have asked Nathan to stay with him.

Loren stepped back but kept an eye on Nathan's form in case he decided to dive for the ground.

"What do you do?"

Nathan's sultry tone wrapped around Loren's brain, and he briefly closed his eyes. This was such a bad idea. "I'm an accountant." He was unable to see the expression on Nathan's face. Loren was about to ask—he was sure—an inappropriate question when he heard the taxi driver shout from the mouth of the alleyway. "We're coming!" he bellowed back.

Stepping forward, Loren wrapped his arm around Nathan's waist, gripping his right hip, and threw Nathan's left arm over his shoulder, holding onto his wrist for leverage. Together they slogged towards the street. When Nathan stumbled, he grabbed hold of Loren's hand on his waist and never removed it. Loren tried to ignore the cold palm, though it felt so right against his hand.

Loren paused at the taxi as the driver opened the door to the back seat for them. "Is he alright?" the driver asked.

"Yes. He's cut his head, but we're going to get it sorted now." Loren's answer was short and succinct; he told the guy to mind his own business.

Helping Nathan into the low seats was not easy, but they managed without too many problems. Shutting the door, Loren hustled around to the other side and got in. He reached across Nathan to grab the seatbelt and buckled him in, aware of the scrutiny his new roommate gave him. After Loren buckled his own, he repeated his address to the driver, not because the driver didn't know where they were going, but because it gave his address to Nathan without fanfare in case he wanted to let anyone know where he was.

Speaking of, "Do you need to let anyone know where you are?" Loren eyed Nathan, watching him swallow and move his gaze to the passing scenery.

"No," he answered softly.

"What about your friends?"

"There's no way to contact them without going to see them."

"Nathan." He waited until Nathan peered at him. "Do you want to go and tell your friends where you are going to be?"

The only noise in the taxi was the sound of the radio playing softly from the front and the noise of the car on the road. Loren roamed his gaze across Nathan's face as he waited for his answer.

"No."

Loren nodded once and turned to his window, fighting to keep his hands where they were instead of reaching for Nathan.

They arrived at Loren's house quickly; he didn't live far from where he'd found Nathan. Loren paid for the taxi and helped Nathan down the path to his front door, opening it one-handed and holding tight to him as they crossed the threshold. He kicked the door closed behind them and guided Nathan to the stairs, switching lights on as they went.

"Let's take this slow. I don't want your head to hurt more. We'll get you situated in the spare room, and then we'll sort out your head."

Nathan made an acknowledging noise in the back of his throat as he stared at the floor, and Loren concentrated on their destination instead of the red tinges he saw twining through Nathan's strands of lighter-than-expected hair as it fell across his face.

Loren opened the bedroom door, flicking the light and helped Nathan across to the armchair. "Right. Sit here for a few minutes while I get some things sorted." He watched as Nathan rested back, his head naturally falling to one side with his eyes closed. "No falling asleep on me, Nathan," he said sternly.

Nathan's eyes flew open, his gaze finding Loren's immediately. An expression crossed his face, which Loren couldn't decipher, but he sat more upright in the chair. Loren nodded and exited the bedroom for the main bathroom, where he kept a first aid kit and pain relief. Grabbing both, he stalked back to the spare room, finding Nathan in the same position as he left him. *Good boy*.

Loren cleared his throat at the thought and busied himself with sorting through the kit, finding the items he needed to clean the cut. He turned to the young man and, after a brief hesitation, kneeled at his feet, watching as Nathan's eyes flared wide and a flush crept back into his cheeks.

"I need to clean the cut," Loren whispered, not wanting to break the haze of…whatever this was.

Nathan nodded but didn't move.

Taking the nod as agreement, Loren lifted his hand to grip Nathan's chin between his thumb and finger. The first proper feel of Nathan's skin under Loren's fingertips had his breath catching; it was soft and cool, although beginning to warm now that they were inside. He dabbed at the cut, apologising when Nathan hissed and pulled away, but cleaned it out properly. It wasn't as deep as he first thought, but the developing bruise was not going to look pretty on such an unblemished face.

"There you go. It's not as deep as I first thought, but it's going to hurt like hell in the morning, I reckon." Loren stood and reached for the paracetamol, passing over a cup of water he'd also retrieved.

Watching as Nathan took the pain relief, Loren's heart swelled with the unexpected submission.

"Thank you." Nathan's voice was quiet, and Loren hoped he was not having second thoughts.

"You're welcome. I haven't put a bandage on it yet because I wondered if you'd want to wash up a bit before we get your settled into bed?" Loren busied himself with clearing up the contents of the first aid kit, not wanting to hover, even though it went against his instincts.

"Yes, please. I don't…" Nathan stopped, which had Loren glancing at him, eyebrows raised.

When he didn't continue, Loren asked, "You don't, what?" Loren watched as Nathan fiddled with his jacket, studying the floor. "Nathan." Brown eyes flicked up to his immediately, and Loren felt a sense of satisfaction flow through him. He waited.

Nathan swallowed. "I don't have any other clothes," he muttered.

Possessiveness went through Loren. "You get yourself cleaned up, and I'll grab you something to wear. Take a shower if you want one. There is a seat in there you can take into the shower with you." Loren headed to the door, indicating Nathan should follow, although keeping an eye on him to ensure he was steady.

Nathan nodded, feet shuffling towards him. Loren showed him the bathroom and left him to it. He strode to his bedroom and picked out some joggers, boxers and a t-shirt. He took some time and sat on his bed to get his thoughts in order.

Loren rubbed both hands over his face, resting his elbows on his thighs, before dropping his hands. He would admit he was attracted to Nathan. He ticked all the boxes of what Loren wanted from a boy, but there was no way Loren would ever approach him about it. He'd told Nathan he wouldn't expect benefits from this arrangement, and he would stick to it, regardless of how much he wanted to take Nathan down to the mattress and show him exactly what Daddy could do for him.

Pressing against his semi-hard shaft, trying to calm it, Loren took a few breaths. Once he was less aroused, he picked up the clothes and wandered down the hallway. He heard the shower running and left the clothes on a stool outside the door and headed to the kitchen to make something to eat.

Chapter Five

NATHAN

Using the bath chair, Nathan showered carefully, trying to keep the shampoo from entering his cut. His mind wandered to Loren. Initially, he wondered what the guy received from this arrangement, but the way Loren was so careful around him and focused on caring for him made Nathan's stomach flutter, and he was no longer concerned. Hidden under the stream of water as he was, Nathan admitted it was nice being taken care of. It was why he'd agreed. His boy personality loved it, which was exactly the kind of relationship he wanted to be in.

He needed to remember not to get comfortable, though. Loren was being kind, and Nathan would be back out on the streets tomorrow.

Ignoring his semi-hard cock, Nathan dried himself off, wrapping the towel around his waist and inspecting his head. There would be a huge bruise there by tomorrow, without a doubt.

Nathan peered around. There were no clothes in the

bathroom, so he knew Loren hadn't come in when he'd been in the shower. He could've put them in Nathan's room. Clutching at the knot, Nathan opened the door, pausing when he saw the pile on the stool to the side of the door.

Nathan beamed and picked them up, scanning the hallway towards the stairs where he could hear Loren pottering around. Retreating again, he closed the door, placing the garments on the counter. They were too big for him, but Loren had chosen jogging bottoms that could be cinched tighter around the waist, and it would help with keeping them on. As Nathan got to the boxers, he hesitated. Under normal circumstances, he would ignore them and not use them because they belonged to someone else, but because they were Loren's...Nathan bit his lip, his breathing increasing.

The idea of wearing something intimate that belonged to his—temporary—*Daddy* was more than he could take. He slid them on, closing his eyes and rolling his lips inwards to withhold the moan. His cock would be too difficult to ignore if he didn't calm himself down.

Quickly dressing in the other items, Nathan towel-dried his hair once more and rested the towel on the radiator. Barefoot, he wandered slowly towards the stairs, hesitating when he saw Loren ascending.

"You should be getting back into bed, Nathan," Loren chastised, indicating the spare room with his head, carrying a tray in his hands.

Nathan flushed, barely restraining the urge to say, "Yes, Daddy." But, remembering how that went earlier in the evening, he turned on his heels and held the door open for Loren, receiving a pleased look and a "Thank you." The butterfly feeling in his stomach intensified with the praise.

"I brought you a slice of toast and a glass of milk to help you sleep. Jump into bed." The words were not an order, but Nathan felt the need to obey regardless.

"You didn't have to make me anything." Nathan sat against the bed's headboard, legs stretched out in front, hands twiddling in his lap.

"I know, but you need to keep your strength up." Loren sat on the edge of the bed, his thigh resting against Nathan's knee, and placed the tray on Nathan's legs.

Surveying what was in front of him, Nathan watched as they became blurry, and he tried to stop the tears from overflowing.

"Hey, now. What's all this about?" Loren rested his hand on Nathan's forearm, stroking his skin with his thumb.

Nathan used his other hand to wipe under his eyes, brushing away the evidence of his foolishness. "I'm fine." He attempted a smile.

Loren stared at him, gaze strong and resolute. "Tell me what's wrong." His words brooked no argument, although not a firm order.

Nathan sniffed and swallowed, licking his bottom lip, debating what to say. There was no way he would admit to wanting this more with every breath he took. He went with the partial truth and hoped Loren would leave it at that. "I've not had someone look after me for so long, it's difficult to accept."

The hand on his arm squeezed, and a soft inhale preceded Loren's words, "Are you homeless, Nathan?"

Nathan said nothing, eyes fixed on the food this amazing man had made for him.

"Nathan."

Closing his eyes, dislodging a stray tear, Nathan nodded as it rolled down his cheek.

"Okay. Eat up, and we'll get you into bed. A good night's sleep will do you a world of good."

True to his word, Loren watched as Nathan ate and drank every bite. He then attached a dressing to Nathan's forehead and—literally—tucked Nathan into bed. Nathan watched as Loren picked up the empty tray and headed to the door.

"Thank you—" Nathan caught himself before he added a word that would change everything. He couldn't deal with a beating, not after Loren had been so kind up until now.

Loren pivoted around, the grin on his face matching the shine in his eyes. "You're welcome, Nathan. Get some sleep. I'm right down the hall if you need anything." With that, he switched off the light and closed the door, leaving Nathan to sleep.

NATHAN HADN'T THOUGHT he'd be able to sleep with the surroundings being different from his usual, but when he woke the next day, he couldn't remember anything after Loren closed the door. Sitting up, he stretched and yawned, then winced as his forehead pinched. He had no idea what time it was, he only knew it was daytime because the sun peeked past the edges of the closed curtains.

Wanting to find Loren, despite the uncertainty flowing through him, Nathan headed down the stairs after briefly visiting the bathroom. He could smell bacon and toast and followed his nose to the kitchen. Hesitating at the entrance, he watched Loren in motion. The radio played songs Nathan had heard when he'd been in various shops—he assumed it was recent pop music or such— but his eyes were captivated by the man moving his head and hips in time with the music, whilst moving something around in a pan on the stove.

Distracted as Loren was, Nathan took the time to study him. Thick, black hair covered his head, but Nathan noticed a few lighter streaks catching in the light, and a body that was filled out in all the right places as far as Nathan was concerned. Tilting his head, Nathan examined Loren objectively. Nathan considered him to be an average type of guy, especially if he included the dark-rimmed glasses, smart trousers and v-neck jumpers.

All in all, Loren was very appealing.

Nathan must have made some noise because the next thing he knew, he was pinned by the bright blue gaze of the owner of his appreciation.

"Hey. I was going to come and check on you again once I'd made some food. How are you doing?" Loren beamed directly at Nathan, making his knees weak.

"I'm good." All of what Loren said finally registered. "Um…check on me again?"

Loren nodded and turned back to the stove,

removing the bacon from the pan and placing it on a plate. "Yeah, I've been checking on you every two hours all night. Do you know you sleep like the dead!" He laughed, lifting a plate and passing it over to Nathan. "Brunch is served."

Nathan's gaze widened as he scanned the room for a clock, seeing it was eleven in the morning. "Woah. I haven't slept that long in a long time."

"Well, your head injury coupled with a warm bed and painkillers helped." He reached the plate out to Nathan, indicating for him to sit at the breakfast bar. "Here. Eat up."

Nathan sat, floored by the amount of food he had in front of him. "I don't…"

Loren glanced at him when he didn't continue. "Don't what?"

"I don't know if I'm going to be able to eat all this."

Loren smiled. "Eat what you can. But you need to keep your energy up." Loren brought over his plate, which had half the amount of food on it.

Half-wondering why he needed high energy levels, Nathan ate the pancakes, bacon, beans and toast. He had not eaten food like that in a long time. The thought reminded him of Robbie and Daisy. They were probably really worried about him. He hoped Daisy wasn't too sick. He felt bad for not taking any medication back to them, but he knew it couldn't be helped.

"What's wrong?" Loren reached across the space and rested his hand over the top of Nathan's.

Nathan glanced at him and back to the plate. "My friends are likely to be worried about me." He remembered something Loren had said earlier in their conversation and frowned over at Loren. "Why did you check on me every two hours last night?"

Loren's eyebrows rose. "You have a head injury; I needed to be sure you were still breathing whilst in my care."

Mouth falling open, Nathan apologised, "I'm sorry. I never thought about you having to do that. You must be knackered." He put his cutlery down and stood. "I'll get out of your way, and you can get some more rest."

"Sit."

He was sat back in his seat before he'd consciously registered the order. He bit his lip as he stared at Loren.

"Now, firstly, you don't need to be sorry. I was happy to do it. It was more for my peace of mind than anything else. I'm sorry if you feel I intruded on your space, but I had to be sure you were okay."

"No——"

"I should have told you I would be doing it. Although I don't think it mattered because you were delirious every time I woke you." Loren smirked. "It was cute."

"I don't remember waking up at all."

"You were well gone. An alarm right by your ear wouldn't have woken you." Loren snickered.

Nathan flushed. "Sorry. I was comfortable."

Loren's smile softened. "I'm glad." He picked up his fork and prepared to eat again. "Secondly, you don't need to get out of my way. You are welcome to stay for as long as you need to."

Leaving Nathan with those words, Loren shovelled

some food into his mouth, gaze fixed on his plate, leaving Nathan stunned.

"Wha–?" Nathan inhaled, gaze roaming the space in front of him. He couldn't understand why this stranger offered him the room to stay in. He would have loved to accept it, but Nathan hated being a burden. "Thank you for the offer, but I'm fine."

Loren nodded slowly but didn't reply, just carried on eating.

Nathan wasn't sure what to say, so he picked up his cutlery and finished off his food. And he was immensely glad he had when Loren gifted him with a grin which lit up the house.

"I've washed and dried your clothes. I thought it would be better to get the dirt off the knees of your jeans rather than let it dry on." Loren picked up the plates and moved back to the kitchen area, placing them in the sink. "Can I have another check of your head?"

"Sure."

Loren stepped to his side, and Nathan twisted on the seat until they were facing each other. Carefully, Loren reached up and peeled off the plaster. "It looks okay, actually. The bruise is nasty, but it doesn't take away from your charm."

Nathan tried to prevent his heart from galloping out of his chest and into the hands of the man in front of him. His whole body flushed under the scrutiny of this stranger, but he couldn't stop the feelings brewing up. He wished Loren could be his Daddy, and he had no idea if Loren knew what a Daddy was, let alone was interested in him that way. He needed to get out of there.

Loren stepped back, and Nathan missed his nearness. "Sorry, I shouldn't have said that. I was trying to make you laugh."

Frowning, Nathan eyed Loren, recalling what he'd said, he flushed again. "It's fine."

"Right. I have to go to work." Nathan's heart fell at his words. He watched as Loren went to the front door, reached for something out of the tray on the entrance table and strolled back to him. Loren held out his hand. "Here is a spare key. Make yourself comfortable and get some more rest. I'm not sure exactly what time I'll be back, but I'll bring some food with me."

Shaking his head, Nathan stood. "I don't need a key. I'll get ready to leave now."

"No. You need more rest before you head out into this weather."

"I've been in worse."

"That may be the case, but I would like you to stay out of the rain while your head is healing." Loren's gaze hooked him in.

Nathan worried his bottom lip, torn between being warm and sheltered, and not being a burden.

"It's not up for debate." Loren pushed the key into his palm. "In case you need it. At any time. Now or the future."

"But—"

Loren silenced him with a finger to his lips. "No, Nathan. Rest, relax, eat, sleep. I will be back later."

Nathan lowered his gaze to the floor, nodding slowly, feeling every slide of Loren's finger against his lips and trying not to react. Or at least, trying not to let his body show how he wanted to react.

Loren shuffled away. Nathan was frozen to the spot until he heard the front door close behind Loren. He sank into the seat he had previously occupied and stared around the house. Overwhelmed by the magnitude of the gift Loren had given him, he couldn't do anything but think over their entire interaction since the previous night.

Now that he was alone and somewhat rested, he could see Loren being the perfect Daddy for him. But there was no way Nathan would bring it up into the conversation. No way at all. That's the first way to get yourself kicked out—as the prior incident highlighted.

But it didn't stop Nathan from wanting Loren with a fierce ache. Nathan stood on shaky knees, deciding he would enjoy a peaceful day.

Several hours later, after a small lunch, which was a feast to him, he elected to shower. Two showers in less than twenty-four hours was a record for him, but he would enjoy every minute of it before he had to go back out there.

Flicking the shower to hot, Nathan stripped out of the clothes, resting them on the counter to wear again afterwards. It might seem stupid to put clothes on he'd worn before the shower, but he was used to being in clothes with several days' dirt on them. He didn't want to rifle through Loren's stuff for more, and Loren hadn't told him where he'd put his newly cleaned clothes.

Nathan stood under the spray, groaning with the luxury of hot water provided at pressure. It soothed his muscles more than anything else. Well, almost anything else. With that in mind, his cock hardened. Rubbing soap over his body in leisurely strokes heightened his arousal. He slid a finger across a nipple, dropping his head back with the stiffening of his already hard shaft. His hands smoothed over his slick body, his palms caressing his nubs each time he passed, getting closer and closer to his target.

"Fuck," he breathed. When he finally circled the base of his cock, he squeezed, staving off the threatening orgasm. Nathan rested one palm against the tiled wall, shifted to let the water beat onto his back and stroked his other hand up to the head of his cock. Using the tips of his finger, he teased his head repeatedly before sliding his fingers around to grasp himself then he slid them down his cock. His knees trembled with the pleasure streaming through his body, and he knew he wouldn't be able to hold back much longer.

Sliding his whole palm around his cock, he stroked in earnest, his mind taking him to the one thing he knew he couldn't have but wanted all the same. Loren—his Daddy—behind him, allowing Nathan the ecstasy of Loren's hands on his cock, giving him pleasure.

Permitting him to come.

"Fuck! Yes! Ah, god, yes!"

Nathan painted the tile with his release, barely keeping himself upright with the strength of it. Panting heavily, he rested his head against the wall.

Chapter Six

LOREN

Loren entered the house, hoping to find Nathan in residence, although his head told him Nathan had gone. He stood in the hallway, listening, his whole body relaxing at the sound of the shower. Exhaling softly, he closed his eyes briefly, nodded and, balancing the bags in his arms, strode to the kitchen.

He'd picked up Chinese on the way home, and not knowing what Nathan enjoyed, he'd bought a variety. Setting it up on the table with plates and cutlery, he ascended the stairs to tell Nathan the food was ready, but his feet froze on the top step when the sounds of heavy breathing, curse words and pleasurable sounds filtered through the closed door.

Inhaling roughly, it took everything in him to turn around and go back to the kitchen. He'd managed to stay at the café a lot longer than he thought he would, but he was home earlier than he usually as it was only three-thirty. Loren needed to ignore what he'd heard and carry on as normal.

Easier said than done when the man in question entered the room with a deer in headlights expression. Schooling his features, Loren smiled. "I brought Chinese. Hope you like it."

Nathan swallowed, then nodded.

"I think tonight we should put on a movie and eat Chinese. What do you think?" Loren was trying to keep Nathan here; he knew he was. He also knew Nathan would have to leave at some point, but Loren wasn't ready for it to be now. He'd figure out some way of keeping Nathan here for another day, at least.

"Sounds good," came the quiet reply.

"Come, choose what you want, and I'll get the trays. We can eat in the living room." Loren indicated the food, turning his back to open the cupboard for the lap trays he often used when he was on his own. When he faced Nathan again, it was to find him hovering over the dishes, not having chosen anything. "Do you not like them?" Loren was worried because Nathan had been on the street that his taste buds had changed.

"I…" Nathan swallowed audibly. "I wasn't sure what I could have."

Inwardly, Loren preened at the idea Nathan needed reassurance from him. Outwardly, he smiled. "Whatever you want—" He cut off his final words, *sweet boy*.

Biting his lip, Nathan took a small sample of each dish, which was not close to enough for him, but Loren would rectify it later. He watched Nathan's movements to determine which ones he enjoyed best and would fix him another plate. Loren had a strong need to take care of him while he was here.

The thought soured his mood some. He created his plate and directed Nathan to the living room. "What would you like to watch?"

"Anything. I'm not up on new films. You pick."

Loren didn't like the reminder Nathan hadn't had the luxuries he was entitled to. He picked a comedy with some action in it as well.

They settled on the two-seater sofa, close but not close enough according to Loren's mind. Loren kept his awareness on Nathan throughout the first part of the film, though. After around half an hour, Loren stood, gathering the plates. "I'm going to get a drink. Keep watching, I'll be back in a few."

He stalked to the kitchen. First, he made a cup of tea for himself, which he added to the tray with a couple of bottles of water and a glass of milk, then he made Nathan another plate of food. He stood at the island counter, breathing deeply several times, trying to brush away the feeling of rightness permeating the air. It wasn't an easy situation to be in, and he had no idea how to navigate his way through the maze. He'd love to see where this could go, but how could he bring up the fact he was a Daddy. Nobody outside of the clubs had ever heard about it, except obviously Ben.

Taking a final breath, Loren carted the tray back to the living room, finding Nathan sitting with his legs tucked underneath him.

"Are you cold?" Loren asked, frowning.

"A little."

Loren placed the tray on the coffee table and grabbed the throw from the armchair. He laid it over Nathan's legs, and, asking him to lift his arms, tucked it around his torso. Turning back to the table, he reached for the plate of food and passed it over, resting the cup of milk on the small side table next to where Nathan sat.

"What—?" Nathan's puckered brow expressed his confusion.

"I thought you might be hungry. There's plenty left." Loren sat himself back on his side of the sofa, ignoring the scrutiny Nathan gave him and drank his tea. Out of the corner of his eye, he saw Nathan hesitate then dig into the food. Loren hid his grin in his cup.

By the time the film had finished, Nathan was fast asleep, neck tilted at the most uncomfortable angle. Loren knew what he wanted to do—carry him to bed—but he needed to try and wake him instead.

"Nathan?" Loren shook the boy's shoulder. All he received was a slight change of position. He hadn't been joking when he'd told Nathan he slept like the dead; apparently, this wouldn't be any different. Loren would get his wish after all.

Standing, he gently pulled the throw off, discarding it into his empty seat, and, for a moment, studied the enigma that was Nathan. Smiling gently, he reached down, sliding one hand beneath his knees and the other around his back.

As Loren pulled Nathan against him, Nathan rested his head on his shoulder, making a snuffling noise into his neck. Loren's heart grew more. Gently shifting Nathan closer, Loren drifted towards the stairs. As light as

Nathan was, Loren would have no problem climbing them. He took his time, wanting to keep Nathan in his arms as long as possible. Loren laid Nathan on the soft mattress, lifting the duvet from beneath to cover him. He crouched next to the bed, watching as Nathan shifted, clutching the pillow closer and snuggling down.

Loren stayed there, listening to Nathan's breathing and reached a hand forward to brush gently at his hair. Pulling back once more, Loren rubbed a hand across his mouth, hiding his frown. He wanted nothing more than to be able to keep Nathan. Not in the kidnapping sense, but to care for him…feed him…love him.

He watched Nathan for a few more breaths, rising with reluctance. Standing in the open doorway, he glanced back, his heart overwhelmed with the emotion rising towards this…boy…after such a short time. Sighing, he closed the door and wandered back to the living room, cleaning up their dishes and taking them to the kitchen. His mouth turned up at the corners when he realised Nathan had cleared his plate the second time and drank all the milk.

Setting the kitchen to rights, the dishwasher rumbling in the background, he grabbed his work bag and settled himself at the table. There was no way he'd be able to sleep right at that moment, and the usual monotony of his job should be able to take his mind off the dilemma he found himself in.

LOREN ENTERED the house to an eerie silence, his heart hammering once more at the thought Nathan might have left. His bag fell softly to the floor as his shoulders dropped. That morning had started with an apology from Nathan for staying another night when he'd planned on heading out. Loren had reassured him he was welcome to stay as long as he needed to, as Loren had told him previously. Nathan had seemed unsure, and Loren had sweetened the deal by enticing Nathan with a home-cooked meal that night. By the time Loren had left for work—at the library, this time—he'd persuaded Nathan to stay until after they'd eaten at least.

Or so he'd thought.

He climbed the stairs with leaden feet, not wanting to see the proof of the emptiness of the house but needing to all the same. He headed towards the spare room, halting when a sound caught his attention. Spinning his head towards the bathroom, Loren paused, listening for more sounds. When another small noise sounded, Loren changed direction. He stood outside the bathroom door, hearing heavy breathing and movement inside.

Heart beating rapidly, his breathing increased as he connected what he heard with the images they could represent. He'd ignored hearing Nathan masturbate the previous day, but he was too close to leave now. Not in control of his movements at that point, Loren leaned forward. The sounds intensified, words becoming more distinguishable, shocking him with their content.

"Fuck, Daddy. Yes, that's it. Harder, please, Daddy, harder!" Nathan's voice was heavy with arousal, and

Loren could imagine the expression of ecstasy on his face.

He leaned his forehead against the door, trying to curb his arousal, though, his cock was more than evident in his trousers. He pressed a palm against it, trying to ease the pressure, with the sounds of pleasure heightening on the other side of the door.

As he did, the door shifted and swung open, Loren just stopping himself falling inside.

His gaze landed on a vision that would forever be etched into his memory.

Nathan kneeled in the empty bath, naked, and fucking himself on a dildo. *Loren's* dildo. The one which can be stuck to certain surfaces to give the user a better experience.

"Fuck," he breathed, gaze locked with Nathan's movements.

Nathan's gaze flicked to his, his eyes widening then narrowing. Loren wondered why, until he heard it, "Yes, Daddy. Fuck, yes!" Nathan's cry of release reverberated around the tiled room, and Loren wanted to hear the sound forever. He watched as Nathan's release painted the bath and Nathan's hand, which had been wrapped around his thick cock.

Once the sound died down, the only thing Loren could hear was their united breathing. Gaze locked with Nathan's, Loren took a chance.

"Did I say you could come?" Silence greeted his words.

Loren backed out of the door until Nathan whispered, "Sorry, Daddy."

Breathing a sigh of relief, Loren let his Daddy personality take control. "Get dried and wait in your bedroom." Loren left to retrieve the clothes he'd bought Nathan the previous day. And to calm down a little until he faced Nathan again. He noticed the top drawer of his chest was cracked open and understanding came. Loren nodded, the decision made, and headed to Nathan, this time with a different dynamic in mind for them.

Entering, he saw Nathan waiting in the room, towel around his waist, shuffling from foot to foot, vibrating with energy despite his recent release.

"Good boy." He placed the bag on the bed, standing close to Nathan, but not near enough to touch. They needed to clear the air first. "Why were you in my room?" he demanded.

Turning wide eyes towards Loren, Nathan wrung his hands together. Loren stepped in front of him, reaching to hold his hands still. Nathan stared at him, licking his lips. "I…I spilt coffee on the top I was wearing, and I wasn't sure where you had put my clothes. I didn't think you'd mind if I got another one. When I saw…" Nathan trailed off, a beautiful blush suffusing his cheeks and neck. "I'm sorry. It was wrong. I'll get dressed and leave." Nathan tried to turn, but Loren gripped his hands tighter. Their gazes locked once more, a wealth of information being taken and received.

Loren squeezed Nathan's hands, then let go. "Let's get you dressed, shall we?" Loren reached for the bag, riffling through the contents and choosing a pair of grey joggers and a blue short-sleeved t-shirt with a cartoon character on them. "Would you like to choose your underwear?" He laid out several pairs of briefs in different colours, so Nathan could choose.

Nathan frowned at the clothes before smiling softly and biting his lip, a trait Loren would cure him of. Nobody bruised that lip but him—he hoped. He watched as Nathan reached his hands across the selection and picked up the orange pair, surprising Loren. He'd expected him to be a bit more subdued.

"Perfect." Loren took the briefs from Nathan and crouched near his feet, so close to Nathan's cock, he had to use all his restraint not to touch. "Rest your hands on my shoulders and lift your foot." Nathan obeyed, and Loren pulled the briefs to Nathan's shin. "Other leg." Nathan replaced his left foot and lifted his right, repeating the process. As his foot found the floor once more, Loren slid the underwear up Nathan's legs, discarding the towel and pulling the waistband over his ass and cock. "Are you comfortable?"

"Yes, Daddy," was the soft reply.

Loren turned back to the chosen clothes, briefly closing his eyes with the pleasure strumming through him at those words. "Let's do it again with your trousers, sweet boy." They repeated their actions, this time, Loren slid his hands up along the outside of Nathan's thighs, watching the goosebumps follow in his wake and feeling Nathan tremble. Loren swallowed and stood quickly, his arousal humming along his veins. "Arms up." He pulled the t-shirt over Nathan's head and arms. "There we go, sweet boy. Let's get you some food." Ignoring his arousal, Loren took Nathan's hand and pulled him out of the room and towards the breakfast bar in the kitchen. "Sit."

Loren didn't think about what he did, other than to acknowledge he needed to show Nathan what he wanted, and this was the only way he knew of doing it. He needed Nathan to understand what Loren offered.

Bustling around the kitchen, trying to settle his nerves, Loren cut up some vegetables, throwing them in the tray with the chicken and placing it in the oven. After, he retrieved some fruit. He paused, momentarily, then pivoted towards a drawer. Pulling out a brand-new colouring book and crayons, he hesitated before sliding them across to Nathan. Not making eye contact, he turned back to making the dinner.

Loren knew what he wanted, but he needed to see what Nathan wanted, too. They had not talked yet; he didn't know what Nathan wanted out of this. But Loren needed to get it all out in the open, which he would do as soon as they'd eaten. He pulled down a cup, filled it with milk and twisted around to place it next to Nathan.

He froze in place when he saw Nathan sat there, arms wrapped around the colouring book with tears running down his face.

Hurrying to round the counter, Loren put the cup down. "Sweetheart, what's wrong?" He sat on the seat next to Nathan, smoothing a hand along his back. He had no idea what he'd done wrong. Maybe Nathan wasn't a boy who liked colouring. "I'm sorry if I—"

"No!" Nathan's voice was wet with tears, and he audibly swallowed. "No. You don't need to be sorry. I… I…" He cleared his throat. "I've never had anyone care for me the way you have while I've been here. I…I know some of what I want but finding someone who under-stands has never happened."

"What do you want, Nathan?" Apparently, they were talking about this now rather than later.

"I want someone to help me look after myself. I want to be able to…" he indicated the colouring book with his chin, "do some colouring or read comics to relax and forget about things." He rushed on, "I don't want the nappies and toys…at least I don't think so." Nathan frowned. "I'm not sure about that."

"You don't have to know everything right now, Nate." The nickname rolled off Loren's tongue but sounded right. Seeing the grin on Nathan's face as he lifted his chin, it appeared he liked the sound of it, too. "We can work it out as we go along. If you want to." Loren hoped Nathan did.

"I would."

Loren's heart soared at the words. "The things I need you to be sure about are that you want to try this and that you are honest about things. If, at any time, you are unsure or overwhelmed, you need to tell me."

"Yes, Daddy," Nathan replied shyly.

"Good boy." Loren wanted to seal the deal with a kiss but thought it better if he waited for Nathan to indicate he was ready. He stood. "Let me finish cooking, okay."

"Okay, Daddy." Nathan wiped at his face and placed the book in front of him. Loren moved the chopping board and fruit over to the breakfast bar; he could watch Nathan while he cut up the fruit. Nathan opened the colouring book to the first page and flattened the cover until it stayed flat. He pulled out the crayons, choosing blue, and rested his right hand against the book. Loren paused. He hadn't realised Nathan was left-handed. Not that it mattered, but it was a new piece of Nathan for Loren to file away for later.

He watched as Nathan meticulously coloured the balloon, the tip of his tongue visible through his teeth, wholly focused as he was. Loren tilted his head; he hadn't been this content for a long while. Refocusing on the fruit, he finished the fruit bowls and turned to the oven. Pulling out the tray, he checked the contents, replacing them as they needed a little longer. Loren took a breath and pivoted around to face Nathan, finding him watching Loren.

"Are you okay, sweet boy?" Loren tilted his head.

"Yes, Daddy. I made a picture for you."

"Thank you, Nate." He took the proffered book, seeing the neat colouring of several balloons being held in a young boy's hand. "It's great. Thank you so much." Loren slid the book back to Nathan. "Let's get this cleared away."

Nathan nodded and with a serene expression, replaced the crayons he had used in their box and pushed them across the table to Loren, who put them in the drawer where they lived.

"Good boy. Now, let's wash our hands. Dinner will be ready in a couple of minutes."

Chapter Seven

NATHAN

Nathan's heart felt full to bursting with everything that had happened over the last couple of hours. Naturally, Loren catching him using the dildo in the bathroom was *not* what he had planned, but it ended up with a result he couldn't argue with. Loren was a Daddy. Nathan could not believe his luck. He felt a little silly about his mini-breakdown, but Loren was so understanding—as a Daddy should be. And being able to colour, under Loren's watchful eye, was such an amazing experience.

Dinner was blissful. Not only because he was able to have a meal without having to *work* for it first, but because they talked. Not about anything in particular, but about the things they both enjoyed. Nathan had opened up about Robbie and Daisy—the only nod to the homelessness situation he was in—talking about them as a couple. He felt bad about not having been to see them to explain.

"We could go there tonight if you want to?" Loren's

voice broke into his musings. "You could collect some of your things."

They had yet to discuss what the plan was for them. Nathan had assumed he'd head back out tonight and, over the next few weeks, get to know Loren more before progressing any further. Loren had a different idea.

Nathan bit his lip. "What things do I need to collect?"

Loren put his knife and fork down, crossing his arms loosely and resting his elbows on the table edge. "I don't like the idea of you being out there. I've been thinking about whether you might want to move in here. Into the spare room." Loren held up a hand when Nathan began to talk. "You don't have to start any kind of relationship with me. I'm not forcing you to do it in payment for the room. The room is yours, free and clear, regardless of our…situation."

Nathan studied his plate, moving the food around with his fork as he thought about what Loren had said. His life would be more comfortable if he stayed here, but he felt…unworthy. He'd done some demeaning things since he'd been on the streets. Yes, they ensured his survival, but it didn't mean they were any less embarrassing. He couldn't believe Loren would want anything to do with him, but it sounded as if Loren wanted him there.

Thoughts were tumbling around and around in his brain.

"Nathan." The quiet but authoritative voice captured Nathan's attention once more, encouraging him to face Loren. "You don't have to make a big decision right now. You are welcome to think about it, but I would love it if I could make your life a little easier while you do think."

Nathan's gaze roamed Loren's face, seeing the wrinkled brow, ocean blue eyes under sexy thick black glasses and the full lips which spoke with so much care. He nodded with a bite of his lip. "I'll stay while I decide."

Watching as he was, Nathan saw pure joy spread across Loren's features, making him appear immediately younger than…whatever age he was.

"Shall we visit with Robbie and Daisy?" Loren pressed, reclaiming his cutlery and continuing to eat.

"Yes, please, Daddy." Nathan had lots to tell them.

***

"HERE."

Nathan saw the coat Loren held out towards him. "What's this?"

"Something a little warmer than your jacket." Loren held the coat open for Nathan to slide his arms into, and immediately warmth encased him, more so when Loren turned him to face him and proceeded to zip up said coat.

"Thank you." Nathan couldn't remember a time he had been warm—well, when he was on his way outside, that is.

"You're welcome. Now, are you sure you don't want anything else to take to Robbie and Daisy? A couple of blankets and some tinned fruit doesn't seem enough for what they're going through. I wish I—"

"I know what you wish you could do, but this is more

than enough for the moment." Nathan cut Loren off, earning a narrowed eyed stare. "Sorry, Daddy. I don't want you to feel like you need to do more. We've looked after ourselves for many years now. Too much would hinder, not help."

Loren nodded. "You're right. I don't know enough about these things. I'm trusting you to show me the way."

Nathan's mouth widened until he beamed. "Thank you, Daddy." Unable to stop himself, he threw his arms around Loren's neck in a hug he never wanted to end. Loren's arms came around him, holding him tightly against his form.

"Let's get going."

Nathan reluctantly pulled back, wanting to keep hold for longer, but knowing he had things to think about.

They had decided to take a stroll with the shack being close and Nathan feeling better. Nathan decided he needed to speak to Robbie about the situation and get his advice.

Within twenty minutes, they were at the wire fence. Nathan bit his lip again. "You don't have to come—"

"I'm coming," Loren replied, voice firm.

Nathan inhaled deeply then ducked through the hole, holding it open for Loren to get through. Worrying his lips, Nathan led the way around the edge, relaxing minutely as the shack came into view. He hoped they were still there and hadn't moved on. Stopping at the door, he exhaled and knocked twice, opening the door slowly.

Seeing Robbie crouched in front of Daisy, protecting her, had Nathan slumping in relief.

"Nathan!" Daisy pushed Robbie to one side, scrambling up and running to him, throwing her arms around him. "I thought something had happened to you. I'm glad you're alright."

"Hey, Daisy. Yeah, I'm okay. Sorry to worry you."

"What happened to you?" Robbie came forward, frowning, hesitation clear on his face as he inspected Loren up and down. "Nice bruise." He nodded towards Nathan's forehead.

Nathan ran his fingers across the lingering evidence and grimaced. "Yeah, things took a turn for the worse the other night."

"What happened?" Daisy asked, fingers gripping Nathan's coat sleeve.

"Some guy left him injured in an alley. I happened to be walking past and heard him in pain. I helped." Loren filled in the blanks succinctly enough Robbie and Daisy's eyebrows rose.

"What did he do?" Robbie's eyes narrowed, and his lips thinned.

"Doesn't matter. I've been staying with Loren for the last couple of days to recuperate…" Nathan paused, unsure of how to explain everything.

Robbie tilted his head, locking gazes with Nathan. "You're heading out, aren't you?"

It was what those on the streets called it when someone left the homeless situation.

Nathan bit his lip. "For the moment."

Daisy piped up. "And can you give him what he deserves?" The question was directed at Loren as she manoeuvred around Nathan to stand in front of him.

"I'll give my boy everything he needs."

Robbie and Daisy gasped jointly, redirecting their gazes back to Nathan. He blushed under their perusal. They knew what he wanted from a relationship, so to them, this would be perfect for him. Nathan was unsure because it felt a little like Loren was rescuing him.

He cleared his throat. "Robbie, can I have a word?" He indicated the opposite side of the small space; it wouldn't give them a huge amount of privacy, but enough for what Nathan needed.

Nathan stood with his back to Loren, knowing it would be more difficult if he could see him.

"What's up?"

Running his hand through his hair, he lowered his voice. "I don't know if I'm making a mistake."

Robbie's eyebrows rose again. "Why would you say that?"

Nathan squinted off to one side, focusing inwards instead of outwards. "Am I rushing into this because of how I live my life? On the streets? I can't decide if I'm… seeing what I want to see instead of what is actually there."

"What's happened between you so far?"

Nathan felt his cheeks flush again. "Nothing sexual." He didn't mention the bathroom scene, it was too embarrassing. "He's taken care of me, took the lead in things we do, cooked for me. Generally taken care of me." He paused, peeking back at Robbie. "He gave me colouring to do while he cooked tonight."

Robbie's mouth curled at the corners. "Grab onto him, Nathan. You'll never know for definite unless you try. We'll be here for you if you need anything." Robbie rubbed the back of his neck, something he did when he was thinking. "Trust yourself. You wouldn't have gone back to his place the other day if you didn't believe he was a good guy, would you?"

Nathan pondered his words and shook his head. "No, I would've told him to piss off."

"Exactly. If the worst comes, come back to us." Robbie reached a hand to Nathan's shoulder, squeezing gently.

"Thanks." Nathan turned, seeing Loren going through the bag they'd brought with them with Daisy. He smiled, turning to his stuff and packing some little bits into a backpack he kept ready for a quick exit. Once he had everything, he pivoted back to Loren. "I'm ready."

Loren nodded, glancing at his friends. "If it eases your concern, Nathan is welcome to leave at any time. He is not being held prisoner, and, although I will try to change his mind, I will never keep him from his freedom." He hesitated. "I put my—our—address in there in case you need anything or want to stop by. You're welcome any time."

Daisy came forward, throwing her arms around Loren, who's eyes widened. Nathan and Robbie guffawed.

As she pulled back, she threw over her shoulder towards Nathan, "He's a keeper."

They said their goodbyes after several more minutes, and Nathan and Loren headed back the way they came.

"I wish I could do more for them." Loren's tone was laced with regret.

"You've done plenty. Giving them a place to come to if they're not safe is one of the best things you could've given them." Nathan sidled up next to Loren and linked his arm around his elbow, resting his head on Loren's shoulder as they ambled back to the house. After a few minutes, Nathan realised what he'd done, and he tensed.

"What's wrong?" Loren asked.

Nathan hesitated. "Nothing. I…I've never felt so at ease with someone as quickly as I have done with you. It's a little unsettling sometimes," he admitted.

"Thank you, Nate."

"For what?" Nathan tilted his head to see Loren's profile.

"For telling me the truth. Where possible, I always want the truth from you, even if you think it will hurt my feelings. Okay?"

"Yes, Daddy," he whispered.

"Good boy."

They continued in silence until they reached Loren's house. Nathan could feel the butterflies beginning in his stomach because he wasn't sure what they were supposed to do tonight.

Loren led the way, helping Nathan out of his coat and shoes then removing his own. Then he held out his hand to Nathan, who grabbed it eagerly.

"Let's go watch TV for a little while before bed."

At the word bed, Nathan pulse skyrocketed, he inhaled and exhaled to slow it. He didn't know what he should be doing. This was new to him, except where he'd had a few interactions with Daddies previously, but nothing to this degree. Those previous meetings had been in a bar and for a release, nothing more.

As they sat, Nathan stared at the TV with fascination, fiddling with his fingers in his lap as Loren found something to watch. The film chosen, Loren sat back, and they watched in silence. Every second that ticked by without conversation, fed Nathan's anxiety.

When a hand rested on his shoulder and pulled him towards Loren with a "Relax, Nate," he went without a fight. Resting his head once more on Loren's shoulder, he tucked his feet under him on the sofa and relaxed into the position.

A gentle shaking motion along with a slide of a hand along his arm woke him gradually. He became aware of a fruity scent and nosed himself further into it, being rewarded with a rumbling chuckle felt through the chest he burrowed into. At the noise, Nathan's eyes opened, instantly taking in his surroundings and finding himself laid on top of Loren on the sofa. He glanced up at Loren, seeing a smirk on his face.

"You were tired, it seemed." Loren's voice was husky, as if he, too, had been asleep, though, Nathan doubted it. Why? He wasn't sure, but he didn't think Loren would've slept while Nathan had.

Nathan pulled back, cheeks flushing with mortification at their positions, which were undoubtedly his fault. "I'm sorry. I didn't mean to fall—"

"Hey, hey. You've nothing to be sorry for." Loren sat up, hands cupping Nathan's jaw and tilting his head until they locked gazes. "You were tired. I loved holding you. You gave me the best gift tonight."

Nathan's brow creased, and he tried to figure out what Loren was trying to say. "I don't—"

"You gave me your trust when you fell asleep on me. You trusted me not to hurt you. You trusted me to keep you safe. That's…" Loren exhaled, "everything."

Nathan checked the truth of his words through his expression. There was a softening in Loren's eyes, a smile on his mouth, and he held Nathan gently.

"Please, Daddy." Nathan wasn't sure exactly what he asked for.

"What do you need, my sweet boy?"

"Could I have a kiss, please, Daddy?" Nathan hadn't known what he wanted until he said the words. Then it was all he wanted. He needed to feel Loren's lips on his. Claiming him. Their first kiss.

Loren's gaze roamed Nathan's face as he smoothed his thumb across Nathan's bottom lip, to which Nathan replied with a quick swipe of his tongue. Loren's gaze darkened, eyes narrowing. He pulled Nathan towards him in infinite slowness. When he got close, Loren went fuzzy, Nathan's eyelashes swept to his cheeks as his breathing increased.

The first press of their lips together was a mere brushing, but when Loren pulled back, Nathan grumbled until Loren returned. The sweet torture continued as Loren pressed kisses across his mouth, jaw and cheeks, returning to his lips and *devoured* Nathan. He could do nothing more than grip the back of Loren's shirt as their lips smashed together, and Loren's tongue explored every inch of Nathan's mouth.

Light-headed but not wanting the kiss to end, Nathan

allowed himself to fall deeper into Loren. The movement must have registered because Loren slowed the kiss then pulled back.

Nathan was unable to open his eyes, drunk on passion as he was. He allowed his head to fall back as he struggled to inhale enough air to make him coherent again. When his eyes finally fluttered open, he saw Loren staring at him, lips glistening, eyes shining and mouth grinning.

"You are perfect," his Daddy said.

"Thank you, Daddy."

"Time for bed."

Loren stood, jerking Nathan up by his hands and steadying him when his knees, initially, proved too weak. Once he stood strong, Loren released one hand but kept the other, leading Nathan down the hallway. Outside the spare room, Loren hesitated and turned to him.

"I don't want to assume you are at the same place I am right now. Tonight, you have a choice of where you want to sleep. In the spare room, or with me?"

Nathan rolled his lips, trying to hide his smile. Loren was so considerate. Nathan didn't know why he'd had any reservations about this. "Your room, please, Daddy."

"We're not doing anything else tonight, but I'd love to hold you all night," Loren replied with a pleased expression.

"Yes, Daddy. Please hold me."

"Okay. Do you need anything from the room? Or from your backpack?"

Nathan shook his head.

"Let's get some sleep." They continued down the

hallway, Loren opening the door and guiding Nathan to the bed. "Wait here for me."

Nathan stood, fidgeting, gaze roaming the room. He'd been in here earlier in the day but didn't take the time to investigate his surroundings. Instead, he'd gone straight to the drawers to get a t-shirt and found something enticing instead. Nathan smiled, realising his choice that afternoon had led to where he was now, and he couldn't bring himself to regret it. Not that he'd tell his Daddy, of course.

He watched as Loren returned carrying some clothes. "Lift your arms for me, sweetheart." Nathan complied, and Loren removed his t-shirt. "I'm going to change your trousers now." Loren's fingers curled into the waistband of the joggers and slowly nudged them down his legs. "Lift your foot." Nathan rested his hands on Loren's shoulders as he did as he was told. "Other foot."

Once Nathan was naked, Loren reached for the trousers on the bed. He held them out for Nathan to step into and slid the soft, warm fabric up his legs and over his ass. Nathan couldn't help the way his cock jerked, being semi-hard as he was. Loren picked up a top and indicated for Nathan to lift his arms again. Once the pyjama top was in place, Nathan dropped his arms.

"Come on. Jump into bed." Loren reached around him to pull back the duvet, encouraging Nathan to get in and then covering him. "I'm going to get ready. I'll be in after." He pressed a kiss to Nathan's forehead and disappeared into the en-suite.

Chapter Eight

For the first time in a long time, Loren stayed at home to work, content to hear Nathan potter around the house from his vantage point at the kitchen table. He hadn't made a conscious decision to stay home, and he trusted Nathan, but he also wanted to be close to him. He was aware he was not getting as much work done as he would've done if he'd been at the café or the library, and he knew he would have to head there most days; otherwise, he would get behind on his schedule. But he understood himself and knew he needed to be at home that day.

The previous evening had been a revelation. Loren knew Nathan trusted him enough to allow him to stay in his house alone, but he hadn't been sure if Nathan had trusted *him*. He proved the trust last night. Falling asleep on him had turned Loren to tears, and he had been unable to fall asleep alongside him initially, the emotions overwhelming him.

And when Nathan had asked for a kiss, Loren would have done anything to fulfill his wish at that moment.

"Daddy?" A soft voice interrupted his thoughts. He glanced up to see Nathan stood near him, wringing his hands and stepping from foot to foot.

"What do you need, Nate?"

"Would you like a drink?"

Loren tilted his head, scrutinising Nathan as he turned the question over and over in his mind. There was an underlying meaning behind the words, but Loren wasn't sure what they were. Not knowing where Nathan was going with the question had Loren thinking about the correct way to answer.

Being a boy didn't necessarily stop Nathan from doing adult jobs, like helping with meals or making a drink, but Nathan had proved he enjoyed colouring and doing jigsaws, putting him on the lower age limit of being a boy. It was something they had not properly talked about, which Loren would have to rectify that evening.

Taking a chance, he went with his gut instinct. "Yes, please. A cup of tea would be great."

The answering beam was enough of a reply, at least for the moment. Loren watched as Nathan sashayed to the counter, a bounce in his step, settling into his task. He tried to concentrate on the work he'd been completing but found himself watching Nathan's movements instead.

When Nathan turned with a mug in his hand and began drifting towards Loren, his gaze on the mug, Loren saw the tip of his tongue peek out between his lips in concentration. He grinned and thanked Nathan when it was placed next to him.

"You're welcome, Daddy." Nathan twisted to leave the room, but Loren called him back. "Yes, Daddy?"

"Come here, sweet boy."

Nathan returned to him without hesitation, and his heart felt full to bursting.

"I'd love to reward you." Loren crooked a finger at Nathan, enticing him to come closer, which Nathan did. Loren reached a hand up to Nathan's neck and pulled him in for a kiss. As their lips touched, Loren felt a fire begin in the pit of his stomach, which flamed higher when Nathan moaned into his mouth. Keeping it chaste was hard work, but Loren pulled away after a few minutes, keeping hold of Nathan's neck until he opened his eyes and regained his balance.

"Thank you, Daddy," Nathan whispered.

"You're welcome. Now, go have fun while I get some more work done."

Nathan grinned. "I will, Daddy." He skipped to the doorway, pausing when Loren called his name again.

"You don't have to call me Daddy all the time if you don't want to, you know." Loren had been curious about that since Nathan had started saying the word; it seemed to be in every sentence he spoke. He didn't want Nathan to think he had to call him Daddy in every interaction. Loren watched as a flush tinted Nathan's cheeks as he ducked his head and mumbled his response. "I didn't hear you, Nate."

Nathan inhaled and peered at Loren. "I love saying it, Daddy."

Loren's mouth curled up. "Okay, then."

Nathan beamed and exited the kitchen. A few minutes later, Loren heard the TV, and he relaxed back into his seat. He was concerned Nathan accepted their… relationship…because Loren had helped him, and he didn't want that to be the reason.

Turning back to his accounts, Loren got to work, promising himself they would have a discussion after their meal that evening.

LOREN STIRRED the chicken together with the sauce, mentally creating bullet points of the things he needed to talk to Nathan about, a conversation they should have had yesterday. It wasn't a conversation he'd had more than a few times so trying to cover everything was pointless, and some of it they would have to work out as they went along. If Nathan decided to stay. And there was the crux of the matter. Loren wanted Nathan to stay and be his boy, but he needed Nathan to want to stay.

He recalled his earlier conversation with Ben on the phone. Loren had called him to tell him about having found his boy, and, while they were overjoyed about it, Ben cautioned him about jumping in with both feet. He understood Ben's reservations, but Loren needed to speak to Nathan before anything was agreed.

"Nate?"

A few seconds later, Nathan poked his head through the kitchen doorway. "Yes, Daddy?"

"Could you set the table, please?"

Nathan, wearing the same clothes Loren had dressed him in that morning, reached up for the plates and glasses and placed them on the table, then returned for cutlery.

Loren emptied the pan contents into a serving bowl and carried it to the table. "Thank you, Nate. Enjoy your food." Loren spooned some of the chicken pasta onto Nathan's plate, passing it to him, offering him the salad bowl as well.

"This looks and smells delicious. Thank you, Daddy."

"You're welcome. Eat up."

Loren watched as Nathan picked up his fork and speared pieces of chicken and pasta onto it, placing it in his mouth, pulling the tines out again and licking his lips before chewing with a puckered brow. Loren didn't interrupt his musings. If Nathan had questions, Loren wanted him to ask when he was ready.

They ate in silence—comfortable silence—until Nathan had finished his plate. Seemingly snapping out of a daze, Nathan glanced to Loren, eyes wide.

"What's wrong?"

"I'm sorry, Daddy!" Nathan spoke in a rush as he dropped his fork to the table.

"Calm down, Nathan. What are you sorry about?" Loren reached a hand forward and covered Nathan's trembling one.

"I've not spoken to you since we sat. I didn't mean to be so quiet. I was thinking about everything that has happened since I met you, and I thought about Robbie and Daisy and the things I had to do…previously. I didn't realise how long I'd been thinking until I saw my plate was empty. I didn't mean to ignore you. I would never do—"

Loren stood, halting Nathan's words, crouching next to Nathan's chair. "Shhh, sweet boy. Calm down. Take a breath for me, okay? Breathe, that's it." Loren rubbed a circle on Nathan's back while holding a hand over both of Nathan's in his lap. "Right, one more. That's it." He waited until Nathan had followed the instruction. "Have you finished your dinner?" Nathan nodded, eyes downcast. "Okay. Let's sit on the sofa and talk for a while, alright, sweetheart?"

Loren pulled him to standing, and, not letting go of his hand, led him to the sofa where he sat and pulled Nathan onto his lap. At first, Nathan sat upright until Loren placed a hand on his back again and tugged him closer.

"Right, now. Let's have a chat." Nathan tensed in his arms again, and although Nathan was snuggled under his chin, Loren knew he was about to apologise again. "You have nothing to apologise for," Loren cut in before Nathan could say a word. "You don't have to talk if you don't want to. I have lived most of my life without someone to chat at the kitchen table. It's not a new scenario for me. You don't need to worry about offending me. I will say, however, if there is something you want to talk to me about or something you are worried about, I would love it if you could share it with me. I fully believe in 'a problem shared is a problem halved,' but," he continued, rubbing Nathan's back again, "you don't *have* to. My role as your Daddy is to look after your wellbeing, but also, to be there when you need someone. Do you understand what I'm trying to say?"

There was silence for a few seconds, then Nathan nodded against Loren's chest. "I think I understand, Daddy."

"Good. We need to talk through a few things, and there's no better time than now. Sit up for me, Nate." Loren helped Nathan rise from his position and sat him right next to him so he could see Nathan's face. "I know you told me a little about what you wanted yesterday. Is there anything else you want from this relationship, Nathan?"

Loren watched emotions fly across Nathan's face, then Nathan's gaze dropped to the floor; he was pleased Nathan considered his answer, rather than automatically replying.

"I would like someone to take care of me and to help me figure out how to take care of myself properly. I would like an emotional connection with someone. And to have hugs and cuddles whenever I want them."

Smiling, Loren cupped Nathan's jaw. "I would love to be that person for you."

Nathan's gaze locked to his as he whispered, "I would love that person to be you."

Loren leaned in, placing a chaste kiss to Nathan's lips. "There are many things we need to discuss. For example, what do you want to happen about sex?"

Nathan blushed and ducked his head again. "I…I would like to have sex with you. I want you to give me what you think I need, Daddy. I don't have experience of emotional sex, only…" Nathan trailed off, waving a hand around.

"I understand. We can figure it out together, how about that? And we will both get tested, so you know I'm safe."

Nathan ducked his head. "And to check if I am, too, Daddy."

"We'll check us both, so we know we are both safe." He paused. "You seem to be content with the 'Daddy' word since we started this. What do you want to do about our dynamic when we go out in public?" Loren had no preferences either way when it came to his public persona.

Cocking his head, Nathan bit his lip. "I think I would like to keep calling you Daddy. But…can we see when we do it? If it doesn't feel comfortable, I won't say it."

"That's fine, Nate. Thank you for taking the time to answer honestly."

"What would you like me to do as your boy, Daddy?" Nathan stared at him with such openness and curiosity.

"I want you to be yourself. I don't want you to change who you are for me. This will only work if we are honest with each other."

"And what happens if I do something I shouldn't?" Nathan bit his lip again, something Loren would need to curb him of; he hated the idea Nathan was hurting himself.

"Well, that is something we need to decide upon. We can have certain boundaries you need to work within or certain tasks, which need to be undertaken to make sure you are healthy and strong. And if your behaviour needs to be corrected, I will think of appropriate punishment."

Loren heard an audible intake of breath and chuckled. His boy liked the idea of punishment, it seemed. He knew it wouldn't take long for Nathan's behaviour to *challenge* the boundaries, whatever they may be.

"Okay, Daddy."

"Good boy." Lifting his hand to cup Nathan's jaw again, he pulled him closer. "I think it's time we sealed the deal."

Their lips met in a sweet caress until Nathan groaned, and Loren dragged Nathan across his lap, deepening the kiss. Nathan wrapped his arms around Loren's neck, straddling him properly. Loren slid his tongue along the roof of Nathan's mouth, gripping the back of his head, and moving him where Loren wanted him, Nathan providing a background noise of moans and groans.

Running a hand down Nathan's back, Loren teased his fingers into the top of the waistband of his trousers, pawing at the top of his ass cheeks, letting one finger stray to the tip of his crack. Nathan arched his ass back towards Loren's hands.

"That's what you want, is it, sweet boy? Hmm? You'll have to be good to get it, won't you?" Loren didn't expect any answer to be forthcoming with the haze covering Nathan's expression. Sliding his finger closer to Nathan's hole, Loren licked a strip up Nathan's neck, sucking a bruise under his jaw, marking him for all to see. A little caveman mentality there, but he couldn't resist.

At Nathan's next needy groan, Loren pulled away gently, taking Nathan's chin into his hand to focus his attention. "Let's head to bed." Not planning on sealing the deal tonight, Loren lifted Nathan off his lap, grabbed his hand and dragged him up the stairs to the bedroom, straight into the en-suite. "Shower time, sweetheart."

After helping Nathan out of his clothes and switching on the shower, Loren indicated for Nathan to get in. When Nathan hesitated, he asked if something was wrong.

Nathan bit his lip and stared to one side. "Can you shower with me, please, Daddy?"

Loren reached forward, running his fingers through Nathan's hair. "Of course. You jump in. I don't want you getting cold. I'll join you in a moment."

Nodding, Nathan did as instructed. Loren had the best of intentions of not doing anything else that night, but it appeared as if something would happen, after all. There was no way he would be able to deny the boy, especially with how good he was being. A reward was in order.

He removed his clothes, throwing them into the hamper by the door and sliding into the shower behind Nathan, who stepped back into him and rested his head on Loren's shoulder. Loren stroked his hands across Nathan's wet skin, teasing his nipples, and the needy sounds escaping from Nathan, hardening his cock more than it already was.

Their heights, as they were, enabled Loren to rest his swollen cock against the crack of Nathan's ass. Every time the boy arched into the fingers teasing his nipples, his ass pressed harder against Loren's shaft.

There was no way Loren would last long in this

scenario. As he went to change their positions, Nathan mouthed at his ear, "Please, can I suck your cock, Daddy?"

Loren let out a shaky breath and swallowed. Hard. "You ask so nicely, sweet boy, and you have been good for me. Yes, you can."

He watched as a delighted expression crossed Nathan's face, and he immediately whirled around to face Loren and dropped to his knees. When water sprayed onto his face, Loren pulled Nathan up again, smiling. He reversed their positions, the water pounded against his back, sheltering Nathan.

Nathan kneeled at his feet, his big doe eyes peering up at Loren as if he was as innocent as they come. A good disguise, but Loren had already seen behind the expression and knew Nathan could be a brat if he wasn't trying so hard to please. Time would tell.

Nathan ran his hands up Loren's legs, both surrounding the base of his cock at their finishing position. Using one hand, Nathan encircled the purple shaft, pulling it to his mouth, where he licked the tip repeatedly, teasing the slit. Minutes, or seconds, later, Nathan wrapped his lips around the head, using his tongue to drive Loren crazy, alternating between the tip and the nerves under the crown of his dick. Loren felt every swipe of the talented tongue as small electrical shocks filtered through his system. He tried his hardest not to grab hold of Nathan and keep him where he wanted him. This was Nathan's time for exploring. But Nathan had other ideas. He grabbed Loren's hands, guiding them to his hair, pushing against them as he took Loren's weeping dick further into his mouth.

Loren got the idea. He gripped Nathan's head in his hands and pulled him forward, sinking further into the warm, wet mouth before pulling away again. He was conscious of not going too far in and choking Nathan. He repeated the action several times and he felt a vibration on his cock, making his eyes roll back in his head. When he guided Nathan back down once more, Nathan pulled away from his hands and sank Loren's shaft straight down his throat and swallowed.

"Fuck!" Loren lost it. After that manoeuvre, Loren had no control, he fucked Nathan's mouth and throat, then blew his load, barely warning Nathan. Never had he ever lost control like that. With anyone. He rested against the tiled wall, catching his breath, watching Nathan rise from under lowered eyelids.

"Was it okay?"

Loren snorted. "Fuck, yes, Nate. It was…" He couldn't finish. He could barely think. Wrapping his boy in his arms, they stayed locked together while Loren recuperated. When Nathan shivered, he turned Nathan back into the stream of the shower, facing forward. It was time he rewarded his boy.

Sliding his hand down Nathan's abs and gripping his cock, his other hand reached further down to play with his balls and synchronising his movements with Nathan's answering groans, he quickly had Nathan on the edge.

"Please, Daddy!"

"What do you want, Nate?" Loren knew exactly what

he craved, but he wanted Nathan to ask for it. He wanted Nathan to wait until *Daddy* said he could come.

"Please! Can I come, Daddy? Please, can I come?" Nathan's fingernails were embedded in Loren's forearms, his head resting back against Loren's shoulder as his hips thrust in time with Loren's motions. "Please, Daddy?"

Loren waited for a beat more and replied, "Come for me, my sweet boy." He hadn't finished his words when Nathan's release painted the tiles, his groans loud in Loren's ear but musical all the same.

When Nathan's knees refused to keep him upright, Loren banded an arm around his waist and proceeded to wash him with infinite care in the now-lukewarm water. Switching off the shower, Loren managed to dry Nathan off partially and danced him towards the bed. Flicking the cover to the side, he helped Nathan to lay down and pulled the cover back over him. Loren leaned down to kiss his forehead, wishing him a good sleep.

He finished drying himself, checked everything was locked up properly and strode back to his bed…and his boy, tucking up tight against Nathan's back.

Chapter Nine

NATHAN

Nathan wandered around the empty house, wanting to search from top to bottom to see what he could find out about Loren. But, although Loren had said to treat the house as his own, Nathan couldn't do it. It wasn't his home; he was staying there for a short time.

That morning, before Loren had left for the library, he had woken Nathan with sweet kisses along his neck, cheeks and mouth.

"Good morning, sweet boy. Did you sleep well?" Loren braced himself on his elbow, tracing Nathan's stomach with his free hand.

Nathan's mouth curled in a content smile. "Yes, thank you, Daddy. Our bed is comfy." He snuggled his head into the pillow and closer to Loren's naked chest, taking a deep breath.

"I'm glad you think so. I am going to spend the day at the library today. I have a bit of work to complete by the end of the week."

Nathan opened his eyes, blinking sleepily. "What should I do?"

"You can do whatever you'd like to do, Nate. Make yourself at

home." Loren kissed his nose. "What would you like for breakfast? Pancakes? Toast?"

Biting his lips, Nathan replied, "Pancakes, please, Daddy."

"Pancakes, it is."

Nathan reached up a hand to cup Loren's cheek but hesitated before he made contact. Loren covered the hand and pressed it to his cheek, turning to kiss Nathan's palm, the scratchy stubble tickling the sensitive skin.

"Are you okay?"

Nathan's gaze roamed the expanse of Loren's face, noticing the dips and valleys in his skin and loving every one of them. Loving? What was he thinking? He cleared his throat. "Yes, Daddy. I'm okay."

"Good." Loren leaned down and kissed Nathan once more. "Let me get breakfast done, and we'll shower and get you dressed for the day."

After circuiting the house once more, he decided to go and visit Robbie and Daisy again. Not wanting to ruin his new clothes, he re-dressed in his old street clothes, as he called them now, and packed a few pieces of fruit and a couple of yoghurts, along with some tinned meat, into his backpack and, grabbing the spare set of keys from where Loren had pointed them out, he locked the house and drifted down the road.

He did have a small amount of money in his pocket, but he didn't want to waste it on a taxi; therefore, he took a meandering stroll, watching as the houses changed to shops, then to high-rises. In no time, he was at the fence, cutting his way across the open space and knocking on the door in the pattern they had all agreed on.

Daisy opened the door hesitantly, beaming when she

saw him, making him feel settled once more.

She pulled the door wider. "Come on in. Why didn't you come in? You know you're always welcome here."

"I wasn't sure if you two had planned to find somewhere else to stay. I didn't want to intrude on someone else." Nathan glanced around. "Where's Robbie?"

Daisy went back to her blanket, sitting against the wall. "He went to see if there were any job openings listed at the shelter."

Nathan raised his eyebrows. "I thought he didn't want to?" He made himself comfortable on the floor, stretching his legs out in front of him and setting the backpack down.

Daisy stared at her hands, rubbing them together in slow motion. "He doesn't, but…"

Nathan frowned when Daisy stopped talking. His stomach cramped. "Daisy? What's wrong? Why is Robbie searching for work when you both have been vocal about being happy as you are?" His breathing came faster. His thoughts were on the worst scenarios, one being Daisy was ill, and they needed the money for medical expenses. Surely, they would ask him for help if they needed something. He was in a better position to help them now, and he would be able to get a job himself to help pay for it.

Daisy peered up at him, tears in her eyes, a small smile on her face. "I'm pregnant," she whispered.

Nathan stared at her, mouth flapping. All of the difficulties they were about to face ran through his mind. He could now understand why Robbie was out looking for a job. "Wow. Congratulations?" He said the word as a question because, although he'd seen her contentment, he wasn't sure if it was something they were happy about or not.

Daisy snickered. "Yes, thanks. It's a happy thing. Unexpected but happy."

Nathan moved over next to Daisy and wrapped an arm around her shoulder. Kissing the side of her head, he murmured, "You'll be great parents."

"Thanks, Nathan."

"Have you talked about what you plan to do?"

"A little. Enough that Robbie is job hunting. We're not sure what the plans about housing are yet. We need to speak with the shelter and see if they have any ideas of what we could do and where we could go. But it's little yet; we have a bit of time to sort things out."

Nathan squeezed her shoulders and rested his head on top of hers.

They stayed in that position for a short time until Nathan remembered what he'd brought with him. "I come bearing gifts." He reached for his bag, pulling out the food and showing Daisy.

She pressed her nose against the oranges and inhaled, eyes closing. She held the oranges as if they were precious, which, in some ways, they were. "Thanks, Nathan," she repeated. Still holding the fruit, she settled back against the wall again as Nathan placed the other items on the small box next to him. "How are things with Loren?"

"Good. I think."

"What do you mean, you think? Is he hurting you?" She sat upright, eyes narrowed.

"Hold fire, mama-bear." Nathan snorted at her automatic defensive stand. "No, he's not hurting me. It's...a lot to get used to. I've been on the streets for so long, it's difficult to get comfortable somewhere where it can all be taken away again. I wonder whether I should stay on the streets, then I won't have to worry about it every minute of the day."

He felt awful saying these things. He knew Loren wouldn't throw him out, even if their relationship didn't work, but it was difficult to remove those thoughts from his head. On the streets, he had to work for everything he needed, and he only owned a few things. If they had been taken from him, all he would have to do is *work* to be able to get them again. Whereas staying with Loren in comfort made him forget how difficult living on the streets was...and he didn't think it was a good thing.

"Oh, Nathan. I could tell Loren feels deeply for you. I don't think you have to worry about it all crashing down around you. And I can see you care for him." She paused. "Does he give you what you need? Emotionally, I mean?"

Nathan's smile grew. "Yeah, he's amazing."

"More information than I needed!" Daisy pretended to block her ears.

Swatting at her, he laughed. "No, I don't mean that way. We've not..." he stopped, examining the floor.

Daisy turned towards him, crossing her legs, holding the oranges on her lap. "You've not had sex yet?"

"No. Well, technically, yes, if you call a blowjob sex. But not...all the way." Nathan's cheeks warmed under Daisy's scrutiny.

She snorted. "I can't believe you're blushing when we're talking about sex! Who are you?"

"Shut up!" He pushed against her shoulder in mock irritation, then they both burst out laughing.

"What's all this noise?"

Nathan's gaze swung to the door, heart in his throat at the possibility of their shelter being taken away from them, but his shoulders sagged when he saw Robbie. "If it wouldn't be a waste of food, I would throw this fruit at you, asshole! You scared the shit out of me."

Robbie laughed. "Serves you right, pushing my girl-friend like that." He shut the door behind him, dropping his bag near the entrance and hurrying over to Daisy, planting a kiss on her lips. "Hey, sweetheart, how are you feeling?"

Daisy blushed, ducking her chin. "I'm good." She held up the oranges. "Nathan brought vitamin C."

Robbie glanced at him with a grin. "Thanks, man."

"I hear congratulations is in order?" Nathan smirked.

Robbie beamed, a light shining brighter in his eyes. "Thanks." He dropped to a seated position next to Daisy, linking their fingers. "What brings you out here, anyway? Not that we mind the company."

"He was asking for sex advice," Daisy said with a straight face.

Robbie's mouth gaped, eyebrows raised. "What?"

"Shut up, Daisy! No, I wasn't. You started it." Nathan pouted, crossing his arms over his chest.

Daisy and Robbie cracked up, and Nathan rolled his eyes, joining in.

When they regained their breath, Nathan explained,

"I didn't specifically ask for advice. I was saying, Loren and I hadn't had sex yet if you didn't include a blowjob as sex."

"Why haven't you slept with him?"

"It's not for lack of wanting to, Robbie! God!" Nathan snorted, then continued quieter, "You know who he is to me. He's taking it slowly. Not wanting to take advantage of the situation. And we're waiting for test results, too. I want to be sure I'm not…Anyway, it's…great."

Robbie cocked his head. "You want him to ravish you."

The deadpan tone hit the nail on the head. "Yes! My feelings are all mixed up. I feel cared for but also unsure and, in some ways, unwanted. Mainly the latter when he's not around. Maybe it's my issue and nothing to do with him."

"I disagree," Daisy said. "It has everything to do with him. He needs to make sure he takes care of you when he's not around as well. It's part of his job. And he should know that."

"Has he punished you yet?" Robbie smirked.

Nathan chuckled. "No."

"How come?" Robbie frowned.

"I've been a good boy." Nathan leered.

"Doesn't sound like you. What's stopping you from being yourself, apart from being unsure?"

Nathan hesitated, biting his lip. He loved being a good boy for Loren. The attention he received was amazing, but…something was missing.

"You don't want to take things too far and risk him throwing you away?"

Once more, Daisy hit it spot on. Nathan nodded.

"He wouldn't, you know." Daisy wrapped her arm around his shoulders.

"You need to speak to him about it. You both need to be on the same page. Is he waiting for you to get home?"

Nathan shook his head, clearing his throat. "No, he went to work at the library today, as he usually does. I felt weird staying there by myself, so I came to see you."

Robbie's eyebrows rose as the corners of his mouth turned up. "Did you tell him where you were going?"

"No. I don't have a phone to message him on, do I?" Nathan frowned, not understanding what Robbie's expression was about.

"You didn't think to leave a note on the table or something?"

Nathan's eyes widened, he scrambled to his feet. "Shit. I best get back. Loren doesn't usually finish work until around four, I have time."

"Nathan, calm down. I think you did this as a test. You knew exactly what you were doing when you left. Even if you didn't realise it at the time."

He paused what he was doing and stared at Robbie, brow creased. "What do you mean?"

"Well, you said you've not had sex yet. You also said you're not sure how you feel about everything, and you said you have yet to be punished." Robbie paused and sighed when no one said anything. "I think you are trying to provoke a reaction from Loren."

"No! I...I'm not used to...I didn't think...fuck!"

Nathan sat back, his hands gripping his hair. He closed his eyes and calmed his breathing, examining his earlier thoughts when he was at the house. Yes, he had been all turned around and hadn't known what to do with himself, but did he want to be punished?

He worried his bottom lip as he thought through everything. His shoulders sagged, and his head rested back against the wall, hands dropping into his lap. "You're right. I didn't realise it at the time, but I was annoyed at Loren for leaving me alone without any idea of what I should be doing. He told me to treat the house as my own, but I have no idea what I enjoy doing anymore. The idea of leaving a note did briefly cross my mind, but I believed I'd be home before he was." He sighed.

"What are you planning on doing now you've realised what you want?" Daisy asked.

Nathan stared at the roof of the shelter, feeling the cool breeze from one of the gaps in the wooden shack as he considered his options. It was unlikely Loren would be home before Nathan, but if he was, did it matter whether Nathan was home earlier...or later? He'd still get punished.

"I'm planning on hanging out with my friends for a while longer, then I'll head home." He rolled his head towards them, a smirk crossing his face. "May as well make the punishment worthwhile."

They all laughed at Nathan's answer, who, despite his words, was unsure if it was the correct course of action. He guessed he'd see when he returned.

Chapter Ten

LOREN

Loren entered the house to complete stillness, a complete and utter lack of presence, and he knew instinctively Nathan wasn't there.

He closed the door behind him, wandering to the kitchen table to drop his bag and keys. Glancing around, he studied the kitchen, seeing nothing out of place. He continued his perusal through the rest of the downstairs, climbing the stairs, a lump in his throat, making it difficult to breathe. He checked the bathroom first, then their bedroom, and when he saw nothing to indicate anyone was here, he trudged towards the spare room.

The door was closed, and Loren stood in front of it, pulse skyrocketing, sweat gathering at the base of his spine. He didn't know what he wished for: Nathan to be in there or not. If he was, Loren was unsure why he'd prefer the spare room to their bedroom. If he wasn't, he had no idea where Nathan would be.

Heart pounding, Loren turned the handle and

pushed the door open. Standing at the threshold, he saw no one. Shoulders sagging, he caught himself on the doorframe, breathing deeply and stumbling towards the bed, where he fell to his knees in front of the clothes he had dressed Nathan in that morning.

The clothes were thrown haphazardly across the bed as if Nathan had been in a rush. Loren scanned the room for Nathan's street clothes and his backpack, and, seeing neither, he turned and sat on the floor by the bed.

Stretching his legs out in front, he dropped his hands to his lap and rested his head back, staring at the ceiling. As tears rolled into his hairline, he tried to understand what he'd done wrong. When he'd left this morning, Nathan had been smiling and seemingly happy. There was nothing to indicate Nathan had wanted to leave him. Lifting his head, he bent his knees, crossing his arms across the top and resting his forehead on them.

He had no idea how long he'd sat there, or how many tears he had cried when he heard the front door open. Staying in the same position, he ignored it, thinking he imagined things. It was only when he heard footsteps mounting the stairs that his heart began hammering once more.

"Loren?" The voice was quiet but clear and coming from the doorway. "Loren? Is everything okay?"

Loren lifted his tear-stained face to the doorway, not knowing whether to believe the apparition or not.

"Loren?" Nathan stepped further into the room.

With that movement, Loren sprang up from the floor and flew towards Nathan, enfolding him in his arms and tucking his face into Nathan's neck. As Nathan's arms came around him, Loren lost it. They stood in the embrace for several minutes before Loren became aware of Nathan rubbing a hand up and down his back and speaking.

"I'm sorry, Daddy. So sorry. I should've left you a note. I didn't think things through. I'm sorry," Nathan repeated the words over and over again.

Loren inhaled, opened his eyes and pulled back. Cupping Nathan's jaw, he gazed into the apologetic chestnut-brown eyes. "You will be punished for this bad behaviour, boy." He felt Nathan swallow. "But later. I need you too much, right now." Lips met in a fierce clash as Loren took what he needed from Nathan. Nathan's hand went from stroking his back to gripping his shirt, little moans sounding from the back of his throat while Loren unleashed his frantic need. The overwhelming pressure of holding back was now being released, and Nathan stood in the centre of it.

Loren strode forward, making Nathan stumble back as he clung to Loren as he directed them to their bedroom, all the while kissing Nathan until he was light-headed. When Nathan stumbled again, Loren gripped the back of his thighs and lifted his legs to wrap around Loren's waist. Nathan changed his grasp, encircling his arms around Loren's head. Opening his eyes partially to see where they were in the hallway, Loren stomped towards the bedroom door, which, thankfully, was open from his earlier search.

Pausing at the side of the bed, Loren lowered Nathan to the floor, ripping his mouth away and gasping for breath. They stood staring, hands holding each other.

Loren lifted a hand and rubbed at the bruised, wet lips gracing Nathan's face. Nathan's eyelids lowered, and he licked at Loren's finger.

"Let's get you undressed." Sliding his hand down the column of Nathan's neck, he pushed the jacket off his shoulders, allowing it to drop heavily to the floor, then found the hem of his t-shirt, pulling it up and over Nathan's head and threw it down. Nathan's eyebrows rose as he glanced between the discarded t-shirt and Loren. Smirking, Loren leaned in for another kiss, distracting Nathan from whatever thoughts were going through his head. A shiver went through Nathan's body, breaking Loren from their kiss. "Lay down, sweetheart."

Watching as Nathan obeyed, Loren began undressing, dropping his clothes to the floor. He kept his boxers on and crawled on all fours to Nathan's prone body. Stopping next to him, Loren ran a hand from Nathan's waistband to his navel, up his abs to his chest, bypassing the nubs seeking attention. Continuing to slide his hand upwards, he cupped Nathan's jaw, leaning on his elbow to sip at the swollen lips.

"Are you okay, Nathan?" Loren whispered against his mouth. Nathan nodded. "I need words, my boy."

Clearing his throat, Nathan uttered, "Yes, Daddy."

"We can stop anytime, just say the word, alright?"

"Please, don't stop, Daddy." Nathan closed his eyes, a bodily shiver running through him again when Loren grazed a nipple. "Please, don't stop."

Loren grinned. "As you wish." He replaced his fingers with his mouth, using the firm tip of his tongue to lash at the erect nub and watching as Nathan's hands fisted the sheets below. Nathan's voice rose when Loren's hand found his other nipple, giving it a similar treatment.

"Daddy!"

Loren's free hand slid to the button of Nathan's trousers, undoing it and relieving some pressure on Nathan's cock. Removing his hand from Nathan's nipple, he tucked both hands into the sides of Nathan's trousers, pushing them down as Loren's mouth moved to the opposite nub. When he couldn't push them any further, his mouth left the sensitive peak and kissed down Nathan's abs where the trousers were pulled off, the underwear closely following, and thrown in the vicinity of the rest.

From his position, it was difficult to miss Nathan's erect cock, standing proud. Eyes locked onto Nathan's face, Loren slowly pushed Nathan's legs apart, revelling in the pupil-blown expression. "I'm going to take care of you, now, Nate." He removed his boxers and crawled in between Nathan's spread legs after reaching for the items from the bedside table.

Sliding his hands up Nathan's shins, knees and thighs, Loren marvelled at the smoothness of his skin until his gaze was caught on his weeping shaft.

"You're beautiful, Nate."

"Thank you, Daddy," Nathan choked, arousal lowering his voice.

Loren situated himself on his stomach, his face close to the swollen cock. Unable to resist, Loren licked a strip up the shaft, earning a groan from Nathan, enticing Loren to do it again, finishing with a swipe of his tongue to collect the precome. He grabbed the lube he'd retrieved and squeezed some onto his fingers, making sure to keep Nathan's focus on his cock. Rubbing around his hole, Loren sucked the head of Nathan's cock, swallowing him down as Loren breached him.

"Yes! More, Daddy!"

From his position, Loren could see Nathan's head pressed back into the pillow, fists still clenched in the sheets. Loren lifted and lowered his head on the swollen shaft as he prepared Nathan's ass. They had not spoken about what Nathan preferred, but Loren was unwilling to take him without the proper preparation, no matter how much of a rush he was in to claim his boy.

When Nathan could take three fingers, Loren deemed him ready, especially with the incoherent noises Nathan was making. Loren released Nathan's cock and lifted to his knees, grabbed the condom, rolled it on and slicked it.

Loren leaned his hands either side of Nathan's torso and brought their faces close together. "Look at me, sweet boy." He gazed at the sheen of sweat coating Nathan's skin and similarly at the blissed expression when those eyes met his. "Are you ready for me?"

"Yes, please, Daddy. Make me yours," Nathan breathed.

Loren's heart soared at the words, and he dipped down to kiss those delectable lips. "As you wish." Kneeling back again, he pushed Nathan's legs further apart, and bracing one hand on the bed and one holding his cock, he pressed forward against Nathan's hole.

Unable to decide where to look, Loren flicked his gaze between where his cock was and Nathan's face, watching every nuance of muscle movement for pain. When he saw nothing except pleasure, he surged forward, claiming every inch of Nathan he could.

"Fuck, Nate, you feel amazing." Staying fully inside of Nathan, Loren lowered to his elbows, covering Nathan's body, getting as close as he could. "Wrap your arms around me, Nate."

Nathan blinked his eyes up at Loren, then complied, sliding them around his neck and one hand into Loren's hair. Loren closed the distance between their lips, unable to resist, and as they explored, he began to move his hips in a slow, torturous rhythm.

Loren could feel Nathan's hard cock rubbing between their stomachs, and by the twitching in the stomach muscles, he knew Nathan wouldn't last long. He slid his arms underneath Nathan's back, one hand resting against his shoulder, the other gripping his ass cheeks, holding him close and tilting him exactly right. He thrust his hips harder.

"Oh my god! Oh! Please, Daddy." Nathan's moans escaped when he tore his mouth from Loren's and arched his head back. "Right there! Oh, please, Daddy! Can I come? Please!"

Nibbling at the muscle straining between his shoulder and neck, Loren increased his speed. "Fuck! Yes, Nate! Come! Now!"

With the order, Nathan's body seized, the rhythmic clenching on Loren's cock blinding him with his orgasm.

Loren rested his weight on his arms once more so Nathan could breathe but stayed plastered against him, inhaling his sweaty, sex-scented smell. After a few minutes, he lifted his head, smiling when he saw Nathan with his eyes closed, mouth open and a gorgeous flush to his skin. Loren pressed a kiss to his collarbone and rose off him, laughing when Nathan's arms flopped to the bed.

"Come on, sweetheart. It's time for a bath."

"Mmm," was the response he received.

Chuckling, he strode to the en-suite and cleaned himself off before plugging the bath and turning on the taps. Throwing in some relaxing salts, he returned to the bedroom, shaking his head when he found Nathan in the same position.

"You'll get sore if you stay in that position all night. Let me help you up." He placed one knee on the bed and slid his hands under Nathan's knees and shoulders, lifting him with ease. Manoeuvring Nathan through the door and into the tub was easy…waking him up was not. "Come on, Nate, wake a little, so I can wash you properly without you drowning." With one arm wrapped under his shoulders to keep him from sinking, Loren grabbed a sponge and soap and lathered it, gently stroking it across Nathan's skin. Loren shook his head again when there was no response other than a small sniffle.

Giving up, Loren forewent washing Nathan's hair and scrubbed his body clean as best he could. Popping the plug out, the bathwater emptied as he grabbed a towel and pulled Nathan to a semi-sitting position. Having to bear the brunt of his, albeit light, weight, Loren rested the towel over the top of Nathan and grabbed another, doing the same. Lifting him from the bath, Loren strode back to the bed, crouching to spread a towel on the sheets, laying Nathan on it, and placing another towel over the top.

Loren snorted at the sight. Nathan had to be fast asleep; otherwise, there was no way he would've slept through everything. Loren should take it as a compliment, perhaps.

He dried Nathan off as best he could under the circumstances, pulling the towel from underneath him when he was done, then tucked the covers around him. Returning to the bathroom, he tidied up in there, then switched off the light and picked up the clothes from the floor of the bedroom. He didn't want Nathan tripping over them in the middle of the night. Checking the house was locked up, he returned to the bed and slid in behind Nathan, curling himself around him tightly.

Inhaling Nathan's sweet scent, Loren held him a little tighter, remembering what had happened earlier. He had been certain Nathan had left and wouldn't be coming back. When Nathan had appeared in the doorway, Loren had been relieved, he hadn't considered a punishment. At least until a little anger had shown up. Tomorrow would be the test of their relationship, if Nathan wanted a relationship. Their first conversation the next morning would be about their expectations, then, and only then, will they discuss the need for Nathan to be punished for what he had put Loren through. After all, although they had not specified what they were doing, Nathan should have thought about the consequences of him leaving without mentioning where he was going.

Loren frowned. Should he expect Nathan to tell him where he is every minute of the day? Ideally, yes. It's what the Daddy in him needed. But could he punish Nathan when it hadn't been discussed before it happened? Loren wasn't sure.

Nathan moved in his sleep, snuggling deeper into Loren's embrace. He didn't want to risk scaring Nathan away. But he also had to put everything on the line to explain what he needed from a relationship. And he didn't know what he would do if Nathan turned and walked away.

LEAVING Nathan warm and content in their bed that morning had been excruciating, but Loren wanted to cook Nathan a rejuvenating breakfast and ready him for the conversation to come.

"Daddy?" Nathan's sleepy voice broke into Loren's musings, and he twisted towards the doorway to find his boy dressed in joggers and a large t-shirt—one of his.

"Good morning, sweet boy. Did you sleep well?" He drifted over to kiss Nathan on the side of his head, his cheek and, finally, his mouth.

A rush of red filled Nathan's cheeks as he nodded. "Yes, thank you, Daddy."

"Good. Sit. Let's get some breakfast inside you." Loren shared out the cooked breakfast he'd made and placed a plate in front of Nathan, whose eyes widened.

"Wow. That is a lot of food, Daddy."

Loren chuckled. "Don't worry if you can't eat it all, Nate. Eat what you can. I wasn't sure how hungry you would be this morning."

"Thank you, Daddy." Nathan picked up his fork and began shovelling the contents into his mouth, moaning with every bite.

Snorting, Loren chided, "Not so fast, Nate. The food isn't going anywhere." Nathan ducked his head and slowed his chewing, apologising when his mouth was empty. "It's okay. I don't want you getting a poorly stomach later."

They ate in comfortable silence, locking gazes often, swapping smiles and small caresses. Loren tidied away the plates when they were finished.

"We need to have another conversation, Nate."

Not meeting his gaze, Nathan nodded. "I know, Daddy. I'm sorry—"

"Wait. Let's get comfortable on the sofa first. I'm not sure how long this will take, and I don't want you getting sore or cold." Holding out his hand, Loren waited patiently for Nathan to decide if he wanted the support or not. Closing his eyes briefly when Nathan grabbed on, Loren led him to the sofa, snuggling Nathan into his body to keep him close. He knew they would need to be face to face for some of the conversation, but for the moment, Nathan was right where Loren needed him.

"Okay. What were you going to say in the kitchen?"

"I'm sorry about not leaving a note yesterday. It was after I spoke to Robbie that I realised I hadn't thought you might get home earlier than you said." Nathan glanced up at him.

Loren contemplated his answer. "Were you upset because you'd been out without telling me, or were you upset because you didn't want me to know?" The distinction was small but significant.

"Oh god, no! I didn't care if you knew I'd been out. I was upset because I didn't tell you." Nathan's gaze slid away from his. "There may have been another reason."

"Which is?" Loren had a feeling he knew what bothered Nathan, but he waited to see if his hunch was correct.

"I think I wanted to be punished," he muttered.

Loren's mouth curled up. Yeah, exactly what he thought. "You did it on purpose?"

"No, not consciously. Not at first, anyway." Nathan fiddled with the fabric of Loren's t-shirt.

"What do you mean, not at first?"

"Well, I left the house thinking I'd be back before you finished your work, so it didn't matter if I left a note or not. But when I spoke to Robbie, he told me I'd be punished for not telling you. By that point…" Nathan paused, then continued in a whisper, "I thought I may as well stay longer if I was going to get punished anyway."

Loren rolled his lips inwards to stop the smile spreading across his mouth. When he'd gained control, he replied, "I'm glad you told me. You will be punished, and you will not enjoy it, but you will also remember not to do it again. But after we have finished our conversation."

Chapter Eleven

NATHAN

Nathan was devastated when he found Loren curled up on the bedroom floor, something he never thought he'd see. And the way Loren had held him when he realised Nathan was there, it about broke his heart. If nothing else got through to him about how he felt about Loren… that did. He was falling hard for his Daddy. Telling him the truth about his thoughts had been difficult, but he felt better for it, although he was unsure about the rest of the conversation.

"What else do we need to talk about?"

Loren shifted, and Nathan sat up, facing him. "I'm going to put everything out there, Nathan. And you need to think about it and decide if you can put up with me as I am."

Gaze roaming the face of the man who had made Nathan feel complete for the first time, Nathan nodded.

"I need to care for a boy. I have to be in control of a lot of things most people wouldn't need to be in control of. I would like to help my boy to wash and dress, prepare his food, know where he is at all times, give him time to destress from his day-to-day issues, love him, care for him, punish him when he needs it." Loren cupped Nathan's jaw, gazing intently into his eyes. "I want to help him become the best version of himself he can be."

Unexpectedly, tears welled in Nathan's eyes and slid down his cheeks. Loren wiped them off.

"What's wrong, Nathan?"

Swallowing against the lump in his throat, Nathan decided to be honest, "I'd love that, too. I want to become the best I can be."

Loren beamed. "And you shall." He leaned forward, pulling Nathan towards him and pressed their lips together. "I will help you if you'll allow it."

"I'd love your help," he whispered.

Wrapping him in his arms, Loren pulled them back to their original position. "Nathan?"

"Yes, Daddy?"

"Will you stay here with me? I know it's quick, but I don't like the idea of you living on the streets when there is a place here for you."

Overwhelmed by the generosity, Nathan wanted to grab with both hands, but he was unsure if it was the right thing to do. "I'd love to, but…" He trailed off, not knowing how to explain his reservations.

"But, what, sweetheart?" Loren brushed his fingers through Nathan's hair.

"I don't want to take advantage of what you have here. I don't have a job, so won't be able to contribute to the bills. I can't cook, so can't help with it. I could clean but have never had to." Nathan felt like a failure in life.

"Nathan, look at me." Loren's voice brooked no argument. "You don't *have* to do anything. But," he continued when he saw Nathan was going to interrupt, "if you want to work, I can help you. What would you like to do?"

Nathan blinked at him. He hadn't thought about what he'd wanted to do for many years. He'd always thought about the things he would be *able* to do rather than what he *wanted* to do. Back when he was a teenager living at home, he had been good at school, and he'd wanted to do something to keep him interested. The only subject had been was mathematics. He'd planned on going to college in a mathematical field and seeing what jobs came up. But when he got kicked out, college went out of the window.

"I like maths, although I haven't done anything with it for years, it was something that interested me at school. I can add in my head quickly. I did it a lot when I went shopping for food to make sure I didn't go over what money I had."

"Budgeting, that's good. Anything else?"

"I didn't have any huge issues with schoolwork, but maths always held my attention." Loren chuckled. "What?"

"A man after my own heart."

Nathan snorted, realising, stupidly, Loren was right, being an accountant dealt with a lot of maths. "Yeah. I never thought about it before."

They were quiet for a moment, then Loren started

talking, "If maths is what you're interested in, I can teach you what I know. You can see whether accounting is something you might enjoy. If not, we can search for other job opportunities and see what is needed for them. You have a lot of options open to you, Nate, and I will be more than happy to help you if you want me to."

Nathan felt the prick of tears again but pushed it back. He crawled into Loren's lap, straddling his lap and burrowing his head into Loren's neck. "I'd love that," he whispered against his skin.

Loren rubbed a hand up and down his spine. "Would you like to stay?"

Nathan held him tighter. "Yes, please, Daddy." He felt a whoosh of air leave Loren's body, and Loren's arms coming around him to hold him as tightly as he held Loren.

"Thank you," Loren mumbled.

They stayed wrapped together for a while, and Nathan could feel himself becoming sleepy again, until Loren patted his ass.

"Time for your punishment, boy."

Nathan tensed but pulled away, resigned to his fate. "Yes, Daddy."

"Stand up." Nathan did reluctantly and watched as Loren moved to an armchair. "Joggers off and lay over my lap."

Nathan swallowed, briefly hesitated, then dropped his joggers and trailed over. He leaned his stomach on Loren's thighs, his head and arms down.

"Move up a bit." Nathan was shifted into position by warm, strong hands, his head closer to the ground, his ass higher in the air. Not the most comfortable of positions, but that was the point. Loren smoothed a hand over his ass, and Nathan arched against him. "No moving. Your punishment is ten smacks. They will not be pleasant. They will hurt, but you will learn your lesson. And next time, we can do this for fun instead. Understand?"

"Yes, Daddy," Nathan replied with a tremor in his voice.

"Good." Loren slid his hand across his skin again. The heat left briefly. A sharp pain spread from the base of his ass outwards as Loren's palm connected. No soothing this time. Nine rapid successive smacks were administered, bringing tears to Nathan's eyes, but once the tenth was finished, a hand soothed his skin once more. "Well done, sweet boy. Well done."

Loren assisted Nathan to rise, the blood rushing from his head, making him dizzy. He stumbled, and Loren helped him lie on the sofa. Once he was settled, Loren disappeared for a moment, returning with a drink.

"Drink this." Loren took it from him once he'd finished and brushed his fingers through Nathan's hair again. "You did so well, Nathan. You're such a good boy for me."

Pleasure spread through Nathan's system; he had pleased his Daddy. "Thank you, Daddy."

"Rest there for a bit while I clean the kitchen." Loren pressed a kiss to Nathan's lips and drifted away.

Despite the sting in his ass, Nathan was relaxed and content, a feeling he hadn't felt for a long time.

He awoke warm and sleepy. A blanket was spread over him, and although he was naked from the waist down beneath it, he was toasty. He kept his eyes closed, relaxed as he was, but listened for sounds around him. There were repeated tapping and clicking noises which he eventually identified as typing and mouse buttons, and it came from the direction of the kitchen. He assumed Loren was working. Nathan blinked open his eyes, not wanting to emerge from his sleepy cocoon.

He snuggled deeper, wincing when his ass protested but smiling all the same. When his bladder wouldn't hold any longer, he untangled himself, standing immediately to not put pressure on his no doubt red ass and pulled on his joggers to visit the downstairs bathroom.

Studying himself in the mirror as he washed his hands, Nathan saw a brightness to his eyes he hadn't seen for a while, and he had Loren to thank for it. Thinking of Loren had Nathan seeking him out.

"Hello, Nate. Did you have a nice sleep?" Loren's gaze met his as he stopped his work.

"Yes, thank you, Daddy. Sorry. I didn't mean to sleep."

"It's okay, Nate. You needed the rest." Loren stood, coming towards him and pressing a kiss to his forehead. "Are you hungry?"

"A little."

"Okay." He returned to the table, picking up some paper and placing it in Nathan's hands. "Sit and read this while I make us a snack." He veered Nathan towards a chair next to where he'd been sitting.

Frowning, Nathan studied the paper. It was an offer of an apprenticeship working for March Accountants.

Nathan couldn't believe it. "What…?" He glanced over at Loren, who peered over his shoulder with a smile.

"You don't have to accept it, but I spoke to an acquaintance of mine. They have been searching for people to learn accounting from the beginning in the hopes those employees will stay with the company afterwards. They are a good company."

Nathan read over the offer again. He'd get minimal pay, naturally, but he would be taught everything there was to know about accounting. His breathing increased as he bit his lip, withholding the grin wanting to escape. "Why do they want me?"

"I put in a good word. I explained you didn't have any qualifications, but I would vouch for you." Loren shrugged as if it was no big deal.

"Why?" Nathan didn't understand why Loren would vouch for him when Loren had no idea what Nathan was capable of.

Loren turned and rested back against the counter, crossing his arms over his chest. "Because I know you'll work hard. And I believe if you begin to struggle, you will ask for help." He paused. "Am I wrong?"

"No!" Nathan shook his head vehemently. "I will work hard. I…Wow. Thank you."

Loren nodded in acknowledgement of the thanks. "Do you want to know the best part? Or at least, I think it's the best part."

"What?"

"I'm the one training you."

The wealth of emotion was too much for Nathan to hold in at that point, and he burst into tears. He felt

Loren's arms come around him, then he was lifted from the chair and settled into Loren's lap. He gripped the shirt below him, pressing his face into Loren's neck as the tears escaped. All he'd ever wanted was the opportunity to try and become something. Nathan had applied for hundreds of jobs over the last eleven years to no avail because they didn't want to take a chance on someone who was homeless. He was overwhelmed by the changes happening so quickly from a chance meeting in a dark alley.

He knew he would never be able to repay Loren for what he had given Nathan: a chance at a better life with someone who cared enough to help him.

Nathan took a cleansing breath, exhaling roughly but less shaky than the earlier one. Pulling back from Loren, he cupped his Daddy's jaw. "Thank you. From the bottom of my heart, thank you."

"You are welcome, Nathan."

Nathan became aware of the sting in his ass the longer he sat on Loren's lap. Wriggling to get more comfortable, he felt a chuckle run through Loren's chest.

"Are you uncomfortable, by any chance?"

"Yes, Daddy," Nathan whispered.

"Okay, let's stand. I can finish getting your snack ready."

Nathan followed him into the kitchen and washed his hands, ready to eat.

"Here we are." Loren passed a plate to him filled with melon slices, orange segments, apple slices and a little pot of yoghurt in the middle. "This should fill you up until lunchtime."

"Thank you, Daddy." Nathan rested back, making sure his lower back touched the edge of the counter but not his ass, and proceeded to eat. Out the corner of his eye, he could see Loren watching him over a cup of coffee. He wasn't sure what the perusal was about, but he enjoyed being the focus of his attention.

When Nathan had cleared the plate, Loren took it from his hands, rinsed it off and stacked it in the dish-washer. Loren stood in front of Nathan, lifting his chin.

"Are you okay with everything that has happened over the last few days? It's a lot to take in, I know. But I need to know if you're okay with it all."

Nathan rested his palms against Loren's chest, running them up and down the fabric as he watched. He thought through everything that had happened since the incident in the alley. "I am fine with it." He met Loren's troubled gaze. "It's a bit of an adjustment after eleven years, but I am coping. You are being amazingly patient with me, and I love it." *I love you.* Nathan dropped his gaze, biting his lip to stop the words from escaping. They weren't there yet, but Nathan realised how true his feelings were.

Loren was a good man and an amazing Daddy. He took care of Nathan, always making sure he had what he needed and helped him to figure out what he wanted for the rest of his life. And trying to make it happen.

Nathan's body filled with emotion, and he felt light as air. Nobody had ever made him feel like this.

Loren lifted his chin once more and pressed their lips together in a sweet meeting, kissing his top lip, then his bottom lip and sipping from his mouth before pulling away.

"I have some more work to do. Why don't you go have a bath? Soak your behind a little," he said with a smirk.

"Yes, Daddy." Nathan felt his cheeks heat.

Loren snickered, kissed him once more and let him go.

Nathan drifted to the en-suite, set the bath running and stood, staring at his reflection. His life had changed dramatically in the last few days, but Robbie and Daisy's had, too. He needed to speak to Loren about what he could do to help them, especially with their baby on the way. He knew Daisy had said there was time, but life on the streets was hard for adults. For children or adults with babies, it was terrible. He needed to figure out his options.

The apprenticeship Loren had secured was an amazing start at getting where he wanted to be—a valuable member of the relationship and a working person—but he wanted to help more homeless people. He didn't know if his maths could help, but they could think of something together.

Together.

That was another thing. He now had someone to care about what happened to him. Don't get him wrong, Robbie and Daisy would've cared, but they had each other. It was slightly different.

His brain went round and round in circles, so he stepped into the bathwater and gingerly sat, hissing at the temperature when it hit his ass. Once he was settled, he rested his head back and relaxed. His body, including his ass, soon got used to the heat, and his limbs turned heavy. He couldn't believe how much he'd slept today already, but he could easily sleep again.

Returning his thoughts to Loren, Nathan smiled. He'd been searching for a Daddy for a long time, and a chance encounter found him one perfect for him.

Eight Months Later

Loren dreamed of the tongue-lashing Nathan had given him the previous day, the wet heat surrounding his cock as he thrust into Nathan's throat. He couldn't think; he could only act. Reaching down, he gripped the light brown strands, watching the red tinges appear in the slight glow of the light.

As his orgasm came to fruition, he awoke, opening his eyes and locking gazes with the beautiful chestnut-brown eyes of his boy. The muscles in his torso clenched in time with his climax, but he couldn't pull his gaze away as Nathan swallowed everything his Daddy gave him. When his brain had calmed, and his breath had returned to normal, he narrowed his gaze at the naughty boy lying between his legs.

"You, boy, are in big trouble."

Nathan batted his eyelashes in a fake apology. "Sorry, Daddy. You were aroused, and I couldn't resist."

"Uh-huh. Go have a shower, boy. Your guests will be arriving soon; therefore, your punishment will be doled out later." Loren gave him a small push, making Nathan jump off the bed, talking a mile a minute.

"I can't wait to see them. Robbie has done well with the job the shelter found him, and though he'd not been there for long, they gave him the paternity leave. He does have to go back in a couple of days, but it will be nice to see them again. I hope Daisy is getting some sleep. She looked terrible the last time I saw her. I told Robbie he needed to help out more because Daisy didn't seem well. Hopefully, he's..."

The dialogue continued as Nathan stepped into the shower, but Loren had no hope of hearing what was said.

How his boy had changed since they first met. Gone was the quiet, reserved boy who didn't want to impose, and in his place was a talkative, social butterfly. And Loren loved it. Their dynamic was pretty much the same as it had been from the start, except for Nathan pushing the boundaries a lot more.

Loren pulled on his boxers and padded over to the en-suite.

"...see about getting a house nearby or something. I said I'd speak to you because I have no idea about properties."

"Nathan."

Nathan stopped soaping his body and glanced over his shoulder. "Yes, Daddy."

"Breathe." Loren watched as Nathan's chest expanded and collapsed twice, nodding. "Better. I know you are excited about them visiting, but you need to calm down. When you've finished your shower, I will help you get dressed, and you can colour while I make breakfast."

Nathan closed his eyes briefly. "Thank you, Daddy."

Loren retraced his steps, heading for the drawers and pulling out a navy-blue t-shirt, black jeans, blue socks and underwear. When Loren had found out the blue was Nathan's favourite colour, he had purposefully bought several clothes in varying shades for him; it appeared to help him relax and be more confident. Laying them out on the bed, Loren pulled on his own clothes.

Exiting the bathroom in a cloud of steam, Nathan was naked as the day he was born, drying his hair with a towel. It wasn't as long as it had been but long enough for Loren to grab in his fist.

"Come here, sweet boy."

Nathan strode over after dropping the towel in the laundry basket. He stood in front of Loren, eyes and face smiling, limbs loose.

Picking up the underwear, Loren kneeled at Nathan's feet, holding them out for him to step into then slid them slowly up his legs. Goosebumps followed in his wake, earning a smirk from Loren. He tucked Nathan's semi-hard cock into the underwear, patting it gently as he finished and grabbed the trousers, repeating the process. As he fastened the button and zip, Loren could hear Nathan's rapid breathing and noticed his fists were clenched at his sides. Willing to have Nathan squirming for a while as part of his punishment, Loren helped him with his socks, each movement excruciatingly slow. Lastly,

Loren stood with the t-shirt. Lifting Nathan's arms over his head, Loren pulled it down over his arms and covering his face. Before pulling it on, and while Nathan's face was covered, he leaned down and nibbled at both Nathan's nipples in turn, earning a growl in response. He tugged the material into place, revealing the pained gaze of his boy.

"Time for breakfast."

"Daddy!"

"Come on, sweet boy. Let's go." Loren led the way out of the room and down the stairs. He rounded the counter, pulling out the colouring book and pencils and placing them in front of Nathan. "I think today is the day for pancakes and syrup. What do you think, Nate?"

Nathan did a little victory dance on the stool and pumped his arms in the air. "Yes, please, Daddy!"

Loren snorted and shook his head at Nathan's antics, inwardly over the moon at the response. As he prepared the batter mix, he glanced over at Nathan, occasionally smiling at the tip of his tongue peeking through his teeth as he concentrated on colouring. Although Nathan didn't regress to being a little, he enjoyed the mindless tasks, which helped his mind to settle and recuperate from everyday life.

By chance, Loren had found trains were something Nathan liked, so they'd ended up with a toy train track and some accessories much to Nathan's delight. It wasn't a young boy's toy; it was for older children and had remote-controlled trains instead of push-along ones. Regardless of the age for the toy, Nathan loved it and often brought it out to watch the trains going round and round the track endlessly. On those days, Loren knew Nathan needed extra time to destress. It wasn't often Nathan needed the trains, but when he did, he'd had a busy day.

Flipping the final pancake onto the plate, Loren turned off the oven. "Time to tidy up, Nate."

"Okay, Daddy." Nathan began repacking the crayons straight away, and Loren knew he hadn't been in the zone. He was too excited to see his friends.

Placing a plate in front of Nathan when the table was clear, he dribbled some syrup over the top just as Nathan liked and watched him grin as the syrup ran down like lava.

"Thank you, Daddy."

"You're welcome."

They ate in silence, Nathan finishing his pile before Loren was halfway through. He didn't say anything. Out the corner of his eye, he watched Nathan fidget, his gaze bouncing around the room, and Loren withheld his smile as he continued eating.

When the doorbell rang, his eardrum was blasted by Nathan shouting, "They're here!" and running towards the front door. Loren snorted and shook his head, a regular occurrence for him.

Putting the plates in the sink, he heard multiple voices and wandered down the hall to greet the visitors.

"Good morning, Robbie, Daisy. How are things?" Loren shook hands with Robbie and hugged Daisy, seeing she was indeed looking a lot healthier for this visit.

"Great, thanks, Loren," Robbie replied.

"Easy for you to say, Mr Heavy-Sleeper," Daisy raised one eyebrow in Robbie's direction, and Loren chuckled.

"Can I see my beautiful goddaughter?" Nathan asked, bouncing on his toes.

Daisy laughed. "Sure." She twisted the car seat around, revealing a tiny pink bundle fast asleep.

"She's so cute," Nathan whispered, kneeling next to Baby Lexi on the floor.

"Nathan? Why don't we take her into the living room, and you can sit next to her on the rug? You'll be more comfortable there than on the hard floor," Loren advised.

"Okay, Daddy." Nathan jumped up from the floor, and, carefully, picked up the seat, trailing slowly towards the living room.

Loren smirked. Nathan had never been around babies and didn't understand their resilience. Every time he saw Lexi, he treated her like a china doll. Every movement he made was slow, careful and measured around her. He adored the eight-day-old baby.

Loren knew Nathan would make a great father one day. And Loren wouldn't object to the idea either. But that was in the distant future, anyhow.

"Would you like something to drink?"

"A cup of tea would be nice, if it's not too much trouble?"

"Not at all, Daisy. Robbie?"

"Coffee if you have some, if not, tea is fine. Thanks, Loren." Robbie sat on the sofa next to Daisy and rested his head on the back. If anything, Robbie appeared more tired and Daisy less so.

The morning was spent in great company and with great conversation. Much to Nathan's unhappiness, his friends left in the early afternoon, citing the need for more sleep. Loren prepared a snack for Nathan, hoping to boost his mood, but he sat on the sofa, crossed legged, staring at the TV.

Loren knew how to take his mind off things.

"Nathan?" When he peered over at Loren, he continued, "Go to the bedroom and strip. Leave your clothes tidy and lay on the bed on your front."

Nathan's eyes widened, and he scrambled to do what Loren asked.

Grabbing a bottle from the cupboard in the kitchen, Loren followed at a more sedate pace, giving Nathan time to do as asked. When he entered the room, Nathan was in the perfect position. Loren wandered to the end of the bed and dropped the bottle on the cover. He stripped out of his clothes, folding them and placing them on the chair with Nathan's and crawled onto the bed, straddling Nathan's thighs.

Clicking open the bottle, he poured a little of the contents into his palm, sealed the bottle again and began rubbing his hands together. The lavender oil warmed, and he placed his hands on Nathan's back. Rubbing in long movements up and down his spine, he made sure every expanse of skin was covered, sometimes rubbing firm, sometimes soft.

Loren's cock was hard, and he purposefully teased Nathan's crack every time he pushed his hands to Nathan's shoulders, then pulled away when he lowered them. The moans, groans and pleas falling from Nathan's lips made Loren leer. Punishment could be enacted in different ways.

Bucking his hips into the mattress below, Nathan pleaded for relief, but Loren refused, even when Loren's hands descended to massage Nathan's ass cheeks and upper thighs.

"Please, Daddy."

Deciding to give Nathan some relief, but only minor, Loren told him he could turn over.

"Thank you, Daddy."

Loren smirked. He filled his palm again and proceeded to repeat the whole process on the front of Nathan's body, this time Loren's cock pressed against Nathan's cock, making Nathan bite his lip. No doubt withholding the curses he wanted to say.

When Nathan's body trembled so hard, he was practically vibrating and his cock streamed precome, Loren felt his control falter. He turned Nathan onto his front once more, lifting him to his knees, and prepared him. Loren knew Nathan enjoyed a small bite of pain with the initial entry. He used two fingers then lubed his shaft, leaning over his back.

"Mine!" Loren called as he breached Nathan's hole.

"Yes, Daddy! Yours! Always yours!" Nathan braced himself on his hands, pushing back against Loren.

Thrusting his hips in a punishing rhythm, Loren lost himself to the feeling of Nathan. One hand gripped Nathan's hip, the other his shoulder, giving him more leverage. His orgasm was fast approaching, he canted his hips slightly, knowing the correct angle and was rewarded with a cry of release. The vice clenching his cock brought his climax forward, and he shouted Nathan's name.

When their legs could no longer hold them up, they cuddled up with Nathan's back to Loren's chest, regaining their breath.

"I love you, Daddy."

"I love you, sweet boy."

SOOTHE ME, DADDY

ISAAC & HENLEY

Acknowledgements

I want to thank several people who have helped me get this book ready to go:

Emma, thank you so much for believing in me and being my cheerleader. You are amazing.

Maria, my fantastic editor, who helps me keep things straight, gives me advice when I'm lost and an ear when I need it. Keep strong. You're the best.

Renee, who keeps me on the straight and narrow with her evilly helpful deeds. I don't think I would have been able to make everything run as smoothly without you by my side.

Chapter One

Henley James had watched him for the past six months: he asked colleagues about their families, he brought items into the office that had been discussed previously, he brought cards and gifts on birthdays, he helped colleagues when they were under the weather. This acquaintance…this stranger freely gave other people what Henley longed for. To be taken care of.

When he first began working in customer services at the uniform manufacturing company, Henley thought it would be a short stop before he decided where to focus his attention. At thirty-three, he should have known what he wanted to be when he grew up, but he didn't. He struggled to find jobs that held his attention for more than a few years, which meant his resume was not the best example of a reliable employee.

Fortunately for him, EasyFit Uniforms Ltd was an amazing company to work for. Each day was different from the last—regarding the small details of the calls, not the actual day to day process—and he had fun with his colleagues. Anne had trained him for a week, and now, she sat next to him, answering the calls as he did but laughing and joking in between. As soon as he'd finished his training, Anne had included him in their bi-monthly nights out, which always ended up as a display of drunken wandering through the streets before he found his way home.

Best nights ever.

Isaac Chapman never joined them. When Henley had brought up the question of why others didn't join in, Neil, another customer service assistant, explained that each department had their own little groups that ventured out together. It was only during big company events that the groups mixed. Henley thought it a shame because he wanted to get to know Isaac better.

It was the only reason he could think of as to why he was sat in a comfortable visitor's chair in the manager's office answering questions about why he thought he was a good fit for the customer service executive position.

The job title sounded much fancier than the job description did. The job was travelling throughout the country, assisting different stores in their uniform needs. That was the baseline, anyway. There were other responsibilities included, but Henley knew he wouldn't have a problem doing them.

"Well, Henley. Unless you have any questions for me, I think we're finished." Derek Sanders studied him, but Henley shook his head.

"You seem to have answered everything I thought about. Thank you."

"Very well. I have two more applicants to see before the end of the day, and tomorrow, I will be making my decision. I'll let you know before you finish work tomorrow for definite."

Henley nodded his understanding and stood, holding out his hand. "Thank you for the opportunity."

"You're welcome, Henley. Now, go grab a coffee before you head back to work." Mr Sanders smiled, showing the gap in his front teeth.

Grinning in response, Henley pivoted and left the room, closing the door quietly behind him before aiming towards the staff kitchen. Finding the surprisingly large room empty, Henley trailed to the kettle and set it boiling.

Most people would say that applying for a new job for the sole purpose of getting to spend more time with another person was crazy, but Henley honestly believed he would enjoy the role. He had no qualms about spending long hours driving or travelling on various public transport, he could happily talk the ear off anyone who would listen, and he knew about fashion. Regardless of the outcome of his infatuation with Isaac, Henley knew he wouldn't let the company down.

Lifting his mug for a scalding sip of his tea, he carried it up two flights of stairs to the customer service department, the ringing of phones and mechanical sounds of printers reaching his ears before the doors became visible. He strode to his seat, placing his mug on the unicorn coaster Anne had given him as a "welcome to the team" present, and dropped down into his chair, bending forward to stretch out his back before sitting upright again.

"How did it go?" Anne whispered before returning to her caller. "Yes. Once you've filled out the correct sizes, click submit, and the order will be sent through. I will put a hurry on it this end for you. You should have it delivered in three days at most."

Henley waited until she bid goodbye to the caller before answering, "It seemed to go alright. I'll find out tomorrow."

"It's good that you don't have to wait too long. When do they want someone to start?"

Henley logged onto the computer. "Two weeks."

Anne whistled. "That's not long to find a replacement for you."

"Aww. You think I have the job. That's so sweet." Henley fluttered his eyelashes at her, receiving a backhanded slap to his shoulder. "Hey, no damaging the merchandise. I need to be pretty for tomorrow."

Anne chuckled. "Why? Do you think your looks are what will get you the job?"

"No, don't be silly. It's our night out! I'm so looking forward to letting loose for a few hours."

"Are you bringing your sisters with you? They were a hoot last time."

Snickering at the thought of the night to which she was referring, he shook his head. "Not this time. Ariel and Arianne might be double the fun, but they are also double the hassle when they're hungover. Who knew that twins would have different but equally gross results to excessive alcohol?" He shuddered in mock horror.

"You know you love them," Bernie teased from across the desk.

"Yes, but even I have my limits. I dropped them off at Dad and Pops the following morning." He cackled and rubbed his hands with glee. "Served them right for doing the same thing to me with Rebecca when we were younger. I swear I still smell the vomit whenever I hoover my living room carpet."

"Gross." Anne grimaced.

Henley slid on his headphones, ensuring they didn't mess with his hairdo or snag on his earrings. He'd done that a few times before, and it wasn't pleasant. Adjusting his sleeves and fidgeting to get comfortable, he inhaled and signed on, immediately answering a call with a manicured finger.

"Good afternoon. EasyFit Uniforms. My name is Henley. How can I help you today?"

The afternoon hours flew by, and when Henley disconnected his final call of the day, he blew out a breath. Anne had gone home half an hour ago, leaving a quarter of the staff left in the department. The company believed having staggered start and finish times made more sense with the number of calls received at those times. Henley was one of the last people to leave the building each day.

He descended the stairs as he pulled on his jacket, his bracelets jingling and glittering in the spotlights. Henley wasn't an overly feminine guy, but he knew what he liked and what looked good on him, so he went with *his* flow. He refused to acknowledge anyone who told him otherwise. He had his dads and sisters to thank for that.

Waving goodbye to Leah, the receptionist, Henley jogged to his car, wanting to avoid the fine mist of rain. Enclosing himself in the warm interior, he decided to visit his parents. He could let them know about the job interview while checking up on them.

Twenty-five minutes later, he pushed through the front door, calling out his usual jovial greeting, "Yo! Henley's in the house!" Guaranteed to receive groans or chuckles every single time.

"Hey! I wasn't expecting to see you tonight. How are you?" His dad, Lewis, had been a sprightly man in his younger days, but as the years wore on, Henley could see that time was taking its toll. At seventy-five years young, his dad used a cane and walked as fast as his arthritic joints would allow. Never a day went by when he didn't have a smile, though.

Henley hopped over to hug him, holding him tight. "I'm good, thanks, Dad. I had a job interview today."

"Oh, are you searching for a new place already? I thought you liked it there."

Henley linked his dad's arm through his as they aimed for the kitchen, where pots and pans were crashing and clanking. "Oh, I do. It's an internal position. A step up the ladder, if you like."

"That's amazing! Well done, you."

"I haven't got it yet." Henley snorted and rolled his eyes.

"Haven't got what yet?" a gruff voice asked.

Henley deposited his dad on a chair at the table and hurried around to wrap his arms around Pops' neck from behind. "Hey, Pops."

A hand patted his arms in affection, but the voice repeated the question.

"The job I interviewed for today. I find out tomorrow." He stepped over to the cooker, placing a kiss on his sister's cheek. "Hey, Becca."

Becca smiled as she dished up dinner. Henley grabbed himself a plate and added it to the counter with the others before grabbing a pan to help serve. He never had to worry about there not being enough food for unexpected visitors. The family made extras whenever they cooked, and if there ended up being leftovers, it was frozen for another time. With them being such a big family, large quantities had always been necessary. At least, as long as Henley could remember, but he was the youngest of the five of them and didn't know any better.

"So, what was the job?" Pops asked, digging into the fluffy mashed potatoes.

Henley brought over glasses for each of them before answering, "There was a position for someone to travel and visit stores up and down the country, helping them out. It seemed a good fit for someone as socially extroverted as I am." Henley chuckled.

"Is that another name for a flirt?" Becca asked around a mouthful of food.

Henley threw his napkin in her direction. "I don't need another name for it. I am a flirt. But the position needed someone who could talk to anyone. I think I can do that." He held his hand up and smirked.

"You could talk their ear off. The problem is getting you to stop," groused Pops.

Henley pouted, forehead creasing. "Hey! I stop." He lifted his nose in the air before smirking again. "When I'm asleep."

They snorted their agreement before continuing to eat.

"Are you staying over tonight?" Dad asked.

Henley shook his head. "No, it was just a short visit. I need to get my beauty sleep ready for the work night out tomorrow." However ungentlemanly it was, Henley devoured his meal. Becca was the best cook out of them, Tracey came next, and Ariel and Arianne…well, he was surprised they didn't wither away from lack of edible options was all he could say about them. It was one thing the twins did have in common.

After pleasant conversation and helping with the washing up so Becca could rest, Henley said his good-nights and drove towards home. He needed to visit the gym, but he was too full after dinner. He'd have to get up early and head there before work. Not his favourite time to go but much needed.

After locking up the house behind him, Henley climbed the stairs as a yawn stole his breath. He strode into the bathroom, rubbing his eyes and stifling another yawn. Now that he was home, he didn't care about his hairstyle, so he threaded his hands through the longer blue-green tinted strands and scratched at his scalp. He glanced in the mirror and removed his earrings, necklace and bracelet, placing them on the counter for the next day. After another yawn escaped, he shook his head and moved into his bedroom. He removed his clothes, throwing them in the wash basket before sinking into his expensive but totally worth it mattress, naked as the day he was born.

Having retrieved his phone before discarding his trousers, he plugged it into the charger, double-checked his alarm and turned over.

KATY PERRY BLARED through the silence at five o'clock the next morning. Instantly awake, Henley sat up, rubbing his face free of sleep before dismissing the wake-up call. Knowing if he sat there too long, he'd fall back asleep, he flung the covers off and got ready for the gym.

Henley worked hard on his body and wouldn't let anything mess it up. Not even interested in the vanity side of exercising, he did it because he liked how he felt after he'd worked up a sweat. Energy pulsed through his muscles, giving him a buzz. He usually had a lot of get-up-and-go anyway, but the gym amped it up further, and by the time he arrived at work, he was ready to take on the world and win.

Unfortunately, the day didn't agree with his outlook and time dawdled. Several times, he requested additional work to keep him busy until he received a request for his presence in the manager's office. Taking a deep inhale, he danced his way down the hallways and staircases, expending far too little energy before arriving at the door.

Mr Sanders called him in, and Henley sat in the same seat he'd sat in not even twenty-four hours prior.

"Okay, Henley. I have good news. I would like to offer you the position." Mr Sanders sat back in his seat, resting his linked fingers on his stomach.

Henley beamed. "Seriously? That's fantastic. Thank you so much."

"You're more than welcome." He leaned forward again, reaching for some papers. "We will get you sorted out with a new contract shortly, but in the meantime, I thought I'd run through a few things with you today if that's okay?"

"Definitely."

"So, you're starting date will be two weeks on Monday, and you will be trained by the same person for eight weeks and then given free rein to work by yourself. During your training period, you will either be picked up by your trainer, or you will need to meet him at a desig-nated point, but you can discuss those details with him."

At the word "him," Henley sat up a bit straighter. There were only three guys on the executive team: Isaac, Blake and Leon. Clearing his throat, he asked, "Can I ask who my trainer will be?"

"Of course. Sorry, I should've mentioned that. Isaac will be training you."

Henley inhaled through his teeth slowly, hoping to withhold his reaction to those words. When he'd applied for the position, he never actually thought Isaac would be training him. He'd only ever seen Trish train executives before. There was no way on this earth he was going to complain about it, though. He was about to spend eight hours a day, five days a week, for eight weeks in the company of the one man who intrigued him so much, he applied for a new job.

If that didn't show his interest, he didn't know what did.

Chapter Two

ISAAC

Isaac Chapman coughed as he reached the third floor of his apartment building, breathing in much-needed air. He'd let his exercise regime go after his last failed relationship, not caring about anything for such a long time. Unfortunately, he was feeling the effects now and needed to start doing something about it.

If only he could find someone like Lisa had. He smiled as he remembered the expression on her face when he gave her some flowers. The previous day, she had announced she was expecting her first child, and everyone was ecstatic for her. Anyone who carried a human being inside their body for nine months, or however long the baby decided to stay in there, deserved to be treated throughout, so he would ensure to grab her little gifts over the coming months to keep her upbeat and comfortable.

Doing little things for his colleagues settled something inside him, something that was usually centred around having a boy to take care of. Being between relationships made him feel a loss that was not easily filled.

It was not easy for boys to accept Isaac's need to be a Daddy all day long, inside the home environment and outside in the world. He was particular about the boy he needed, too. They had to be on the older side of the scale, not young enough to be infants. Isaac had attempted that type of relationship before, and it didn't fit in with his personality. Every Daddy was different, as every boy was different.

Unlocking his front door, he exhaled heavily, finally regaining enough calm to breathe unhindered. He needed to start at the gym again. Maybe it was something he could begin after he'd finished training the newbie executive.

Isaac had seen him around the office—who could miss the shock of blue hair—but hadn't been introduced until today. Henley certainly wasn't shy, which would be a benefit, but he seemed…fidgety. Isaac couldn't put his finger on it, but he supposed he'd find out next week. In three days, he would be collecting Henley for his first day of training.

Flicking the light on, Isaac divested himself of his coat and shoes before shuffling to his kitchen to shelve the leftovers his mother had foisted on him earlier that evening. Friday night was family night, and he and his three siblings and their families all congregated at their parents' house for dinner. Isaac rarely missed them, only on the occasion when his work nights out couldn't be organised for the Saturday as they usually were. Most people would think him strange for bowing out of a family dinner to go on a work night out, but for him, family nights happened every week, whereas the work nights were bi-monthly, and he believed it was important to ensure a good working relationship with those around him.

His thoughts took him to Henley again. Isaac wondered whether Henley would continue to go out with the customer service staff as well as the executives. He appeared to have a good relationship with them, so Isaac would be surprised if he brushed them off now he'd changed jobs. Not that Isaac knew Henley well yet.

He stretched his arms above his head as he strode down the hallway to his bedroom. It was only ten o'clock, but he was shattered. It had been a long week of driving to the extreme edges of Britain. Most of the time, he was able to schedule appointments that were close together in location, meaning he could get a hotel and save himself some driving. Unfortunately, this week hadn't been one of those weeks. He'd been in Sheffield, Brighton, spent two days in Cardiff and then up to York. Sleep was the first thing on his agenda this weekend. Starting after he'd had a shower.

"WE WANTED to see if you'd come for breakfast with us."

Isaac blinked his eyes blearily as he tried to decipher the time on the clock beside him. As the number eight swam into view, he groaned and rolled to his back. "It. Is.

Eight. On. A. Saturday. Morning. Felicity." Every word was punctuated with a growl.

"I know! We'll buy you breakfast, though. We're at Pete's Café on Main Street. We'll have coffee waiting…?" Felicity sing-songed the last sentence, earning another growl from Isaac, although he wavered.

"Fine. Give me half an hour or so."

"Yay! See you soon, Is." Her nickname for him made him smile despite the early wake-up call. She must have something to tell him if she was waking him up as the sun barely peeked over the horizon when she knew he normally slept in on a Saturday. He blew out a breath and pushed to a seated position. With his eyes still wanting to close, he rubbed a hand across them, bringing his fingers towards the middle to wipe the sleep away.

It was only as he shuffled to the bathroom that he realised Felicity had said "we." Isaac doubted she was talking about her husband, Van, so it was more than likely Sarah, his other sister. Double trouble indeed. There had better be coffee waiting.

An hour later, he finally made it through the door of the café to find his two sisters, chittering like old ladies across a table from each other. His sisters could easily have passed as twins: their dual blue-black hair hanging to their shoulders, and their slim frames reminiscent of their mother's appearance made him smile. Their whole family took after their mother, so she would never be able to disown any of them.

"Isaac!" Felicity jumped up from the chair and flung her arms around his neck.

He stumbled backwards under her attack, chuckling

in her ear. "Anyone would think you hadn't seen me for years when, in fact, it was only last night."

"I know, but I have news that I couldn't share last night."

Isaac pulled back, narrowing his gaze on Felicity's face. "And…"

She smiled wide. "We found a surrogate." She bit her bottom lip, trying to contain the excitement on her face that her body had already shown.

"That's great news." He dragged her in for another tight hug, rubbing his hand up and down her back as he felt her breath hitch.

Doctors had told Felicity several years prior that she was unable to have kids, and it broke her heart as well as her husband's. After attending counselling for a year or so, they had finally begun talking about other ways of expanding their family. They had originally chosen the adoption route until Felicity acknowledged her wish to have something that was a part of Van if it couldn't also be a part of her. They'd been through another few difficult sessions with the psychologist before agreeing to the surrogacy route.

Their first attempt to find someone had failed when the surrogate pulled away after a few meetings. Although Felicity knew that there were others out there, it had been a difficult time for them all. Both Felicity and Van agreed to take a step back for a few months to reconnect as a couple before delving back into anything. Neither wanted their relationship to suffer, and Isaac was damn proud of them for it.

"I hadn't told anyone before because I didn't want to

jinx it," she admitted as she dropped back into her seat. "But the contracts have been signed, and everything has been given the go-ahead. As soon as Shelby's ready, we'll start."

"I'm so happy for you. Are you going to tell Mum and Dad?" Isaac sat beside Sarah, wrapping her in a one-armed hug.

"Not yet." She played with her coffee cup, turning it around in place as she lowered her gaze. "I want to wait until I have something else to tell them."

"Understandable." Isaac smiled at her, resting his hand over hers. "I'm so pleased for you."

"Me, too," Sarah added.

"Well, you know where I am if you need anything." Isaac would be there whatever the weather to help if she needed it. If any of them needed it. "Have you told Jeremy?"

Felicity snorted. "No. He'd go straight to Mum about it if I did. He can wait like they have to."

"He's going to be so pissed at you when he finds out." Sarah rolled her lips inwards, attempting to hide her glee.

Felicity shrugged.

"Anyway, where's my coffee?" Isaac mock growled.

Sarah pushed at his shoulder, moving him so she could scramble out. "I'll get it."

Felicity hooted as Sarah skipped across the tiled floor.

"What's all that about?" Isaac asked, watching his little sister gesture wildly when she reached the counter.

"She has the hots for the barista. Every time we come in here, she's the only one who's allowed to order."

Isaac grinned. He might pass by the counter on his

way out and see what he could do for her, obviously, without her knowledge. He could honestly go for a couple of cakes to takeaway. Anything for the chance to make her happy.

And he did just that. After an hour of catching up on the topics that were not parent-friendly, he made his excuses and expressed an interest in some bakery items. Sarah attempted to come with him until he gave Felicity a significant look, and she ushered Sarah out of the door quickly, "remembering" something they had to do. He'd have to thank Felicity later.

"Good morning, sir. What can I get for you today?"

Isaac leaned his elbows on the counter as he stared at the delicious looking sweet treats. Indicating two of them, he casually asked, "Do you have a girlfriend?"

The barista, Miller, his nametag said, glanced across at him with raised eyebrows and an increasing blush on his cheeks. "No, sir."

"A boyfriend?"

The colour increased as he cleared his throat. "No, sir."

"What do you think of my sister? The one who ordered for us?"

Miller concentrated heavily on his movements, but Isaac could see his jaw clenching. "She's…beautiful."

"That she is." He paused, standing upright once more. "Would you like to go on a date with her?"

Miller's surprised gaze found his as he pushed the cake box over the counter. "What? Really?" At Isaac's nod, he beamed. "I'd love to."

Isaac smiled. "Are you free tonight?"

Miller nodded emphatically.

"Alright. Meet her at Romano's at eight. I'll make sure she's there." He hesitated, narrowing his gaze at Miller. "Don't mess her around or stand her up. Got it?"

"Yes, sir. No, sir. I'll be there."

"Good." Isaac paid for his treats, nodded and left the café.

As he reached his car, he texted Felicity and told her the news, indicating it was up to Felicity to get Sarah to Romano's at eight. When she complained, he cited the fact that she got him out of bed on his sleep-in day. She soon acquiesced.

Driving home, Isaac was content. He was happy with how his life was for the most part. He wished for someone to share it with, though.

MONDAY MORNING DAWNED FAR TOO EARLY for Isaac's liking. Being a night owl made waking up difficult, but every damn morning, he obediently woke at five-thirty to ensure he had time to get a shower and some breakfast before getting on the road. Today, however, he had to leave slightly earlier to collect Henley first. Henley had offered to drive to Isaac's place, but Isaac had told him not to worry.

By seven, he was outside Henley's house. He had planned to knock on the door, but Henley came bounding down the path, swinging a backpack onto his shoulder and a lunch bag by his side.

Isaac raised his eyebrows at the exuberant display so early in the morning but didn't comment.

Flinging open Isaac's passenger door, Henley dropped heavily into the seat. "Good morning, Isaac." Henley grinned as he stuffed the two bags into the footwell between his legs.

"Morning." Isaac's eyebrows had yet to lower. He could see that Henley was a morning person, and he wasn't sure if he could handle so much energy at that time of day.

Running his gaze over Henley's outfit, Isaac decided that he fit the look required for being an executive. He wore grey trousers paired with a matching waistcoat and a light pink shirt. Small earrings in the shape of the infinity symbol dangled from his earlobes. Through the open neck of the shirt, Isaac caught a glimpse of a braided necklace but couldn't see anymore, and when Henley moved his arms, Isaac heard jangling. With the other visible jewellery, Isaac was led to believe Henley also wore bracelets. All the items were allowed as part of the uniform, so Isaac was pleased with what he saw.

"Are you happy with how I look?"

Isaac flicked his gaze to Henley, noting the eager light in his eyes. "Very much so. You'll fit in well."

"Thank you," Henley uttered. "Are we leaving now?"

Isaac wondered for a moment what Henley meant until he realised they were still parked outside his house. Clearing his throat, Isaac thought quickly. "I'm waiting for you to put your seatbelt on. We need to keep you safe."

Henley's eyes closed for the briefest moment, then he

twisted to reach the belt and slid it across his body, clicking it into place. When his gaze met Isaac's once more, Isaac's breath caught. He wasn't entirely sure what the look was about, but it was powerful enough that he blinked away from the spell and put the car in gear.

As he drove towards the motorway, Isaac flicked through what he knew about Henley. Mr Sanders hadn't given Isaac a lot of information to work with, other than Henley was a sociable guy and would do a good job. That was great, but Isaac needed more. He supposed he could go straight to the source as he *was* sat right next to him.

"What made you decide you wanted to do this job and not stay in customer services?" Isaac asked as he merged onto the dual carriageway, keeping his eyes straight ahead or on his mirrors.

"Well, I'm talkative. Although you probably didn't know that because I haven't said much since we've been in the car. But that was because I thought you wanted to concentrate on the road. Apart from that, usually, I like talking to other people and getting to know them better. And with this position, it felt like I'd be able to do that every day. Also, I like fashion, so clothes…yeah. I think I can do a good job of it."

Isaac waited to see if Henley had anything else to add to his dialogue, but when nothing else came, he smiled and said, "You'll be able to see over the next few weeks what's involved, but talking to people is a must."

Chapter Three

HENLEY

Henley wasn't sure if he detected a teasing note in Isaac's tone, but if there was, he ignored it because he didn't want to get off on the wrong foot. When he'd been waiting for Isaac to show up, he'd been pacing the hallway by the front door for at least half an hour, trying to remind himself not to overshare—or rather over-talk —straight away.

That lasted all of around twenty minutes. It was Isaac's fault, though. He'd asked the question. It would've been rude not to answer it.

"How long have you been doing this job?" Henley asked, crossing his right arm over his waist and leaning his left elbow on it as he fiddled with his earring while staring across at Isaac. He was a gorgeous specimen, and not just on the outside. Henley always believed that kindness bled through into how other people saw you regardless of your outer appearance. Ignoring his thoughts on Isaac, Henley studied him in a detached manner as he had done when he'd first seen him. Now, he was closer, though.

Isaac wore some extra weight around his waist, but his basic build was solid, so it wasn't as easy to see. His face was lined in the right places, indicating he had plenty of laughter in his life, although some of those lines were harder to see as they blended in with his stubble, which was about the same length as his salt and pepper hair. Henley hadn't thought Isaac was old enough to have grey hair, but maybe he was. It had him wondering how old he was.

"I've been doing this for fifteen years now. I came into the role straight away, without working in the customer service department first."

"Wow. You must have started here straight after school. How did you know what you wanted to do at that age?" Henley rested part of his upper lip between his teeth as he fought back a smile. Isaac had given him the perfect opening to talk about ages.

Briefly glancing across the car to Henley, Isaac's mouth curled up. "Thank you for the compliment, but I was twenty-nine when I started. I'm forty-four now." He sniffed. "If you wanted to know my age, you could've asked."

Henley snorted, covering his smile with his hand. "Sorry."

"You don't need to be sorry. You need to be upfront. If you want to know the answer to something, ask. It's important to be open about things."

Turning his gaze to the passing scenery, Henley thought about that. He wasn't sure he could be honest about everything, especially his reasoning behind applying for the job, but he could be as open as possible about most other things.

"Did I lose you?"

Isaac's voice washed over him, and he forced himself to concentrate. "No. I was thinking about what you said. You're right."

They were silent again for a moment, an unusual occurrence for Henley until Isaac broke it with a question of his own.

"Do you have any family?"

"How much time do you have?" Henley sniggered.

"Around two hours, give or take."

"I wasn't…" Henley paused when he noticed the smirk on Isaac's face. "Funny." He held his hand out in front of him, counting off his fingers. "I have four older sisters: Tracey, Ariel, Arianne and Rebecca. My dads chose a mixture of adoption and surrogacy to welcome us all into the family. Ariel and Arianne are twins born of a surrogate, and when they were four, Tracey was adopted into the family. She was eight at the time and had been bounced around the system for too long." He didn't know the whole story about Tracey's life before she came to them, but he knew it wasn't an easy one. "Rebecca came as a surprise into the family at age one. Dad and Pops hadn't planned on adopting another child because their surrogate was already pregnant with me. But they told us they'd talked it over and decided that if they had managed with twins, they should be able to manage with a one-year-old and a newborn. And that was that."

"A very eclectic family."

"Definitely. We're really close. Dad and Pops are getting on in years now, so Rebecca lives with them, helping them out and looking after them when they allow it. I try to help out when I can."

"Sounds like you all do a lot for each other."

"I certainly wouldn't be like I am today if it wasn't for them all, that's for certain."

"What do you mean?"

Henley grinned, twisting in his seat to face Isaac. "I had four sisters to show me how to dress, how to do makeup, how to wear jewellery, what colours go to together, how to do my hair. Everything. Can you imagine me as anything but what I am now?"

Isaac flicked his gaze over to Henley's again for a brief second before returning to the road ahead. "I withhold judgement until I get to know you a bit better."

Henley giggled. "Excuses, excuses." He paused, regaining his breath. "Anyway, what about you?"

"What about me, what?"

"Say that twice as fast," Henley murmured before answering Isaac's question, "What about your family?"

Isaac cleared his throat. "I have two younger sisters and a younger brother and my mum and dad."

Henley waited for more information, but Isaac remained silent. "That's it? That's all you're going to tell me?"

"Yes."

Henley pouted. "Why? I told you my whole sordid family past."

"I didn't ask you to."

"What happened to being open and honest?"

Isaac grinned. "I thought you'd throw that back in my face." He sighed. "Alright. Jeremy is the child next down from me, Sarah then Felicity. Felicity is married to Van and has something in common with your family. They've just found their surrogate."

Henley clapped his hands together in small but fast movements. "Yay! That's wonderful news! Oh, wow. I know you're likely to already do this, but make sure you pamper Felicity throughout the pregnancy. She'll feel the loss of not being the one bringing the child into the world."

"How do you know?"

"When I first found out about our circumstances, I researched surrogacy and adoption, trying to figure out the differences and what that made us as a family. It was when I was a teenager and feeling a little…lost, I guess. I finally approached someone for more information, and they suggested I speak to a surrogate to get their side of the story. You know, why they chose to give another couple a family and all that. It was one of the things the surrogate said to me. People who were unable to carry their babies felt at a loss, useless almost, but they are the most important because they can rest and get everything ready for when the baby comes. Naturally, they'll need their energy."

Isaac was silent for a moment. "That was a brave thing you did."

Henley studied his hands that were linked in his lap, a small smile playing on his face as he preened at the pleasure of Isaac's words.

"I will say, though, my question was about how you knew I would already do it."

How was he going to answer the question without giving away his obsession with Isaac? "I've noticed you bring gifts in for people in the office." He wouldn't expand on his answer.

"Hmm."

Henley threw himself into the topic of work, asking questions about what would happen when they got there and what he would need to do. Before too long, they had arrived at the store, parking close to the staff entrance. Isaac slid a laminated sheet onto the dashboard, which Henley quickly picked up and read before replacing. It told the car park attendants that they were there for work.

Unclipping his seat belt, Henley exited the car. He left his backpack but grabbed his lunch bag before joining Isaac at the boot, where Isaac was going through several bits of paperwork. When Henley began questioning him again, Isaac pivoted to face him and rested both hands against Henley's shoulders.

"Henley?" At Henley's nod, Isaac said, "Breathe."

Henley inhaled a shaky breath, exhaling slowly.

"Good. There is plenty of time to learn everything. Do not worry. Calm yourself. I will show you everything. Eventually."

Nodding his head, Henley gave a cheeky smile. "Everything?" he asked, raising one eyebrow.

Isaac snorted and shook his head, returning to his papers, ignoring Henley's words. Henley wondered how long it would take for him to get under Isaac's skin.

When they entered the store, signed in and clipped visitor's badges to their shirts, they were led to a sizable room filled with cardboard boxes, tables and a few chairs. Henley's eyebrows rose at the sight of so many boxes, especially as he knew this was one of the smaller stores.

"Henley?"

Henley glanced across to where Isaac was placing his bag on the table. When his gaze connected with Isaac's, Isaac spoke, "Breathe."

Chuckling at the second reminder, he danced to the table. "Henley, reporting for duty, sir," he pronounced, standing tall. He smiled at the snort that escaped Isaac's mouth.

"Right, first things first. We have to go through all these boxes and sort them into alphabetical order."

Henley's eyes widened. "What?"

Isaac grinned. "Welcome to the world of executives." Isaac strode over to the first box, opened it and pulled out a plastic covered item of clothing. "The best way to start is to open a few boxes first and sort them onto the tables into piles. Once some of the boxes are empty, we can start filling them up with certain letters of the alphabet. So, a and b together, c and d together, and so on."

"Could they not have been put in the boxes in alphabetical order?" Henley pondered aloud.

"Possibly, but the warehouse works out *their* best way to get *their* job done as fast as they can while doing what they should be doing. Then it's our turn to do our best job with what we have to work with."

"Surely, it wouldn't be too difficult to print the name labels off in alphabetical order; the clothes would be put in boxes the same way." Henley opened a box several down from Isaac and started sorting.

"It's something to speak to the warehouse about when we go visit them."

Henley worked solidly for the next few hours, chatting about anything and everything that came to mind. Several times throughout the morning, Isaac retrieved hot or cold drinks for them and ensured that Henley took breaks. If Henley had been alone, he would've continued working and probably finished it all before stopping for anything. Inwardly, he glowed from the care Isaac showed. He decided it must come naturally to Isaac, possibly because he had younger siblings. No doubt, he spent his time taking care of them when he was younger, as well as now.

When their day ended, Henley had met a huge number of people, engaging with each one he could and helping them find their uniform, checking that they fit and ordering new if not. As he packed away their order forms, Henley exhaled.

"You alright?" Isaac asked, appearing next to him.

Henley smiled and nodded. "Yeah. I am. This was amazing."

Isaac's mouth curled. "I knew you'd be a natural."

Ducking his head away from the scrutiny and compliment, Henley closed the bag. "All set."

Isaac silently observed Henley for a moment before he inclined his head and indicated the door with a wave of his hand. "After you."

On the journey home, Henley was quieter than usual. The day, however great as it had been, was tiring, and he was ready for sleep. The scenery passed by in a blur of green interspersed with grey as they raced down the motorway towards home.

"Henley?"

Henley blinked his eyes open, lifting his head with a wince when his neck protested loudly. Yawning and rubbing a hand over his face, he tried to get his bearings. Glancing across at Isaac, he saw a line appear between his brows as Isaac studied him.

"Sorry. Guess I was more tired than I thought." Henley peered at their surroundings, finding them parked outside his house. "How long did I sleep for?" He turned back to Isaac with raised eyebrows.

"Around an hour. You might want to head straight to bed when you get in; otherwise, you will end up with a headache for sleeping so little after such a long day. Try not to do anything to perk you up too much. Maybe clean up and get some sleep. It's been a long day."

Henley nodded, his brain not functioning yet. "I will," he said distractedly.

"I'll pick you up again tomorrow, same time. Alright?"

Henley nodded again.

"Henley?" He focused on Isaac's face. "Go straight to bed, okay?"

The forcefulness of Isaac's words pierced the cloud surrounding his brain, and Henley answered, "Yes, sir," before he even realised what he was going to say. Eyes widening, Henley murmured, "Thanks," and got out of the car, wrestling with his bags. When they finally came free with Isaac's help, Henley waved and whirled around.

As he climbed the steps to his sanctuary, he thought about what Isaac said. He could feel pressure behind his eyes, so he knew a headache would be coming just as Isaac predicted. Henley locked the door behind him, dropped his bags by the door and strode for the bathroom. After a quick visit, he trudged to his room and stripped, throwing his clothes in the vicinity of the wash basket. He faceplanted on his bed, then struggled to get the covers from underneath him, cursing himself for not moving them before he laid down.

Thankful that his alarm was programmed to ring every weekday, so he didn't have to remember to set it, he tucked the duvet around him, resting one hand under his pillow as he nestled into it.

Exhaling deeply, Henley smiled as he remembered Isaac's words. Obeying him was something Henley had no problem doing, in fact, he relished the idea of doing it. He only hoped it would continue, and potentially, become more. From what he'd seen of Isaac's behaviour today, and factoring in what Henley had witnessed previously, Isaac would make a fantastic Daddy.

Chapter Four

ISAAC

As the weeks passed, Isaac determined several things about Henley. Firstly, he was a quick learner. Everything Isaac explained to him was picked up straight away with rare occurrences when it needed repeating. Secondly, Henley was a social butterfly. He could coax the quietest employee out of their shell enough to get the job done with the least amount of fuss. Thirdly, he could talk the ear off anyone in the vicinity. Finally, and possibly the most important, at least to Isaac, Henley was the most obedient person Isaac had ever met. Even his past partners had nothing on Henley.

And damn if he didn't want to see how far that obedience went.

He didn't test it, though.

Isaac pulled up outside Henley's house. The executives were heading for a bar in Cambridge city centre that night, and Isaac was the designated driver for five of them, with Blake driving the other four. The bars were used to their little group now as they always visited the same venues, although alternating between them each time.

Isaac climbed the step to get to the front door and pressed the doorbell.

"Hold on!" Henley shouted from inside, and Isaac's mouth twitched at the usual exuberance.

When the door swung open, Isaac turned from his perusal of the neighbourhood to view the guy in front of him. Struck speechless, Isaac's gaze roamed over the vision that was Henley. Dressed in light blue skinny jeans tucked into what Isaac knew were Converse trainers and a white t-shirt with rainbow colours dripping from the top, Henley looked fantastic. But that wasn't what caught Isaac's attention.

Henley's face was painted to perfection. With a slight blush to his cheeks, whether natural or artificial, and pink painted lips, he looked divine, but his eyes shone the most. He had blue eyeshadow, the same colour as his jeans; long black eyelashes, darkened and lengthened by mascara; and shimmer underneath his eyebrows. Combined with the slight wave of his styled blue-green hair, the effect was stunning.

A jangling noise brought Isaac out of his observation, and he glanced down to see a myriad of bracelets adorning Henley's arms.

Isaac swallowed hard and returned his gaze to Henley. "Ready?" he croaked.

Henley beamed. "Definitely."

Isaac pivoted and drifted to his car, trying to settle the butterflies that had suddenly taken flight in his stomach.

He didn't want to cross lines with a colleague; thus, he had to tamper down on all these new realisations and be the designated driver he was supposed to be.

"I'm so looking forward to this. There are some execs I've not met yet, aren't there?"

Henley started talking before he'd even sat in the car. Isaac briefly wondered whether alcohol would change Henley's personality at all. Some people became more confident—which Henley didn't need because he had confidence in spades—some became maudlin, some violent and probably other changes, too. He doubted Henley would become violent. It would be eye-opening to see the result of tonight's get-together.

"Yes, Henley. There are two you haven't met, but I will introduce you to them all again tonight to make sure, alright. You don't need to worry."

"Who are we picking up first?" Henley didn't need reminding to put his seat belt on anymore, Isaac noted.

"Sierra. Then Maddie and Jo," he added, anticipating Henley's next question. Thinking about their team, Isaac smiled. "We're more evened out now. Four guys, five women." There had been more men at one point.

"And it's Frankie and Leon I haven't met, isn't it?"

Isaac smiled, noting Henley's anxious tone. "Yes, that's right. They are great. Frankie has been with us for around two years, and Leon came onboard last year. He will be glad to not be the newbie anymore." Isaac chuckled.

"I won't be drinking much, so you don't need to worry about me," Henley said into the short silence.

"I'm not concerned. That's why I'm the designated driver. You can have as much fun as you want to, and I will be there to ensure you get home safely. If you want to drink, then do."

"I'm not a big drinker anyway, except for special occasions, I suppose. Ariel and Arianne's birthday party last year was one to behold, I must admit. Maybe I should start drinking more."

From the corner of his eye, Isaac saw Henley tapping his forefinger against his chin. "You don't need to drink more. You have enough confidence to talk to anyone and enough energy to fuel a house for a year. Alcohol won't give you anything you need. Only drink if you enjoy it and want to."

They picked up the three women before Isaac drove to the car park where he was leaving his car. They chatted and laughed through the streets to the bar, weaving their way through the Saturday night crowds to find the others, who had sent a message to Isaac saying they'd found a table. After guiding everyone to the rest of the team, Isaac quickly introduced Henley to everyone, took the drink order and battled his way through the masses once more.

He delivered his order to the bartender and the drinks to the table, and finally sat down on a spare chair to the left of Henley. As was ritual, the team had ordered shots and beer for their first round, so with a cheer, they were downed by everyone except Isaac and Blake. Henley coughed into his elbow after, following it with a healthy gulp of beer.

"God, that was awful!" He grimaced, swallowing several times.

Isaac grinned. "It will put some hair on your chest."

Henley smirked in his direction. "How do you know what I have on my chest?"

Nostrils flaring, Isaac narrowed his gaze, watching as Henley rolled his lips inwards to prevent a smile.

"Hey, Henley!" Trish shouted from the other end of the table. "Are you seeing anyone?"

"Why? I'm afraid you've got the wrong equipment for me, honey." Henley shook his head sadly.

The table erupted into laughter, and Henley received a weakly tossed napkin in his direction.

"No, you idiot. I wondered if you needed help finding someone," Trish replied.

"I'm single, but I'm good."

Henley glanced at him briefly before continuing with the new topic of conversation.

By the time they left that bar to walk to the other one, Isaac could see Henley had a buzz going. He'd kept track of what Henley had been drinking and ensured that he didn't mix his drinks. It wasn't Isaac's job to prevent Henley from getting a hangover, but he did his best to make sure Henley wouldn't feel worse.

All nine of them arrived at the new venue with little to no fanfare, where Trish, Sierra and Blake pulled Henley onto the dance floor. The rest of them found a small table with a few chairs and perched with drinks as the conversation continued.

Isaac was pushed forward when someone fell onto his

back, arms wrapping around his neck and a Henley-scented face rested against Isaac's cheek.

"Isaac! Come dance with me?"

Isaac smiled and patted Henley's arms, moving his head to the side as much as he could to gain eye contact. Blown pupils met his, and he shook his head.

"I'm not much of a dancer, Henley. Go enjoy yourself."

"Oh! Please, Isie! Ooh! Isie is going to be your new nickname." Henley nodded once, lips pressed together in satisfaction at his pronouncement. "Come on, Isie. Come dance!"

"No, thank you, Henley. Go. Have fun."

Isaac pulled Henley's arms away from his neck and gave him a small push in the dance floor's direction. He might need to grab a couple of glasses of water to help sober some of the team up. They were going to feel awful tomorrow.

Watching as Henley pouted his way back to Trish and Sierra, Isaac couldn't look away as Henley's hips began to sway to the rhythm of the beat. Henley's arms rose above his head, and Isaac saw his eyes were closed, lost to the music.

"He doesn't care what anyone thinks, does he?" A voice filled with admiration, and if Isaac wasn't wrong, envy spoke into his ear.

Twisting to face her, Isaac studied her expression. Frankie gazed in Henley's direction, a crease on her forehead as she followed his movements.

"No. A lot of people should take a leaf out of his book, in my opinion."

Frankie met his gaze, a small smile taking the place of the uncertainty. "Yeah, we definitely should. I'd love to have his confidence."

Isaac laughed at that. "Trust me, you could take some of his, and he'd still have more than enough to go around."

Frankie chuckled, leaning her arms on the round table. "How is he doing?"

"Really well. He has taken to it like a duck to water if I borrow my mum's phrase." Isaac squinted in Henley's direction, noting he had a fan dancing around him.

"You have your hands full with him," Frankie said, nudging his shoulder with her own.

Snorting, he shook his head. "Only for a few more weeks. Then he's on his own." He glanced at Frankie again, noticing the same faraway look on her face. "Is everything alright with you?"

She tilted her head and smiled. "I'm getting there. Maybe I need to rub up against Henley." She coughed and added, "That came out wrong. I meant maybe some of his confidence would come off on me if I did."

Grinning, Isaac patted her hand. "Yeah, yeah. That's what you meant. I believe you. I'm sure Henley wouldn't be opposed to having you dancing with him. Why not go join in?"

"Nah, I'm not good with rhythm. And he's coming back anyway."

"Isie! Come on. Dance with me." Henley pulled on Isaac's hand, trying to drag him to the dance floor.

"You don't want me out there. I'd ruin your…whatever you've got going on." Isaac spread his free hand, warding Henley off.

"But you're so good to me. You look after me all the time. Please, Isie?" Henley pouted, eyelashes batting at him.

"No," Isaac said firmly.

Henley sniffed and let go of his hand. "You're such a mean D…person."

Isaac quirked his mouth up at the change of wording. He would have loved to know what word Henley was going to use, but seeing his wide eyes and gaping mouth, Henley was shocked by what he'd nearly said.

His expression of horror slowly faded until Henley quietly said, "I think I need some water."

Standing, Isaac manoeuvred Henley into the seat he'd just vacated. "I'll get some. Stay there." He glanced at Frankie. "Talk to him. See if you can get some of the…whatever from him." Isaac smirked and elbowed his way through to the bar.

He wanted to know what Henley had been about to say, though, he had a feeling he knew what it was. Everything in Henley screamed boy, and everything in Isaac screamed for him to look after Henley. Thinking over Henley's behaviour during the last four weeks, Isaac could see he shone whenever Isaac gave him something to do or showered praised on him. Henley tried his hardest to do whatever Isaac wanted to the best of his ability.

Isaac wanted to take things further with Henley, but there needed to be a heavy conversation before anything happened between them. It was something he would discuss with Henley when he was sober.

When Isaac dropped Henley back at his house around one in the morning, he was second-guessing leaving him alone. He helped Henley into his house and ordered him to lock the door behind him, waiting on the step until he heard the click before returning to his car. He sat there for a few moments, weighing up his options until he saw the light upstairs switch on. Trusting his instincts, which said Henley was not drunk enough to do anything stupid, he drove off, reminding himself to ring Henley in the late morning to check on him.

"BUT ISAAC—"

"But nothing, Henley. Do as you're told."

Isaac watched as Henley pouted before pivoting on his feet and marching to the other side of the room where he dropped into a chair and opened his lunch bag. Henley had been a whiny brat for the last two days, and enough was enough. Isaac hoped that eating his lunch would reduce some of the emotions bleeding into his work. Henley didn't show it while staff was in the room, but as soon as it was empty, he went on and on about Saturday night and how there should be more days like that.

After explaining for the fourth time that people didn't have enough time to go out every week because of family commitments, Henley had begun pouting and whining about it.

When it continued even after his lunch, Isaac took a chance. "Sit down!" he ordered, pointing to the chair Henley had used previously.

Stunned into place for a second, Henley glanced at Isaac and shuffled over to take a seat.

Checking no one else had entered the room, Isaac spoke, "Right. I am going to give you an option now, and you need to think hard about it before you give me your answer." He paused until Henley nodded. "Choice one. Keep whining about everything, and I will continue to ignore it, which will get you more annoyed as the week goes on and may earn you a spanking. Choice two. Stop whining, and I will take you out for dinner on Saturday." He held up his hand as Henley tried to interrupt. "Just dinner. There is a conversation we need to have."

Henley's eyes lit up as his mouth began to curve up into a smile.

"Your answer?"

Closing his eyes briefly, no doubt contemplating the thought of a spanking, Henley returned his gaze to Isaac's, his eyes glistening in the lights. "Choice two, please," he whispered.

Isaac nodded. "Good choice. Now, please, cheer up and stop whining." Isaac held Henley's gaze until he nodded.

For the rest of the day, things went back to how there had been in previous weeks. Although Henley didn't stop talking, that was usual for him, and Isaac admitted, only to himself, it was endearing, and he was getting used to the constant narration throughout his day.

When he dropped Henley back home that afternoon,

he practically danced to his door, turning to wave over his shoulder before shutting himself inside. Isaac shook his head, the movement being used more and more often in relation to Henley. He hoped Henley could last another four days, but if he was honest with himself, he was just as eager to get to Saturday as Henley probably was. It had been a while since he'd had a date and one where he'd have to do a lot of explaining, laying it all on the line.

He hoped with everything in him that Henley liked the same things he did, and that Henley wanted more than a fling.

Chapter Five

He couldn't believe Isaac was taking him on a date. Or at least he would be if Henley could keep his mouth shut for the rest of the week. Henley honestly had no idea whether he would be able to, but because Isaac had asked him to, he would try.

By the time Friday came around, Henley was about to self-combust. He had so many questions about what was going to happen on Saturday, he was more fidgety than usual. He was driving himself to the store that day, in a company car he'd picked up the day before. It was a bit nerve-wracking meeting Isaac there instead of having the safety net of Isaac being with him, but he supposed he'd have to get used to it with only three weeks of his training left.

As he pulled into the store and parked his car, Henley scanned around but couldn't see Isaac. It meant he'd have to get into the building by himself. Inhaling deeply, knowing Isaac wanted him to do this, Henley put the sign on his dashboard and climbed out the car, locking it behind him. Hooking his bag over his shoulder, he strode to the staff entrance.

With his pulse pounding a thumping rhythm, he spoke to the receptionist and gained entry, following her directions to the room where, blessedly, Isaac waited. When he entered, Isaac beamed at him.

"I knew you'd be fine," Isaac muttered before waving him over. "Come on, we have our work cut out for us today."

Henley groaned, dropping his head back and squeezing his eyes shut. "Okay." He put his bag with Isaac's, listening to his instructions. His voice was amazing, not gravelly but deep, like plucking a low note on a guitar, and it vibrated up his spine.

"Do you know what needs to be done before this can all happen?"

Isaac's voice cut into his musings, and Henley realised he hadn't heard everything Isaac had said. He rolled his lips inwards, trying to remember what the last thing was Isaac said as he raked his necklace along the chain from one side to the other.

"You didn't hear me, did you?" Isaac narrowed his gaze, pinning Henley with his grey eyes.

Henley licked his lips but knew he couldn't lie to him. He shook his head before lowering it. He hated disappointing Isaac. He didn't mean to be all over the place. It was no excuse, but Rebecca had been on the phone the previous night in tears because of some guy, so he'd headed over there to keep her company. They'd talked until the early hours of the morning, so he wasn't completely with it anyway.

"What do we do after checking all the stock is here?"

"If the items do not have names on them, we put them in size order in individual boxes." Henley smiled.

Isaac nodded. "Well done. Let's get to it."

They worked silently for a change, the tiredness bleeding through Henley into his work.

"God, I'm so tired. Can this be the end of the day already? I want it to be Saturday." Henley sat in a chair and hunched over, resting his head on his crossed arms.

"Come on. A little tiredness never killed anyone. You should go to bed earlier." Isaac continued sorting the final few boxes.

"I would've done that, but Becca needed me. We ended up talking for longer than planned. Everything takes so much effort," he whined, rising to his feet. Staring at the box in front of him, he half-heartedly opened it and pulled items out, trudging over to each box he had to put them into before slogging back.

"I'll be back in a few minutes." Isaac strode out of the room, leaving Henley to continue working.

He grumbled the whole time Isaac was gone.

"Why can't it be Saturday already?" Henley leaned his arms on the box and dropped his head.

"Why can't you stop whining. I warned you."

Henley swung around, his gaze locking onto Isaac, who walked towards him, holding two cups of steaming liquid. He watched as Isaac placed them on a table away from the boxes, then stalked back to the door, putting something on the front and shutting and locking it.

"What—"

"Shush." Isaac's dark gaze rooted Henley to the spot as he wandered back towards him. "What did I say to you the other day?"

Henley remained silent because he honestly couldn't remember anything at that moment.

"I said if you kept whining, you would earn yourself a spanking." Isaac pointed to the floor in front of him. "Come here."

The command in his voice made Henley want to crawl, but he didn't think that was what Isaac wanted, so he sauntered over, trying to hide his reaction. There was no reason to because Isaac could see through him, he was sure.

"Trousers down and bend over the table."

Henley glanced at the table in the centre of the room and back at Isaac, his mouth suddenly dry at the idea of being spanked.

"Now."

Henley's gaze flicked from the door to the table before he inhaled and moved his hands to his button. Staring at the table as he pulled them down, along with his boxers, he rested his elbows and linked his fingers, his necklace clanking to the surface. The table chilled his lower stomach, where it met the bare skin. Henley felt goosebumps rise along his ass cheeks as he waited.

"We're going for ten. Red for stop, yellow for slow down. Agreed?"

"Yes." Henley felt Isaac's hand smooth over his skin before leaving. Not even a second later, it was back, the sharp slap sending waves of heat out from where Isaac's palm had landed. He bit his lip, waiting for the next blow.

Isaac spanked his other cheek this time, and Henley whimpered. The gentle jangle of his bracelets and the scrape of his necklace across the surface of the table were loud in the quiet.

"No noises. Remember where we are."

Where they were? He had no idea. Keep quiet? He wasn't sure about that either.

Each smack radiated heat through his body, and the table scraped forward across the floor, the noise piercing.

A knock on the door sounded.

"Yes?" Isaac called.

"Do you have everything you need?" a voice replied.

"Yes, thank you. We're rearranging a few things."

If Henley hadn't been trying to muffle his moans, he would've laughed.

"Okay. Let me know if you need anything."

"Will do, thanks." Both were silent for a few beats before Isaac continued talking but to Henley this time. "Two more."

The smacks came fast and hard, and Henley knew he'd be feeling them for days. He squirmed as his cock rubbed against the table with the movement of Isaac's hands across his sensitive skin.

"Hmm. Maybe that sting will remind you to listen to me when I tell you to do or not do something. What do you think?" Isaac punctuated his words with a squeeze, sending fire through Henley's ass once more.

"Yes." Henley gasped for breath, trying to keep his voice down.

"Yes, what?"

Henley licked his lips. "Yes, sir."

"Good. Right. Let's get you up and suitable for company. We have work to do."

Isaac slid an arm under Henley's chest and helped him to stand, each movement sending needle-like stings through his ass. When he was upright, Isaac reached down and pulled up his boxers, being careful of his behind and his cock, and repeated with his trousers, gently tucking his cock away before zipping them up. When he'd finished, Isaac stood in front of Henley, holding him by the waist.

"Good boy." He cupped Henley's jaw, rubbing his thumb across his cheek. "You did well."

Henley inhaled deeply and smiled. "Thank you," he whispered.

The rest of the day passed without a whimper of pain or tiredness. It was as if the spanking had revived Henley. As Isaac and he parted ways at the end of the day, Isaac squeezed his shoulder and smiled at him, reminding him to put some lotion on his ass before he slept. He looked so proud. It was that picture that kept Henley blissfully happy for the journey home and the rest of the evening, despite it being a short one because he crashed when he finally got home.

Friday night traffic was no joke.

Apart from removing his jewellery, a quick cool shower and applying the lotion, Henley did nothing more than drop to his bed and sleep.

A STING, starting from his ass and venturing wider through his body, woke him, and he blearily glanced at the clock. Seeing it was eleven in the morning was a shock Henley was not prepared for. He only ever slept that late when he was drunk.

He sat upright, wincing when he put his weight on the one place he couldn't avoid easily. Isaac had been correct. He would remember the reason for the stinging in the future. He would never whine again…maybe. Henley smirked as he stood. He might do so just to get a similar result.

But now he had to get himself ready. He had no idea what he was going to wear to dinner that night. He didn't even know where they were going. Should he go flashy? Or demure? Or plain? Maybe he needed to message Isaac to find out where they were going.

Good morning! Where are we going tonight? I need to plan my accessories, lol x

He replaced his phone on the bedside table and sashayed to the bathroom, brushed his teeth before heading back. Checking his phone quickly, he saw no reply, so he decided to search through his wardrobe and see what options he had.

After several go throughs and still no reply from Isaac, he called his sister.

"I need your help," he said in lieu of a greeting.

"What'cha need?" Ariel asked.

"You, here, now. I have a dinner date tonight and have no idea what to wear."

Clapping sounds came through the line, and he grinned. "Yay! Alright, we'll be over in a few. Bye!"

We. That meant Arianne was coming, too. Bonus. He could persuade her to do his makeup.

His phone beeped, and he snatched it up from where he'd just put it back.

It's a surprise, but I know how you like to dress appropriately, so I will tell you that you will need to look smart, but not over the top. Hope that helps. I'll be there to pick you up at six.

Henley grinned at the response. So like Isaac.

I'll be ready x

He heard the front door open and his sisters' voices floating up the stairs as they climbed, chatting constantly.

"Hey, girls. Thanks so much for this." Henley was suddenly extremely glad he'd put boxers on before he'd called them, they didn't need to see his ass moonlighting as a rescue beacon.

"You know we love to help choose outfits. So, where are you going, and who is it with?" Arianne said, lying on her side on Henley's bed.

Henley proceeded to tell them all about Isaac, minus the spanking, and what he'd said in the message as they worked through his wardrobe choices.

"How about your skinny leather trousers with a white shirt, cinched with a large black belt. The shirt sleeves could be rolled up your forearms so your bangles will show. Then you can add some darker shading to your face and eyes to make you more mysterious looking." Ariel waved her hands across her face as if to demonstrate mystery, but it just set them off laughing.

Once they recovered, Henley agreed. "That sounds good. We'll do it. He's picking me up at six, so I need to be buffed and ready before that."

"You have us to help. You'll be fine. First thing, though. Go get in the shower and get shined up. We can see what we have to work with." Arianne stood, heading to his dresser.

After scrubbing himself raw, Henley dried off and pulled on some clean boxers. He returned to his bedroom to find the girls arguing over two white shirts.

"It needs to be looser to get the right image!" Ariel insisted, waving one shirt.

Arianne shook her head. "No, tighter will show off his body to the best advantage."

"For twins, you certainly don't have the same opinions. Doesn't the world think twins are the same in every way?" He chuckled. "All I need to do is show them you two, and everyone's beliefs would be thrown upside down."

"Shut up!"

"Hey, that's no way to talk to your brother!" he joked. He pulled on some pyjama bottoms and walked back out of the room, yelling over his shoulder, "If either of you wants lunch, I would come and tell me what you want. I'm calling an order in now."

As he knew they would, they were by his side within seconds. He placed the order with the local deli who delivered. While they waited, he made some tea and coffee. His sisters—all four of them—lived on coffee and couldn't stand tea while he was the other way round.

Lunch was spent catching up on his sisters' lives, who lived quite separately. They shared the same house, but that was as far as it went. Arianne worked in a beauty salon, doing makeup and nails, whereas Ariel worked as a receptionist for a large manufacturing company. Arianne liked to go clubbing with her friends, whereas Ariel preferred the cinema or staying home with hers. Even when they were little, their dads would receive comments about why they were not dressed in the same clothes because it was "so cute," but they had insisted on the girls having their own identity, one separate from their twin.

Once the trio had filled their stomachs, they began the long road to getting him ready. It took longer than usual because they could never agree on things, and there was always an argument before a decision was made, usually by Henley. He never complained, though. He loved that they were here with him.

Ariel had lost the battle with the shirt. She concentrated on making sure every hair on his head was in the correct place, spraying it until Henley was sure it would crack if so much as a breeze touched it. Arianne, on the other hand, made sure to make his face match his outfit and hair colour. She needed to fix a couple of his nails, too. Working with boxes did not make his manicure last as it had done before.

When he was ready, apart from his clothing, he checked his reflection, marvelling at Arianne's ability to make his eyes look smoky, yet blue. It looked like his eyes were sparkling, which they quite possibly were. Clothes were next.

It was only after he was going to put the trousers on that he realised he needed to go commando. He had never dressed privately before. They had always been happy to dress in front of each other, and it would look suspicious if he did it now.

He shrugged as he dropped his boxers. Let the questions commence.

Chapter Six

Isaac waited on the step outside Henley's door. He'd rung the bell and received a female shout asking him to wait, so he stood there, flicking the keys around in his hand. He was surprisingly nervous about this date. The conversation he planned to have with Henley hadn't been vocalised for many years, and Isaac was a little unsure about Henley's reaction to it.

He knew from Henley's behaviour over the past five weeks that he was a Daddy's dream boy, but that didn't mean Henley knew anything about the lifestyle and what was involved. There were two ways this conversation could go after he explained what a Daddy and boy relationship was: either Henley would look at him as if he was delusional, which had happened in the past, or he would accept what he'd been told and be willing to try.

They would have to traverse the work route carefully. As far as Isaac was aware, there were no rules about workplace romances, but he wasn't certain.

Once he knew where their relationship stood, he would make sure to speak to Mr Sanders and explain the situation. Everything needed to be out in the open. He refused to hide. Although the decision to show or hide what type of relationship they had would be up to Henley.

The sound of the door opening brought his attention back to the house. A female with striking blue eyes and long blonde, wavy hair stood with her hand on her cocked hip as she tilted her head to study him.

"You must be Isaac," she said, indicating for him to enter.

"Yes. Nice to meet you…" He held out his hand in greeting.

"Arianne."

"Nice to meet you, Arianne. Is Henley ready?"

"Almost. Bear with us for a couple of minutes more." Her heels clicked against the wooden floor as he watched her walk into a room to the left.

Unsure what to do, he followed, hesitating in the doorway.

"You can come in if you want to. I won't bite."

Isaac chuckled and stepped forward. He wandered around the living room, looking at the photos on the walls and resting on the shelves, many depicting Henley's large family at different stages of their lives.

"Henley said your destination is a surprise for him. He doesn't have any allergies, so you should be fine no matter where it is."

Isaac refrained from smiling but only just. "Is that your polite way of asking where we're going?"

Arianne's cheeks flushed under her flawless appearance. "Yes," she replied with a smile.

"The Italian on Church Street. Nothing fancy."

"Ooh, nice. I'm jealous."

"Jealous of what?"

Henley's voice had Isaac pivoting around, finding himself as speechless as he had been the last time he'd picked Henley up for a night out. Their gazes locked, and Isaac felt something pass between them.

"Jealous of your destination, which I am not going to tell you about." As Arianne spoke, Isaac pulled his gaze away and saw as she mimed zipping her lips and throwing away the key.

He met Henley's gaze again when Henley said, "Oh, that's how it is, is it? You'll tell my sister, but you won't tell me. I see. I'm going to have to keep my eyes on you both."

Isaac moved towards Henley. "You look magnificent," he stated, watching the blush work its way down Henley's cheeks and neck.

"Thank you," he mumbled, looking at the floor.

"Let's go." He rested a hand on Henley's back, guiding him to the door.

"Lock up for me, please, girls," Henley called over his shoulder as he grabbed his keys from the table in the hall.

"Sure thing." Ariel waved as they exited the house.

Isaac opened the passenger door for Henley, leaning over him to fasten his belt after he was seated, closed the door and hustled around to the driver's side. As they got on the road, he studied Henley from the corner of his eye.

"Are you okay?"

Henley glanced across at him and smiled. "Yes. I'm excited."

"You're quiet, though."

Henley was silent, and Isaac quickly peered over at him, seeing him biting his bottom lip until he sighed. "I want this date to go well. I keep thinking that I talk too much, and so I've been trying to not say a lot." He hesitated before licking his lips and straightening his spine. "I want this to go well. I want *us* to go well together."

Isaac's mouth curled up. "I understand. But I want you to remember something."

"What?"

"I asked *you* on a date, not someone you think I want you to be. *You.*"

"Oh!"

Isaac stayed silent, waiting for any questions or comments Henley might have. It appeared he was lost in thought, so Isaac didn't interrupt. When they arrived at the restaurant, Henley's mouth gaped.

"Seriously? I've never been here but always wanted to."

"I'm glad I could bring you. Wait there."

He climbed out of the car and strode around the front to open the passenger door, presenting his hand to help Henley stand.

"Thank you."

"You're welcome." Isaac locked the car and linking their fingers together, guided Henley to the entrance.

Upon entering, he gave his name to the hostess who

seated them with menus, letting them know their server would be with them shortly.

"This looks so posh," Henley said, surveying the room with wide eyes. "It's beautiful in here."

"I agree." But Isaac didn't mean the restaurant. Whatever makeup Henley had put on shimmered in the lights, making him appear otherworldly. Now if only Isaac could figure out a way to start the conversation they needed to have.

"Choose what you'd like. Do you drink wine?"

"God, no. I've drunk all I need to for the next few weeks." Henley shuddered in his seat. "Water is fine. Or maybe a lemonade."

"Fizzy drinks are not good for you, so if you have one, the rest will be water." Isaac hadn't thought about his words, they'd just escaped, and he tensed wondering what Henley's reaction would be.

"Okay. One lemonade then water," he agreed without argument.

Pride swelled inside Isaac as he watched Henley peruse the menu, alternating between biting and licking his lips.

"Would it be okay if I had the spaghetti alla puttanesca?"

"Of course." Isaac wondered if Henley knew he was deferring to Isaac for his decisions.

When the waiter arrived, Isaac placed their order and leaned back in his seat to study Henley. He wasn't sure where to start.

"Isaac?"

"Yes, Henley."

"Do you know what a Daddy is?" Henley's gaze was across the restaurant, not on Isaac, but he wouldn't stand for that. Especially as Henley brought up the subject Isaac had been struggling to start.

"Look at me," Isaac demanded.

Henley turned to him immediately, loosening something inside Isaac.

"Tell me what you know about a Daddy."

He inhaled. "Well, a Daddy takes care of a boy, tells him what he can and can't do, makes sure he's safe and looked after, punishes him when he needs it. And the boy does what he's told."

Isaac tilted his head side to side. "Roughly, yes. Is that what you need?"

"Yes."

"Have you been part of a Daddy and boy relationship before?" Isaac was curious as to where Henley's knowledge came from.

"Not in a relationship, no, but I have been to a club and had a scene before. I realised it resonated with something inside me, but I didn't like the idea of finding someone at the club. I have been sure I wasn't going to find anyone until I saw you seven months ago."

Isaac frowned. "Seven months ago?"

Henley nodded. "When I started working at EasyFit, I saw you visit with the staff, talk to them, interact with them. You were always so caring, gentle and considerate. I wanted that. I wanted you." With those words, he blushed fiercely, the blood rising to the surface of his skin all the way to his chest.

"How did you know that was what I was?"

"I didn't!" Henley shook his head, eyes wide. "Are you?"

Isaac nodded slowly, and Henley beamed.

"I had hoped to get to know you and introduce you to the lifestyle in case it was something that appealed to you. I didn't realise you were actually a Daddy!" He brought his hands to his cheeks, fingers fanning over his mouth as he stared at Isaac.

They were interrupted by the arrival of their drinks, but once the waiter retreated, Henley burst out, "Seriously? You're not joking with me right now?"

Frowning, Isaac leaned forward. "I would never joke about something so serious. I have been a Daddy for a long time and been in several long-term relationships. I just…lost hope after the last one ended." He rubbed his thumb through the condensation on his glass, watching the movement.

"Is this what you brought me here to talk about?"

"Yes, and we still have things to discuss. Such as, how deep into being a boy do you like to go?"

Henley's brows drew together. "I don't like playing with toys or wearing nappies. That doesn't appeal at all. But I like the idea of someone looking after me, taking control, helping to calm me when my thoughts get all messed up."

"I have noticed that you're obedient, for the most part. So, you like being told what to do. If we try this, you will be listening to and obeying me."

"Yes. Please."

Their conversation paused once more as their food arrived, and they ate in near silence, which was strange from Isaac's point of view. He was so used to the constant chatter from Henley.

"I don't want you to change yourself for me, Henley."

"What do you mean?"

"You need to be yourself from the beginning. Don't act or speak how you think I want you to. If I think something about your behaviour needs correcting, I will discuss it with you and help you alter it."

"Through punishments?" Henley asked, eyebrows raising.

"If I believe that is the best way to remind you, yes." Isaac hesitated. "For me, being a Daddy is a twenty-four-seven responsibility. I would need you to realise that everything I do for or to you is for your own benefit. I want to help you become all that you can be, and in return, you need to trust me wholeheartedly. Telling me the truth at all times, even when it scares you. You need to trust that I will catch you should you fall. I will hold you close and protect you with everything I am."

Isaac gazed at Henley, seeing a shimmer begin in his eyes before they filled and overflowed.

"Come here." Isaac issued the order, and they both scooted out of their opposite seats, Isaac guiding Henley to slide over in the booth seat so he could sit next to him. Isaac wrapped his arm around Henley's shoulder, hugging him close and resting his fingers against the side of his face as his tears continued to fall soundlessly.

Once Henley had calmed, Isaac lifted his face. "Are you okay?" Henley nodded. "I need your words, sweetheart."

"I'm okay," he croaked. "I…You…It's everything I want."

"Alright. Let's eat our food, and once we're full, we can talk some more."

Isaac reached for Henley's plate from the opposite side of the table and placed it in front of Henley. Henley smiled, and though a little watery, it filled Isaac's heart with joy. He couldn't believe he had found someone who already knew about Daddies and boys, and in fact, was one.

After they had finished their meal and Isaac deduced Henley *didn't* want a dessert, he gripped Henley's hand and left the restaurant. It wasn't particularly late, and the air was warm, so he suggested a short walk.

"For a relationship to work with me, I would need to give you a routine to stick to—"

"What kind of routine?"

Isaac raised his eyebrows at Henley, waiting until he apologised for interrupting before continuing, "Things like when you'd need to go to sleep, when to wake, when to eat. I don't do this because I think you are incapable of doing them yourself. I do it because then I will know you are looking after yourself like I have asked you to. I trust that if I ask you to do something, you will do it. For example, if I ask you to eat at midday, and you agree, I expect you to eat at midday, barring any unforeseen circumstances."

"That sounds good." Henley glanced up at Isaac from underneath his eyelashes. "I do sometimes forget whether I've eaten or not."

"Good to know, and thank you for being honest with

me. I have seen that you can be a little excitable at times. I would like to help you find a way to manage that. I think your work, however amazing you already are at it, would benefit a great deal from you being calmer and more in control of your actions." He paused and smirked. "And mouth."

"Hey!" Henley pouted for a second before grinning. "Yes, okay. I know I can be a chatterbox. But I have so much to say."

"And I wouldn't ever want to stop you from saying it, but I do think there is a time and place for certain topics of conversation."

Henley scrunched his nose up. "Is there really?"

"Yes," Isaac said firmly.

They walked in silence for a few steps before Henley asked, "What should I call you?"

Isaac exhaled deeply. "I would love for you to call me Daddy. But you don't have to. Isaac is fine, too."

Henley rested his head against Isaac's shoulder, wrapping his free hand around his biceps. "I would love to call you Daddy."

"Does everything sound okay so far?"

Henley nodded, and when Isaac raised his eyebrows, he added, "Yes…Daddy."

Isaac inhaled and briefly closed his eyes, his pulse skyrocketing at the word. "Perfect." He pressed a kiss to the side of Henley's forehead, pulling him close. "Let's head back."

Changing the subject on the stroll back to the car, Isaac found out that Henley was visiting his family the following day. All of them were congregating at their dads' house for his sister Tracey's birthday.

Isaac pulled up at Henley's house, seeing it in darkness, and assumed his sisters had gone home. He walked around to the passenger door and opened it, helping Henley out once more. Linking their fingers again, he wandered up the garden path, stepping onto the porch and turning to face Henley.

"Thank you for tonight, Henley." Isaac's gaze roamed his face, taking in the glacial blue eyes, strong nose and full lips before returning to his eyes.

"Thank you for taking me out for dinner…Daddy," Henley whispered.

"You're welcome."

Isaac reached a hand to the back of Henley's neck before leaning in and pressing their lips together in a soft kiss. He sipped at Henley's top lip, then his bottom lip before pressing a small kiss to the corner of his mouth.

"Goodnight, Henley."

Walking away was the hardest thing he'd had to do for a long time.

Chapter Seven

HENLEY

"You're goddamn right I did," replied Henley, still seething from being left on his porch without the goodbye he had been hoping for. "I lost count how many times I came once I'd run upstairs. I don't care if he punishes me for it. You don't leave a man hanging, Ariel. It's not kind."

"You'll survive." Henley wasn't so sure.

Actually, he did care. He didn't want to get punished for masturbating all night long, but he had been so horny, and every time the images from their date came to mind, he became hard again. Even now, he felt his cock twitch despite the numerous orgasms.

He was pissed off with Isaac, that was for certain. He had no idea how he was going to face him the following day without screeching at him.

Henley knew their relationship had only just begun, but why did Isaac have to leave? He could've stayed, and they could've had some fun. But no, he was being all gentlemanly.

By the time he met Isaac at the warehouse on Monday morning, he was less angry but more upset. Last night, he had wondered if there was something wrong with him, and that was why Isaac hadn't wanted him. His mood had plummeted, and he'd struggled to sleep. So, an early morning of lugging boxes from the warehouse to a van was not the best idea. Still, it was his job, and he'd do it, even if he moped along the way.

"Is everything okay, Henley?" Isaac asked.

"Yes, thanks," he replied, picking up another box. He knew he was a lot quieter than usual. It was a mixture of being upset about the weekend and lack of sleep. He also knew that Isaac would pick up on it, but there was nothing he could do to prevent that.

"Did you sleep well?"

"Not really."

"Why not?"

"Not sure."

What he was sure about was that his two-word answers were grating on Isaac because Isaac's tone became more clipped with each exchange, and Henley felt an obscene amount of pleasure from it.

Once the van was loaded, Isaac slid into the driver's seat and Henley the passenger seat, pouting some more when he had to do it himself, without the assistance Isaac had provided Saturday night. They got on the road quickly, speeding towards a new store that would be opening in three weeks.

"Right. Now that we are away from prying eyes and

ears, what's the matter? And don't say nothing because you have been sulking all morning."

Henley didn't say anything for the moment. He didn't know what to say.

Isaac sighed. "When we were talking on Saturday, you said you understood that I needed you to always tell the truth. Did you lie to me?"

"No!" Henley swung his gaze around to Isaac. "I wouldn't do that."

"Then why are you hiding behind silence today?"

Henley shifted in his seat, pushing his hands under his thighs as he thought about his answer. "I'm… annoyed," he muttered.

"That's a start. What are you annoyed about?"

Henley heaved a breath. "Because I wanted more on Saturday. And you left me standing there with nothing but a small kiss! I wanted…" Henley paused, brow furrowing. "That's why. Because I wasn't ready. I need to start thinking about both of us, not just me." He glanced across at Isaac, seeing a small smile playing on his lips. "You didn't want to rush us into anything. You wanted to go slow."

"Correct."

"Why didn't you tell me that?"

"I did."

"When?"

"Think about our conversation, Henley. I'll wait."

Henley gazed out of the window, not seeing anything as he played back their date. There were lots of talking about trust, and then he remembered specific words: *"Everything I do for or to you is for your benefit."*

"I have to trust that you know me better than I know myself when it comes to certain things."

"Well done, Henley. I'm proud of you for figuring it out."

Henley closed his eyes and grinned, sitting taller in his seat with the praise.

"I wanted to be with you," Henley said.

"I know. And I wanted to be with you, too. But we need to make sure we're happy with our decisions before we cross that line, okay?"

"Okay." Henley waited a few seconds. "When will we know that we are happy with our decisions? Because I feel happy about it."

Isaac chuckled. "I'm sure you do."

"When can we go out again?" Henley asked.

"We're going out with the execs this weekend, remember."

"I know. I mean you and me. Maybe we could go to the cinema or bowling or something? I've not been to the cinema for a while. Not sure what's on either, I'd have to check. Do you like the cinema? Or would you prefer dinner again? I'm easy, rea—"

"Henley? Relax."

Henley inhaled and exhaled shakily, resting his head back and rolling it towards Isaac. "Sorry."

"It's fine. Just remember to breathe in between sentences or questions. How will anyone be able to answer you if you don't give them time?" Isaac chuckled, gentling the reprimand.

"I get so…"

"Excited?" Isaac supplied with a smile.

"Yeah, I suppose."

"It's not a bad thing, Henley. Life is for living. If you can't be excited about it, you're not enjoying it."

"Do you enjoy your life?"

"Very much so. I have a loving family, fantastic colleagues, amazing career. What more could I ask for than what has been given to me already?" He flicked his gaze over to Henley then back to the road. "Including you."

Henley smiled. "Thank you."

That conversation, however settling it was that day, proved to be only one of two of its kind that week. They were inundated with getting the store up and running, and with two unexpected trips making for long days, they had no time to breathe.

The second conversation consisted of Isaac asking Henley if he had any toys. After clarification was needed regarding which type of toys, Henley snorted and told Isaac he had plenty. Isaac detailed specifically what he wanted Henley to do that night to remove some of his stress, and two of those toys got used so much, the batteries died. But he went to work on Thursday feeling much better.

By Friday afternoon, though, Henley wanted to cry. Isaac had been amazing with him: rubbing his back to calm him when needed, being stern when he pushed too hard or whined too much, reminding him to eat and drink, asking about his family and friends. But he hadn't *touched* him in any other way. No kisses, no petting, no not-so-innocent touches. Nothing.

Although he felt settled in some ways, he was lively in

others. He wanted Isaac something fierce and couldn't decide how to make it happen. Every time his thoughts turned to the idea of pushing things to make Isaac snap, his brain reminded him that Isaac knew what he was doing. His heart didn't agree, though.

When he drove home after dropping the leftover uniforms back at the warehouse, he was ready to hibernate for the weekend. Forget going out anywhere, he was going to hide away and get centred once more.

Unfortunately, someone else had other ideas.

Henley was submerged in a luxuriously hot bath with plenty of lavender bubbles when someone knocked on his front door. At first, Henley ignored them. He wasn't expecting anyone, and those who he wanted to see had a key and could let themselves in. But when the knocking continued and his phone began ringing, he realised he needed to sort it so he could get back to his bath.

Grumbling when the cool air hit his overheated skin, Henley draped a dressing gown around him, and dripping, went to the door.

"Who is it?" he asked.

"Open the door, Henley."

Henley quickly unlocked the door and opened it wide, eyebrows raised at his unexpected visitor.

"Can I come in? I don't want you catching a chill."

Henley nodded, and Isaac manoeuvred past him into the hallway.

"I've brought some dinner. Why don't you finish your bath or shower? It will be ready for when you've finished."

"Okay."

He watched as Isaac's gaze roamed across his face and down to his bare feet and back up again. "Go on. Enjoy the water."

"Yes." Henley drifted to the stairs before turning back with his hand on the bannister. "Thank you, Daddy," he whispered, tears threatening to fall.

"You're welcome. Go. Enjoy."

Henley climbed the stairs, careful of his wet feet, and slowly sank back into the warmth. He couldn't believe Isaac was at his house, making dinner. Or maybe he was just serving it, he wasn't sure, but regardless, Isaac was in his house.

Trying to relax when the object of his affection was on the floor below him was next to impossible, but the heat seeping into his muscles did the trick until a knock on the bathroom door.

"Yes?"

"Would you like something to drink?" Isaac called.

If he answered yes, Isaac would come in while he was in the bath. If he answered no, Isaac would go back downstairs. If Isaac wanted to take things slow, why would he ask to come in when Henley was only dressed in bubbles?

"Henley? It's not a trick question." There was humour in his tone.

Taking a breath, he answered, "Yes, please."

Watching as the door handle turned, Henley swallowed hard, trying to affect a calm appearance when, in fact, his heart was racing. Isaac entered, holding a beer bottle and a glass of water.

"I wasn't sure which you would prefer."

"Water, please."

Isaac settled the bottle on the sink and brought the glass to him, crouching next to the bath. "Let me hold it. Your hands will be slippery."

Henley nodded, and Isaac rested the glass against his bottom lip. As Henley moulded his mouth to it, Isaac carefully tilted it, allowing the cool liquid to fill his mouth. Not realising how thirsty he had been, Henley gulped down several swallows before locking gazes with Isaac and lifting his head. A small drop dripped onto his warmed skin, causing his breath to hitch, and Isaac wiped it away with his finger.

"Thank you."

"You're welcome. Dinner is ready as soon as you are. Don't rush, though. Enjoy yourself." Isaac stood, turning away from Henley, and Henley felt a moment of panic.

"Stay!"

Grey eyes met his, and Isaac must have seen something in his expression because he laid a folded towel on the toilet seat and sat, resting his elbows on his knees.

They were silent for a long while, and when the bath had cooled enough that Henley developed goosebumps, he decided he'd had enough.

"I'm finished."

"Have you washed?" Isaac asked, sitting upright.

"Yes. I always wash first and relax when I'm done."

Isaac smiled. "My clever boy."

Henley didn't think he would ever get tired of hearing that.

"Come on. Let's get you dry."

Isaac lifted another towel off the radiator and held it

out for Henley, who had a moment of indecision before pulling the plug and standing up. The water flowed off him like a waterfall, and he refused to meet Isaac's gaze, not wanting to see disappointment *or* lust. He couldn't handle either now as bare as he was, physically and emotionally.

With Isaac towelling him off in a no-nonsense manner, Henley felt more secure, and once the towel was wrapped around his waist, he found his equilibrium again.

"Thank you, Daddy."

Isaac leaned forward and pressed a kiss to his forehead. "You're welcome, sweetheart. Why don't you go and get dressed—pyjama bottoms or joggers and a t-shirt would be good—and come down and meet me in the kitchen."

"Okay."

Picking up the half-empty glass and the full beer bottle, Isaac gave a half-smile before exiting the room.

Henley inhaled and exhaled slowly before following. As he passed the stairs, he saw Isaac was already at the bottom, and Henley smiled as he continued to his room. Entering his space always soothed him. Painted light blue walls, and royal blue curtains and duvet cover matched well with the pine floorboards and furniture. He loved his room. It never failed to calm his excitable nature and was the perfect place to fall asleep.

The drawers contained his trousers and pyjamas, so he chose his favourite pyjama bottoms: dark blue flannel with Tweety Pie on them. They were a gift from Becca a few years ago when she started calling him "sweetie pie," and he'd misheard her and asked why she was calling him Tweety Pie. Soon after that, the pyjamas appeared. They made him smile every time.

Flinging the towel towards the washing basket, Henley pulled them on, going commando underneath. He didn't usually wear a t-shirt when he was at home, but Isaac had asked him to, so he slid on a light grey round-neck one.

He checked his hair in the mirror, running his fingers through it to tidy it up and reminding himself he needed to dye his hair again soon. The blue colour was beginning to fade. He wasn't sure what colour he would go for next. Maybe he could ask Isaac.

Thinking of Isaac had him hurrying out of his room and down the stairs. The kitchen smelled heavenly, and as he entered, he saw the table had been set for two with candles in the middle.

"Feeling better after your bath?" Isaac asked over his shoulder.

"Yes, thank you. You didn't have to go to all this trouble."

Isaac smiled as he pivoted towards him, carrying two plates. "It's no trouble. Anyway, you know I like to look after you." He set the plates down. "Sit down, sweetheart. What would you like to drink?"

"Would I be allowed some juice, please?"

"Of course. Good choice." Isaac filled a small glass and placed it in front of Henley. "We can't have dinner out or takeaways too often, but we've had a busy week, so I thought this would be good for us."

"It's wonderful. Thank you, Daddy." Henley was

feeling a lot more confident in using the word and accepting that someone else wanted to look after him. He knew his family did, but this was different. Sometimes it seemed wrong that another adult took care of him in ways that he should be able to do for himself. But he reminded himself, it wasn't that he couldn't do it, he enjoyed allowing someone else to do so *only* if they enjoyed doing it. It was a difficult concept for some people to understand when, as children, they were taught to become independent and self-sufficient.

They spoke about little things while they ate, enjoying the calm atmosphere after a hectic week at work. The closer Henley came to finishing his food, the more distracted he became about what would happen afterwards. He wanted them to take this further tonight, but after last weekend, he didn't dare to hope. Isaac turned the conversation to their relationship.

"So, we talked a bit about what I want from us. What do you want?"

"I want someone to help me be *me*, without the fall-outs I usually get from when I become overexuberant or excitable. When I get like that, I can't control what happens. I'd like someone to help me to learn control, even if it's through obeying the rules they have set. I need the rigidity of it, I think."

Isaac nodded. "You've thought about this. I'm glad." He leaned forward, resting his elbows on the table and reaching one hand forward to encircle his glass. "What about punishments? I know you're okay with spankings. What else?"

Chapter Eight

ISAAC

Isaac watched Henley's cheeks colour as he studied his plate.

"I like it when my Daddy controls everything."

He waited for more information to come, but nothing did. "What do you mean by *everything*?"

Isaac couldn't attempt to dissect that sentence. He needed it broken down for him. It was too important to get wrong.

"I like being told what and when to eat and how much. Sometimes, I find I either miss meals or eat too much. There doesn't seem to be any middle ground. I also like it when I'm not allowed to orgasm without Daddy saying I can. I like it when he tells me what punishments I can take and what I can't."

Surprise flared through him at the punishments state-ment. "Alright. We would need to decide on your hard limits, though. That's non-negotiable." He knew Henley needed structure in his life. Consideration needed to be given to his family, work and friends. He didn't want to take anything away from Henley; Isaac wanted to enrich what he had and make his life more settled.

"Okay."

"Let me clean up and we'll go watch a movie." Isaac stood, picking up their finished plates and taking them over to the dishwasher. "You finish your juice. Would you like any ice cream for your dessert?"

Isaac rested a hip against the counter while he waited for Henley's answer, watching as his mouth curved into a beautiful smile.

"You have ice cream?" Henley questioned, eyes sparkling.

"I do. Cookie dough or chocolate brownie? I think maybe cookie dough would be a good choice this evening."

"Perfect."

Isaac filled a small bowl and placed it in front of Henley, holding out a spoon.

"Thanks, Daddy."

His hand reached forward to rub over Henley's hair, and he smiled when Henley pushed into it. He liked being petted. Isaac filed that away for future reference.

Returning to the dishwasher, Isaac filled it and, by the time he was ready to set it going, Henley had finished and brought the bowl to him.

"Thank you, sweetheart." He put the last items in and started it. "Right, let's go see what's on TV."

The living room was surprisingly spotless, as it had been the previous weekend when he'd had a chance to study it before their date. Knowing Henley as he did, he would've immediately assumed he had a chaotic house, but the whole house was in a similar tidy condition. Henley took good care of his home, which Isaac appreciated.

"What would you like to watch?"

"Could we watch Drag Race?" Henley asked with a hopeful look on his face.

Inwardly cringing, Isaac agreed. He was never one for watching reality-style shows, preferring to watch documentaries instead, but if Henley enjoyed them, he would learn to live with it. Sometimes.

Isaac sat in the corner of the sofa and patted the seat next to him. Beaming, Henley snuggled up beside him, his head resting on his shoulder as his legs curled up underneath him. Isaac picked up the remote from the side table and switched the TV on, passing it to Henley for him to find his programme. As it started up, Isaac found himself drifting. His hand leisurely rubbed up and down Henley's arm, and he repeatedly caressed Henley's hair with his cheek.

Henley squirmed and wriggled increasingly as time went on, and Isaac could feel his erection pressing into his thigh. He didn't think Henley was even aware of what he was doing, but Isaac knew he needed rest, not getting worked up.

They watched two episodes of the show before Isaac deemed it enough and switched it off. "Come on. Time for bed."

Hope lit Henley's eyes, and Isaac fought a smile. Henley wasn't getting what he thought he was, and Isaac could imagine what response he would get when Henley figured it out.

"Head up and get ready for bed. I will switch everything off down here and grab us some drinks. I'll be up in a moment."

Henley nodded and climbed the stairs. Isaac wanted to give Henley some time to sort himself out, especially this first time, but it chafed a bit because he wanted to be the one to help him. There would be time for that, though. As he ascended the stairs carrying two glasses of water, he contemplated Henley's reaction to the plan for them to sleep and only sleep.

When he entered Henley's bedroom, Henley was stood in the middle of the room, appearing a little lost.

"Is everything okay?" Isaac asked as he placed the drinks on the bedside table.

"I…I'd…"

When Henley couldn't finish, Isaac took a guess, "Would you like some help getting ready for bed?"

Henley nodded, biting his lip.

"I need your words, sweetheart."

"Yes. Please."

Isaac smiled. "What do you normally sleep in?"

"Just pyjama bottoms. Or boxers if it's warm."

"Alright. Those were clean on after your bath, correct?"

"Yes."

"Would you like to sleep in those?"

"Okay."

Isaac stepped towards Henley, and although Henley's gaze was averted, Isaac knew he was aware of every movement Isaac made. When the hem of his t-shirt was within reach, Isaac lifted it slowly, following Henley's arms as he lifted them until it was free. Glancing around, he saw the washing basket and threw it in. He teased the waistband of the pyjamas, feeling for underwear but not finding any. His pulse rocketed at the realisation Henley had been commando all night.

"Head to the bathroom to brush your teeth. I need to fetch something, and I'll be right back."

Henley ducked his head and shimmied past Isaac, disappearing through the door. After a minute, Isaac exited the room and hustled down the stairs and back up again after picking up the overnight bag he'd brought with him. He hadn't been one hundred per cent certain he would use it, so hadn't drawn attention to it, but knowing Henley was alright with how the evening was turning out, made him sure of his actions.

He shucked his jeans and briefs, pulling on some pyjama bottoms and grabbed his toiletry bag. He waited until he heard Henley open the bathroom door before leaving the bedroom.

"Good boy. I'm going to the bathroom, then I'll be in." Henley looked much younger when he had no jewellery or makeup on.

Henley didn't reply but continued on to the room. Isaac hurried through his nightly routine and returned to the bedroom, finding Henley sitting on the bed with his back against the headboard.

"We've had a long week, haven't we?" Isaac said, stepping towards the bed and Henley.

"Yes. It's been busy, but I've enjoyed it, too."

"I'm glad. You're a natural at the job."

Henley glowed from the praise.

"Let's get you tucked up, and we can talk for a few minutes."

When Henley lifted his hips so the duvet could be pulled out from underneath, Isaac chuckled. He pulled the cover over Henley, grabbed one of the glasses of water and walked around to the other side of the bed. After placing the drink down and resting his phone there, too, he lifted the covers and slid onto the cool fabric. Switching off the lamp before moving onto his side to face Henley, Isaac rested his head in his hand, his other hand reaching over to pull Henley closer.

Deciding to reward his obedience that evening, Isaac's free hand traced the contours of Henley's face, gaze roaming the strong features. Pinching Henley's chin between his fingers and thumb, Isaac leaned down, capturing the gasp that left Henley. He was unhurried with his kisses, teasing and giving, then retreating and playing. When Isaac moved to retreat again, Henley grasped the back of his head and pressed their lips together harder. Isaac allowed it for a short time but gentled it once more before pulling completely away.

Henley groaned and whimpered. "Please. I need…"

"You need some sleep," Isaac finished, and as antici-pated, Henley disagreed.

"No, I don't. I need you!"

"Henley," Isaac said sternly.

"You can't leave me like this! Not again!" Henley whined, going for the full effect with a pout and puppy dog eyes, too.

"We are not doing anything tonight. It's time for rest. Tomorrow is another day."

Henley's jaw dropped. "You're really going to leave me like this."

"Yes. You will be fine. Tomorrow, we will talk a little more, and once we are happy with how things are, we can further our relationship."

Isaac was giving himself a case of blue balls. He wanted nothing more than to bury his cock inside Henley, but he needed to think about Henley first, and Henley was exhausted. He could see it in his eyes.

"But…Why…That's…not fair!"

"It is fair. We are both tired and need to rest. Tomorrow will be here before you know it."

As much as it killed him to do it, he moved Henley onto his side, facing away and tucked him against his chest. As he rested his head on the pillow, he wasn't sure how much sleep either of them would be able to get.

"We will also talk about your punishment for talking back to me. I know what you need, Henley. Don't push me."

Henley didn't reply, but Isaac could feel the tension in his body. Slowly, though, the rigidity of Henley's muscles lessened, and Isaac knew he was asleep. He kept his own breathing steady, so he didn't disturb Henley, but his thoughts were going a mile a minute. Everything seemed to be too good to be true, and he hated that he second-guessed everything Henley did or said. Experience had taught Isaac to be careful, but Henley didn't deserve that distrust. Isaac was asking Henley to trust him, so he needed to trust Henley in return and leave everything else behind.

Henley fidgeted in his sleep, which had Isaac wondering with a small smile if he was ever still. It wasn't until he caught the hitch of breath and the minute movement in Henley's upper arm that he realised something was amiss. Isaac pretended to move position, lowering his hand further down Henley's front but not far enough to touch anything but his stomach. Henley's movements and breathing ceased. After a few seconds of Isaac being still once more, Henley began again.

Refraining from chuckling at Henley's audacity, though he should not be surprised in all honesty, Isaac let him continue for a short time. When he felt Henley's pulse and breath increase, Isaac softly said, "What do you think you're doing?"

Henley flinched violently, gasping as he twisted his head towards Isaac. "I…I…" He sighed. "I'm so horny, I couldn't sleep."

"Thank you for being honest. But you told me earlier this evening that I was in control of everything. That meant your orgasms, too."

"I know. I'm sorry."

Isaac considered the problem. If he let Henley come, he was allowing him pleasure when he should be punished, but if he didn't let him come, he would lose sleep, which was vital to his wellbeing. He decided to allow Henley to come, but with the understanding that the punishment he received the following day would be harsher. He gave Henley the choice.

"I will take the worse punishment tomorrow. Please!"

"Alright. Part one of your punishment will be taking yourself to the edge, but you will *not* come until I tell you to. Part two, we will discuss tomorrow."

Henley made a little noise in the back of his throat, but Isaac couldn't tell if it was in reaction to part one or part two of the plan.

Rolling to his back, Henley pushed his pyjamas beneath his balls and wrapped his hand around his cock with a groan, his hand stroking fast. His lip was caught between his teeth, his hips thrusting to meet his hand as his pleasure built. Isaac could see the flush darkening the skin of his chest and cheeks.

When Henley's back bowed and his head writhed on the pillow, Isaac said, "Stop!"

Henley's hand flinched away from his cock, grasping at the sheets beneath him with a white-knuckled grip as his body shivered and twitched. "Oh, god! Please!"

Isaac studied Henley, waiting until he was no longer twisting on the bed before commanding, "Again."

Henley sighed and encircled his cock, hissing with his first caress and panting as his pleasure increased with each movement. His left hand was clutching the sheets at his side.

"Pinch your nipples."

An expression of torture passed over Henley's face as he followed the instruction, his dominant hand creating friction on his dick. He gasped as the sensations, undoubtedly, grew fierce. Isaac watched him for the point of no return, and before Henley reached it, "Stop!"

Henley's body twisted and clenched and grabbed at nothing as he puffed his way through backing away from his orgasm. Isaac was so proud of him for doing as he said. All it would take is for Henley to ignore him for a second or two more, and it would all be over.

"Please, Daddy! Please let me come!"

"Not yet. This is a punishment, remember. Again." The command in Isaac's voice was unmistakable, and Henley moaned in response but encircled his cock once more.

Henley's toes curled, his legs couldn't keep still, and his head pressed hard into the pillow as his hand worked his shaft. Isaac leaned over to the bedside table, opening a drawer and seeing a variety of toys, but also the lube which had been what he was after before he faced Henley again, unclicking the lid.

"Stop!"

Henley made a keening sound full of pleasurable pain as he let go and jack-knifed when Isaac squirted some lube directly onto his cock.

"Again."

Blowing out a breath, Henley's hand shook as he wrapped it around his length, the purple head so angry, Isaac was sure he couldn't last much longer. Henley hummed as the lube slicked his way. Isaac licked his lips as he watched Henley work himself, twisting as he reached the head. The thick cock emerging from Henley's hand was an erotic picture Isaac that would not forget any time soon.

"Please! Oh, please, Daddy! Let me come this time! Please! I'll be good. Please! I promise!"

Isaac noted the hoarseness of Henley's voice and

eyed Henley's free hand, clutching at the sheets as it was. "Come."

The hitch of Henley's breath, the gasps, the muffled sounds of pleasure ramped up Isaac's need, but he refused to do anything about it. A particularly violent flinch from Henley advertised his release, and Isaac's gaze was riveted. Henley's hips bucked several times as his release painted his stomach. His rough breathing sounded loud in the quiet room.

"Ah! Oh, fuck!"

Isaac let out a breath, trying to calm his own libido as Henley finally slumped onto the mattress. Henley would likely be the death of him.

"I'm sorry, Daddy," he mumbled, the sound forlorn. "I should have been stronger."

Isaac pulled him closer, letting him rest his head on Isaac's shoulder. "You are strong, Henley. Don't ever think otherwise. If a release is what you need before you can sleep, we will factor that in. If you wanted to push the boundaries, that is another matter."

"No! I honestly can't sleep when I have a hard-on. If I'm relaxed, I can sleep fine without climaxing, but if I'm worked up, I can't."

"Okay. I'm glad you told me. This will help in the future. But from now on, you need to listen to me. No more trying to sneak orgasms when you think I won't know. I will be able to tell on your face whether you are lying to me when I ask you the question."

"Yes, Daddy."

Those words coming from Henley sounded so right, Isaac couldn't help but smile into the darkness. He had been alone for long enough now, and he needed someone to care for to enrich his own life, as well as his boy's. He only hoped Henley would last. He'd had the same hope for Mateo, though, and look where that ended up. Three years down the drain because Mateo had found someone who gave him what Isaac couldn't. The problem was, Mateo hadn't explained what that something was; therefore, Isaac had been unable to figure out if it was something he could give him.

In hindsight, Mateo probably used it as an excuse to end their relationship and place the blame on Isaac instead of Mateo. It was all water under the bridge now. Apart from a slight sting he felt from not knowing, he was over it. At least over that relationship. He wasn't over the hurt that had been caused by the breakup.

It was why he'd been so hesitant to find another boy. At forty-four, Isaac wasn't getting any younger, and some boys didn't like a huge age gap, whereas others preferred a bigger age gap. Mid-forties was a dead zone when it came to boys looking for Daddies.

His friends in the community had rallied around him when Mateo left, giving him hope that he would find someone, but after several years, he couldn't keep the hope alive, so he had distanced himself from those friends. He didn't think he'd spoken to Steven and Claude for at least a year. He'd have to remedy that—if they wanted to hear from him at all.

Not long after Henley had returned from cleaning up in the bathroom, soft snores met Isaac's ears, and he smiled again at the weight of the boy he was fast becoming enamoured with. He'd never expected to be interested in someone as comfortable in their skin as Henley was; he'd always gone for boys who were more timid or new to the community. Maybe that was where he'd gone wrong.

Maybe he'd just needed someone to shake *him* up a little. To get *him* out of his usual routine.

Maybe he just needed Henley.

Chapter Nine

HENLEY

"Yes, Dad. I promise I'm fine. This week has been hectic, so I'm a little worn out. I'll be there for lunch tomorrow." Henley switched the phone to his other ear.

"You seem to be enjoying the work."

Nodding, though his dad couldn't see him, Henley answered, "Yes, I do. I get to meet some awesome people from all over the country. It's fantastic." He cut his gaze towards Isaac, seeing him smiling as he drank his coffee and studied his phone. Henley wasn't sure if he was smiling because of Henley's words or what he was looking at.

"Sounds like the perfect job for your personality, son." His dad chuckled, and Henley joined in.

Staring at Isaac, Henley couldn't withhold his words. "I've met someone, too."

Isaac's gaze flicked to his, eyebrows raised.

"You have? That's great news! When can we meet him?"

"It's new, so give me a few more weeks before you send in the cavalry." He grinned.

"What's he like? Let me know something about him before I meet him, at least." His dad stopped to cough before coming back on. "I may need to research things if he's interested in stuff I'm not."

Henley shook his head, snorting. "You'll be fine. He's amazing, Dad. He takes care of me. Keeps me in line. Reminds me to eat." He snickered.

"He's a keeper if he can get you to eat three meals a day." His dad sighed. "Even when you were younger, you were a nightmare to get to eat. In the end, we figured you'd eat when you were hungry, or when it was dinner time and the family sat down. At least you were eating one meal."

"I ate more than one meal." Henley paused, furrowing his brow. "Most of the time," he added.

"Well, make sure you bring him home when you're ready to. You know we'll greet him with open arms so long as he's looking after you."

"He is. Very much so."

Isaac's gaze had not left Henley's the whole time he'd been talking about him, but he raised his eyebrows again with that last remark. Henley smirked. He'd have to wonder about that. Henley heard Pops' voice in the back-ground, and his dad called back.

"Right, I'm going to have to go, son. Remember what I said. Whenever you're ready."

"Thanks, Dad. Say hi, bye and love you to Pops for me."

"Will do. Take care. Love you."

"Love you, too, Dad."

Henley cancelled the call and shifted down on the sofa, jingling all the way, until he covered the entire area. Isaac was sitting in the armchair across from him, which was too far away as far as Henley was concerned. He played with his bangles, spinning them around and around.

"Is everyone well?" Isaac asked, putting his phone on the arm of the chair and tipping his mug up to drain his coffee.

"Yeah. Dad has a cold, which has given him an awful cough, but he's alright. Pops is as lively as ever, so I'm told."

"Talking of eating, it's lunchtime." Isaac stood, tucking his phone into his jeans pocket and carrying his cup as he ventured into the kitchen.

Henley sat upright, ready to follow. Isaac had not brought up the punishment Henley would have to do, but he was not going to remind him. He didn't think Isaac had forgotten. Maybe he was biding his time.

"Henley? Please come into the kitchen."

Standing, he threaded his fingers through his untamed hair as he followed the instruction.

"Yes, Daddy?"

"I've made a plate for you. Please wash your hands and have a seat."

Henley traipsed to the sink and washed his hands, glancing over and seeing an array of rainbow colours spread on two dinner plates. "That looks amazing!"

"Thank you, sweetheart. A rainbow of salad, meat and dairy to keep your energy levels up. It will help you when we go out tonight." Isaac picked up the plates and deposited them on the table.

They sat in the same seats as the previous night and dug into the food, Henley moaning with the fresh taste of everything. When Henley had cleared his plate, he sat back, resting his fingers on his stomach and groaning.

"I'm so full!"

Isaac chuckled. "That means you will be ready for a nap. We were awake early this morning."

Glowering, Henley agreed. "There was no need for the postman to knock so loudly."

"He was doing his job. You had something to sign for."

"That's not the point."

Shaking his head, Isaac stood, taking the plates with him and placing them in the dishwasher. "I'm going to head home shortly. I have a few errands to run before we go out tonight, but I will be back to pick you up, maybe before if I'm finished earlier."

He still hadn't mentioned anything about punishment, and despite his eagerness not to remind him, Henley wanted to know what to expect.

"Daddy?"

"Yes, sweetheart."

"Am I going to have my punishment soon?" He nibbled on his lip as he asked.

"I wondered how long it would take you to ask about that." Isaac grinned. "Your punishment is three-fold today." He stalked to the table, retaking his seat. "Firstly, you are not allowed to come at all tonight, even if it means you stay awake the whole night. Secondly, you will not be drinking when we go out. You need to be aware of everything and everyone around you and not use being drunk as an excuse to do things you shouldn't, like getting off. Thirdly, you will be wearing a plug. All night."

Henley wished he'd never asked, and he pursed his lips, wanting to argue. He'd made a promise to Isaac, though, and he would try to keep to it. Isaac knew what he was doing, and he was trying to help Henley be the best person he could be. It was Henley's job to help Isaac do that by listening and obeying, despite how unfair it seemed.

"Do you have anything to say?"

Henley glared at Isaac but shook his head.

"Use your words, please."

His nose crinkled as he withheld his snarky comments. "No, Daddy."

"Good boy."

Henley was silent for a moment before he thought of something else. "Daddy?"

"Yes, Henley," Isaac said with a smile.

"May I have a kiss?"

"You will always be allowed a kiss, my sweet boy." Isaac leaned forward, resting one arm on the table and resting his other fingers underneath Henley's jawline to tilt his head up. He paused right before touching and blew against his lips, making Henley open. As soon as he did, Isaac swooped in. Their tongues twined together, Isaac tasting of their lunch and something that was purely Isaac.

Henley's head fell back as Isaac devoured him, lying prone under Isaac's attack but wanting every bit of it. As he began to get lightheaded, Henley felt himself tipping to the side before being lifted until he was straddling Isaac's lap with his strong, sure hands resting against his back and ass, pressing him closer. Henley wrapped his arms around Isaac's neck, taking everything that Isaac was giving him.

Pleasure streamed through his body, and he undulated against Isaac, feeling his erection, hard and thick behind his zipper. His own shaft ached, seeking release. Isaac pressed their hips closer, groaning before yanking his mouth away.

"You are dangerous, my boy. I can't get enough of you," Isaac muttered, resting their foreheads together.

Henley tried to get closer, thrusting against Isaac until Isaac grasped his hips and stopped him.

"Calm down, sweetheart. We have all the time in the world."

"Please?"

Isaac chuckled. "Remember your punishment," he whispered into Henley's ear.

It froze Henley's body, and he closed his eyes and bit his lip, refraining from screaming his frustration. He wanted nothing more than to argue, but look where that got him yesterday.

He exhaled through gritted teeth several times to calm his libido, Isaac rubbing a calming hand up and down his back.

"Well done, Henley. I'm proud of you."

Henley wrapped his arms tight around Isaac and nestled his head against his neck. Inhaling Isaac's scent calmed him more, and when he was in control, he pulled back.

"I will be ready for six o'clock unless you come by earlier."

Isaac beamed at him and kissed his nose. "Perfect."

Henley rubbed his hands over Isaac's closely cropped hair, feeling the soft texture tickling his palm. "I love the feel of your hair," he murmured, staring at his movements. He could sense Isaac's gaze on him as he continued, but he didn't waver. If Isaac allowed him to play, then play he would. One hand rested at the base of Isaac's head, his thumb smoothing back and forth while his other hand moved in circles around the top of Isaac's head.

"Having fun?" Isaac asked, and Henley heard the grin in his voice.

Henley smiled. "Yes, thanks."

Isaac chuckled and dug his fingers gently into Henley's sides, making him laugh out loud and cringe away from his tickle attack.

"Stop! No!" Henley couldn't contain his shouts of laughter or pleas to stop. They fell to the floor, but Isaac didn't stop.

When they were both breathing heavily, Isaac paused, and Henley stared up at him from his position on the floor. Isaac was braced over him. At any other time, it would be a sexual position, but Henley knew that wasn't what this was. Isaac was showing Henley that he could be fun, that Henley could have fun with him, that he wasn't all about routine, structure and punishments. Henley appreciated the reminder.

Isaac leaned down, pressing a gentle, chaste kiss on Henley's lips before sitting up and pulling Henley with him.

"Come on, sweetheart. Up you get. I need to get going."

"Okay, Daddy."

Henley felt much better about Isaac heading out now than he had, and Isaac had probably realised Henley had been postponing the inevitable.

Isaac threaded their fingers together as they walked towards the front door. "Right, what I would like you to do while I'm gone is to do whatever you'd like to do for a couple of hours, even if that's sleep, then I want you to exercise as you normally would. You told me before that you liked going to the gym or using your equipment at home. So, do one of those. Afterwards, have a nice long bath before getting ready for tonight. I don't want you to have any sore muscles from working out." Isaac let go when he reached for his coat, slipping it on as he turned to face Henley. "And remember your punishment." He gripped Henley's chin, lifting it for him to plant one more kiss on his mouth and wrapping his arms around Henley for a tight hug before moving to the door.

"See you later," Henley said a little forlornly.

"Not too long at all, sweetheart." Isaac smiled and exited the house with his bag, closing the door with a soft snick.

Henley sighed, his shoulders drooping. Well, he did need to get some laundry on, and it was Saturday, which was his cleaning day. He had two hours to get some done before heading off to the gym. He didn't think a home workout would be the best idea for him today. Too many things to distract him.

SEVERAL HOURS LATER, Henley slid on his favourite outfit: a black tank covered with a black transparent short sleeve t-shirt, tucked into jeans, which were also black with multi-coloured dragons and flowers all over them. Completing his outfit were black combat boots, bracelets, two rings and a silver chain necklace. He had styled his hair in a side parting, allowing his hair to flow into a natural wave. Obviously, he put some hairspray on as well. There was no way he'd be able to keep it looking this fantastic without *some* help.

Checking the watch he'd just clipped onto his wrist, he saw it was ten past five. He had just under an hour before Isaac would be back to pick him up. Maybe he could fit in one episode of his favourite drag show.

The thought had him hauling his ass down the stairs and to the sofa. He dropped down, snatching the remote from the coffee table and set the programme running. It wasn't even five minutes later when the doorbell rang. Henley jumped up from the sofa and ran to the door, flinging it open in eagerness.

There Isaac stood wearing a light blue shirt, which was open at the neck, black jeans and boots. But what cinched the gorgeous factor was the leather jacket. He looked fantastic. In his hands were a bouquet of freesias and a small box.

"Hello again, sweetheart. You look amazing."

Henley felt his cheeks heat with the compliment, and he ducked his head. He was usually so confident when it came to how he looked and acted, but from Isaac, who meant so much to him, it felt more personal, for obvious reasons.

Closing the door behind Isaac, Henley whipped around him to pause the show and faced him once more, a little shy. "I'm excited to go out again. I haven't seen many of the execs these past two weeks."

"Yeah, we've been busy with all the stores opening. Everyone will be letting off steam tonight." Isaac stepped closer to Henley, holding out the flowers. "These are for you."

"How did you know they were my favourite?" Henley lowered his head and breathed deeply of their scent.

"I noticed you have several pictures with them in, so I took a chance. I wasn't certain until your face lit up when you saw them." Isaac lifted his hand, cupping the box in his palm as he offered it to Henley. "And this is for you, too."

"You didn't have to buy me anything."

"I know, but I liked this when I saw it."

Henley smiled as he undid the purple ribbon, laying it over the arm of the sofa before lifting the gold lid. Nestled inside was a key chain. Henley pulled it out and held it up in the air. It was a gold circle, and the middle spun around. The centre picture was clear glass filled with rainbow colours. As he held it up to the light, it shone brilliantly.

"It's beautiful," Henley breathed.

"I thought it might go nicely with your keys."

Henley nodded. "It would look great, but for tonight, I know exactly where it's going."

Isaac lifted his eyebrows as Henley put down the box and lifted his necklace. Looking down at his fingers, he clipped the keyring onto one of the links of the necklace and dropped it against his chest. It was heavy against him, but he loved it. Every time he looked down, he would see it and remember.

"Thank you, Daddy. I love it." He wrapped his arms around Isaac's waist and snuggled into his chest.

Isaac's arms came around him, and he rested his cheek on Henley's head. "You're welcome, my sweet boy." Kissing the top of his head, Isaac continued, "Now to finish getting you ready for our night out." He pulled away, leaving Henley frowning. "You told me you had toys. I'm assuming you have a plug?"

Henley nodded slowly, remembering part three of the punishment. "Upstairs," he mumbled.

Isaac linked their fingers together and pulled Henley up the stairs. "Show me."

Henley blushed as he opened two of his bedside drawers. Both had several different toys. Isaac looked through them and chose a thick purple plug. Grabbing the lube that was in the same drawer, Isaac turned to Henley.

"Lower your trousers and underwear and bend over the bed."

Henley stood and did as instructed, remembering a similar position when he'd been spanked in the store. Facing away from Isaac as he was, his hearing picked up sounds easier: the click of the lid, the tap as the bottle was put down, the wet slippery sound of the lube being spread, the scuff of Isaac's shoes on the rug. When Isaac's warm hand touched his ass cheek, Henley breathed deeply, wanting more than what he knew he was going to get.

A cool, slippery finger rubbed against his hole, and Henley instinctively pressed back, biting his lip to withhold a moan. A sharp smack to his ass had him stilling. The finger pressed in, and Henley bore down. He closed his eyes and licked his lips, wanting to move but knowing he wasn't allowed.

"Good boy, Henley. You're doing so well." Isaac's praise made Henley fly and relax at the same time, completely at odds with each other.

After he'd been sufficiently prepared, Isaac pressed the tip of the plug to his hole, and once more, Henley bore down to allow entrance. The further it filled him, the lower his head dropped. The pleasure was exquisite. As it was secured, Isaac tapped on the base, making Henley flinch and moan. Then, he helped Henley to stand and dressed him again.

Once he was dressed, Isaac turned him around and embraced him tightly. "You were amazing, Henley. Such a good boy taking your punishment."

Henley breathed deeply, trying to calm his racing heart. He knew tonight would be testing for him, but he was determined to make Isaac proud.

Chapter Ten

The bass thundered through the seat Isaac was sat on, and, not for the first time, he wondered whether he was getting too old to be out with these youngsters. Sierra, Maddie, Frankie, Trish and Henley were all on the dance floor, moving to the beat. Next time Frankie denied being any good at dancing, Isaac knew to ignore her. He couldn't take his eyes off Henley, though. If Isaac hadn't known better, he'd say Henley wasn't wearing a plug at all. It must be moving with every shift of his body.

Despite pouting when he'd been reminded of his punishment, Henley appeared to be having fun. He'd become close with Sierra and Frankie, often texting and calling them, no matter the time of day. Isaac was glad for that. Henley needed some friends, and from what he gathered from their previous conversations, the only people he ever went out with, apart from his sisters, were three people from the customer service department.

Henley had gone out with them last weekend, dragging his sisters along for the ride.

Isaac smiled when he remembered Henley's description of the first time he took Ariel and Arianne out with them. A disaster was putting it politely.

"What are you smiling about?" Leon's nasally voice spoke next to his ear.

Isaac's smile dimmed a little, but he held it as he turned to face Leon. "Just seeing how much fun they're having out there," he answered, thumbing over his shoulder.

There was nothing wrong with Leon per se, but Isaac hadn't taken to him like he had the other execs. It didn't mean Leon was awful. Isaac felt there was something *off* about him. Nobody else had mentioned anything, so he'd ignored his feelings and tried to get to know the man better.

"You can tell right off that Henley's gay," Leon said, gaze riveted on the group. "He certainly doesn't hide it, does he?"

Isaac bristled. "Why does he need to?"

Leon must have noticed the tension or tone because he immediately backtracked. "No, of course, he doesn't. I meant—"

"You meant to keep your nose out of his business. That's good to know," Isaac smoothly interrupted.

"Yes, of course." Leon swallowed and scooted back, leaving more of a gap between them. His gaze kept flicking between Isaac and the group on the dance floor, but Isaac couldn't interpret what his expression said.

He jumped when a more-than-slightly inebriated

Sierra fell into his lap and wrapped her arms around his neck. "Isaac! Do you wanna come and dance? The music's fantastic!"

"No. You go have fun, though. I'm enjoying watching you all."

"Okay! Watch me!"

Isaac did watch as she careened towards the group, and Henley caught her with a laugh. He spoke to her for a moment, wrapped his arm around her shoulder and started moving with the beat once more. Their eyes met briefly, and Isaac nodded to him, hoping Henley would understand he was proud of him for taking care of her.

"Hey, Isaac!" Jo called over to him. "We're going to grab something to eat from the Chinese restaurant down the road after this. Do you fancy coming with us?"

"Who's us?" Isaac asked. As he was the designated driver, if any of the people he had driven had agreed, he would naturally go as well.

"Me, Trish, Blake, Leon and Maddie. I hadn't asked the ones you drove in case you needed to get home."

The thoughtfulness made him smile. That was Jo, always thinking about others. She would make a good Mummy to a little. "I'm happy for you to ask them, although I think my passengers are worn out." He chuckled as he saw Sierra and Frankie leaning against each other, and Henley with his arms around both of their shoulders.

Jo laughed. "Yeah, possibly. I'll give them the option, though. Is that okay?"

"Of course, it is."

Jo wandered off to the dance floor, and Isaac

watched the animated conversation. He had a feeling Sierra would want to go, but Frankie and Henley appeared to have had enough. Sierra was completely off her face, so he didn't think it wise. Jo strode back to him.

"Sierra wanted to stay, but I persuaded her to go home instead. She's wasted. And Frankie and Henley were happy to go home."

"Thanks, Jo. We'll bow out this time. But next time you decide to, we'll be there."

"Alright. Do you need any help getting them into the car?"

"No, don't worry. Henley hasn't been drinking, so he'll help me."

"Yeah, what's up with that? Last time, he was sozzled." Leon chuckled.

Isaac assumed it was an attempt at a joke. "Henley doesn't need to drink to have a good time, unlike some people," Isaac all but snarled at him. He could see Leon was on his way to the land of unpleasant mornings. Maybe that was the cause for his words earlier.

Leon stared at Isaac, making him second-guess his opinion of how drunk he was until Leon giggled like a small child. Isaac shook his head and ignored him. When he turned back to the dance floor, he saw the group walking towards him, or rather Henley and Frankie holding Sierra between them. Isaac stood quickly.

"We'll say goodbye now, folks," Isaac called to the rest of the group. "Thanks for the great night. We'll see you soon, or in two weeks, depending on how busy we all are." He waved.

"Night, guys and gals," Henley added.

"Let's get these two to the car." Isaac pointed at Sierra and Frankie, and they each took one woman. Frankie was less drunk but not by much. Isaac heard her jabbering away to Henley, and Henley softly answering her, but the music was too loud for him to hear what was said. When they exited the bar, Isaac's ears were ringing.

He led the way to his car and helped Sierra sit in the back seat, buckling her in tight. Henley did the same with Frankie, and they both got in the front.

"Well, that was an interesting night." Henley laughed.

"I find it's always more interesting and amusing when you're sober." Isaac grinned. "And there are fewer consequences, too."

"True that."

"Did you have a good time?" Henley had appeared to enjoy himself, but he wanted to be certain. He needed to know if drinking was a game-changer for Henley or not.

"It was great," he said enthusiastically. "I love that bar. It's one of my regulars when I go out with my sisters. We also go to that Chinese place that they talked about. The food there is delicious. Do you think we could maybe get something to eat when we get home?"

Henley's eyes grew round as he realised what he'd said, and he quickly glanced in the back seat.

Isaac grinned. "I think you're okay. They look like they're asleep."

"God, I'm so sorry. I didn't think. I just spewed."

"Yes, we don't want spewing of any kind in my car, thanks," Isaac replied, straight-faced.

Henley was quiet for a moment before snickering quietly. "I can't guarantee that," he sputtered.

"Let's hope they sleep the whole journey home."

"If they do, be ready to open the door quickly when we stop."

"Why?" Isaac asked, brows drawn low.

"Because the motion of the car coming to a stop is more likely to cause sickness than anything else. Their brain still thinks they're moving even though they aren't. Mixed brain signals usually mean vomiting."

"Who taught you that?"

"Dad and Pops. They taught us how to look after each other and look out for symptoms of all manners of things. It helped on more than one occasion." He chuckled.

"Full of surprises," Isaac muttered.

They dropped Sierra off first, and as Henley predicted, she vomited within seconds of the car stopping. Luckily, Isaac had listened to Henley and jumped out, opening the car door immediately. And also, luckily, the vomit landed on the path, not in his car. Isaac deposited Sierra into the loving arms of her husband and bid goodnight.

Frankie lived several streets away from Sierra, so it didn't take long for her to be home and left with her waiting girlfriend. Isaac saw Henley's eyebrows rise, but he said nothing until they were in the car.

After they had been driving a few minutes, Henley said, "Why didn't you tell me Frankie was a transwoman?"

Isaac didn't miss a beat. "It's not my place to say. It's

up to Frankie who she trusts with her information. You should be honoured that she gave that much of herself to you."

"Oh, I am! Don't get me wrong. I meant…"

He trailed off, and Isaac allowed him time to think through what he was going to say.

"Yeah, you're right. I shouldn't have assumed you'd spill all the beans about everyone. I wouldn't want people talking about me behind my back, so why should I expect you to tell me those things?" He ducked his head. "Sorry, Daddy."

"You have nothing to be sorry for. I could see you were thinking about why you had made the assumption, and you came to the right conclusion. I can't ask for more than that from you." Isaac laid his hand on Henley's thigh and squeezed. "I'm proud of you."

Henley grinned as Isaac knew he would and concentrated on driving. Not to Henley's home, though. When Isaac parked the car in the designated parking area for the apartment building, Henley's forehead was furrowed as he inspected his surroundings.

"Where are we?"

"My place."

Henley's head whipped around to Isaac. "Seriously?" he asked with a grin.

Isaac nodded, barely containing his own smile as Henley's exuberance began to shine through.

Clapping his hands together, Henley exited the car, uncaring of the brisk breeze, and danced around the car to Isaac. "I can't wait to see it."

"Well, you haven't got much longer, sweetheart."

"What floor are you on?"

"Three."

Henley grabbed Isaac's hand and followed in his wake as he guided them to his front door. Unlocking it, he waved his hand for Henley to enter first. He had nothing to hide. Henley practically skipped into the apartment, stopping before the step down into the living area.

Isaac removed his leather coat, hanging it on a peg beside the door and toed off his boots. When Henley had still not said a word, he ambled to his side and cocked his head at him. "Problem?"

Henley shook his head slowly.

"It's not often I've seen you speechless. What are you thinking, sweetheart?" Isaac moved behind Henley, gripping his thin denim jacket and pulling it off his shoulders. He moved to hang it up, then returned, bending down to remove Henley's boots, which took a little longer with the number of laces he had. When Henley was finally free of them, Isaac placed them next to his own, thinking how good they looked together, and he returned once more to Henley's side.

"It's gorgeous," Henley breathed, gaze slowly roaming across the space.

Isaac tried to study the area as if he'd never seen it before. It was an open plan, apart from two bedrooms and a bathroom. In front of them was the dining area, where the table and chairs were—not often used, he had to admit. To their immediate left was a large kitchen with a squared breakfast bar dividing the kitchen from the dining area.

Looking between the two spaces and into the far corner of the apartment was a lowered living area that you had to step down into. It was a large space with a corner window as well as windows running the length of the whole apartment. The natural light he received was phenomenal.

When Isaac had purchased the apartment many, many years ago, he'd received an amazing deal on it. He wouldn't want to move and leave the views any time soon. Tomorrow, he might be able to show Henley the sunrise.

"Right, Mr James. Let's get you ready for bed." Isaac smoothed a hand along Henley's back and pressed against his spine to move him away from the view and towards the bedroom. His bedroom door was already open, so he reached in to switch the light on and indicated for Henley to go first.

"I knew you liked blue," Henley stated.

Caught off guard by the random comment, Isaac chuffed. "Yes, I do. Why do you say that?" Isaac made his way over to the drawers and removed his watch before turning and bracing his back against it as he watched Henley wander around the room.

"You always seem to have something blue on you. Either a shirt, a suit, or a tie. Something blue. Now, I find your room is blue, as well. Is that your favourite colour, Daddy?"

"Yes, sweetheart, the blue of your eyes, especially." Isaac stared at him, wondering how he got so lucky. He would love nothing more than to make love to Henley, but he couldn't. Not tonight. He had to be firm with his punishments, or Henley would rebel every time. "Come here."

Henley glanced over at him and changed direction, sashaying his way across the floor until he was close enough for Isaac to grab his belt hooks and pull him close. He could feel Henley's hard cock between them. Isaac dipped his head, pausing before he kissed Henley to get lost in those glacial pools, then fused their lips together. He planned to make things a little more difficult for Henley, and he couldn't resist his mouth any longer.

Sipping, licking and nibbling at Henley's lips, Isaac groaned when he was given entrance. Isaac used his tongue to explore every inch of Henley's mouth as his hands roamed across every inch of Henley's body, pressing against the plug when he reached his ass, causing Henley to moan. Henley was trying to pull their clothes off, but Isaac held firm. Henley probably hadn't remembered his punishment, and if he became any more aroused, Isaac would bear the brunt of Henley being awake and pouting all night.

Gentling the kiss, Isaac pulled away, both were breathing heavily.

"Why did you stop?" Henley asked.

"Because it's time for bed." As Isaac knew he would, Henley scowled, so Isaac reminded him once more. "Remember your punishment."

Henley's mouth dropped open, and he spluttered, but sighed and dropped his shoulders. "Yes, Daddy."

"Good boy. Let's get cleaned up. I have spare toiletries and some boxers you can wear for tonight."

Isaac turned and opened the top drawer, finding the

smaller sizes he had worn several years ago but had not touched as much lately. They might be too big for Henley, but they would work for now. He strode into the bathroom with Henley following. It was big enough for the two of them to stand comfortably without being unable to manoeuvre.

"Let's get you changed first. Arms up." Isaac grabbed the hem of Henley's t-shirt and lifted it off, making sure his necklace didn't get tangled. "And again." He did the same thing with the tank top. Having Henley's naked chest right in front of him was as much torture for Isaac as it was for Henley to have to wait to come.

The buttons on Henley's jeans came undone easily, and Isaac pulled them and his briefs down at the same time, dropping to his knees to help Henley step out of them. As he reached for the boxers to slip on, Henley's cock stood proud, inches from his mouth. He licked his lips and swallowed, tearing his gaze away when Henley's hand gripped the base of his shaft.

Chapter Eleven

HENLEY

"Sorry, I'm trying not to come. It's difficult when you look at me like that!" Henley's voice was pained, and his eyes were screwed tightly shut.

"Foot up." Isaac tapped his left foot, hooking the boxers over, and tapped the right foot before repeating. He slid the material up Henley's legs but stopped short of tucking his cock away. "Hands resting on the bath, legs spread."

Henley swallowed and obeyed, opening himself for Isaac. He couldn't see him, but Isaac's hands were smoothing across his skin until one hand gripped the base of the plug. Isaac twisted it around a couple of times before pulling on it and slowly withdrawing it from Henley's highly-strung body. Henley gasped and tried to breathe through the sensations, gritting his teeth against the need to come when the plug finally came free, and he slumped forward.

"Stand up."

Legs wobbling, Henley stood as best he could, and Isaac twisted him around. Reaching for the boxers, Isaac slid them up and over his angry looking cock. "Right, let's wash up. There are spare toothbrushes under here." He opened the cupboard under the sink and backed away from him. "Go ahead and come out when you're finished."

Isaac shut the door as he left, giving Henley a chance to calm down.

Henley inhaled then exhaled slowly. Resting his hands on the sink, he hung his head. It was going to be a long torturous night. He was tempted to stroke himself to completion right now and get it over with, but the thought of disappointing his Daddy made him reconsider.

Straightening up, he glanced in the mirror, seeing the tension bracketing his face. His eyes caught on the chain still encircling his neck, and he lifted the rainbow, spinning the centre around and around. It was beautiful the way the light caught the different colours. He unclipped the chain, setting it aside, slid off each of the bangles and rings and left them in a pile on the counter. He washed up and brushed his teeth before setting everything back down.

One more deep breath centred him, so he took a chance and left the bathroom, entering the empty bedroom. He could hear running water and assumed Isaac was in the other bathroom, getting ready for bed. Now that he was alone in the room, Henley felt a little unsure of himself. He didn't want to get into bed without Isaac being there. Which was probably a silly thing to worry about, but it was Isaac's house, after all.

When Isaac entered the bedroom, Henley waited at the end of the bed.

"Everything okay?" Isaac asked as he slipped off his shirt.

"Yes, Daddy. I wasn't sure which side you slept on, so I didn't want to take your space," Henley uttered, eyes captivated.

"I'd like it if you could sleep on the left."

Henley nodded, smiling as he relaxed in Isaac's presence, and walked over to slide under the covers. He knew Isaac was watching him as he got comfortable, and Henley stared at Isaac as Isaac studied him, a bit like a bug under a microscope.

Shaking his head as if pulling himself from a dream, Isaac pointed to the bedside table. "I brought some water for you in case you were thirsty." He wandered over to the bed, lifting the covers and crawling in next to Henley. The minute he was situated, Isaac lifted his arm for Henley to snuggle in, and they both sighed.

"You do realise I probably won't be able to sleep, don't you?" Henley whispered, his hard shaft pressing against Isaac's hip.

"Hopefully, you will, but if you don't, I'll keep you company."

Henley ran his hand up and down Isaac's chest, loving the feel of the minimal hair which would feel amazing against his skin. He'd had a fantastic night, even without the alcohol. It was one of the only times he'd been out and not thrown back at least one alcoholic drink. He hadn't minded, surprisingly. Sierra and Frankie were fantastic, and when Frankie had admitted, drunkenly, that she was a transwoman, it had shocked him initially but had no bearing on her as a person. He would have to tread carefully when he next saw her, though. She may not remember telling him.

Losing himself in the feeling of being so close to Isaac and in the rhythmic stroking of Isaac's hand on his upper arm, he relaxed further.

Movement woke him, and he groaned, rolling over onto his other side and burrowing into the pillow. When a chuckle reached his ear, he blearily opened his eyes a fraction, seeing Isaac facing him with his head rested in his hands.

"Good morning, sweetheart." Isaac ran his fingers down the side of Henley's face before cupping his jaw and lifting him to Isaac's kiss.

Henley groaned once more, pressing closer, wanting more. Isaac smiled against his lips and licked the seam of Henley's mouth, demanding entry. Henley granted him access, and Isaac pushed forward, forcing Henley onto his back as the kiss went from nought to sixty in seconds. Maybe they were both feeling the lack of activity the previous night, but this morning all bets were off.

Isaac slid a leg in between Henley's thighs, pressing up to massage against his balls and cock. Henley moaned into Isaac's mouth and wrapped his arms around Isaac's neck, keeping them as close as humanly possible. Isaac's hands were roaming all over Henley's body, skimming across his skin, leaving goosebumps and heat trails in his wake. It was all Henley could do to hold on and take whatever Isaac dished out.

Henley's rock-hard shaft gained friction from being squashed between their bodies, and he didn't think he was going to last long.

Isaac pulled off, both gasping for breath, and reached for the drawer in the bedside table. Henley couldn't help but keep thrusting against Isaac's stomach until his Daddy's voice demanded he stopped. Visibly shaking with restraint, Henley gripped the sheets below him as Isaac lifted to his knees, lube held in his hand.

Sighing with relief, Henley spread his legs and licked his lips as he eyed the container and the person holding it.

"Now we're going to take this slowly this first time, Henley. I want the first time that we come together to be amazing for us both. Try to be patient," Isaac remarked.

"Yes, Daddy," Henley whispered.

"Good boy. Let me see you more. Lift your legs a little higher." Henley did so. "Great. Wow, look at you," Isaac said with awe in his voice. Isaac ran a finger from his taint to his hole, and Henley fought not to react, except for a gasping inhale. "You're gorgeous, even here." He slid onto his stomach, his face level with Henley's ass, which Henley felt clench in response. "So eager to have something in here." Isaac rubbed a circle around his hole without penetrating. "Grip the backs of your thighs. I want a taste."

Henley's eyes rolled into the back of his head as he did as he was told, exposing himself completely to Isaac. Exquisite torture followed as Isaac licked a stripe down from his balls and ending at his hole. Isaac proceeded to lap at it repeatedly before firming his tongue and pressing against the rim several times. Isaac returned to lapping, more pressure than before, then stuck his tongue in Henley's hole again, withdrawing and entering, withdrawing and entering.

Henley was out of his mind. He'd been rimmed before, but nothing like this. He slammed his head back against the pillow when Isaac raked his teeth over the area in gentle bites before licking at him again.

When Isaac pulled back, Henley whimpered, but a cool finger replaced Isaac's mouth. When Isaac had lubed it, Henley had no idea, blissed out as he was, but he no longer cared when said finger was inserted into his hole. Henley gasped as pleasure began tingling up and down his spine. A second then a third finger quickly followed, Henley humming with delight at the stretch he felt. The stretch he always associated with pleasure that was soon to follow.

As the fingers left him bereft, Isaac rose to his knees once more. He ripped open a condom packet with his teeth and deftly rolled it on before smearing it with lube. Bracing one hand next to Henley's head, the other guiding his cock, Isaac lifted his gaze to Henley.

"You still with me, Henley?" Isaac's voice was strained and deep, the tension in his shoulders belying his control.

Henley nodded emphatically. "Please! Please! I want you so bad!"

"You have been such a good boy, Henley."

With those words, Isaac sank slowly but without stopping until he was balls deep. He leaned down onto his forearms and cupped Henley's head. Henley lifted his legs and wrapped them around Isaac's lower back, crossing his ankles, repeating it with his arms around Isaac's upper back.

"Henley." Isaac's tone was reverent as his lips teased Henley's mouth.

Wound around each other as they were meant to be, Isaac could only move in small increments, which he did. His hips pulled back before flexing forward over and over as his mouth and tongue explored Henley's mouth.

As their pleasure grew, Henley loosened his legs, resting his feet back on the bed, allowing Isaac more room. As if that was his cue, Isaac rose onto his hands, bracing himself as his hips snapped forward, deeper and harder than before.

"Wrap your hand around your cock, sweetheart."

Henley blinked up at him and encircled his dripping shaft. He gasped at the arousal spiralling through his body.

"That's it." Isaac shifted his hands, so Henley's legs were resting on his forearms, opening him up further.

"Fuck! Daddy! Please, let me come!" Henley panted.

Isaac pounded into Henley, leaning forward to seal their lips together in a brief kiss before lifting and grunting, "Come, Henley."

Isaac hadn't even finished speaking when Henley

keened through his climax. As he came down from his high, he felt Isaac's rhythm falter before he bellowed Henley's name and snapped his hips forward one more time before stilling. After what felt like an age, Isaac relaxed, gasping heavily and, holding onto the condom, withdrew with a wince from Henley.

As Isaac crawled off the bed, he murmured, "You're going to be the death of me." To which, Henley grinned.

"In such a nice way, though."

Isaac snorted and disappeared into the bathroom, returning with a damp, warm cloth. He carefully wiped Henley's ass, balls, stomach and sensitive cock then threw it into the wash basket. Climbing back into bed, Isaac opened his arms for Henley, who turned and snuggled into what was fast becoming his favourite position. Isaac pulled the covers over them and wrapped Henley tight.

"Thank you, Daddy."

"What for?" Isaac pressed a kiss to the top of Henley's head.

"For taking care of me. I think that helped me to fall asleep last night. Usually, if I am worked up and hard, I wouldn't be able to think about anything else, making the night so long unless I did something about it. But with you…I felt content. I knew I would be fine."

"That's my job, sweet boy. To care for you, and I love that I can do that for you."

"HENLEY? Can I speak to you, please?" Mr Sanders leaned down close to where Henley was sitting in the office. They had been back from the warehouse for a little over half an hour when Isaac was called into the manager's office. Ten minutes ago, he came storming out of the room, face looking like thunder, and walked straight out of the office without saying anything.

"Sure. Is everything okay?"

"Let's speak in my office, please."

Henley followed him to the spacious room with several large windows overlooking the surrounding trees. Where the office was based was on the edge of an industrial estate, and the trees were there to offset the environmental effects of having the buildings there. Almost as if the companies were apologising to the earth for taking over nature.

As he sat, he noticed Mr Sanders leaning his elbows against his desk with a frown on his face.

"Henley. There has been a claim of sexual harassment against Isaac."

"What! No way! He—"

"The claimant says *you* are the victim."

Henley was stunned to silence, his mouth gaping as he gawked at his boss.

"I can see that has shocked you."

Henley snorted. "Yeah, a little. Who would say that? And why?"

"I need to ask you a few questions." Henley nodded. "Has Isaac ever made any sexual advances towards you that you did not wish for?"

Trying to withhold his smirk at how the question was phrased, Henley swallowed before answering, "None that were not wanted."

Mr Sanders smiled. "Are you in a relationship with Isaac?"

Henley grimaced. As far as he knew, there were no rules about colleagues dating, but he was hesitant to get them into trouble if he'd missed something. He had to go with the truth, though. "Yes."

His boss nodded. "Thank you for being honest. As you are probably aware, it is not against the rules, though, we request that PDA's are kept to a minimum. I've spoken to Isaac, who, understandably, is upset about the claim. I must admit, I had never put much faith in it, but I had to follow the protocol. I have a feeling the claimant has an axe to grind against Isaac, so keep an eye on him for me."

Henley blew out a breath. "Who would do that to him? Isaac has never hurt anyone. He is probably the best of all of us."

"You're right there, which is another reason why I was so uneasy about the claim." His boss sighed. "I told Isaac he wasn't allowed to speak with you before I did, which is probably why he stormed out of the office. So, I permit you to grab all your stuff—yours and his—and head home. Forget about work for the rest of the day. I will be dealing with the claimant anyway, so it would be better if you weren't around."

"Yes, sir. And thank you for believing in Isaac."

Mr Sanders grinned. "He's a good one. Keep tight hold of him."

"I plan to," Henley replied with a laugh.

Henley exited the office to find several eyes tracking his movements, but he ignored them all. He switched off his laptop after saving what he'd been working on, did the same to Isaac's laptop, closed them both down and placed them in their bags. Flinging both bags over his shoulders, grabbing their lunch bags and coats, he felt like a packhorse, but he headed out of the office to find Isaac. First stop was at the car, which was where he hoped to find Isaac.

And he was correct. The passenger door was wide open, and Isaac was sitting sideways in the seat with his feet on the ground outside, elbows on his thighs, head in his hands.

"Hey, troublemaker," Henley spoke softly so as not to make Isaac jump. When there was no response, he moved to stand in front of him, carefully setting the bags on the ground next to his feet, then crouched down, resting his hands on Isaac's clenched ones.

"Who would do that?" Isaac's tone caused Henley's heart to break. Whoever thought that this man in front of him could harm a fly was well out of order.

"No one who matters. I straightened it all out with Mr Sanders. He knows we are in a relationship, and he's happy with it."

Isaac peeked up at him at that. "He is?"

Henley nodded. "Yep. Even told me to keep tight hold of you and never let you go." He smirked. "It was part of my plan all along so..." He shrugged. "Oh, and bonus, he let us finish work already. So, we can head home. Whatever will we do with ourselves?" He waggled his eyebrows up and down and stuck his tongue out the corner of his mouth.

Shaking his head, Isaac rubbed his hands over his

face and sat upright. Henley leaned forward, pressing a kiss to Isaac's mouth, and pulled away. "Boss said PDA's must be kept to a minimum but didn't say we couldn't do anything at all."

Isaac laughed. "Come on, sweetheart. Let's go home."

Chapter Twelve

ISAAC

"Yeah, he's mine, so you can't have him," Henley stated as he strode over to Isaac and wrapped his arms around his waist.

"Henley!" Isaac admonished.

"She was asking!"

"You're also asking…" He left the rest of that sentence out, knowing exactly what conclusion Henley would come to.

Henley bit his lip, and Isaac knew he wanted to say, "Yes, Daddy," but wouldn't while they were working. Since Mr Sanders had confirmed their relationship was fine two weeks ago, Henley had been a lot more visibly flirtatious at work, and although Isaac didn't mind, he didn't want their work to suffer, or for the stores they were visiting to complain. Their boss hadn't named names for the claimant of the sexual harassment accusation, but he wanted to keep his head down, nonetheless.

"Aww, that's so cute!" the brown-haired woman said, clasping her hands at her chest.

They worked through the sudden influx of staff before there was a break, and Isaac took the opportunity to talk to Henley about the following week.

"So, do you have any questions about next week? Anything you're unsure about?" Isaac carried the cups to Henley, setting Henley's tea in front of him and wrapping his hands around his coffee.

"What's next week?" Henley's brow furrowed.

"The end of your training. You'll be on your own from next week."

"I…You…" Henley ducked his head, appearing to be lost for words.

"You knew it was coming. You can't work with me all the time." Isaac sat down next to him, resting his hand on his back.

"I know. I just…it seems like it's gone so quickly." Henley smiled, a fake one if ever there was, and added, "But I'll be fine. I can't think of anything I may have problems with, and you're at the end of a phone if there is."

Isaac knew Henley was trying to sound cheerful, but he was failing abysmally.

"You will be absolutely fine, Henley. I have no worries about you at all." Except for his current reaction to working alone, which was concerning. As Isaac had told Henley, he knew it was coming, it was part of the job description that execs worked alone unless the store was a large one, when usually two execs worked together, but it didn't happen often.

Henley appeared more subdued for the rest of the day, and Isaac decided he needed to rest and relax when they got home. Luckily, Isaac had driven them both that day, so he could drive them home and allow Henley to work through whatever was bugging him. Although that was what he did, Isaac was unused to the quiet interior for the three-hour journey. It was funny how easy it was to get comfortable with a new normal.

There wasn't a murmur of protest from Henley when Isaac parked at his apartment. He exited the car, grabbed his bag and followed Isaac up. When they entered, Isaac did what he'd wanted to do all day, he began pampering his boy. He helped him out of his coat and shoes, took his bag from him, grabbed him a glass of juice and hustled him to the bathroom. Isaac was becoming concerned with how quiet Henley was.

Sitting Henley on the closed toilet seat, Isaac plugged the bath and turned on the taps. As he squirted in some muscle relaxing bubble bath, the scent of lavender filled the room.

Isaac noticed Henley had not drunk his juice. "Drink, sweetheart." He furrowed his brow at the vacant expression on Henley's face. Isaac made a decision. If Henley was not talking or responding by the time the bath was ready, he would call in reinforcements.

At his push, Henley drank the juice, a few sips before draining the whole glass. Isaac exhaled for the first time since entering the apartment. The whole Daddy lifestyle was different for each person, and although there were some similarities between relationships, most of it was fine-tuned for the specific boy. So, what worked for Mateo wouldn't necessarily be what Henley needed. It was Isaac's job to figure out the best way to take care of Henley, and if he needed help to do that, so be it.

When Henley had finished his juice, Isaac took the glass from him and pulled him up to stand. The buttons on his pale blue shirt were small, and Isaac fumbled a bit, but before long, they were undone. Sliding his hands up Henley's chest and over his shoulders, he pushed the shirt off and let it fall to the floor. Henley's gaze was now on Isaac, a little spark kindling in the blue depths.

Isaac glanced down, pulling the belt from its clasp and removing it from the belt loops before dropping it with the shirt. Gaze still on his hands, Isaac unfastened the trouser buttons and zipper, allowing them to drop to the floor. Henley was left in his briefs, which enclosed a semi-hard cock. Isaac raised an eyebrow. If Henley was only partially hard at this point, something was definitely weighing on his mind.

Seemingly without thought, Isaac's hands found their way into the waistband of Henley's underwear and pushed them under his ass, sliding his hands forward to lift it over his shaft. Inhaling and clenching his jaw to withhold from reaching for the beautiful sight, Isaac dropped to his knees…for a different reason. He tapped Henley's left foot, removing the layers of material and his sock, and repeated on the other side.

Once Henley was stripped, Isaac switched off the taps and grabbed Henley's hand, leading him to the soothing warmth. Helping him into the bath, Isaac crouched and propped a bath pillow behind his head.

"Rest, sweetheart. I will be back in a few minutes. Alright?" He brushed his hand across Henley's hair.

"Yes, Daddy," Henley mumbled, eyes closed.

"Don't fall asleep, though," Isaac whispered as he pressed a kiss to the side of his head.

A ghost of a smile formed on Henley's mouth, so Isaac called that a win. He exited the bathroom and strode to the front door, where he had left his coat and phone. Unlocking his phone, he called up a contact, dialled and pressed it to his ear.

"Hey, Isaac. Is everything alright?"

"I hope so, Ariel, but I need your help."

"Is Henley okay? What can I do?" She shushed someone—probably Arianne—on the other end of the line.

"He's…alright, but he's gone silent on me. I mentioned that next week he would be working by himself, and he withdrew into himself. I'm dealing with it as I would, but I wondered whether having his sisters, family or friends around him would be better? What do you think?"

"He certainly doesn't need to go out," she said in a motherly tone. "I think if you had a couple of people over to distract him, he might open up later on."

Isaac nodded, though she couldn't see him. "That's what I thought. Who is best, though? Sisters?"

"Yes. Arianne and I will come over, and I'll see if I can get Becca to come as well. Tracey is out of town, but we can always get her on video call if needed."

"Thanks, Ariel. I appreciate this."

"You're welcome, Isaac. You've been looking after him so well, let us take some of the burdens for now."

Isaac didn't mention that none of this was considered a burden as far as he was concerned, he wanted what was best for Henley, and he was still learning what that was. At this moment, Henley was unable to tell him what he wanted, so he had to go to another source.

He gave Ariel his address, and she promised to be there in an hour. It gave him enough time to get Henley cleaned and dressed in comfortable clothes.

He put a few snacks and another juice on a tray and took it to the sofa. When Henley was out, he'd sit down with him and feed him a few bites until his sisters arrived when he would order takeaway for them all.

The bathroom was overly warm when he returned, and he rolled up his sleeves before kneeling next to the bath.

"Hey, sweetheart. How are you feeling?"

"Like a limp noodle," came the response, causing Isaac to chuckle and his tension to release a little. If Henley was making jokes, he was coming back to earth.

"Perfect. Let's get you cleaned up." He reached for a sponge and the body wash, soaping it up and rubbing it across every inch of skin he could reach. Sliding his arm behind Henley and lifting him forward so he could wash his back, Isaac understood what Henley meant about being so relaxed. He was a lot heavier than usual, but he managed.

After cleaning and rinsing his back, Isaac helped him sit back again and brushed the sponge down his stomach to his groin. The soft cock perked up a little, but Isaac purposefully avoided that area, for now. He lifted each of Henley's legs then moved back up to his shaft. This time he grabbed Henley's cock to clean all around and under it and his balls, sliding the sponge into his crack, as well.

By the time he was finished, Henley's cock was happy to see him. Leaning back to check the clock through the open door, which was situated on the wall of the bedroom, he realised they had a bit of time.

Isaac grasped Henley's cock in a tight fist, stroking up and down in slow movements. As he reached the head, he added a twist of his hand, like he'd seen Henley do previously, before retracing his path. Henley's hips twitched in response to the stimulus, and his throaty moans were escalating. He increased his speed, and Henley's hands reached up to grasp the handles on the side of the bath, gripping them tightly.

"Please, Daddy. I'm so close." Henley's head thrashed on the pillow as the water rippled around his body in time with Henley's thrusts up into Isaac's hand.

"Come, sweet boy. Come for me."

Isaac watched the expressions crossing Henley's face as the orgasm ripped through him. His mouth gaped open, and his back arched just before his climax hit, then his stomach contracted, and he curled in on himself as his cock released his come. Henley's eyes were squeezed shut, his breathing laboured, and a flush coated his body. Beads of perspiration slid down his cheeks as his arms dropped into the bath, and his head rested back.

Complete and utter relaxation. Mission accomplished.

Isaac smiled at Henley and stood to grab a towel

from the radiator. "Come on, sleepyhead. Time to get out." Hooking the towel over his forearm, Isaac held out his hands for Henley's, taking his weight and pulling him to stand when he grabbed on. Once he had stepped out of the bath, Isaac quickly towelled him off and wrapped the towel around his waist.

Linking their fingers together, Isaac dragged Henley to the bedroom and sat him on the end of the bed. Turning to the drawers, he contemplated the options. Henley had brought a few clothes to keep here over the last couple of weeks, so he had a change of clothes if he needed them, so at least Isaac didn't have to find something of his own to fit him.

Choosing a tank, a fluffy jumper and some pyjama bottoms, Isaac pivoted back to Henley. He kneeled in front of him once more, gazing into his eyes.

"How do you feel, sweetheart?" he asked as he slid the pyjamas on, helping Henley to stand momentarily when he removed the towel and pulled up the trousers.

Henley sniffed as he sat. "Cared for." He lifted his gaze to Isaac's. "Loved," he whispered.

Isaac smiled and cupped his cheek. "You are."

Tears shimmered in Henley's eyes, but a beautiful grin lit up his face. There was his boy. Henley was coming back to him.

Isaac helped Henley into the tank and jumper and watched as Henley snuggled himself into it. He made a mental note that the jumper was a comfort for Henley. He might need that information in the future.

"I've got some snacks ready. Come on." Threading their fingers once more, Isaac led the way to the sofa, sitting and positioning Henley's side to his chest, Henley's back against the arm of the sofa. The tray was within reach, so he passed Henley the juice, encouraging him to drink it all, and picked up some grapes. One by one, he fed them to Henley, enjoying each time Henley took a piece from his hand and rested his head on Isaac's shoulder as he chewed it.

Once the food and juice were gone, Isaac pushed the tray away and wrapped his arms fully around Henley. They stayed that way until the doorbell rang. Henley lifted his head, his forehead creased.

"Who's that?"

Isaac smiled. "We won't know unless we open the door."

Henley chuckled and stood. Isaac helped steady him before shuffling in the direction of the door. He opened it with a flourish, beckoning everyone in when he saw Henley's three sisters. "Welcome, ladies."

"What are you girls doing here?" Henley gaped, a slow smile spreading across his face as he saw Ariel, Arianne and Becca.

Ariel came forward and wrapped Henley in a hug. "A little bird told us we might be needed."

Isaac caught Henley's gaze over her shoulder, and Henley mouthed, "Thank you." Isaac waved it away.

"I thought we could order some takeaway. What's everyone's choice?" Isaac said, heading to the kitchen counter.

"Chinese!" Several voices shouted at once.

Isaac chuckled. "I think the answer might be Chinese. But each of you needs to be a little more specific." He finally managed to finagle their preferences and placed the order. "They said it should be around forty minutes."

"Perfect. Time for a pampering session, Henley!" Arianne clapped. "Your hair needs a little colour. What do you think, Isaac?"

"I think Henley can have whatever he wants."

"Ooh, keep him, Henley," Becca thumbed over her shoulder.

"I intend to."

"Right. I'll leave you to your hair discussion," Isaac said and wandered towards the hall.

"Wait!" Henley ran to Isaac and threw his arms around his neck. "Thank you! Thank you! Thank you!"

"You're welcome, sweetheart. Have fun. Later, we need to talk."

"I know. We will."

Isaac pressed a kiss to the centre of Henley's forehead, then on his lips before gently pushing him in his sisters' direction. "Enjoy."

Henley grinned and whirled around, sashaying his hips in an exaggerated sway as he moved back to his family. Isaac had no plans for what he would do, but he could listen to some music and read a book while they visited. It was nice to see Henley smiling again.

Chapter Thirteen

HENLEY

Henley was overwhelmed by how generous Isaac was. Not just with his money, but with his time. He knew Isaac wanted to spend time with him to talk him through his issues, but instead, Isaac gave him what he knew Henley needed to help him find his equilibrium again. His family.

His sisters stayed for a couple of hours, making sure his hair was perfectly coloured, and his nails were manicured. Isaac had only joined them when the food had arrived, then he'd retreated to the bedroom.

Henley now stood in the doorway to the bedroom, watching as Isaac nodded his head to whatever music was playing through the headphones. He was on his laptop, sitting with his back against the headboard and his legs stretched out. Henley knew Isaac was conscious of the weight he carried around his waist, but Henley loved it. And as for the rest of the package…Henley wouldn't be complaining. Ever.

His heart raced as he realised how much he hoped their relationship would last. He was falling for—had fallen for—this amazing person, and he didn't want to ever let him go.

Isaac noticed him, and his mouth curled as he pulled off the headphones. "Hey. Everything okay?"

"Yes. They've gone. They said to say goodbye."

"Did you have fun?" Isaac swung his legs off the bed, coming upright and pushed the laptop closed.

"It was amazing, thank you so much, Daddy!" Now that Isaac had hold of nothing that would break, Henley skipped across the room and flung his arms around Isaac as he had done earlier. "I can't believe you did that for me. Thank you."

"I would do anything for you, sweetheart. I told you right from the beginning that my job is to take care of you. I have your best interests at heart, and if it's something I can't give you myself, I will find someone who can. Tonight, you needed to unwind with your sisters." Isaac ruffled his hair. "I love the colour, by the way."

Henley pulled away and ran his hands through his hair. "It's your favourite colour."

"I know, but you didn't have to do that for me."

"I wanted it. I like blue a whole lot more now that I know you do."

Isaac snickered. "So long as you're happy with it, that's all that matters."

"Very happy."

Isaac rubbed a hand up and down Henley's back. "We need to talk. I know it's late, but it would be better to get this conversation done so we can start sorting it out."

"I know."

"Let's get ready for bed, and we'll snuggle up and talk it through, okay?"

"Yes, Daddy."

They went through their usual routine, Isaac helping Henley get ready as well as himself, and Isaac heading to the kitchen to grab them fresh drinks for overnight. It was something Isaac always did, but Henley had never thought about doing for himself.

When they were settled with Henley draped across Isaac's front, their legs and arms entwined, Isaac asked his first question.

"Can you tell me what happened earlier?"

Henley thought back to earlier in the day, although now, it seemed a lot longer ago. "I guess I forgot I would be working alone. I'm so used to working alongside you, it escaped my notice that it would soon be over."

"It's not over, Henley. I promise you."

"No, I don't mean us. I mean working together. I've had so much fun these last few weeks, I guess...I'm worried that I won't like the job as much if you're not there with me. And that I won't see you as much because of where we will be working."

Isaac was silent for a moment. "It's true we won't see as much of each other as we do now. There's nothing we can do about that, unfortunately. But we can figure out other stuff. Since we started our relationship, we have been together almost all day, every day. We've not spent a night apart." He hurried on before Henley could get lost in his head again, "And I love it. But the job demands some nights away. If that happens, we will sort out a routine for you to follow, we will be on the phone to each other or video calling. There are ways around it."

Henley considered Isaac's words. "It's not the same as when you're with me, though."

"No. It won't be the same. But we will manage because when we see each other again, it will be amazing. I'm not at all concerned about you being able to do the job. I know you can do it. You are fantastic with the staff and everything else that the job entails."

Henley preened under the praise. "I am good, aren't I?"

"And so modest, too." Isaac snorted then sobered. "If something happens and one of us is unhappy with how things are working, we will talk about it and find a solution. The only way this will work is if we communicate."

"Okay. I understand."

"Do you feel better about next week now?"

Henley smoothed his hand across Isaac's chest, above his heart. "I do. We just need to talk."

Isaac pressed a kiss to the top of his head and held him tighter.

***

"AS WE HAVE a bit of time before we have to leave, you need to take your punishment," Isaac declared the following morning.

Henley spun around, eyes wide. "What! What did I do?"

Isaac raised his eyebrows. "Going silent on me yesterday. What did I tell you when we first started this relationship?"

"That you do what's in my best interests." Henley twisted his hands around each other and bit his lip.

"Yes, and what else?"

Henley studied the floor, trying to remember everything they had talked about. He could feel himself getting flustered because he couldn't remember.

"That you need to tell me the truth at all times, even when it scares you," Isaac answered his own question when Henley fumbled for a response. Henley ducked his head. Isaac's hand brought his chin back up. "I'm not cross with you. We talked it out last night and fixed it. But I would've preferred to sort it out immediately. You had me worried for a long while yesterday. You need to remember to trust me, trust us, trust in this." Isaac pointed from Henley to himself several times.

"Yes, Daddy. It's hard sometimes. I've been on my own for so long…"

"I know. But that's why I need to remind you." Isaac got a glimmer in his eye that Henley wasn't sure he could trust. He squinted at Isaac, trying to gauge what he was thinking as his stomach somersaulted. "Stand facing the wall, hands braced, legs apart."

Henley walked over to the wall on shaky legs and assumed the position. His breathing increased, and he could feel rivulets of sweat running down the side of his face.

"Good boy."

Isaac stood behind him. Henley could feel his presence. Isaac reached around to undo Henley's trousers, letting them fall to his knees, where his position prevented them from dropping to the floor. Isaac pulled his briefs out of the way in the same manner, leaving his ass bare to Isaac's roaming hands. He squeezed one cheek then the other before announcing, "Ready?"

"Yes, Daddy." He bit his lip to contain the sob that wanted to break free. He hated that he'd disappointed Isaac. That hurt worse than the pain of the spanking would, he was sure.

Isaac's hand left his skin and returned with a short, sharp smack on the fleshy part of his ass. Henley grimaced at the sting, holding his breath until the pain reduced. The second smack smarted his other cheek, and he clenched his ass and thrust forward, away from the pain. As he settled back into his original position, a third slap caught his lower buttock and upper thigh, quickly followed by a fourth on the opposite side. Henley blinked back tears and gritted his teeth as Isaac smoothed his hands across the sensitive skin.

When Isaac's hand left his ass, Henley braced for more. Locking his knees as the next threatened to take him down, Henley's tears cascaded down his face. He swallowed against the lump in his throat, knowing this spanking *was* a punishment rather than pleasure. He had scared his Daddy, and his Daddy needed to remind him.

Henley rested his head against the wall, writhing in place with every stinging smack, but knowing it was for the best. A sob left him, although he tried to stifle it.

Isaac's hands smoothed across his undoubtedly reddened skin, the sensitivity making it feel like pins were sticking in him. "Good boy. Such a good boy for your Daddy," he whispered in Henley's ear as he wrapped his arms around him from behind. Henley turned, wanting the full embrace, and he snuggled his face into Isaac's neck and cried.

"I'm sorry, Daddy. I'm sorry," he repeated.

Isaac stroked his hair and back until Henley calmed. Taking a large inhale and a cathartic exhale, Henley lifted his head. He felt rejuvenated, which he hadn't expected.

"All is forgiven, sweetheart. Done and dusted. Well done, sweet boy."

"Thank you, Daddy."

A sense of calm and pride flowed through him.

"Turn back to the wall for a minute. I want to put some lotion on you," Isaac said.

Henley obeyed as he always would, and the cold cream made him jump before soothing his ass as it was rubbed into his sensitive skin.

"All done. Let's get to work. We're running a little behind schedule now." Isaac reached down and pulled Henley's briefs back over his ass and did the same with his trousers.

The material rubbed annoyingly against his ass, and he knew it would be a hundred times worse when he sat in the car. Henley grabbed the things he needed for the day, and they headed out. As he'd predicted, his ass felt like it was on fire as soon as he was seated, but he breathed through the pain, remembering the lesson he was being taught.

It was remembering the lesson that gave Henley the

courage to ask Isaac for something he'd been thinking about for a while.

"Daddy?"

"Yes, sweetheart."

"Would you…Will you…" He breathed deeply and started again, "I'd like you to meet Dad and Pops."

"Sure. Whenever you want me to."

No shock. No horror. No denying him. Just, "Sure." A weight lifted off his shoulders that he never realised was there. He'd wanted to ask for a while but had thought it was too soon. Although Isaac had met all but one of his sisters now.

"Thank you. I'll speak to them and ask."

"Perfect. You can meet my family whenever you would like to. We have a Friday family dinner, which, as you know, is why early evenings on Fridays is always a tricky time for me. You are more than welcome to meet them as soon as you are ready."

Henley thought about this. He wanted to know what his dads thought first. "Maybe after you've met mine?"

"Okay."

Henley had an idea. "I think we should join our work nights out together." Henley had been going out once with the execs and once with the customer service staff. It made sense, at least to him, that they should join forces. More people, more fun.

Isaac's forehead creased, his brows knitting in the middle. "I'm not sure. We usually get together at the Christmas party or some other company celebration, but I don't know if the departments will mix well."

"Could we ask them and try?"

Isaac's face cleared as he smiled. "We can ask. The worst they can say is no."

"Yay!" Henley clapped his hands together, wincing when his fidgeting caused his ass to burn.

"You okay?" Isaac asked, glancing over.

"Yeah. I'm fine."

Their journey was a short one that day, only an hour away, and soon they were busy with boxes, clothing, orders and complaints. Henley loved every minute of it. When he first applied for it, he knew he would be able to do the job, but he didn't realise how much he would enjoy meeting new people each day. Even travelling, although tedious some days, was fun. However, maybe that was because he had been with Isaac for most of it.

He knew the following week—four more days— would be his first visit to a store alone. Despite being anxious about not seeing Isaac as much, Henley was looking forward to the actual work.

At lunchtime, he saw he'd received a text from Tracey, so he decided to call her and see if he could catch her before she was busy again.

"Hey! I got your message. How are you doing, stranger?" he said with a grin.

"You can talk, Mr I've-got-a-new-guy," she countered.

"Oi! I see you all!"

"Not as much as you did."

"And I bet you're glad about that!" He giggled.

"Too right, troublemaker."

"Anyway, how are you?" Henley was worried about Tracey. She had been more distant than usual over the last few weeks, missing more of their family time than ever before.

"I'm alright." Henley heard her sigh. "I've taken a new job, but I haven't told Dad and Pops yet."

"Why not? You're not a call girl, are you?"

"What! No, you asswipe! Jeez! I'm a PA still, but it's for a larger company, and I'm the first port of call for the owner. He travels a lot; hence, I do now. It's a twenty-four-hour day thing. I don't want Dad and Pops worrying about me working too hard."

Henley understood the undertones of what she was trying to say. Dad and Pops, while they meant well, if they get a bugbear about something they thought was harming their children, there was no stopping them. If they believed Tracey's new job was too much for her, they would go on and on at her about it. They wanted the best for them, but they don't like their children doing more than they needed to.

"Congrats. It sounds like a good job. You always wanted to travel, now you get to do that. But be careful, please, Trace. I love you, and I don't want you working yourself to the bone for this guy."

"I love you, too. And I will be careful. I will also do everything in my power to be fan-fucking-tastic at this job because I love it."

Henley laughed. "Good. Anyway, loser, some of us have to work. I'll catch you later, gator."

"See ya, Hen."

Though their conversation was short, it was bittersweet. Henley often thought Tracey pictured herself as an outsider because she was brought into their family when she was older, but none of the other family members thought of her that way. Every one of them tried to show her she was perfect for their family. Unfortunately, her gremlins got in the way sometimes.

Henley switched off his phone and shook his head.

"You're worried about her, aren't you?" Isaac said, coming to crouch next to Henley's chair.

Nodding slowly, Henley gave a lopsided grin. "She works too hard, but she loves it. Who am I to complain?"

"You're not complaining, you're worried and have every right to be. She's your sister." Isaac rubbed Henley's back soothingly. "I set Sarah up on a date with a guy from a café we went to once. I didn't know him but when I spoke to him, I trusted my instincts and got him to take her out. They're getting on well, but I still worry about her. Same for Felicity. Doesn't matter what age they are, you will always worry about family. Nothing you can do apart from loving and supporting her."

Isaac was right, as usual.

Chapter Fourteen

ISAAC

Henley had been working alone for the past three weeks. Every time they spoke on the phone, Isaac could tell he was having a good day and was excited about what he was doing. He could also hear the melancholy of not having Isaac with him.

As Isaac had predicted, Henley came to Isaac's house any night they were both at home. They had only been apart four nights.

It was because of this that Isaac decided to change things. Or, at least, to ask Henley an important question, despite having only been together for a short time, Isaac knew it was the right decision.

He had been to Henley's parents' house the week before, and they had welcomed him with open arms. Isaac had decided there and then, he needed Henley in his life for as long as he could have him.

Pops, as he asked Isaac to call him, cornered him in the hallway after dinner. Isaac could tell something was on his mind, and he was happy to listen and talk through anything they needed. He would do anything for Henley.

"Henley is incredibly special, Isaac. You need to treat him with care and consideration, especially with the age difference. I'm not saying I disagree with it because I don't, but please be careful with him. He's a soft soul."

"I know he is, and he's precious to me. I would like to ask him to move in with me. He's been struggling with our work schedule, and I think having a place that is ours to come home to each time, even when I can't be there, would be helpful to him. Do you agree?"

He hadn't planned on asking Pops for his advice, but the words just came out.

"Don't you think that's a little soon?"

"Not really. We spend so much of our time together already. If something is going to go wrong in our relationship, it would more than likely happen once we're living together. God forbid, but if that happens, why not figure it out sooner rather than later?"

Pops paused, gaze roaming Isaac's face. "I think that's an incredibly good idea. I like that you take care of him, Isaac."

"It's who I am," Isaac replied.

After that, they did not mention it again, but he could see a new light shining in Pops' eyes, and he was happy he'd been able to give Henley's parents some peace of mind.

So, tonight, he was planning on asking Henley to move in, officially. Henley already had a key, but Isaac wanted to do it properly. If he ever got home. Henley had rung from the road saying the traffic was awful because of an accident on the motorway, and with it being Friday as well, tailbacks were miles long. Isaac had been keeping an eye on the travel news and traffic reports. He'd not heard from Henley in over half an hour, though, so he tried calling him. No answer.

He began pacing the floor, worry flooding his body until a key turned in the latch. He whirled towards the door, seeing a haggard, tired-looking Henley entering. Isaac hustled over to him and wrapped him in his arms, squeezing him tight.

"I missed you, Daddy," Henley said, voice strained.

"I missed you, too, sweetheart."

They stayed in the embrace for several long minutes, Isaac breathing in Henley's scent, reaffirming he was there and safe. Isaac pulled back, cupping Henley's face and pressing their lips together in a sweet kiss.

"Dinner is ready. I just need to warm it up. Are you ready for it now?"

"Yes, please, Daddy. I'm starving!"

"I thought you might be." Isaac leaned down to help Henley with his shoes, led him to the breakfast bar and sat him down with a brief kiss. Isaac filled a glass with juice and placed it in front of Henley. "Drink up while I warm your food. Tell me about your day."

Henley's voice was excited as he spoke about the store he'd visited that day. He and the manager got on well together, which was great news. A good rapport with managers always went a long way to building good relationships.

When Henley's food was ready, Isaac gave it to him and sat next to him at the counter. In between bites, Henley continued his story. Once he had finished, Henley appeared to wilt.

"You're worn out."

"I'm so glad it's Friday. I love the job, but god!"

Isaac chuckled. "Well, I have something I want to talk to you about." Henley looked at him, and Isaac could see the worry creeping into his eyes. "Nothing bad." He twisted on the stool to face Henley and took his hands in his. "As my mother would say, this may be locking the stable door after the horse has bolted, but I would like you to consider moving in with me."

Henley gaped, mouth opening and closing. Isaac gave him a moment for the idea to sink in before saying any more.

"Seriously?"

For once, there wasn't much of an expression on Henley's face, apart from surprise. "Yes. I'd like you to move in."

"Move in here?"

Isaac nodded, trying not to feel uneasy with how long it was taking Henley to give him an answer.

"Hell, yes!" Henley shouted as he jumped up and wrapped his arms around Isaac's neck.

Isaac's breath came easier, knowing Henley wanted this. "If you'd prefer, we can move to your house instead? I don't want you to feel like you have to live here because I asked."

"No! I love it here. This apartment feels more like home than my house does. Don't get me wrong, I've done what I could with it, but we've made so many memories here." Henley surveyed the apartment, arms loosely encircling his neck.

Henley was right. Although they had spent time at Henley's house, most of their time had been here. "You could rent out your house. It would give you a bit more income on top of your wages." He knew the house meant a lot to Henley, too. Isaac didn't want Henley to get rid of it unless he had no other choice. And in the unlikely event, they didn't work out, Henley would still have the house. Isaac refused to take away his independence.

"When can I move in?" Henley beamed as he asked.

"Well…funnily enough, we don't have any plans this weekend, for once. No Friday night family dinner, no Saturday work night out, no Sunday family time. We have a whole two days, all to ourselves."

"But wouldn't you prefer using that time to do something we want to do instead of moving my stuff."

"There is nothing I would love better than making sure my boy knows his home is right here. And if that means we move your things in, we move your things in."

Henley bit his lip as his gaze roamed Isaac's face. "How about…we grab some people to help move me tomorrow and use Sunday as a rest day?"

"I think that sounds like a good plan, sweet boy. Tonight, however, I think you need to be rewarded." Henley's gaze lit up. "You have worked so hard this week. I am so proud of you, Henley." Isaac slid his hand up Henley's spine to cradle the back of his head before taking his mouth in a hard, desperate kiss. Isaac wanted to reaffirm to himself that Henley was home, safe and *his*. But first, he needed to take care of his boy.

With one hand on the back of Henley's thigh, he pulled Henley's leg to his waist before running his other hand down to do the same for the other leg. Once

Henley was off-balance, Isaac picked him up and sat him on the breakfast bar, lips never leaving each other.

Isaac unfastened Henley's trousers, pulling his shirt free and unbuttoning it enough for him to pull it over Henley's head. His lips went to Henley's jaw, down the column of his neck to his chest. Once there, he painted it with his tongue, circling his nipples as Henley gripped the back of Isaac's head.

"Brace your hands behind you," Isaac instructed, and as Henley did, Isaac yanked his trousers and briefs off in one go, quickly shucking the socks, too. The apartment was nice and warm, so he was not concerned with Henley getting cold. "Keep your hands there."

"Yes, Daddy," Henley moaned.

Isaac returned to kissing Henley's chest, and after some more teasing finally flicked his tongue over the nubs, he alternated between licking and sucking until Henley's hips were thrusting up into the air with nothing to gain friction against.

Still fully dressed apart from his jacket and tie, Isaac made sure to keep his body away from Henley. This was for Henley to relax, which he would do once he had climaxed.

Isaac nibbled his way down Henley's abs, licking along the defined muscles until he reached his destination, which was rising to meet him with an angry looking head.

"Please, Daddy."

Isaac could see Henley's hands clawing at the counter, knuckles white, and as Isaac blew across the top of his cock, Henley's arms failed him, and he dropped back to his elbows. Smiling, Isaac locked gazes with Henley and lapped up the precome seeping from the tip.

"Oh god! Oh god!" Henley chanted, his chest heaving with the force of his breaths.

Isaac wrapped his lips around Henley's shaft, flicking his tongue against the head and sank Henley's cock into his mouth. Isaac's hands had been sliding across every expanse of skin he could reach until he used one to push Henley's legs wider and the other to fondle his balls, pulling and rolling them in his palm.

Henley called out his name and thrust his hips upwards as Isaac's tongue found the sensitive area on the underside of his cock. Isaac slid a finger into his mouth and found Henley's hole. He rubbed a circle around it when he sucked Henley's cock down into his throat, and Henley's hips thrust up once more.

"Please, Daddy. I'm not going to last! Please!" Henley panted with the effort of holding back, so Isaac decided to let him have this. He pulled off briefly.

"Come!" he commanded, swallowing Henley's cock as soon as the words were free.

"Fuck! Oh shit!"

Henley's spine hit the counter, and his hands went over his head to grip the edge of the bar as his orgasm hit. His feet were curled on a stool either side of Isaac's body. Isaac drank him down, the slightly bitter taste, not unpleasant but not strawberries and cream either.

When Henley's body became completely boneless where he lay, Isaac pulled off, earning a whimper and a twitch from Henley. He slid his hands over Henley's exposed body, calming, soothing, relaxing.

"I can't move," mumbled Henley.

Isaac chuckled and slid a hand under Henley's back, lifting him to a seated position, or at least he tried to, but Henley was like a ragdoll. He rested Henley forward against his chest and wrapped his hands under his thighs to lift him. He stumbled to the bedroom—their bedroom —lying Henley on the already turned down bed.

"Rest, sweetheart. You've had a long week."

Henley snored in response, and, snickering, Isaac pulled the covers over him.

When he entered the kitchen, he picked his phone up and dialled.

"Hi. He's agreed to move in. Would you mind asking his sisters if they could help us pack up his house tomorrow."

"Of course, I can. All four are here tonight, so that works well." Pops paused. "Ariel, I will tell you in a minute. Be patient, girl. Sorry about that. Yes, I'm sure it won't be a problem. Lewis and I will be there, too, even if we just direct everyone."

"Perfect, thanks. I'm going to call in some more rein-forcements as well. The quicker we get it done, the quicker everyone can have their weekend free."

"See you tomorrow."

"Bye, Pops."

He cancelled the call and made another.

"Hey, Blake. Are you busy tomorrow by any chance?"

"Not at all. What do you need?"

"Henley's moving in. We need some assistance to get it done quickly."

"No problem, text me his address, and I'll be there."

"I'm ringing the rest of them, too. I want him in here asap."

Blake laughed. "Knew you'd be a goner when you found someone."

"What can I say?" Isaac laughed.

"Tell you what, you call Frankie, Jo and Sierra, I'll call the others. I'll text you with who's free."

"Thanks, Blake."

"No problem."

They rang off. Isaac reached for Henley's phone. Pulling up the contacts, he dialled.

"Henley! Nice to hear from you!"

"Sorry, Anne. It's Isaac."

"What's wrong? Is Henley okay?" Her voice was panicked.

"Yes, yes! He's fine. Sorry, I didn't mean to scare you. I was calling to ask for a favour." He explained yet again what he needed, and Anne agreed to help. Her twin sons were home from university, so she would get them to help, too. She also said she'd call Bernie and Neil.

For the final time, he dialled from his phone. "Hey, Dad. I'm calling in the cavalry."

"What did you do?"

Isaac laughed. "I didn't do anything. Henley's moving in. We need some muscle tomorrow to get it done. I've got a fair number of people already, but I wondered if you could ask around who of the family is free and send them over tomorrow."

"Of course, I can."

"I'll text you Henley's address. Thanks, Dad."

"You're welcome, son. It will be nice to meet him finally."

They said their goodbyes, and Isaac blew out a breath. If he counted correctly, and everyone he'd called was able to come, there should be approximately thirty people helping. He wasn't joking when he said he wanted it done quickly. He didn't want Henley to have the chance to change his mind, although if he did, Isaac wouldn't argue; he would ensure everything was returned to where Henley wanted it and back away slowly.

Isaac also wanted it done quickly so they would have more time together. It wasn't often their weekends were this empty, which, although it was a shame they had chosen to do it this weekend, it was the best weekend to do it.

Soon, he would have Henley to come home to or to have Henley come home to him. He couldn't wait to take care of his boy, twenty-four-seven.

Chapter Fifteen

HENLEY

Looking around the apartment—his home—Henley saw a mess, not to put too fine a point on it. Boxes were everywhere, the dining table couldn't be seen from the amount of stuff that was on it, and there were paths created between boxes so they could get from one area to the other. Despite that, though, Henley beamed.

He had decided to leave a lot of the furniture at the house, apart from the things he didn't want damaged. They were safely ensconced in the spare room at Isaac's apartment. The rest of the furniture would stay at the house so he could rent it out as part-furnished, gaining a higher income, at least in theory.

When Isaac and he had pulled up outside his house that morning, Henley had been overwhelmed with how busy it was. He'd never seen so many cars and people milling around. But they had all been fantastic, and the place had been cleared in next to no time. As a thank you, Henley ordered a variety of food from different places, so everyone had a choice of something for lunch. Becca had also baked up a storm with cookies and biscuits to tend to those with a sweet tooth.

As the afternoon had drawn on, Henley had watched their families interact with each other and their friends, and he was reminded of his idea of mixing the work nights. He'd spoken to Anne about it, and she'd been up for it. She said she'd bring her sons, too, which made Henley laugh. Her two sons had their eye on his twin sisters if he wasn't mistaken. Good luck to them.

Henley sighed as arms drew around his waist and pulled him closer to a warm, solid body.

"Having second thoughts?"

"No! Not at all. I was thinking about how everyone helped today. They were amazing."

"That they were." Isaac nuzzled his nose against Henley's neck, and Henley tilted his head to the side. "You smell delicious."

Henley laughed. "I'm sure sweat smells divine," he deadpanned.

"On you, it does." Isaac licked a strip up the column of Henley's neck, enclosing his earlobe in his lips and tugging. "You're mine, now, sweet boy," he whispered.

"Yours. Always and forever."

"I like the sound of that," Isaac growled, the sound sending tingles down Henley's spine and tenting his shorts.

Henley smoothed his hands along Isaac's forearms, which were still banded around him, protecting him, loving him. "I love you, Isaac." It was the first time he'd said it, but he knew it was true weeks ago.

Isaac stilled and rested his chin against Henley's shoulder. "I love you, too, sweetheart."

As soon as the words were spoken, Isaac spun him around and devoured him. One hand cupped his jaw, the other his ass, pulling him as close as possible, rocking their hips together.

Henley slid his hands to the hem of Isaac's t-shirt and underneath, pushing it up his body as his hands rose. When it was bunched under Isaac's armpits, Henley pulled away to yank it over his head before rejoining their mouths. Henley did the same with his own, causing Isaac to growl when he lifted his head once more. With a grin, Henley dived back in, wanting to give Isaac everything he could.

The sensation of their chests rubbing against each other, Isaac's light dusting of hair abrading Henley's skin deliciously, had Henley swaying so he could feel it more.

Isaac's hand found Henley's waistband and tugged the trousers off his hips. He kicked them free and found himself being walked backwards. Henley held on tight, knowing that, although there were boxes everywhere, Isaac would keep him safe from injury. When his ass rested against the sofa, he linked his hands at the back of Isaac's neck and concentrated on their kiss. Isaac's lips were perfection, giving and taking in equal measure. His tongue explored every part of Henley's mouth, leaving no area untouched.

As he became lightheaded, Henley lifted his head to break the seal, and Isaac kissed down his neck. Henley's cock was rock hard, as was Isaac's, so he reached for

Isaac's trousers, attempting to remove them, but Isaac pushed his hands away and turned him to face the sofa.

Isaac pressed his covered cock into the valley between Henley's ass cheeks and held him upright and still. As much as Henley wanted to thrust against the sofa, Isaac held him tight.

"You're mine, Henley."

"Yours," Henley breathed.

Isaac bit his earlobe and released him, pushing against his upper back until he was leaning over the back of the sofa, his hands resting on the cushions. Hands grazed over his back, blunt nails causing goosebumps to follow in their wake. When they reached Henley's briefs, Isaac peeled them over his ass, pressing a kiss to each cheek before pulling them off completely.

Henley gasped as the fabric of the sofa chafed against his cock and the front of his thighs, but seconds later, he didn't care. Isaac's hands were back on his ass, kneading and spreading him while Isaac nibbled at his skin and licked it better. He heard Isaac spit, and his mouth was on his hole, licking, pressing, sucking, kissing repeatedly until Henley's mind was fuzzy from the pleasure. The sofa no longer scraped him, or if it did, he couldn't feel it. All his senses were focused on that one part of him that was being teased beyond anything he'd ever felt before.

Hands and lips left him bereft, and he whimpered, pressing back for more, but when he heard the click of a cap, he settled, knowing Isaac would be back. A hand slid across his ass, spreading him again, and Henley stuck his ass out further. The cool gel made him jump when it was applied to his hole, but he soon didn't care. With Isaac's finger probing and finding entry, Henley was up in the clouds.

He lost all sense of time, only coming back to himself when he heard the rip of a wrapper and the click of the tube once more. The press of Isaac's cock against his hole had Henley gasping and pressing back. He wanted more. He wanted it all.

Words tumbled out of him. He had no idea what he was saying, but Isaac's hands rubbed up and down his back in a soothing gesture. Henley fell to his forearms, changing the position and allowing Isaac to slip further inside him. Henley wanted more. Pressing with his hands, he moved back, allowing Isaac to slide completely in.

"Fuck, Henley."

"Please!" Henley tried to move, but he was pinned between Isaac and the sofa. "Please, Daddy! Move, please!"

"I'll take care of you, sweetheart. Don't you worry, boy." Isaac withdrew and slammed back in, the screech of the sofa moving on the wooden floor echoing loudly. Neither cared because Isaac continued to thrust his hips in a quick, deep rhythm, holding tight to Henley's hips.

Henley received plenty of friction to his cock, and he was on the verge of coming, trying to pull back because his Daddy hadn't permitted him to come.

"Daddy! Please!"

Isaac reached under Henley's chest and pulled him upright, the change in position a relief on his cock but an explosion on his prostate. Henley reached his hands back, touching whatever skin he could reach of Isaac as he continued to pound into him, tweaking his nipples at the same time.

"Oh, fuck! Daddy! I'm going to come! Please!"

Isaac growled as he swore, and his cock emptied into Henley, his rhythm stuttering. "Come, Henley."

As soon as the words were spoken, Henley obeyed. No hands required. He rested his head back on Isaac's shoulder as the spasms flowed through him, and his cock released. Isaac caught him when his knees finally gave out, swinging him up into his arms and carrying him out of the room.

Henley wrapped his arms around Isaac's neck and rested his head on his shoulder again, content to be carried anywhere Isaac deemed necessary. Which happened to be the shower.

Isaac slid Henley down, keeping tight hold until he was certain Henley's legs would keep him upright, then reached to switch the shower on. Isaac kept his arms around Henley, smoothing his hands over his sweat-soaked skin, until the shower was ready, and helped Henley in, following straight after.

"I'm going to be asleep after this," Henley groused.

"Fine by me." Isaac yawned.

Henley snorted and burrowed further into Isaac's chest.

"We can sort everything out tomorrow." Isaac paused. "Although I will need to clean up the sofa. Either that or get it replaced."

Henley sniggered. "Sorry, Daddy."

"Don't need to be sorry, sweetheart. However, we

can't go buying a new sofa every time that happens. It might be worthwhile getting a leather one or something."

Henley dropped his head back, staring up at his Daddy. "You're amazing," he sighed. Never had he felt more relaxed and content as he did at that moment.

Once they were in bed, the stain mopped up as best as they could, Henley snuggled into his favourite position.

"I love your family. They seemed to fit perfectly with mine, too. I never expected that."

"Why not?" Isaac slid his fingertips up and down his arm.

"Because we're so different. But maybe there's something to this nature versus nurture debate everyone talks about."

"As far as I'm concerned, our families got on. That's a win. End of." Isaac laughed.

"Yeah, I suppose there are plenty of people out there who hate their partner's family." Henley thought about everyone who turned up to help. He had been surprised to see the people from work—both departments. Henley hadn't expected them to work together. What with everything Isaac said about them not mixing well. "I think we should reconsider that dual night out, you know. Both departments worked well together today."

"Hmm." Isaac's tone was non-committal.

"At least let's ask the execs if they're interested. If they say no, fine. But we won't know until we ask."

"Alright, alright. We'll see what they say. But if they say no, you need to leave it alone," commanded Isaac.

"Yes, Daddy. I promise."

SEVERAL WEEKS LATER, Henley looked around the bar, seeing the execs and customer service department mingling quite nicely together. He gave himself a mental pat on the back.

"You look far too smug," Isaac said, sliding his hand around Henley's shoulders and handing him a drink.

"I think I did good, don't you?" Henley ducked his head but peered up at Isaac through his eyelashes.

"You're a brat."

"I am not!"

"Yes, you are. You suckered me in by being sweet and obedient, and after moving in, you began pouting and doing things you knew you shouldn't." Isaac raised his eyebrows as he stared back at Henley.

"I was too close to the edge! I couldn't hold it in! If I had so much as tried to put my trousers on, I would've come anyway. I thought it better to make sure my trousers stayed clean."

"Exactly. A brat." Isaac sipped his drink. "Which is why you're now wearing that." He nodded his head towards Henley's groin.

Henley had not been happy when Isaac's punishment had been a cock cage. He'd never worn one before, and he certainly wasn't planning on wearing one again. Which meant the punishment had worked as a deterrent. Isaac would be so pleased. Henley snorted.

"What?"

"I was thinking about how you'd be happy because the cage has worked as a punishment. I hate wearing it."

"Good. Maybe you will listen next time when I say…" Isaac leaned in, his mouth resting by Henley's ear as he growled, "your cock and orgasms belong to me."

Henley shivered as pleasure streamed through him, unable to go anywhere. He closed his eyes, cleared his throat and breathed deeply before refocusing on Isaac.

"They do seem to be getting along, though."

"It's because of you," Isaac stated bluntly.

Henley turned to him, brows lowered. "Me?"

Isaac nodded, gaze on their friends.

"What did I do?"

Isaac turned his body to face Henley and cupped his jaw. "You're the glue that brings us together. Without you, this merging would not have happened. You bridged two departments and refused to sever ties—which is a good thing, by the way—therefore, bringing both together. No one else has done that. If anyone left customer service for execs, they cut away from their previous colleagues." Isaac pressed a chaste kiss to Henley's lips. "I'm so damn proud of you."

Henley loved hearing praise from his Daddy, but this was extra-special. His eyes flooded with tears, which soon rolled down his cheeks to be captured by Isaac's mouth and thumbs. His throat was too thick to say a word, so he clawed his arms around Isaac's body and held him tightly while he cried. It was a happy cry, so when someone came over to ask if he was okay, Isaac sent them away with a nod.

Hands and soothing words brought him back to himself however long later. Henley lifted his head, and a napkin was pressed in his hand, which he used to wipe his face. He couldn't see the state of Isaac's shirt, but he assumed it was tear and snot stained. Nice badge there.

"You okay, Henley?" Anne called from across the table, her forehead creased in concern.

"Yes. I'm fine." He indicated his face. "Happy tears." He chuckled.

Anne smiled. "Glad to hear it."

Isaac tucked Henley against him once more, passed him his drink, crossed his legs and started a conversation with Anne. As Henley looked around, he thought about bringing his sisters, and maybe Isaac's sisters, in on these nights out, too. What a hoot that would be. He could imagine the chaos. Although, Ariel and Arianne had been seeing Anne's sons for the last couple of weeks, so he never knew if those guys would be tagging along as well. At the rate they were going, they'd need to book the whole bar themselves. Now, that's an idea. He smiled into his drink.

"I can hear the cogs working in your brain. What are you up to now?" Isaac groused into his ear.

"Nothing," Henley replied as innocently as he could. They both knew better, but Henley couldn't resist denying it.

"As I said. Brat."

Henley snorted and burst into laughter when Anne joined him, Isaac following not long after.

Eighteen Months Later

ISAAC

He lifted the beer bottle to his mouth, gaze on Henley as he raced around the garden with his sisters. With how they acted when they were together, anyone would have thought they were kids if their actual height and age were taken out of the equation. Arial and Arianne chased after Henley with water guns, spraying far and wide, but luckily far enough away from the food for it not to matter. Several guests might not like it, but they were welcome to move away from the shenanigans.

As far as he was concerned, the joy on their faces was more than enough to counter anything else.

"Isaac!"

He turned to Pops, who was beckoning him over with his head. Isaac stood and ambled over to the older man.

"You okay, Pops?" He crouched down beside his chair, resting his hand on the much frailer arm. A stroke, eight months ago, had taken Pops down for a short while.

Everyone had been shocked that the strong, confident, and yes, grumpy man had been knocked down by the silent attack. Luckily, Becca had been there and dealt with it quickly, although she was understandably shaken by it.

"Yes, son. Taking it easy, you know how it goes." Pops smiled, the left side of his face remaining expressionless. "Can you help Lewis, please. He says he's fine, but you know what he's like."

"Of course, I can, Pops. You stay here and keep an eye on my beer, alright?" Isaac winked at him and stood, stepping over to the barbecue where Lewis was wielding the tongs. "Hey, Dad. Why don't you go sit in the shade with your other half and give me a whirl on this beauty?"

Lewis nodded and drifted over to his husband. When Lewis had told him about and shown him the barbecue, Isaac had been impressed by the size the James family had. Lewis had explained that with five kids and several friends over, they had needed it. Isaac had scoffed at the time, but when everyone had arrived today, he'd understood what Lewis had meant.

The number of people in attendance was astounding, and the reason was nothing more than they had been invited to a barbecue. Simply good food and good company. There was no celebration or anything.

Well, until later, anyway. Isaac smirked and peered at the food over the hot coals. He had a few minutes before things needed to be done, so his gaze wandered around the vast garden, finding his gorgeous boyfriend.

Today, Henley had gone all out with his outfit. With it

being a sunny day, he was wearing a white tank covered with rainbow sequins in random patterns, purple skinny jeans with a black stud belt and silver ballet flats. The outfit was completed with his usual bangles, chain, earrings, rings and the rainbow keyring attached to his belt hoops. All in all, he was mesmerising, and that had nothing to do with the continual flicker of light coming from the reflection on his sequins.

Isaac shook his head and shouted to let guests know the food was ready. Once everyone had something and had found somewhere to sit, Isaac grabbed his own and found a place next to a slightly wet Henley.

"Hey," Henley said, eyes lighting up at seeing Isaac, something he would never get tired of witnessing. Henley leaned to the side for a kiss, which Isaac would never refuse. He tasted of beer, cheese and ketchup.

They leisurely kissed, sipping at each other's lips as Isaac held Henley's chin in place until catcalls and whistles broke them apart with a laugh.

Isaac wrapped his arm around Henley's shoulder, feeling more content than he had in an awfully long time. A few butterflies took flight in his stomach as he thought forward to his surprise for Henley. Nobody knew about it. Absolutely nobody. Isaac had hoped he'd read their situation correctly; otherwise, he was in for a disheartening evening. He needed to keep it together for another hour.

They mingled after the food, Becca taking over the grill. Isaac had been to Henley's parents' place so many times over the last year or so that he knew everyone now. But Henley enjoyed speaking to all the people visiting them. When Isaac had asked several months ago why Henley needed to speak to everyone every time he saw them, Henley replied, "You never know when it will be the last time you'll see that person, so what does it matter if I spend five seconds saying hello if it brightens their day a little." Isaac hadn't been complaining, simply curious, but Henley's explanation had stayed with him. It was so true, and such a simple thing that could mean a lot to someone else.

Henley had a heart of gold, and everyone knew it. Unfortunately, it also meant he could be taken advantage of. Several months after he started working alone as an exec, Henley had come home looking worn out after several days away. He and Leon had been opening a store in Scotland, and as soon as he'd walked through their front door, Isaac knew something was wrong.

When Isaac finally pried every piece of information from Henley that he could, he was furious. Leon hadn't lifted a finger to do anything the whole time they were there. He had left it all on Henley, and if there were complaints, Leon pointed to Henley as being incompetent. Isaac had immediately called Mr Sanders and explained the situation, demanding Leon's immediate dismissal.

Henley had been dealing with harassment for months and hadn't told Isaac, thinking he wouldn't be believed. Leon was particularly good at misdirecting people. Isaac had seen several things on their nights out—mainly Leon's disrespect for the LGBTQ+ community—and had challenged it. But once he'd turned that onto Henley, all bets were off.

That same night, Isaac had pampered and taken care of Henley enough to make up for feeling like a failure. Isaac should've seen what was happening but hadn't. Two days later, he'd finally reconciled everything in his head, and Henley had been punished for keeping it a secret. Henley had been doing so well with communicating between them, but this was too much. Months of secrets agonised Isaac, and he couldn't deal with Henley doing that again. So, he'd punished Henley as he had done at the beginning of their relationship, but poor Henley hadn't been allowed to come for three days—a lifetime in Henley's world.

Isaac returned to the present when the bell sounded. As was routine at these get-togethers now, when the bell rang, everyone had to make a circle—or as best a circle as they could depending on how many were there—and tell everyone something good that happened to them since they had last visited. At first, Isaac had been unsure what to say, because his happiness was so wrapped up in Henley, but with Henley's help, he'd been able to see outside the box.

This time, though, things would be different.

Becca and Ariel helped Pops down the steps to a chair placed in the circle next to Lewis. They both sat on their 'thrones' as the guests gathered around them.

Lewis began, "This is what family is all about. It doesn't have to be about blood. You can choose your family. Everyone here has been chosen by someone to be part of our family. And we love you all."

Everyone cheered. Lewis indicated for Arianne to go first as she stood to his left. After that, each person had their turn, some stumbling with things to say, some glowing with happiness, some unsure, but each managed to say something.

By the time it came around to Henley's turn, Isaac had begun to sweat. Typically, Lewis had started at the opposite side of the circle to what they were on, so he'd had to wait for almost everyone else before it got to him.

"I made my first piece of clothing over the last couple of weeks. And I'm happy with how it turned out. I have decided to make a few more pieces before seeing if this is something I want to take further."

Everyone clapped, and Isaac kissed the side of his head. With Henley's flair for design, Isaac had suggested he make some of his own items when he'd once pouted about something not fitting right. Henley had brushed it off until one day they'd revisited the conversation, and Henley had agreed to give it a go. Eventually, Henley was going to get some advice about where to market it because, although they worked in the clothing sector, uniforms were slightly different from more unique and one-off items.

Then it was Isaac's turn. Heart pounding, he said, "Everyone knows I struggled with what to say when I first started doing these. It's difficult to remember the things that went well and so easy to focus on the bad things. But with Henley by my side, that scale is tipping in the other direction, finally." He inhaled and stepped forward, turning to face Henley, whose eyebrows rose. "Henley is the light in my darkness. Every day, he encourages me to be a better person as I do for him. And because of that…" Isaac lowered to one knee, fumbling to remove the box from his pocket as a gasp went around the circle. "I would like to ask Henley to marry me." Isaac opened the purple velvet box as Henley's hands covered his mouth, and his eyes widened. "Will you marry me, sweetheart?"

Henley nodded over and over, tears sliding down his face. He dropped to his knees in front of Isaac, gaze on the ring. Isaac had commissioned a ring that was pure Henley: a white gold band, representing Isaac, being grey and all, and slithers of coloured gems all around the band, to represent Henley and all his many wonderful attributes. When Isaac had seen the result, he'd been so overwhelmed that *he'd* cried.

Now, he pulled the ring from its box, dropped the box to the floor and grasped Henley's hand. Finding his ring finger, Isaac slid the band to the base before pressing a kiss to it amidst cheering and whistling from the guests.

"Oh my god!" Henley's wet gaze flicked from his hand to Isaac's face and back again. He couldn't seem to decide where to look.

Henley threw his arms around Isaac's neck and held him tight, sobbing his heart out. It was a good thing Isaac knew Henley well enough to know they were happy tears. As people broke free of the circle to congratulate them, they were surrounded by all the people who loved them.

"Yay! A wedding to organise! Are you going to make your outfit, Henley?" Arianne nudged her way into their space, kissing their cheeks.

"Oh god! I don't think I could! Talk about stressful!" Henley laughed, wiping his eyes.

"You look a hot mess." Arianne turned to Isaac. "I'm

going to borrow your *fiancé* for a moment to get him looking his best. Be right back!" She waved her fingers at Isaac as she pulled Henley away.

Although Isaac would've loved for Henley to stay with him, he knew Arianne was taking Henley to speak with his sisters and dads, probably to make sure he was alright with everything that had happened. That was the only reason why Isaac wouldn't complain.

They had the rest of their lives to make up for a few missing minutes.

Isaac's parents finally made their way over to him, laughing about not being able to get to them before Henley was whisked away.

"I'm so happy for you, darling," his mum said, giving him one of those big hugs that a child was never too old for.

"Thanks, Mum." Isaac turned to his dad, who clapped his shoulder.

"Nicely done. You take care of him, now, okay?" he said, laughing.

"Already do, Dad. Already do." Isaac didn't mention how he took care of Henley. A few close people knew the finer details about their relationship but not everyone. Henley had agreed he didn't feel right calling Isaac, "Daddy," in front of family, so they'd decided that was a hard limit, although occasionally it had slipped out unintentionally. They weren't worried, though. "Have you heard any news from Felicity?" His sister had been called by their surrogate, Shelby, and told to go there as she thought she was having contractions. The baby was due any time now, and Felicity and Van had gone to see her. They were all going to go to the hospital as soon as they had news about whether Shelby was in labour or not.

"No, nothing yet," his mum said.

Half an hour later, Isaac was wondering where they all were when he saw Henley hustling towards him. His makeup had been redone, and he looked as gorgeous as ever. Isaac didn't mind whether Henley wore makeup or not, it was whatever Henley wanted to do.

When Henley stopped in front of him, biting his lip, Isaac grew concerned. "Is everything okay?"

"Yes. I…" Henley exhaled, nodded and inhaled again. "You beat me to the punch earlier. I hadn't planned on proposing today, but I had the ring ready for when I did. I sent Ariel to go get it for me." Isaac's eyebrows rose as Henley lifted his hand. "I don't know if it's going to fit but…" Henley opened his fingers, showing a white gold band with a yellow gold stripe around the edge.

Now it was Isaac's turn to be shocked. His smile grew as Henley reached for Isaac's hand and slid the ring on his finger. It was a little loose, but they could get that altered, no problem.

"Thank you, sweet boy." He cupped Henley's face, staring into his eyes, and pressed kisses to his forehead, his nose, each cheek and his lips. After, he smoothed his hands around Henley's back and crushed him to his chest. Their first kiss as fiancés.

They pulled apart when a throat cleared right next to them. Isaac blinked a couple of times before focusing on

Dad and Pops. "Congratulations, boys. I know you will be very happy."

"Thank you, Dad, Pops." Henley gave them each a soft hug before Isaac followed suit.

"And you've made us happy, too," Pops said, smiling at Lewis as he held onto him.

SPOIL ME, DADDY

AARON & ZAIRE

Dedication

To those who think they are not worthy.
You are.

Chapter One

ZAIRE

"Yes, of course. Traffic permitting, I'll be there by eight-thirty." Zaire Morgan listened to the caller, nodding. "Sure. Thank you. Bye."

He closed his phone, rubbing his eyes with his free hand as he yawned. He'd been awake for the past hour but, for some reason, could not wake up properly. At least, he now knew which school he was being sent to. It was one of the downsides to working for an agency. He didn't know where he would be sent until around seven in the morning when he received a call with the location and times he was needed. Sometimes, it was a nice school; other times, it was not.

Thankfully, most of the students he met were adorable. He specialised in helping with special educational needs children of any age up to eighteen. There was always plenty of work available for him because there was a serious lack of specialised teaching assistants in the school environment. Unfortunately, the job took a lot of energy and not only physical energy. Guaranteed, by the end of the week, Zaire was exhausted and seriously in need to play.

Stepping into his kitchen, he flicked the kettle on and filled his takeaway mug with coffee, needing a hit of caffeine if he was going to manage it through the last day of the week, then he got into his car and drove to the special needs school. He didn't know which age of children he'd be working with until he got there, so he psyched himself up for anything.

Arriving, he parked his car, picked up his bag of tricks and his coat and headed to the reception desk. As he walked, he slipped his ID card over his head, settling it around his neck. Upon entering, he signed in electronically, a printed ID given to him to add to his current one, and he strode off to the early years' classroom. Today would be a day of fun and games with five- and six-year-olds.

Another unpleasant side effect of working for an agency was that he never managed to create deep, meaningful friendships the way he would if he worked in the same school permanently, but he was getting used to it after a year.

An upside to the job was he could pick and choose when he worked. If he received a call one morning, and he didn't want to work, he was able to decline it with no repercussions. Or at least, no repercussions as long as he didn't do it all the time.

The day passed by as he'd expected it to: playing a variety of games, calming children down, singing, dancing, climbing outside and reading, plus all the toileting and hygiene tasks which were needed. By the time school ended, Zaire was shattered. He bid goodbye to the staff, signed out and dropped into the driver's seat. He rested his head back for a moment, breathing deeply and closing his eyes.

Knowing he would not get better until he got home, Zaire started his car and left. As soon as he arrived, he stripped off his trousers and polo shirt, got into the hottest shower he could stand and washed off the week's work. When he'd wrapped the towel around his waist, he hustled to his bed, where he'd dropped his phone and opened it to Rod's name.

"Hey, I'm heading out tonight. You coming?" Zaire asked without a greeting.

"Nah, man. I've got a party with Delia, haven't I?" Rod was his best friend, had been since university.

Zaire had forgotten. "Alright, no worries. Have a good night."

"Hey, Z?"

"What?"

"Head over to Infinity. They've got a free-for-all night on. You never know what you'll find." Rod chuckled and rang off.

Zaire rolled his eyes. It was a good idea, so he threw his phone back on the bed and strode to his wardrobe. He pulled out a cute red halter-neck top and a black satin skirt. Hanging them on the wardrobe door handles until he needed them, he sashayed over to the drawers, skimming his hands over the contents of the top drawer. Zaire chose black nylon stockings with a black lace suspender belt and matching lace underwear.

He threw the towel to the floor and sat on the bed, placing his feet into the suspenders and sliding them up his legs, settling it nicely on his hips. He repeated the action with the underwear, making sure the clips were underneath. He adjusted his cock to fill the material better and smoothed his hand over the front of his groin, loving the feel of the lace covering him. He sat on the bed again, lifting one foot and sliding the stocking up his calf and thigh until he secured it with the clip from the belt. As he slid the other stocking on, he felt something inside him unclench, something free from within him.

When he was done, he stood in front of the mirror, admiring the way the lace clung to every part of him. He skimmed his hands across his body, feeling more like himself with every passing moment.

He hated having to be so buttoned up, so prim and proper when he went to the schools, but naturally, there'd be outrage if he turned up wearing what he preferred to wear every day. He only had to think about how his dad reacted to know the truth.

Zaire fetched his outfit and slid both items on, once again, admiring the look. Choosing some red three-inch heels—he knew his limitations when walking was involved—he slid them on and sat in front of his mirror. He rarely wore a lot of makeup, usually some subdued eyeshadow and lip gloss, but tonight he needed more. By the time he was done, his amber-coloured eyes popped from his features, his cheekbones were more defined, and his lips looked divine.

Satisfied with his appearance, Zaire grabbed his phone and called for a taxi. Finding his short leather jacket, he checked his social media while he waited. When the horn sounded, he locked up his house and departed for the evening.

He never knew what to expect at these free-for-all events. There was always a mix of kinks milling around each other, and it wasn't always easy to find someone with the same kink as he had. Despite that, he was excited to let go.

When the taxi deposited him outside the club, he thanked him and headed towards the building, the bass pounding into the night, even through the closed doors. Infinity had been open for several years and catered to many people. There was a membership section to the club as well as a public side. Zairè couldn't afford to pay to be a member, so had to settle with public events like these.

Music blasted his eardrums as he entered, and he strolled towards the kiosk to pay his entry fee. He swapped his coat for a ticket, which he slipped into a discreet pocket of his skirt, along with his phone. He thanked the staff member and waved his way into the club, heading straight for the bar for a stiff drink.

As he arrived, a gap opened, and he slid into it before anyone else could take it, although someone bumped into him.

"Sorry, sweetheart." A muscular guy squeezed Zaire's arm and shuffled on his way.

Zaire rolled his eyes before turning his attention to the bartender. When the guy moved closer, Zaire shouted his order to him, receiving a shout in his ear afterwards.

"Hey! Wait your turn like everyone else."

Zaire twisted his head to an older man who stood beside him. "If you wait, you'll be here for hours. Shout, and you get their attention. Suck it up." He returned to the bartender who had arrived with Zaire's drink, and Zaire quickly waved his card over the machine to pay. "Thanks." He nodded to the bartender and turned back to the guy. "See? If I were you, I'd shout. Loud."

He pivoted on his heels and sashayed over to the dance floor. The problem with the public area of Infinity was the deafeningly loud music, whereas, for the members-only section, it was a lot more subdued. He'd never experienced it himself, but he'd been told when he'd inquired about the membership benefits. Maybe in a couple of years, he'd be able to save enough for a membership, but as it was, he was paying off his car and a mortgage, so money was tight, despite how much he worked.

Rolling his head on his neck to loosen the muscles, Zaire studied the patrons of the club. From what he could see, there were Doms and subs, puppy play, a Mummy and her boy, master and slave to name a few. When they said free-for-all, they really meant it. What Zaire couldn't see was anyone looking like a Daddy. His shoulders slumped, and he blew out a breath. Why was it so difficult to find what he wanted? Soon, he would need to take an ad out to get people to interview for the position. He chuckled at that. It might be quite entertaining to see who turned up to such an advertisement.

"Hey, gorgeous. Are you here with someone or searching for someone?" a voice purred in Zaire's ear.

Glancing over his shoulder, he saw a tall black guy

with huge muscles whose demeanour screamed Master. Zaire smiled and whirled around to greet the guy. He never ignored people who approached him; it was a social nicety. "Hey! I am looking for someone, but I have a feeling you're not going to be what I need, sir."

"So polite. Are you sure?"

"May I ask a question, sir?" Despite not wanting what this Master was so obviously offering, Zaire knew to treat all dominants with respect. Disrespecting others got people kicked out of the club quicker than they could apologise.

"Go ahead."

"Are you a Daddy?"

The Master smiled gently. "No, sweet boy. I know there are a couple here tonight, though I don't know if they have boys themselves." He slid a finger down Zaire's cheek. "Thank you for checking with me. Good luck tonight."

"Thank you, sir. And you."

Zaire watched as the guy moved through the crowd before returning his gaze to the masses, trying to find those elusive Daddies.

After spending a couple of hours circling the hordes, finding a Daddy who, unfortunately, already had a boy and drinking some more but not enough to be drunk, Zaire had decided enough was enough. He stood at the bar, which was not as busy as earlier, and requested one more drink while he waited for his taxi to arrive.

As he brought the tumbler to his mouth, someone bumped into his back, spilling the drink on his shirt and skirt.

"What the fuck! Watch where you're going! It's not like I'm difficult to see wearing a bright red satin shirt! Fucking thing is ruined now." Zaire plucked the wet fabric away from his skin and grimaced. He would be stinking of whiskey for his journey home, and to top it all, his favourite top was toast.

"Sorry. I really am. Let me help…" the guy tried dabbling at the fabric with a napkin, but Zaire batted his hands away.

Zaire sighed. "Leave it. Just be more careful around other people. I'm outta here."

Spinning around, he elbowed his way through the crowds to the entrance, pulling out a wet wardrobe ticket to retrieve his coat before exiting in the warm night. Staring up at the sky, he exhaled, shaking his head. Not only had the night been a total bust, but he'd ruined an outfit. He needed to sleep this night off and start fresh in the morning.

"That was a bit harsh, wasn't it?"

Zaire spun around, gripping the edges of his leather jacket as he identified the guy as being the older man from earlier, who'd called him out for pushing in at the bar.

"What's it to you?"

"I thought the idea was to be polite to people." He was stood outside the entrance doors but close enough Zaire didn't have to strain to hear him.

"Maybe so. But sometimes you also need to tell someone when they're being an ass," Zaire countered.

The guy raised his eyebrows. "Is that so?"

Zaire raised his chin. "Yeah."

"In which case…" he paused, "you were an asshole."

Stunned, Zaire blinked at the guy. He couldn't believe he'd been called out on his behaviour when it was the other guy's fault for knocking into him. He told the guy his thoughts.

"But you could have been nicer about it. He did apologise, and he did try to help clean up. Regardless of how it happened, the behaviour afterwards should have shown he was contrite. Your punishment didn't fit his crime."

The words "punishment" and "crime" wound Zaire up tighter, especially as there was no release in sight. But the guy had a point. "Shit," he muttered, staring at his shoe as he swivelled one foot on his heel.

"Maybe you need to think about your actions before reacting to outside influences."

With the reprimand, the guy whirled and headed back into the club. Under other circumstances, Zaire would've been interested in him, especially the confident air around him. He could almost feel the guy's beard and moustache, the same light-brown colour as his hair, sliding against his skin. Zaire watched until the door closed behind him, the outburst of music muting once more. "Fuck!"

A horn made him flinch, and he twisted around to see a taxi waiting at the kerb. He stalked over, checking the number plate and name with what he had on his phone before entering and slamming the door behind him.

"Rough night?" the driver asked.

Zaire snorted without humour. "Could've been better."

"Ah, there's always tomorrow."

And there was the problem. There was an infinite amount of tomorrows, but Zaire was fed up with waiting for his tomorrow to arrive. He wanted to share his life with someone who would take care of him and help him reduce the stresses in his life. And finding someone would be one less stress for him.

Chapter Two

AARON

He checked the figures once more and rubbed at the back of his neck. Regardless of how many times he reread it, he could see the special needs department was suffering from being understaffed. Aaron needed to bring in more people but also didn't have a huge budget to do so. The best idea would be to get an experienced agency member and see how they go. If they were good, he could offer them a job, reducing the outlay of using an agency—after having to pay the agency exit fee, that was.

Standing, he stuck his head outside his office door and asked Pamela to come in. As he returned to his desk, they entered, sitting opposite him. Pamela had been a fantastic help for him while he was finding his feet in this new position, going above and beyond what was required of them, such as being in the office at seven in the morning when it should have been eight.

"How can I help, Mr Brown?"

"Please. I keep telling you, call me, Aaron. Especially

when there is no one else around." He smiled to lessen the sting of potentially offending them. "I need a list of agencies where we could get some staff experienced with special needs. Being new to the area, I don't know which ones you use."

"Sure thing. I can get you the list. If I recall, there are five or six we have used in the past."

"That would be great. Thanks, Pamela."

They left and, within minutes, returned with a list. Thanking them again, he was left alone. Picking up the phone, he dialled the first number. After going through what he wanted, they said they didn't have anyone available for that day, but they would tomorrow. Aaron thanked them and agreed to keep their school on the agency's books. He bid goodbye and dialled another.

"Yes, we have a couple of teaching assistants available today. Thinking about what you wanted, you probably need our most experienced. He has many years' experience but has only been temping with us for the last year. He comes highly recommended and has been requested the most out of all of our staff."

Aaron knew the agency would increase an assistant's abilities to make sure they get a foot in the door at the school, but he was also desperate. "Fantastic. If we could have him, if he's available, and two others if you have them, we will see how things go from there."

"No problem at all. I will get on the phone to them now and let you know if less than three can make it."

"Thank you."

Aaron put the phone down and sat back in his chair with a sigh. When he had first taken on the role, he had been excited about it, but as soon as the previous principal had left—early and without warning—Aaron had felt like he was drowning. He knew as soon as the place was running smoothly, everything would be fine, but at the moment, he wondered why he'd even agreed to the job.

"Pamela?"

They poked their head through his door.

"We have three agency staff coming in today. One is apparently very experienced. At some point this afternoon, I'd like some feedback from the teacher as to how good he is, please."

"Sure thing. Where do you want him?"

"In the class where an experienced special needs teaching assistant is most needed."

"Year one, then. I'll ask Uma to come and see you before the end of school."

Aaron nodded. "Great, thanks." He scratched his nails across his beard and wished he could head to the gym for a workout, the stress of the day was already getting to him, and it was only seven-forty.

Leaning forward again, he refocused on the paperwork, hoping things would change sooner rather than later.

AT LUNCHTIME, he ate his couscous and salad at his desk so he could continue his work. He didn't feel like he was making any headway, but he must've been. His school was a mixed ability school, which meant it included all children regardless of their protected characteristics or special requirements. He didn't see why he couldn't provide what each child needed with a bit of research and funding. It was the funding that was the problem. He'd argued with the education committee many times already about the need for more cash, but as usual, money was what made the world go round.

Pamela brought him a cup of coffee, for which he was eternally grateful, and slipped out of his office again.

Aaron rested back in his chair with another sigh, probably the fiftieth that day, and thought back to the previous Friday night. He'd gone out with Nora, his best friend of thirty-odd years. They had met in secondary school in Lincoln, and after college, Nora had moved with her then-boyfriend to Cambridge. After Aaron's departure from his previous role, Nora had suggested he relocate. He loved Cambridge, always had whenever he had visited her, and more so now he lived there.

Friday had been the first time in several weeks when he'd had enough energy to venture out. Nora had told him about a free-for-all night at one of the clubs, and as she and her now-husband, Geoff, were in a Mistress and puppy relationship, it allowed Aaron and Nora to go together rather than have to split up as they had to occasionally. Apparently, some clubs thought Daddies and Mummies, and Masters and Mistresses shouldn't mix, which was a rather silly notion, which was, thankfully, not seconded by many places.

He'd been talking to Nora at the bar, waiting to be served when a guy shouted his order near his ear. Despite the pounding music, the voice was piercing and had

Aaron wincing and twisting to tell the guy to wait his turn. The guy, dressed in an eye-catching red halter-neck, gave him the cold hard facts as he'd believed them to be and promptly received his drink within minutes. Giving Aaron a final word, he'd sashayed off, his hips and skirt swaying with the beat of the music.

After the guy had left, Aaron had raised his eyebrows at Nora and shrugged, then shouted their order to the bartender. Several minutes later, their drinks were in front of them, and he'd wished he could thank the guy.

Later that night, he'd seen the same guy give a dressing down to someone who had bumped into him. Okay, his perfectly fitted clothing had possibly been ruined by whiskey, especially as he heard the word satin being bantered around, but the accident-prone guy didn't deserve the words thrown his way.

When the guy had muttered and left, Aaron couldn't help but follow. As he saw the guy stare at the sky, words escaped before he realised what he was going to say. His tongue reprimanded the guy's response, and apart from the initial push back, the guy had taken the slap on the wrist well. It hadn't been Aaron's place, but he couldn't help but make the guy aware his actions had been way over the top.

If he had been his boy, he would've been spanked and denied orgasms and Aaron's cock until Aaron believed he understood. The guy hadn't been, though, and a verbal reprimand was the best he could do.

Aaron shook his head, knowing he needed to find himself a boy, or someone, to hook up with. He struggled to find someone who pushed his buttons because he was more attracted to a person's personality than their looks, and many people hid behind a social curtain instead of being themselves. But maybe getting laid would clear his brain.

When Pamela knocked on his door that afternoon with a report from Uma, Aaron was grateful for the interruption.

"Uma says the sub," Aaron's heart rate increased at that word even though the meaning was different, "is amazing, and can she have him forever?" Pamela smirked as they stood there.

Aaron chuckled. "Okay. Could you see if the guy is around so I can have a chat with him, please?"

"Sure thing, boss."

Ten minutes later, Pamela knocked again. "Are you okay to see him now?"

"Sure."

Aaron closed the file he had been working on and stood from his desk as the guy walked in. As Aaron's gaze lifted to the guy's face, he stalled, eyebrows raising. This should be interesting.

"Thank you, Pamela."

They closed the door behind them. As silence descended, Aaron studied him. The black styled hair; warm, amber-coloured eyes; soft-looking, clean-shaven skin and full lips holding a hint of a smirk.

"We meet again…" Aaron held his hand out as he paused for the guy to finish Aaron's sentence with his name.

"Zaire…Morgan." A hand clasped his in a strong but not challenging grip.

"Aaron Brown. Please take a seat."

They both sat, eyes locked as they sized each other up.

"I apologise for the way I behaved on Friday."

Aaron wasn't sure who was more shocked by Zaire's apology: him or Zaire. He saw Zaire clench his jaw and fidget in his seat, so Aaron took pity on him.

"Thank you. I appreciate you saying that."

Zaire snorted. "I wish I could say it was a one-time thing," he rubbed his fingers across his mouth, "but thinking back on previous nights out, it probably wasn't. I can be…" Zaire paused, his focus moving off to Aaron's right as he seemed to search for a word.

"Temperamental?" Aaron supplied.

Zaire flicked his gaze back to Aaron and laughed. "Yeah, that pretty much covers it. But only outside of work." He held his hand palm forward, letting Aaron know he was serious. "Within work, I am reliable and respectable. I keep the two sides separate."

"So, I've heard. You come highly recommended, Zaire. I don't think those words will inflate your ego any more than it is already," Aaron declared with a smirk.

Zaire's lips twitched. "I come wherever I'm commanded to."

Aaron raised his eyebrow. Did the guy seriously flirt with him?

"Sorry." Zaire linked his fingers in his lap and crossed his legs, gaze dropping.

The undeniable submission Zaire showed sparked a flint in Aaron's chest, and he schooled his features. "No, you're not."

Zaire's gaze rose for a second, a twinkle in his eyes until he dropped his gaze once more. "No, I'm not," he whispered.

"You said you were reliable and respectable. If I can ensure you'll leave the innuendos at the entrance to the school, I would love to have you back again. What do you say?"

Aaron watched as Zaire's jaw tightened again, and he swallowed. "I believe I would enjoy working here."

"That's good news. I'll speak to the agency and request you stay with us for the next two weeks. If you appear to fit within the team, I might extend a permanent job offer, if you'd be interested."

Zaire's expression brightened. "I would. Thank you."

"Don't thank me yet. Thank me if I offer you the job." Aaron grinned.

Smiling, Zaire stood, holding out his hand once more. "Regardless. Thank you. For today and last Friday."

"You're very welcome, Zaire. Just remember what I said."

Their hands clasped for longer than was necessary, and when they parted, Zaire's fingertips slid across Aaron's palm.

"See you tomorrow."

Zaire exited the office, and Aaron breathed deeply before picking up the phone and calling the agency. After explaining his terms, they agreed on a two-week employment for Zaire. Aaron didn't mention anything about the possibility of a job at the end of it. That would be discussed if Zaire behaved.

Aaron thought about Zaire's demeanour as he'd sat in front of him and from Friday night. There was no doubt Zaire had confidence in spades, but he appeared to need reining in a bit. Friday night showed his ego might be a problem, but if he was true to his word and kept the two sides to himself separate, he'd fit nicely. Aaron was concerned about the separation aspect. Surely, it wasn't healthy to keep aspects of his personality in different compartments.

He frowned as he tried to figure out how Zaire worked. The side of Zaire he'd seen on Friday was brash, egocentric, graceful and sexy. Today, he'd seen buttoned-up, clean-shaven, confident with some uneasiness if Aaron wasn't mistaken. Which was the real Zaire Morgan?

Shaking his head, he returned his attention to his workload. Then, hesitating, grabbed his phone.

I need relief. Which club or bar is the best choice for tonight?

He sent the text to Nora, knowing she would reply as soon as she could. Naturally, having lived here for thirty years, she knew the place better than he did and had been on the scene longer. He picked up a file and opened it, trying hard to concentrate on what was inside.

A knock sounded.

"Come in."

Pamela smiled. "It's time for assembly."

"Okay. Thanks. I didn't realise the time."

"No problem. It's what I'm here for." Pamela grinned

and left the office, leaving the door open, presumably to remind him to get his ass up.

Dropping his phone into a drawer and locking it, he stood, heading to the hall ready to give his end of the day assembly. They alternated when they had assemblies and didn't have them every day like a lot of schools did. He found children fidgeted a lot the longer they had to sit still, so he had introduced a few changes.

He waited at the front of the hall, pacing, as the children entered, some smiling at him, some shy. He crouched to make himself smaller, so he didn't appear as scary. One of the first changes he had made was to reverse how the classes sat. Usually, the youngest children sat at the front and the oldest at the back. Aaron had read some research once that younger children would benefit from being further away from a person they may be frightened of, especially if he was pacing in front of them all the time. It had the added effect of making the older kids sit closer to him, where he could see the troublemakers.

Once everyone had settled in, he greeted them, "Good afternoon, students."

"Good afternoon, Mr Brown. Good afternoon, teachers."

"Thank you. Firstly, can I say you are all looking very smart today." He caught the gaze of a few students and smiled. "Today, we are going to talk about books."

As Aaron carried on talking about favourite books and calling on children to talk about theirs, he tried to decide if the two other changes he had made were making a difference. Assemblies now only happened on

Monday and Wednesday afternoons and a Friday morning. And in the middle of each assembly was an active session.

"Right. You know what time it is now. Everyone, stand up." Aaron indicated for the piano teacher to get ready. "Remember, please think about where your feet and hands are. We don't want other children getting hurt if you are too close to them. Go!"

He watched as all the pupils jumped, hopped, danced, shimmied, and whatever else they could think of as the music played. After a three-minute burst, the music ended, and all the children dropped to their bottoms.

"Fantastic work, kids. Now, if you can sit nicely again for me, we will have our story."

Aaron switched on the projector, and the story's pictures filled the wall behind him. As he read through the book in his hand, he scanned the children, seeing them hardly fidgeting at all. Maybe it did work. More research had shown that children found it physically painful to sit still for any length of time, so he'd introduced the physical burst to allow them to shake it off, in the theory they would be able to sit still again afterwards.

Time would tell if it worked.

As he finished the story, he caught Zaire's eye. Aaron couldn't decipher the expression on his face. It was almost as if he was shocked but not. Focusing back on the children, he bid them a good day. After they left the hall, Aaron found his way back to his office, checking his phone immediately.

The best place would be Infinity, again. The membership section is the best bet, but I don't know if you want to do that yet. Otherwise, stay in the public section and see what's there. Any other clubs on a Monday aren't the best idea for Daddies. X

Aaron exhaled and nodded. He was heading back to the club. He needed to scratch this itch, desperately.

Chapter Three

ZAIRE

He couldn't believe the headteacher was the guy who'd told him off on Friday. What were the chances? Zaire smiled, recalling Mr Brown's well-tailored suit and a tie that matched his dark-brown eyes. He was gorgeous. Zaire could admit the guy ticked all of Zaire's boxes. If only he could be a Daddy. The guy must have some kink or fetish to have been in the club on Friday, but what was anyone's guess. He had been with a woman, so he probably wasn't even gay. Zaire tilted his head. Aaron had rebuffed his flirtatious attempts, so he probably was straight.

Driving home, he thought about what it would be like to head to the same place of work every day. The school today had been a breath of fresh air. The teacher had explained the headteacher—Aaron—was moving with the times and willing to listen to their opinions. It wasn't often you found a place like that. If what Uma said was true, he'd love to work there.

The agency rang as he was plating his dinner, and he answered immediately.

"Zaire. I have a proposition for you."

"Go on."

"The school today would like you to stay for two weeks. Are you happy to?"

"Sure, that's fine."

"He didn't say the words, but it might turn into something permanent."

Zaire could almost hear the clink of money in the guy's voice as he thought about the severance fee the school would have to pay if Zaire went permanent. Every company had to pay a lot to take a staff member off the agency's books.

"Maybe. But thanks. Yes. It would be nice to be in the same place for a short while."

"Fantastic. I will leave a message for the head saying you agreed. I'll speak to you at the end of the week."

Zaire clicked off the phone and sighed with relief. He hadn't been lying. Being in one place would be nice but being close to Aaron might be more than he could handle.

Aaron had been amazing in the assembly that afternoon, and the children responded to him. Zaire smiled as he remembered watching Aaron jumping up and down in the physical session. Only a couple of the other teachers had taken part.

For once, Zaire was looking forward to working.

ZAIRE ENTERED the bar with Rod near the end of the week and wished Rod had chosen somewhere else. Infinity was packed, and though Zaire usually didn't mind crowds, he was ready for an easy night out with a friend rather than the happy ending type of night Rod had in mind. He supposed it wouldn't hurt to get laid, reducing his stress levels would be beneficial, but he couldn't get up the energy for the chase.

He also wasn't sure if he was likely to bump into Aaron there, too.

Climbing onto a handily vacated seat when he arrived at the bar, Zaire tried to converse with Rod, who was already searching the sea of people for his conquest.

"I'm assuming things with Delia aren't good." Zaire didn't understand their open relationship, but it wasn't up to him to understand it. He supported Rod when he needed it and hoped things didn't go wrong for him.

"She's being difficult again. I told her where I was going, so it's not like she doesn't know what might happen." Rod's gaze searched the masses as he spoke.

Zaire couldn't imagine sleeping with someone else when the perfect person was waiting at home for him. It didn't sit right with him, but it wasn't his relationship, so he had no right to a say in it. "God, I need a drink. What do you want?"

"Beer, please."

"Two beers and a whiskey, please!" Zaire yelled to the bartender. As he waited, he spun the cardboard coaster advertising a beer brand and yawned. He shouldn't even be here.

"You look like you need a drink."

Zaire turned to face a slim guy with shoulder-length dark hair, bright green eyes and a wicked grin.

"I don't know if it's a good thing or not." He raised his eyebrows in question.

"It's a good thing because it means I can ask you if I can buy you a drink to help."

"I've got one on its way, but maybe next time." Zaire liked the guy's confidence, and his appearance didn't hurt either.

"Sure. I'm happy to hang around until you finish the one you have." The guy held out his hand. "Name's Griff.

"Zaire."

When his drinks arrived, he passed a beer to Rod, placed the whiskey in front of him and slid the other beer over to Griff.

"I thought I was buying you a drink."

"Both of these were for me, but if you help me drink that one, you'll get to buy me a drink a lot faster." Zaire winked and slammed the whiskey back.

Griff chuckled. Zaire saw it in his shoulders rather than heard it, and he watched unabashedly as Griff lifted the bottle to his lips and drank, his Adam's apple repeatedly bobbing as he swallowed. Zaire had not planned on finding a date tonight. He'd decided to go home and sleep as soon as Rod had found someone, but Griff seemed like too good a choice to pass up.

"I love what you're wearing," Griff whispered in Zaire's ear. "You look so fucking sexy."

Zaire grinned. "Thanks. I feel it."

He had chosen tights under three-quarter length teal-coloured trousers and a black off the shoulder chenille jumper. Comfortable but stylish—his own style; he loved mixing it up. His makeup was barely there but with a shimmer to his skin.

Griff's gaze slid over his body again, appreciation evident in his eyes.

A beer bottle slammed down next to him, making him jump. "I'm out," Rod said, and Zaire turned to watch as he stalked towards a woman who eyed him like her next meal.

"A friend of yours?"

"Yeah, best friend. I was the wingman tonight."

"Looks like you both got lucky."

Zaire snorted. "You're full of yourself, aren't you?"

"Would you prefer me to be meek and timid?"

"No. It's refreshing."

Griff leaned forward. "Would you be happy to continue this somewhere else?"

"What about the drink?"

"You can have a drink if you want it." Griff shrugged. "Or we can skip it this time."

Tilting his head, Zaire made a decision. An orgasm or two would help him sleep, even more than whiskey would—without the headache in the morning. At least, in theory.

"We can skip, but I'm going to be honest with you." Griff nodded for him to continue. "We can go to my place, but you're not staying over. Agreed?"

"That's fair. A mutually beneficial transaction and I'm gone."

"Happy with that?" Zaire wanted Griff's word.

Nobody ever stayed overnight at his house. He made sure of it.

"Yes."

Zaire pulled out his phone and ordered a taxi. "Come on." Zaire hopped off the stool and headed to the exit, not bothering to check if Griff was following. He thought he saw Aaron at one point, but when he turned his head, it wasn't him. He was either imagining it or the guy walked fast.

As they waited outside, Zaire took stock of the guy as he messaged Rod to let him know he was taking someone home. Griff seemed honest, but everyone had to be careful, regardless. He lifted his phone to Griff and asked if he could take a photo. Griff looked confused but agreed. Zaire snapped it and sent it with the message to Rod before explaining to Griff.

"I don't know you. If you're a serial killer, my friend now has your picture to give to the police. I'm more inclined to believe you aren't as you let me take your photo in the first place." Zaire smiled at the bemusement on Griff's face. "Although you could quite as easily kill me and go for Rod, I suppose."

Griff burst out laughing. "You're something else. I like it."

"I know what I want, and I know how to be safe. What more can I say?" He was saved from saying anything else by the taxi arriving.

Once they were settled inside Zaire's house, Griff stepped forward. "What do you want me to be?"

Zaire studied Griff's expression, seeing it open and true. "Daddy," he whispered.

Griff smiled and kissed him.

ZAIRE'S ASS smarted as he sat cross-legged on the floor with a child as they prepared for the sensology session. This was one of Zaire's favourites. Five children and three staff members sat or laid on the floor of the spacious room. Each session was based on a different theme. That day, it was The Greatest Showman, and the idea was with each song on the album, staff would use and help the children to use different props to explore the music. Zaire had a box next to him with the props for the child he was helping, and a piece of paper detailing what the recommended activities were.

When the music started, Zaire began brushing a feather over the child's arm, smiling when the child moved their face towards Zaire and grinned. This was one of the most rewarding jobs in the world as far as Zaire was concerned. Children were precious gifts who, hopefully, knew little of how harsh the world could be.

Zaire hoped he would get on well at this school. It would be great if he didn't have to worry about where he would end up being sent every morning. Having one place of work was more convenient, and this school was almost on his doorstep, which he couldn't have chosen better. He hoped his attraction to the headteacher wouldn't prove his undoing.

Aaron had been professional, even when Zaire pushed things and flirted, which he should not have done. It was hardly professional to flirt with your potential boss-to-be. He shook his head at himself. He was an idiot.

After the session had finished, he helped return the children to the classrooms and sat, wincing, with some craft items to help a child make a crown.

"Are you okay, Zaire?" Uma asked, resting a hand on his shoulder. "I've seen you grimace a few times today."

Zaire told himself not to blush. "I pulled a muscle yesterday; whenever I sit or stand, it smarts."

"Ah, not good." She sat beside him. "I know you've only been here a week, but how are you finding it?"

Zaire smiled. "I love it here. I would like to be able to stay for longer."

"Well, we have you for at least another week, Aaron told me, maybe more if everything goes well."

His stomach fluttered at Aaron's name, and he admonished himself silently. "Yes, hopefully."

"I'm glad you're enjoying it. Let me know if you have any problems or questions, okay?"

"Sure thing."

Uma smiled and headed off when she was called away. Zaire wanted to stay there. Everyone seemed great and willing to go to great lengths to help the children. At least in this class, they seemed to. He didn't have any experience with the other classes. Returning to his job as a crown maker, he helped the child glue enough gems on to light a disco ball until they deemed it fit for a king. Once the child had the crown on their head, a cape around their shoulders and a cardboard sword by their side, they knighted Zaire as a soldier, and Zaire received his own cardboard sword.

The rest of the day was interspersed between being a soldier, a ghost and a monster, depending on which child wanted his attention. Zaire had great fun.

Striding to his car, he checked his phone, seeing Rod had messaged him.

Delia is pissed at me. We had a huge argument this morning about yesterday.

Zaire rolled his eyes. If Rod couldn't see what was right in front of him, he didn't deserve Delia. He couldn't remember the last time Rod had mentioned Delia going out and finding someone from outside their relationship. In fact, it had been months, and Zaire had been able to see Delia was falling more and more for his clueless best friend. He thought it was time to let Rod in on some hard truths.

When was the last time Delia went out and had sex with someone other than you?

Several minutes later, after he'd got semi-comfortable in the driver's seat, he received a reply.

What does that mean?

Answer the question.

I don't know. A few weeks?

Try a few months. Do you think there is something you need to talk about? If Delia isn't happy about the way your relationship is now, you need to talk and figure it out. Or you are going to lose the best thing that ever happened to you.

There was no reply straight away, so Zaire drove home, hearing his phone chime after around ten minutes. He didn't check it until he parked in his driveway.

How would I know?

Know what?

If she wanted to change how things were?

ASK HER!!!!

Zaire entered his house, throwing his keys and phone onto the table before hanging up his coat and resting his bag underneath. He kicked off his shoes, picking up his phone when it buzzed.

Fine, I will.

Good, let me know how it goes.

Zaire climbed the stairs, undoing the buttons of his shirt as he went, eager to relax and return to his home self. Stripping completely, he threw his clothes in the wash basket and strode to his drawers. He riffled through, finding a pair of lace shorts and pulled them on, sighing in contentment when they were in place. He grabbed his satin robe and wrapped it around him. It was his security blanket.

Muscles releasing the tension from the day, he danced his way back down the stairs and made himself a cup of warm milk and headed to the living room. The cup was placed on the small side table and a timer set on his phone before he pulled out a blue box from the cupboard. Opening it up, Zaire sighed and removed his cars and building blocks. Then he lost himself in the world of racing.

When his alarm sounded, he pushed up from his stomach and tidied away his toys with reluctance. He would've loved to stay playing for longer, but he had to eat. If he had a Daddy, he wouldn't always have to stop to make dinner. He wanted to share his life with someone who understood what it was he wanted. It was so hard to find, though. He wished Aaron had been a Daddy. Zaire could see Aaron being an amazingly caring Daddy for a boy.

Sighing, he put the box away and returned to reality.

Chapter Four

AARON

Aaron had seen Zaire several times throughout the two weeks. He had purposefully sought him out to see what kind of job he was doing, and putting it mildly, he was great at it. Zaire was patient with the children, a quick learner when it came to new rules or new children, and everyone seemed to adore him.

On the Friday of Zaire's last trial day, Aaron asked Pamela to request Zaire join him in his office. As he waited, Aaron had mixed feelings. One was a professional opinion; the other was purely selfish reasons.

The professional side of things would be discussed in the office. As for the personal feelings…Aaron had more than liked what he'd seen of Zaire, both from the night out and from working there. There seemed to be two sides to Zaire, and Aaron itched to be the one to help Zaire merge the two into one whole personality. He could tell from seeing both sides of him that Zaire kept his private side private and on the down-low from his work side, which he had every right to. But Aaron could see it was wearing on him. He was sure it was one of the reasons for the outburst he'd witnessed at the club.

Aaron would love nothing more than to take Zaire apart and build him back up again into someone Zaire could live with. At the moment, a part of Zaire was hiding no matter what role he was in.

A knock sounded, and he allowed Zaire entry.

"Thanks for coming. Take a seat." Aaron tried to brush away his personal thoughts and focus on the professional.

"I'm always happy to come," Zaire said, gaze demurely dropped away from Aaron's face.

Aaron cleared his throat, refusing to rise to the bait. "I've heard feedback from the teachers you've worked alongside and seen you working myself, and I'm impressed, Zaire. You do a fantastic job."

A flush worked its way onto Zaire's cheeks, and Aaron could see he was trying to withhold a smile, but he could see the sparkle in Zaire's eyes at the acknowledgement of his ability. "Thank you."

"Do you enjoy working with children?"

Zaire's eyebrows lowered. "Of course, I do. I wouldn't be here, otherwise."

Aaron tilted his head back and forth. "Not everyone who comes into these jobs do it because they enjoy it. Sometimes they do it because it's the only thing available to them at the time. I wanted to make sure you were from the first group."

Crossing his legs and threading his fingers together in his lap, Zaire answered, "I love helping the kids. All children, regardless of who they are, have so much love to give people. Others need to stop and see it for what it is."

"Which is?" Aaron asked when Zaire didn't continue.

"Unconditional. Children don't like you because you give them things, they love you because you are there for them, you spend time with them."

Aaron smiled, nodding slowly. "I knew you loved children. I wanted to check."

Zaire snorted. "Check what?"

"Whether you'd be honest with me." Aaron's gaze bored into Zaire's as something passed between them until Aaron cleared his throat again and looked down at his paperwork. "I would like to offer you a position here."

"Thank you. Can I think about it?"

Aaron raised his eyebrows, surprised by Zaire's answer. He thought it would be an immediate agreement. "Of course. If you could let me know as soon as you can, I'd appreciate it. If your answer is no, I need to find a suitable replacement."

"You wouldn't keep me on under the agency?" Zaire asked.

"Unfortunately, not. Funding only lasts so long, and I have enough for short term agency staff, but in the long run, I need to find a permanent member of staff."

"Understandable. Could I let you know on Monday?"

"That would be great. You would be a great addition to the school, Zaire." Aaron smiled at him as he stood, holding out his hand.

Zaire grinned and gripped Aaron's hand. "I know."

Aaron narrowed his eyes on Zaire, silently reprimanding him for his egotistical remark, and receiving widened eyes and a dropped gaze from Zaire. Aaron let go of Zaire's hand, making sure to slide his fingers along Zaire's palm as they slipped apart.

"Have a good weekend, Zaire."

Zaire's gaze locked with his, momentarily. "Thank you, sir."

Aaron clenched his jaw against the words he wanted to say, mainly, "Those words sound perfect on your lips," but he refrained…barely.

The rest of the day was uneventful. Aaron had plenty of paperwork to get through, and his head was pounding by the time everyone had gone home. Packing up the things he would take home to do over the weekend, Aaron switched off his computer and left the building, knowing the cleaning crew would lock everything up at the end of the evening.

After the short drive home, Aaron yawned and dropped his bag in his office before heading for the shower. As much as he'd prefer to faceplant on the bed, he had agreed to go to Infinity for Daddy night. Nora wouldn't be in attendance, but she had arranged for a friend to meet him there, so he wasn't on his own all night. It was her way of pushing him towards what he wanted without arranging a blind date. The only reason he'd agreed was her friend was a Daddy, too, so Aaron knew they wouldn't be leaving together; therefore, not a date.

He didn't hold out much hope because boys were difficult to find at the best of times. But finding one whose needs fit with Aaron's was almost impossible.

Zaire's face flitted through his mind, and Aaron remembered what he'd been wearing the first night Aaron had seen him. He had wondered what Zaire had been wearing underneath, and if it was what he thought it was—wished it was.

Aaron's boy needed to have a love of lace, satin and silk. He loved nothing more than seeing his boy pottering around the house while wearing nothing but lacy underwear, a silk chemise, or even knowing it was underneath their clothing. He needed as close to a twenty-four-seven Daddy and boy relationship, something that was not always possible.

Feeling his body reacting to the visions, Aaron switched the shower on and stepped inside, his cock twitching as the water hit the swollen length. He wet his hair to cool him and gripped his shaft. Knowing it would make his life more difficult when he saw Zaire every day —if he took the job—didn't stop Aaron from thinking about the guy.

Using the tips of his fingers, he played with his foreskin, rubbing back and forth until his cock was rock hard, then he wrapped his hand around it and stroked to images of Zaire dressed in lace underwear and the tights he had worn the first night. Aaron imagined running his hands underneath the skirt, smoothing his hands over the fabric, turning Zaire and bending him over the stool and flipping the skirt up his back to expose his ass encased in lace and the gap where Aaron's cock would so rightly fit. As he took Zaire, he would be able to run his hands across the satin fabric and the naked skin of Zaire's back, feeling the sweat build up there as he pounded into him.

Aaron slapped a hand against the wet tiles, thrusting his hips as his hand gripped his dick firmer. Keeping his hand still, he clenched his ass muscles and snapped his hips repeatedly as he fucked his hand, imagining Zaire was in front of him.

"Fuck! Yes! Ah!" Aaron growled loudly as he came, spurting his release over the tiles. He panted as he rested his forehead against the cool surface, the water beating down on his back. When his legs became stronger again, he unlocked his knees and stood tall, sticking his head under the water again.

If things had been tenuous before due to his attraction to Zaire, now he'd made his life ten thousand times more complicated. He'd have to hope he could have a conversation with Zaire without remembering what he'd stroked off to.

Sighing, he finished washing up and dried off, heading for his wardrobe. Aaron needed to be comfortable. So, he went with his usual outfit: well-worn blue jeans and an emerald green shirt with the top buttons undone. The first time he'd been at the club with Nora, he'd worn a suit and had regretted it the moment he'd arrived. This time, he was determined to be himself. As he told his boys so often, there was no point pretending to be something you're not.

Sliding his wallet and phone into the pockets of his jeans, he headed to the kitchen and grabbed a coffee to go. He was driving because he'd have transport should he find someone to share the evening with. Picking up his keys, he locked the door behind him and strode to his car. He had no idea what the night would bring, but the worst would be a new friend within the community. No one could ask for more.

TWO HOURS LATER, Aaron wished he'd stayed at home. Cord was nice enough, and Aaron would be happy to spend time with him, but there were no boys available. All of them already had Daddies, and that was the problem Aaron found everywhere. Boys were hard to find.

"Is it always like this?" Aaron asked Cord when he returned with some beers.

"Like what?"

"More Daddies than boys? I know it was where I used to live, but I thought it was just there."

"It's been like this for as long as I can remember. Available boys come in on rare occasions, and when they do, they're inundated with choices." Cord sat back in his chair, lifting the beer to his mouth.

Aaron shook his head. "No wonder we can't find anyone. We probably scare them all away."

"There is that. Some of these guys have been single for years. It's so difficult, but what can we do? We are who we are."

Aaron had nothing to say to those whispered words because it was so true. He wiped a hand over his mouth and decided to go home.

"I'm going—" He stopped what he was saying when his gaze snagged on a couple of guys who had entered the bar. No one had come in for a while, so it got his attention.

Cord followed his gaze. "Fuck. I hope they're boys," he whispered reverently.

Inwardly, Aaron was praying, too, especially as one of them was wearing a gorgeous skin-tight emerald green catsuit. Until he saw who it was. Zaire.

"Holy shit," he breathed, hoping he was wrong. If he was right, his life had become a walking disaster. Despite having had an idea Zaire was a boy, this could be the confirmation he needed that they were on the same page.

Zaire examined the whole room, seemingly taking in every person in the club, bypassing Aaron, then flicking back, eyes wide.

Aaron raised his eyebrows and cocked his head. "Excuse me a moment."

"Don't tell me you're…"

He didn't hear anymore because he'd walked over to Zaire. "Fancy seeing you here." He watched Zaire swallow and lick his lips.

"Same could be said for you. I would've said you were stalking me had you not been in here first." He gave a small smile, fidgeting with the belt hooks on his suit.

"You look amazing." Aaron wasn't going to deny the fact.

Crimson highlighted Zaire's cheekbones. "Thank you."

"Am I right in thinking you're a boy? And you're looking for a Daddy?" Aaron needed to know before he got his hopes up, even though he told himself to keep his hands off.

Zaire nodded, and when Aaron raised his eyebrows at him, cleared his throat and said, "Yes, I am. To both."

The tension rose between them as they stayed silent with locked gazes until Zaire blinked away.

"Well, you have plenty of Daddies to choose from. Don't be overwhelmed. Some of us have been waiting a long time to find someone."

"I didn't…You didn't…You're a Daddy?" Zaire couldn't seem to figure out what he wanted to say.

Aaron nodded. "I am. Have been for many years." He paused. "Can I buy you a drink to settle you before your first Daddy comes to visit?"

"What do you mean?" Zaire's brows snapped together.

"I can guarantee as soon as you sit down and I leave your side, you will have several Daddies come and speak to you and your friend and give you their spiel about what they can offer you. I thought you might like a drink before it happens. I don't want you to feel inundated."

Zaire glanced around and nodded. Although Zaire had appeared to be confident the previous times Aaron had seen him, he appeared nervous enough that Aaron's Daddy instincts were kicking in, and he wanted to care for his boy—a boy. Aaron cupped Zaire's elbow and guided him and his friend to the bar, allowing them both to sit while he stood in the middle of them.

"This is Colin." Zaire introduced his friend. "Colin, this is Aaron."

Colin's eyes widened as they flicked back and forth between Aaron and Zaire. It seemed Zaire had been talking about him, but what had he said?

"Nice to meet you, sir."

"You, too, Colin. Now, what would you both like to drink?"

Three beers were ordered, and once they'd arrived, Aaron said, "I mustn't keep you from finding what you came here to find. I'm over at that table," he indicated where Cord was sat, "if you need anything. Please don't think you have no one to help you should you need it. It goes for both of you. Okay?"

Both boys nodded and verbalised their understanding when Aaron indicated he wanted an answer.

He turned to leave when Zaire's voice called him back.

"Could you…" Zaire swallowed and ducked his head. "Never mind."

Aaron returned to him, lifting his chin with his forefinger. "Finish your question, please."

Zaire's gaze locked with his again, and something charged between them. Aaron wanted to kiss him but refused to do so without giving Zaire the choice of Daddies, as much as it killed him to do so. He would've loved to offer to be Zaire's Daddy, but he was obviously a glutton for punishment because he wanted Zaire to choose him.

"Could you stay until we leave?" he whispered.

"I can and will."

Dropping his fingers from Zaire's skin, he nodded at Colin and returned to Cord.

"I see you know one of them. Why not claim him?" Cord leaned his elbows on the table, coming closer.

"It's a little complicated how I know him. As for

claiming him, you should know better. They claim us, not the other way around."

Cord laughed and nodded. "They do."

"I will hang around until they leave. A friendly face and all."

"Yeah." Cord smirked. "A friendly face, okay." Disbelief rang true through his words, but Aaron ignored the implied meaning.

His gaze was on Zaire and the three men surrounding the two boys. Luckily for the men, they kept a respectful distance, and Aaron was not concerned about them pushing too hard. He'd keep an eye on them, even if it killed him.

As much as what he'd said to Cord was true, he also hated the idea Zaire might choose someone else. He wanted Zaire, and he wanted Zaire to want him back.

Chapter Five

ZAIRE

Zaire lost track of how many Daddies had come up to speak to them, but none had given him butterflies in his stomach as Aaron did. He'd been polite, yet honest with each and every one of them. In between visits, he and Colin had spoken about who they liked and who didn't match up with them. Colin had already decided who he wanted, but he refused to leave Zaire until Zaire had made his decision.

He had to get the courage up to ask the one person he wanted. His gaze flicked in Aaron's direction as it had done many times throughout the evening. Once again, he found Aaron's gaze on him, which should be unsettling, but Zaire found it reassuring.

"Why don't you go and speak to him again," Colin murmured, leaning in. "You mentioned him loads before we even arrived here, and that was when you didn't know he was a Daddy."

Knowing Colin was right, Zaire gathered his confidence, which he usually had in spades, and straightened his spine. "Okay. This is fucking scary. I thought I had enough confidence to do this with my eyes closed but the minute it became possible, I'm like a mouse."

"I know, Zaire. I'll be forever glad of your Daddy there helping us out when we first got here."

Zaire didn't reject the ownership comment, wishing it were true. "Do you want to come over with me so your new Daddy, when you tell him, can get Aaron's approval?"

Colin tilted his head. "Hmm. Yes, actually. I think it would be a good idea." Colin stood, indicating with his head to Zaire. "Come on."

Not at all prepared for the conversation he was about to have with Aaron, Zaire left his seat and followed Colin to the men's table.

"Everything okay, boys?" said a voice Zaire didn't recognise.

"We've decided, but we would like some support when we tell them if you wouldn't mind, Sirs?" Colin's respectful attitude was the perfect one for a boy, and Zaire could see why Daddies fell over themselves for him.

"Of course. Why don't you both have a seat and let us know who you've chosen." Aaron was the one who answered that time.

"Thank you, Sirs." Colin moved to sit next to the other guy, leaving the space next to Aaron for Zaire.

Inhaling deeply, Zaire sat, his thigh touching Aaron's in the small booth.

"So, who have you chosen?" the other guy asked.

Zaire looked to Colin, begging with his eyes for Colin to go first.

"I'd like to speak some more with Dave. The guy over there with the bushy beard and grey waistcoat," Colin said in a small voice.

A whistle pierced the air as the guy next to Colin shouted over to Dave and indicated for him to come over.

Colin's face grew warm the closer Dave got to the table.

"Hey, Cord. What's up?"

"Hey, Dave. Colin here would like to speak to you more about him being your boy if you would?"

Dave's face lit up in a beaming smile. "Of course! Do you want to sit here, or shall we move to another table, Colin?"

"Um…another table is fine. I don't want to interrupt Cord and Aaron's evening any more than I have already done."

"You're not interrupting, Colin. I'll be here until you are comfortable. Okay?" Aaron said, gaze locked on Colin's.

"Yes, sir. Thank you."

When Colin smiled at Zaire as he stood and left, Zaire swallowed hard, knowing his turn was next but scared about what was to come from his revelation.

"So, Zaire," said Cord, leaning forward with a smile. "Who can we bring to the table for you?"

Zaire cleared his throat, his stare focused on his interlocked fingers on the table. "No one."

"No one? There's no one you're interested in?" Cord asked.

Zaire shook his head. "No one you need to bring to the table." He inhaled shakily and glanced to the side, locking gazes with Aaron. "He's already here."

"Fuck me," Cord muttered. "I'm going to the bar, Aaron. Have fun."

Zaire was aware of Cord leaving the table, but his focus was on Aaron, who had not stopped staring at him.

"This complicates matters," Aaron stated.

"In what way?"

"Well, there's no legal reason why a headteacher can't date a member of staff, but by offering you the position, I can be accused of favouritism."

"I won't take the job."

Aaron's eyebrows rose. "You'd give up the job for a relationship?"

"In a heartbeat." Zaire was never more certain of anything in his life.

"It's hardly fair to you."

"A good relationship is harder to find than a job." Zaire chuckled.

Aaron studied him, making him fidget. "Offer still stands for the job. We'll work our way through it if you decide to join the team."

"So…you want me?" Zaire asked in a small voice.

Aaron smiled and cupped Zaire's jaw, stroking his thumb back and forth over his cheek. "I do. But where is my confident boy hiding? The one who gives me flirty innuendos while at work. The one who reprimands strangers in bars." Aaron snickered. "Oh, that would be me."

Zaire laughed and ducked his head before lifting it again. Aaron's gaze flicked over Zaire's shoulder and back again. "Is Colin okay?"

Aaron grinned. "He's fine. Looks like you've both found a Daddy tonight."

"You know how I am. I try to be good, but it's so difficult," Zaire admitted.

"I'm here to help you now. What are your hard limits?"

"I don't like being watched. By other people, I mean. PDAs are fine, but anything more, I'm not comfortable with." He needed to stop rambling.

"Okay. What else?" Aaron's hand left his jaw and rested on top of Zaire's wringing hands.

"I don't like being tied up. Restrained. If someone held my wrists, it's fine but nothing…unbending."

"Did something happen to you?"

If any other person had asked, Zaire would've told them to mind their own business. Despite how little they knew each other, Zaire was already beginning to trust Aaron, so he nodded. "A previous partner tied me up and wouldn't undo them."

"Did he hurt you?"

"No, he just laughed and watched me struggle." Zaire swallowed and looked away. "I don't know how long it was until he finally undid the rope," he finished quietly.

"Okay. Thank you for trusting and telling me. Any more limits?"

Zaire thought for a moment. "Can't think of any."

"Okay, we'll see if any more crop up as we go along." When Zaire nodded, Aaron continued, "What type of boy are you?"

"A frustrated one?" Zaire cackled, stifling his laughter under his palm.

"There he is." Aaron smiled at him, his eyes sparkling. "There's the man I know and the boy I want to know."

Zaire shrugged. "I'm a usual boy, wanting someone to take care of him, someone to understand him." To love him. Zaire refused to say that out loud.

"Why do you keep the boy and the man separate?"

"People are unforgiving when it comes to this version of me." He waved his hand in front of himself. "I found it easier to be the working man and relax when I get home."

Aaron nodded. "Maybe we can work on merging the two and see if we can find a happy medium for you. What do you think?"

Studying the man before him, Zaire said, "I don't think we'll be able to, but I'm willing to give it a try."

"It's all I can ask of you."

"What do you want from me?"

"Obedience. Communication. Trust. Do you think you can do that?"

"Can I say I will try?" Zaire didn't want to set himself up to fail from the beginning. If he gave a definitive answer, he would be scared of disappointing them both.

Aaron smiled. "Yes, you can, although communication is vital. If at any point you don't like what's happening or don't understand why something is happening, you need to let me know. It's non-negotiable."

"Fair enough."

"I think you've probably had enough stress tonight, haven't you?" Aaron said, skimming his fingers along Zaire's jaw.

"I am feeling a bit overwhelmed," Zaire agreed.

"Let's get you home."

"What about Colin?" Zaire looked over his shoulder to where Colin sat with Dave.

"We'll ask him what he wants to do before we leave. If he wants to stay, I can get Cord to keep an eye on him. If he wants to leave, he can come with us." Aaron paused. "Did you drive here?"

Zaire shook his head. He hadn't thought it was a good idea to drive when he might need alcohol to settle his nerves. "No, we got a taxi."

"Good choice. I can drive you home."

Zaire slid out of the booth and stepped away so Aaron could do the same. Once Aaron had, he gazed at Zaire and linked their fingers together as if awaiting a rebuttal. When Zaire didn't pull away, the corner of Aaron's mouth lifted, and he directed Zaire to Colin's table.

"Sorry to interrupt, Dave. Colin's friend wanted to check his plans." Aaron glanced at Zaire, indicating with his head.

"Hey, Colin," Zaire said with a quiet voice and a flick

of his gaze to Dave. "I'm getting a lift home. Do you want to come, or are you happy here?"

He watched as twin red patches bloomed on Colin's cheeks as he smiled at Dave, and Zaire knew his answer. "I'm happy to stay. Dave said he would take me home or see me to a taxi when we've finished talking."

"I'll make sure he's safe," Dave agreed.

Aaron nodded and squeezed Zaire's hand.

"Alright. Call me tomorrow, Colin. Okay?" Zaire lifted his eyebrows, hoping Colin understood his meaning.

"I will."

"See you, Dave," Aaron said, clapping his shoulder. To Zaire, he said, "I need to say goodbye to Cord."

Zaire's heels clicked against the wooden floor of the club as he followed behind Aaron. He couldn't believe how much had changed since he'd walked through Infinity's doors. When he'd arrived, he'd hoped to find a Daddy, but he honestly hadn't believed he would. For it to end up being Aaron, who was potentially going to be his boss, was disconcerting.

Sneaking a glance at Aaron as he spoke to Cord, Zaire felt a warm sensation inside him. It was too early to tell if they were a perfect fit, but from what Zaire had witnessed other times, Aaron would be great. Time would tell if Zaire would fit with what Aaron needed. That was where all Zaire's other relationships had failed. They had told him he was an unmovable mountain who wouldn't learn the rules. Zaire stared at the floor, shoulders dropping at the memories from not one, but two Daddies. Maybe he wouldn't ever find someone who could deal with him. Maybe he should leave Aaron now and stop trying.

An arm slipped around his back, tugging him closer, and Zaire peeked up at Aaron.

"Stop thinking so hard. Wherever your mind just went, I don't like it," Aaron whispered in his ear.

Zaire didn't say anything, though he dropped his gaze once more.

"Cord, we're going to go. Zaire's feeling tired." Aaron clapped hands with Cord and guided Zaire to the exit.

Zaire peered over his shoulder for one final check on Colin, who sat in the same place with a huge smile on his face, his hand clasped in Dave's. Zaire smiled. He was so happy for Colin.

"He'll be fine. Cord will keep an eye on them as well."

Moving his gaze to Aaron's, Zaire gave a lopsided grin. "Thank you. It means a lot."

"You're welcome. I'll do anything to make you feel comfortable." They stopped. "This is me."

Aaron opened the car door, indicating for Zaire to get in, which he did. Aaron closed the door and jogged around the front of the car to the driver's side.

After he had given Aaron his home address and the car had pulled out into the night, Zaire watched the scenery in silence. He didn't know what to say. They probably had a huge amount to discuss, but he didn't want to. Zaire wanted their relationship—if they were to have one—to progress as a normal one would. It was difficult for it to happen because there were so many boundaries usually involved in a Daddy and boy relationship.

What Zaire wanted was for his Daddy to take control and stop him from having to think about everything. He wanted to stop second-guessing his choice of outfit. He wanted to stop holding himself inside while he worked. However, as much as Aaron thought he could help Zaire to merge his two sides, Zaire had been doing it so long, he didn't think it could work. He agreed to try and try he would.

"You're thoughtful over there."

Zaire stared across at Aaron. "I'm letting it sink in you're a Daddy, although why I didn't figure it out before, I don't know."

Aaron snorted. "I'm not wearing a sign."

"I know, but most Daddies can't help their protective and caring side from showing in their daily lives. When I think back on the times I've seen you, it all seems glaringly obvious, but at the time..." Zaire shrugged, turning his gaze to the view once more.

"It's often difficult to separate the two, which I believe is why you struggle so much." Zaire gawked at him as he continued, "I don't separate myself. I am who I am. I'm a Daddy in nature, but I don't hide it away when I'm at work. Naturally, I'm not called Daddy, but a lot of the things involved in my job are helped by my personality." He paused and glanced over at Zaire, who was staring at him. "For you, it's a similar notion. Your caring side allows you to do the job you do, but you quietly suffer by hiding away who you are."

"And who am I?" Zaire whispered.

"A boy who has the chance to be a boy with the students he looks after. You get to play with them, help them, support them, just as you would if they were your best friends. If you allowed yourself, you could be a boy ninety per cent of the time."

Zaire snorted. "That won't happen. It's impossible."

"Nothing is impossible if you want it enough and have support," Aaron argued.

Thinking about Aaron's words kept him busy for the remainder of the journey. When he pulled up outside Zaire's house, Aaron stopped the engine and got out, walking around to Zaire's side and opening his door.

"Home sweet home." Aaron smiled, grabbing Zaire's hand and linking it through his arm.

Staring at the ground, Zaire withheld a smile. When they stood outside his door, the security light shining bright, Zaire inhaled. "Thank you for tonight."

"You're welcome. I hope, after you've thought some more, we can do it again and maybe have dinner?" Aaron rested his hands on Zaire's waist.

"I'd like that."

Chapter Six

AARON

Aaron could feel Zaire's body trembling beneath his hands, whether from the cool wind or nerves, he wasn't sure. "I'll ring you tomorrow to see how you are." Regardless of their relationship's status, Aaron would need to make sure Zaire was alright with everything that had happened tonight, even if Zaire declined to go further.

"Okay. Thank you." Zaire's gaze flicked over his face.

Aaron pinched Zaire's chin between his finger and thumb and pressed a chaste kiss to Zaire's lips before pulling back. "Good night, Zaire."

Zaire didn't say anything, just stared, then leaned forward and fused their lips, wrapping his arms around Aaron's head and holding him tight.

Unprepared for the attack, Aaron fell back several steps until he regained his balance. He allowed the forcefulness of Zaire's kiss but slowly gentled it, cupping Zaire's jaw as Aaron held him close with the other hand.

Lifting his head, he held firm when Zaire attempted to kiss him again. They both breathed heavily as they locked gazes.

"I can see I'm going to have my hands full with you," Aaron said with a smile, loving the idea.

Unfortunately, it appeared to be the wrong thing to say because Zaire immediately tensed up. His jaw firmed, and he pulled away.

Aaron frowned, thinking over what he said and seeing nothing wrong with his words. "Zaire?"

"I'm tired. Thank you for bringing me home." His voice was clipped, devoid of all warmth as he unlocked and opened his door.

Before Zaire stepped in, Aaron bit out, "Stop!" in a firm order. Zaire immediately halted, his back facing Aaron. "Turn around." Zaire did, gaze on the ground. "Eyes up." Zaire hesitated but obeyed. Aaron could see pain and strength in the eyes staring at him. "Communication is non-negotiable," he reminded Zaire. "I said something to upset you. I would like an explanation."

He hated he'd inadvertently hurt Zaire, but he couldn't address it until he knew the reason for it. Aaron certainly didn't have any issues with an unruly boy; in fact, he loved being the one to help the boy learn the rules.

As he waited for Zaire to answer, he studied his boy. Zaire's short black hair was perfectly styled; his usually flawless skin was hidden behind a layer of makeup, which made him ready for the catwalk; and his jewellery accentuated his bone structure. In short, he was fucking gorgeous.

"I…" Zaire huffed. "I've been told on more than one occasion I'm a handful and too disobedient for rules. It was why previous Daddies have left me." The last part was said in a whisper.

Aaron could have beat those other Daddies for doing this to Zaire. They were supposed to take care of their boy, not knock him down until he believed all the crap they fed him. He stepped forward, cupping Zaire's face in his hands again and staring into his eyes.

"They were wrong. Not only were they wrong about you, but they were wrong for you. If they couldn't handle you, you were not the right boy for them. I, on the other hand, can't wait to help you remember the rules. I can't wait to help you believe in yourself, to love yourself—to love both sides of yourself. When I said I was going to have my hands full, I said it with joy. I cannot wait."

He punctuated his words with a gentle kiss and wrapped his arms around Zaire, holding him tight and allowing his words to sink in as he rubbed a hand up and down his back. Aaron knew when the words seemed to hit home because Zaire's muscles loosened, and he gripped the back of Aaron's shirt, tucking his face into Aaron's neck.

When Zaire appeared boneless and almost unable to stand by himself, Aaron pulled back, ensuring Zaire was steady. "Get some sleep. I'll call you in the morning."

"Okay, Daddy."

It had seemed an automatic reaction.

Aaron watched as Zaire entered the house and locked the door before leaving. There was a lot to learn about the boy hiding behind those pain-filled eyes.

AARON LEFT the phone call until around eleven the next morning, not wanting to wake Zaire too early. It wasn't easy. He'd been up since seven and had already completed his home workout routine, cleaned the house, done the laundry and made a salad ready for lunch. He was restraining himself as much as possible, but he wanted nothing more than to call Zaire and make sure he was okay. Aaron didn't want Zaire to think too much because he was sure Zaire would talk himself out of their relationship. Aaron would back off if he did, but Aaron believed Zaire needed this as much as Aaron did.

When the clock finally ticked onto the eleven, Aaron already had his phone in hand and ringing.

"Hello?" Zaire's voice was quiet, reserved, so unlike his usual perky, charming self.

"Hey. How are you this morning?"

Zaire's sigh drifted through the phone, and Aaron's heart fell. "I'm a bit tired. I didn't sleep brilliantly."

"Why not, sweetheart?"

"Just…everything. So much to think through, so many decisions to make."

"I understand. Tell you what…get yourself dressed in something comfortable that you can move in easily. I'm going to take you bowling."

"Bowling?" Zaire's tone explained exactly what Zaire thought.

"You don't like bowling?"

"Hmm. It's not usually my thing, but alright."

"Good. I'll be there in an hour. We can have lunch before we go."

"I haven't—"

"I'm bringing it with me. It's already prepared, although do you have any allergies I need to know about?"

"No, I'm fine with anything."

"Okay. Just get yourself ready. Leave everything else to me."

"Yes, Daddy."

"Good boy. See you shortly."

When Aaron ended the call, he blew out a breath. He needed to help Zaire, but he was struggling to figure out the best way to do it. The first thing he needed to do was to teach Zaire to have fun, to relax, to forget about problems for a short time because it would make it easier to deal with them.

Glad he'd already prepared a salad, Aaron quickly sliced the eggs, chopped the ham and added them and the couscous to the bowl. He packed it up with a jar of coffee in case Zaire didn't have any and headed out.

When Zaire opened his door, Aaron raised his eyebrows at his choice of clothing. Zaire's interpretation of something comfortable was black jeans and a red v-neck jumper, which, although looked fantastic on him, lacked his usual extravagance.

"You look good. Wouldn't you prefer to wear something more your style?" Aaron asked as he followed Zaire down the hall to the kitchen.

"Nah, I'm good."

Aaron pursed his lips but let the subject drop, knowing, by the sound of Zaire's voice, he shouldn't push.

The containers were placed on the counter, and Aaron divided the food between two plates, placing both on the kitchen island table along with cutlery. "Do you eat in here or somewhere else?"

Zaire shrugged. "Usually in here or on the sofa. The dining table hardly ever gets used unless people are visiting."

"Alright, here it is."

Aaron perched himself on the seat adjacent to where Zaire was, so their legs could touch if either wanted a source of comfort. To be honest, Aaron wanted to know whether Zaire would take the opportunity if it arose. Time would tell.

Throughout lunch, Aaron peppered Zaire with questions about music and films, which Zaire answered happily as he ate the lunch Aaron had prepared. Seeing it disappear made Aaron extremely satisfied.

Once they'd finished, Aaron washed up what had been used and led Zaire to his car. He opened the passenger door for him and, once he was seated, reached across to click the belt into place before closing his door. Whenever anybody asked about his need to take care of someone, he found it difficult to explain why he needed it so much. It was as if it was in his DNA.

Once they'd arrived, traded their shoes and started their game, Zaire appeared to relax, smiling more, laughing and generally having a good time, so it seemed. Aaron breathed easier knowing he had brought that joy to Zaire, despite Zaire's reluctance to begin with.

They quickly worked their way through two games, which they each won one of, before Aaron took their shoes to trade back before linking their fingers and heading for the food area.

"Would you like a cheeseburger and chips?" Aaron asked

"That would be great."

Aaron ordered two lots of the meal with drinks, paid and carried the tray to one of the high seated tables, where they could see a view of the rest of the bowling alley and people watch.

"I love watching how people act around each other. You can usually tell who has a crush on who, which couples are fighting, and who have recently started seeing each other. Have you ever people watched?"

Zaire shook his head, looking around at the customers. "No. I'm usually too preoccupied."

"Is that what happens when you're not enjoying your-self somewhere, or does it happen all the time?" Aaron asked as he dipped his chips into ketchup.

The chips were poured into the open burger container and the burger in his hands before Zaire answered, "A bit of both, I guess. I struggle to relax when I'm out unless it's somewhere I feel safe, like Infinity. Anywhere else..." He shrugged and took a bite of his burger.

"Hence this afternoon's clothing choice?" Aaron prodded.

Zaire sat back, his brow puckered as he finished what was in his mouth. "Why do you have a problem with how I'm dressed?"

"I don't have a problem with it," Aaron calmly stated. "I know it's not who you are."

"But it is! This is part of me! This is the part of me who can go out on 'normal,'" Zaire used his fingers as quotes, "dates. This is the part who won't get harassed."

"I understand. I'd love for you to be able to feel comfortable in whatever you want to wear, regardless of what other people think or say. I'd love to be your buffer, your sounding board, your reassurance, your caring, everything you need to be yourself."

"How can you? You're not with me all the time." Zaire crossed his arms on the table, gazing at his food.

"I want to give you the tools to be who you are. My support, visible when I'm with you and within your mind when I'm not, will always be there. If you can see a way of being the person you want to be all the time, I will do my best to get you to that point, and I am determined to get you there. I want you happy and whole."

Aaron's heart ached at the expression on Zaire's face. It would take a while for him to believe Aaron could do that for him. Although Aaron needed Zaire's complete trust for it to happen, which he reminded him.

"I'm working on it," Zaire said, his mouth twitching.

Aaron let the subject go, determined to bring it up another time. "What do you like to do when you're not working or at Infinity?" Seeing Zaire had finished his chips, Aaron passed a few from his plate to Zaire's, earning a smile.

"I love rock climbing."

"Rock climbing? Where do you do it? Don't you need

cliffs and mountains for that?" Aaron drank some of his coffee.

Zaire chuckled, and Aaron beamed at the lightness now overtaking his features. "No. I do indoor rock climbing. There's a place on the outskirts of Cambridge which has a huge space full of different sized walls and obstacles for people to try. I've been doing it for several years now."

"You must have good upper body strength."

"Yeah. It is quite intense on the upper body, but your feet support you as well."

"Do you enter any competitions or anything?"

"No, not at the moment. I like doing it to relax. When I have to think about where my hands and feet are going, everything else recedes to the back of my mind. It's how I envisage a Daddy and boy relationship."

"Care to explain?"

Zaire picked up a chip and swirled it around in the sauce but didn't eat it. "The Daddy looks after the boy, doing things for him and giving him time to blank his mind, not worry about everything all the time. I'd love to have that."

"And I'd love to give it to you. You need to learn to trust me. I know what I'm doing, even when it seems like I don't. I want you content, happy and safe." Aaron offered the best reassurance he could, but ultimately, it would be up to Zaire if they continued. "Come on. Let's head back."

They stood in the same places as they had done the evening prior, and Aaron was ready to leave Zaire to think when Zaire opened the house to him. "Come on in."

Aaron didn't hesitate, understanding this was something Zaire needed. He had no plans of taking things to a sexual level, but Aaron was eager to shower Zaire with whatever he would allow.

Zaire was such an enigma, and Aaron wanted to find out every little thing about him. He had his work persona, which seemed to bleed into dates when there were at places deemed unsafe. He had his boy persona, which was louder, and yet, quieter at the same time. It was almost as if Zaire himself didn't know who he wanted to be—or who he was. Aaron would love nothing more than to be the one to help him figure it out.

Even for him, a seasoned Daddy, he was struggling to discern the best way to do it. He needed to speak to Nora. Although she didn't have a boy, she had a pup; there were similarities, and maybe she could see something Aaron had missed.

As he studied the living room, he tried to piece together a bit more information. The room was a neutral colour but had splashes of colour on the walls and fabrics throughout the space—a bit of Zaire thrown out for all to see. The sofas were large and, if Aaron wasn't mistaken, the type which would envelop a person when they sat down and have them wanting to never get back out. Aaron walked to the pictures he could see on the walls, noting Zaire as a young boy with who, he assumed, was family and pictures of various people at different ages. They told a story of a happy childhood, and Aaron sincerely hoped it had been.

"Are these your family?"

"Yes."

"You seem close."

"We were."

Aaron gritted his teeth against the need to reprimand Zaire for the lack of communication. It wasn't the right time for it, although he couldn't refrain from glancing over his shoulder at Zaire with a raised eyebrow and receiving a blush and the ducking of his head.

"Why? Are you not as close now?"

Silence greeted his answer, and when he turned, he saw Zaire clench his jaw and flare his nostrils. This would not be good.

Chapter Seven

ZAIRE

Zaire leaned back in the comfortable sofa, crossing his legs and arms as he plucked up the courage to answer Aaron's question. It wasn't that he was nervous about admitting his past; it would prove what Zaire had been saying all along: he needed to hide away certain parts of himself depending on the situation.

"I have a brother and a sister. We were close when we were younger, always in each other's pockets, especially as we are so close in age, too. Only four years separate us all." He inhaled. "When I came out to our parents, they were amazing about it. Everything a gay man could wish for." Zaire smiled in remembrance. "Zena used to caw about having a gay brother, and Zacary said it didn't change anything."

"Zaire, Zacary and Zena?" Aaron smiled.

Zaire chuckled. "Yes. I'm glad my parents stopped at three kids. Who knows what names they would've come up with?" They chuckled, then Zaire sobered, continuing with his story, "When my love of clothing and makeup began to show, my father took it badly. He stopped talking to me completely. Anything that needed to be said was passed through the other people in the family. He refused to eat at the same table as me."

Aaron came to sit next to him, resting one knee on the sofa, the other braced on the floor as his hand squeezed Zaire's knee.

"There were so many arguments between Mum and Dad," he continued quietly, his mind rolling the films of the past. "So many nights I went to bed crying because I could hear the slurs Dad had shouted about me. So, I began to change. I would only wear the clothes when I was out of sight. I'd wear boring clothes but stop at a friend's house to change. At least, until Mum yelled at me one day for forgetting who I was, for not being true to myself. It was at that point she must have reached her limit." Zaire pulled his legs up to his chest, wrapping his arms around his knees.

"What happened?"

"She kicked Dad out, telling him if he couldn't accept who his son was, he shouldn't be a father," he whispered. "I tried to be the person who they both wanted me to be."

Aaron slid his hand around Zaire's shoulders, pulling him into his body.

Voice hoarse, he forced himself to finish, "Ze blamed me for breaking up our parents' marriage, and thus the second bout of silent treatment began. Car and Mum sided with me, but Dad and Zena..." Zaire shrugged. "I see Mum all the time. Car, I don't see as much because he works abroad, but we're always on the phone."

"Car?"

Zaire chuckled, his spirits lifting a bit. "He hated our names were similar, so he started going by Car instead of Zacary."

They were silent as Aaron held Zaire tight, his cheek rubbing against the top of Zaire's head.

"I need a drink," Zaire said suddenly, sitting up out of Aaron's embrace, feeling the loss immediately. He strode to the kitchen, ready to find a beer.

"Sit down. Let me make us something," Aaron said, guiding Zaire to the chair he'd occupied earlier that day. "You've been on your feet for a while. Tell me where everything is to make hot chocolate."

"I had been thinking of something stronger," Zaire said.

"I know, but you don't need it. You need something warm."

Nodding slowly, Zaire watched as Aaron pottered around the kitchen as if he lived there. It was a fantastic feeling, and he felt his muscles begin to unwind. He rested his head on his fist and studied the sinewy muscles and strips of skin that were exposed as Aaron moved. There were never any hesitant movements, all certain and steady, going a long way to helping Zaire believe Aaron knew what he needed.

Of course, he did. He was a Daddy. He was Zaire's Daddy, and Zaire needed to start believing in him.

Aaron brought the steaming, calorie-filled drinks over to the table and, with a flourish, placed a marshmallow mountain in front of Zaire. Zaire grinned at the display and, after Aaron produced a spoon, dipped right in to taste the gooey mess.

When he'd finished with the spoon, he cupped one hand around the mug, closing his eyes at the warmth soaking into his palm and held his other hand out to Aaron, who quickly threaded their fingers together, rubbing his thumb up and down his skin.

"Your mother was right," Aaron began softly. "You don't need to be anyone but yourself. Even more so when it's just me around. I'd love to see what you're capable of when you allow yourself to be true to your inner self."

Zaire said nothing but thought hard about Aaron's words. He'd been dividing himself for so long now, he wasn't sure if he could stop. He didn't know how.

"Do you have a TV in your bedroom?" Aaron asked, disrupting his thoughts.

Zaire nodded. "Yes."

"Okay. Now we've finished our drinks, let's get you ready for bed. I can see you're tired. We can watch a film before you sleep." Aaron picked up their mugs and set about washing and drying them and the other items he'd used, then held out a hand to Zaire. "Show me the way?"

Zaire said nothing, wanting nothing more than to wrap himself around Aaron and gain a release his cock suddenly needed badly.

When they entered his bedroom, Aaron overtook him and tugged him towards the en-suite, which could be seen from the bedroom door. He motioned for Zaire to sit on the closed toilet seat and opened the cupboards until he found Zaire's makeup remover and cotton wool.

As Aaron wet the fabric and began wiping Zaire's forehead, Zaire swallowed hard and closed his eyes against tears. No one had ever done this for him.

Unsure of how much time had passed as Aaron removed his neutral makeup covering, Zaire remained relaxed and sleepy.

"There. All done. Let's get your jewellery off, now." Aaron, again, helped by removing the one necklace Zaire had allowed under his jumper and his wristwatch. "Do you want a shower before you go to bed? I would normally say you should, but today it's your choice."

"I'd like to leave it for tonight if that's okay?" Zaire's voice was hesitant, not wanting to upset Aaron.

"It's okay for tonight. You've been through a lot today." Aaron led him back into his bedroom, stopping at the drawers. "Do you wear pyjamas?"

Zaire shook his head. "My boxers."

"Alright."

Aaron turned to him and slid his hands to the hem of Zaire's jumper, pulling it up over his head and dropping it to the floor beside them. He went to his knees. Zaire gasped at the sight of Aaron kneeling before him, and despite knowing nothing would happen tonight, Zaire's cock had other ideas. Aaron reached for the button on his jeans and undid them, tugging them down his legs. He removed Zaire's shoes, jeans and socks before standing once more.

"You're gorgeous, sweetheart. Let's get you into bed so you can relax."

Aaron wandered to the bed, lifting the cover for Zaire to climb in and tucked it back around him. He reached for the remote, which was on the bedside table, walked around to the other side of the bed and, after kicking off his shoes, sat on top of the covers with his back against the headboard.

Zaire had no interest in watching anything, but his gaze remained on the film, though he had no idea what it was. He was focused on being so close to Aaron in his bedroom—in his bed—and not having the energy or inclination to do anything about it.

Laid as he was, with his head on his pillow facing Aaron, he could see whenever Aaron shifted position, and he found it reassuring. Aaron's hand came to Zaire's hair and stroked the tips of his fingers through the strands, encouraging Zaire to close his eyes.

"I'm going to let you get some sleep, sweetheart," Aaron whispered from above him.

"Please?"

"What do you want, Zaire?"

"Stay until I fall asleep?" he mumbled, already halfway there.

The hand resumed its movements, and Zaire drifted off.

ZAIRE BLINKED OPEN HIS EYES, his eyelids repeatedly closing as he slowly roused from his sleep the following morning. As he lay there, he felt a deep boneless relaxation from which he could probably fall back to sleep again, but he wanted to bask in the feeling. Never before had anyone soothed him as he fell asleep or taken care of him as well as Aaron had the previous night. Even Zaire himself didn't take good care, though he wouldn't tell Aaron.

The covers rolled with him as he turned to his back and rubbed his eyes free of sleep. He dropped his arms heavily to the bed and stared at the ceiling, a smile curving his mouth as he remembered everything that had happened. It had been an amazing day. Even though he wasn't a fan of bowling, he'd had fun, and maybe he could persuade Aaron to try rock climbing next time.

A knock at the door had him frowning. Preparing to ignore it, he grumbled when it sounded again, so he got out of bed, pulled on some joggers and stumbled down the stairs. Seeing his reflection in the mirror by the front door had him rolling his eyes: his hair was stuck up all over the place, and he had creases on the side of his face from the pillows. Whoever was at the door would have to put up with how he looked because he didn't care.

Another knock had Zaire flinging the door open ready to curse the visitor for being impatient, but the words died on his tongue when a gorgeous headteacher smiled at him and held out a bakery carrier bag.

"Peace offering."

Zaire frowned. "Why do you need a peace offering?"

"In case I woke you up." Aaron grinned at him, and Zaire practically melted at the sight.

Aaron entered, kissing Zaire on the creased cheek and continued through to the kitchen. When Zaire followed, yawning, Aaron passed him a takeaway cup and said, "Why don't you head up for a shower and put something comfortable on. I'll make you some breakfast for when you're finished."

Zaire stared at him for a moment, saying nothing, then he put his cup on the table and walked over to Aaron. "Please, Daddy. Could I have a hug?"

Aaron's face softened, and he graced Zaire with a smile. "Of course, you can." Aaron wrapped his arms around Zaire's back and held him close, rubbing his hand up and down his back and resting his cheek against Zaire's head. Zaire turned his face into Aaron's neck and inhaled, closing his arms around Aaron's waist. Every muscle that had tensed when he'd risen from bed loosened once more, and he returned to his blissful state. What was it about Aaron that was so peaceful?

"Are you okay, Zaire?"

Zaire nodded into his shoulder, holding tighter for a moment before letting go. "Thank you for yesterday. And today."

"You don't need to thank me. I will be taking care of you a lot more now. It will give you a chance to breathe." Aaron pecked a kiss on his lips.

"Will you…" Zaire stopped, not sure if he should be asking for this so soon into their relationship. "Never mind."

"No. It sounds important. Will I what?" Aaron gripped his hands loosely, rubbing his thumb across the back in a soothing gesture.

Zaire ducked his head, second-guessing his words but knowing Aaron wouldn't let it go. Why Zaire was so subdued and quiet when Aaron was around, Zaire had no idea. The thought had him straightening his posture and looking Aaron in the eye. "Will you help me? Shower, I mean."

For a moment, there was no change of expression on Aaron's face as his eyes roamed Zaire's features until the corner of his mouth lifted. "I'd love to."

Zaire rolled his lips inwards, trying to hide the joy he felt at being granted this wish, but he didn't think he was successful.

"Let's take our drinks with us so they don't get cold. We can drink them before we get in."

"Yes, Daddy," Zaire whispered.

Aaron threaded their fingers together and led the way up the stairs, their other hands gripping their coffees.

Zaire had showered with other Daddies, but he wasn't sure what to expect with Aaron, so he was hesitant in his movements. Aaron switched on the shower and pulled the curtain around to stop the spray from hitting the floor, laying the bathmat on the floor after.

"Rest your coffee on the windowsill for a moment." Zaire did and rested back against the sink as Aaron cupped his cheek. "I've got you, Zaire. I've got you."

Tears pricked at the corners of his eyes, and he closed them as Aaron's hands touched the waistband of his trousers, pulling it away from his body and down his legs. His cock, up to now having been soft, went half-hard in seconds as he stepped out of the joggers. Crouched in front of Zaire as he was, Aaron would not be oblivious to his state of arousal. The smirk on his face as he glanced up confirmed it. His hands returned to Zaire's waist, this time sliding his fingers between the boxers and Zaire's skin. Goosebumps rose along his body as Aaron slid the boxers over his now-hard cock and down his legs.

Zaire's hands gripped the edge of the sink behind him, and he gritted his teeth against the need to thrust into the air. How he could be so aroused so quickly, he didn't know.

Aaron stood once more, avoiding touching any part of Zaire as he did. "Drink your coffee." He pressed the cup into Zaire's hand after removing its grip from the sink.

Zaire had no idea what the coffee tasted like because his focus was on the handsome specimen undressing in front of him. Aaron's movements were not a striptease, but his gaze locked with Zaire's until he was as naked as Zaire was. He was fucking gorgeous.

Aaron picked up his cup, breaking eye contact as he drank. When he finished, he placed both their cups on the windowsill and tugged Zaire into the shower, placing him with his back against the spray and facing Aaron. Aaron took Zaire's lips in a heated kiss, his hands in Zaire's hair. It was only when they broke away for air that Zaire realised Aaron had been wetting his hair, ready for the shampoo he had squirted into his hand.

"Step forward a little," Aaron muttered. As Zaire did, Aaron massaged the gel into Zaire's hair, and Zaire's eyes closed in contentment. He repeated the action twice and walked Zaire back under the spray to rinse for the last time. He reached for the body wash.

Zaire was already rock hard. He wasn't sure he could cope with Aarons' hands on his body, but Aaron continued when no protest came from Zaire. Aaron avoided his groin area, washing everywhere else before he lathered up his hands and wrapped his hand around Zaire's cock. Zaire bit back a curse at how sensitive he was and tried to concentrate on not coming.

"Good boy. Let's get you clean, and we can have a nice relaxing day," Aaron murmured as he washed every inch of Zaire's private areas. Once he was content, Aaron guided him back under the spray and washed it all off.

Zaire didn't want to have a relaxing day. He wanted Aaron.

Chapter Eight

AARON

He probably had been a bit of a tease in the shower because he'd spent more time than was necessary on cleaning Zaire's cock and ass, but Zaire looked so blissed out as he'd done it, he couldn't resist. It was coming back to bite him now. As he dried Zaire off, flames were shooting out of his eyes, his cock an angry purple colour. But it was as good a time as any for Zaire to learn Aaron knew what was best for him, and at the moment, their relationship was new. He didn't want to fall into bed with Zaire and potentially ruin everything, even if it did sound old-fashioned.

"Daddy! Please?" Zaire asked again, his hand hovering close to his cock as if he was going to stroke it.

Aaron gripped his wrist. "Later. Maybe. You need to relax today."

"I will relax once I've had an orgasm!" Zaire yelled.

Aaron stood still, eyebrows rising at the volume of Zaire's words. There was no time like the present to begin punishment, but what to choose? He would not let Zaire come, for certain, but maybe some kneeling practice.

He pointed a finger towards the bedroom. "Wait by the bed. Now!" His voice was stern, a tone he used on pupils who needed a stricter talking to.

Zaire's eyes widened, and he swallowed as he shuffled past Aaron and out of the bathroom. Aaron took his time drying himself off and redressing. He'd already had a shower that morning, so he wasn't uncomfortable with wearing the same clothes.

When he entered the bedroom, Zaire stood with his back to Aaron, facing the bed, head lowered. Aaron sat on the edge of the bed, where Zaire could see him.

"I will not have you raise your voice to me. You may not believe I know what's best for you, but I do. I'm your Daddy." He let those words sink in and added, "Kneel."

Zaire's gaze flicked to his and down again before he dropped to the floor.

"We haven't talked about safe words. Do you have any you use other than colours?"

"No, Daddy."

"Okay. We'll use colours. Red for stop, yellow for slow down. Understood?"

"Yes, Daddy," Zaire whispered.

"You will stay kneeling, eyes lowered until your time is up. Let's see how you do with fifteen minutes."

Aaron stayed with Zaire the entire time, not wanting him to be completely alone with this first infraction. He kept silent until the time had passed, and he could kneel with Zaire and pull him off his knees and into his arms.

Tears seeped into his shirt as Aaron rubbed Zaire's back and cooed in his ear.

"You're such a good boy, Zaire. My good boy. You took your punishment so well, sweetheart. Well done. Such a good boy. So good for your Daddy."

Aaron had no idea how long they stayed that way, but when he felt Zaire move, he allowed him to retreat.

"I'm sorry, Daddy. I do know you know best. I'm not used to needing to withhold orgasms. My previous Daddies didn't do that. I didn't know…" Zaire trailed off and tucked his head in Aaron's neck once more.

"I understand, Zaire. I'm here to take some of the burdens now. Try to remember to let me help."

"Yes, Daddy."

"Right. Let's go get some breakfast. Alright?"

"Okay."

He'd felt something settle further inside him when he'd had Zaire in his arms. Something felt so right about this whole situation. He wouldn't let Zaire push him away without a fight.

"Let's get you dressed."

Aaron strode to the drawers, opening the top one to find an assortment of lingerie. He looked through them until he found a lilac high waisted male thong. He closed the drawer, checking in the next, finding pyjama bottoms and chose a black silk version with a tie-pull. Not finding any tops in the drawers, he drifted over to the wardrobe, noting how quiet Zaire was.

"Bingo," he whispered as he found some thin-strapped vests. He chose a dark purple and closed the doors. He'd return for a jumper if Zaire wanted one.

"Right, let's get you up." He laid the clothes on the bed next to Zaire and grabbed his hands to help him stand, which he did with a wince.

Aaron picked up the underwear and crouched down, holding them for Zaire to step into. He didn't say anything about his choice of clothing, wanting to see if Zaire refused them. Carefully, he pulled them over Zaire's ass cheeks and settled the thong in his crack, smoothing his hand over the lace as he adjusted Zaire's semi-hard cock in the front of them. He picked up the vest, helping Zaire into the fabric and settling it over his slim frame. Seeing him in those two items increased Aaron's pulse, and he looked away to regain control.

The trousers were simple to put on, and soon Zaire was covered up, though his cock was semi-hard. Aaron finally glanced at Zaire's face, expecting to find him looking uncomfortable, but to his surprise, Zaire's eyes burned with banked arousal, but the rest of him was a model of relaxed.

Which was what Aaron had been aiming for.

"Let's get breakfast." Aaron strode into the bathroom, returning with their half-full coffee cups, and balancing them in the crook of his arm, he grabbed Zaire's hand with his free hand and led the way downstairs.

Zaire hadn't said anything, but when he'd made breakfast, Aaron would make sure Zaire was alright with what had happened.

As they sat at the table with their sausage sandwiches, Aaron checked in with Zaire, "Are you okay?"

Zaire nodded and, when he'd finished his mouthful, answered, "Yes. I feel calmer than I did before."

"Good. Are any punishments a hard limit for you?"

"None that I'm aware of, apart from what we've discussed already," Zaire replied.

"If at any time you're not happy with something, you need to let me know immediately. I will be upset if I find out you're hiding something."

"Okay."

They moved into the living room, Aaron sat at one end, reading on a book, and Zaire laid on his side with his head on Aaron's lap, tucked under a blanket while he watched You've Been Framed. Aaron hadn't asked what Zaire wanted to watch but thought something easy on the brain would be the best option, and the comedic value of watching people's mishaps was that. If Zaire did have questions, he'd be able to mull them over as he watched or enjoy the show. Which he was if his giggling was anything to go by.

Several times, Aaron found himself watching Zaire's partial expression as he chuckled at the crazy antics. He wondered how often Zaire allowed himself this time to relax fully, and if he was a betting man, it wouldn't be often, if at all.

When Zaire yawned, Aaron decided to get them moving so Zaire didn't ruin his sleep pattern as he had to work the next day. "Hey, sweetheart." He waited until Zaire rolled his head to meet his gaze. "Shall we go for a run?" He smiled when Zaire's eyes lit up.

"Yes, please, Daddy!" Zaire flicked the blanket off and scrambled up, getting tangled in the process.

"Slow down, Zaire!" Aaron laughed as he helped pull the blanket from around his feet. "You'll have an accident, and we won't be able to go anywhere but the hospital." Obviously, Zaire either didn't feel any ache in his knees or didn't care.

"Sorry."

"It's okay. Just be careful, sweetheart." Aaron stood and held out his hand. "Let's find you something to wear."

After entering Zaire's bedroom, Aaron dropped Zaire's hand and strode to the drawers. When he'd chosen boxers, joggers and socks, he grabbed a t-shirt from the wardrobe and went to stand in front of Zaire. He dropped the clothes on the bed and instructed Zaire to lift his arms. As he slid the material over his head, Aaron gritted his teeth against the need to kiss the expanse of skin revealed. Laying the vest on the bed, he picked up the t-shirt and helped Zaire to put it on.

He kneeled. His hands went to the pull cord of the pyjama bottoms and pulled it free, allowing the material to puddle around Zaire's ankles. Aaron glanced up at him, watching as twin red spots bloomed on Zaire's cheeks. Only the knowledge of where they were going enabled Aaron to strip off Zaire's lacy underwear and replace them with boxers, which would be more comfortable when running. It had been warm when he'd arrived at Zaire's that morning, and although it had been several hours, it should be nice enough to run without an outer layer.

"Come on." Aaron stopped by the kitchen to grab

two bottles of water and, passing one to Zaire, indicated the door. "Shall we take a jog along the river?"

Zaire's eyes lit up again, and Aaron decided there and then he would do everything in his power to make sure Zaire had that expression as often as possible.

JOGGING along the River Cam had been enlightening. Aaron had been there many times before but seeing it through Zaire's eyes as he exclaimed at the canoes, rowing boats, ducks, swans and everything else he saw was…educational. It showed Zaire's love of water, which Aaron neatly tucked away for future reference.

After they'd returned, they showered together again, this time quicker and less handsy, but no less clean. Aaron had dressed himself in the clothes he'd had in his car and helped Zaire back into what Aaron had dressed him in after their first shower.

They ordered an Indian takeaway for dinner and argued the merits of several aspects of the school system. It reminded Aaron he'd done none of the work he'd brought home from school over the weekend. Luckily, it wasn't essential. Aaron had only taken it because he'd expected to be alone. He was more than happy with his surprise alternate plans.

A full stomach seemed to sap all of Zaire's energy, or maybe it was the busy day he'd had, but Aaron tugged him up the stairs once more. Zaire groaned as they climbed, grabbing hold of Aaron's hand with both of his and leaning most of his weight on him, so Aaron was literally dragging him up. When they reached the top, Aaron wrapped his arm around Zaire, laughing.

"Did you enjoy that?" he asked, kissing the side of Zaire's head.

"You made me walk up the stairs after eating, so it's your fault," he pouted, lips pursed.

Aaron caught them in a kiss as they stumbled through the bedroom door. Keeping his eyes open, Aaron directed Zaire to the bed, his hands busy roaming across Zaire's satin clad body until they cupped his ass gently.

Breaking away to breathe, Aaron slid his hands upwards, underneath the satin vest top and along Zaire's spine. "You've been such a good boy for me today, Zaire. I think you deserve a treat."

"But I wasn't a good boy this morning. I yelled at you." Zaire's voice was low and tinged with sadness.

"But you took your punishment, and all was forgiven, wasn't it?" Aaron reminded him.

"Yes, but—"

"You don't need to worry about what you think you deserve, my sweet boy. It's my job now. And I say you deserve a treat."

Aaron cupped Zaire's face in his hands and reverently kissed his lips. He licked along the seam of Zaire's mouth, and Zaire dropped his head back on a moan, opening to Aaron's exploration. He felt Zaire sway until Zaire gripped the sides of Aaron's t-shirt, holding himself steady. Leaving his face, Aaron's hands slid down, undoing the cords for Zaire's trousers and allowing them to fall, leaving Zaire clad in a satin vest and lacy thong.

Lack of air had them pulling apart. "On the bed,

sweetheart." He watched as Zaire glanced behind him, sat on the edge of the bed and slid himself over the covers until his head rested on a pillow.

Naughty boy that he was, Zaire proceeded to widen his legs and run his hands over his body in a teasing display. Stripping off his t-shirt and jeans, Aaron allowed the touches until he crawled onto the bed.

"Now, who said you could touch what is mine?" he growled as he caged Zaire between his arms.

Zaire froze, mouth gaping before snapping shut. "Sorry, Daddy. I...I need...I..." He panted, seemingly unable to get his thoughts in order.

Aaron inhaled deeply. If this was how Zaire acted when he'd hardly been touched, how much would he come apart when Aaron was balls deep inside him? Swallowing hard, Aaron leaned down and took Zaire's mouth in a hard kiss, demanding entry and insisting on a reaction. When his arms began to shake with the intensity of the kiss, Aaron lowered to his forearms, sinking his lower body onto Zaire's and groaning into each other's mouths as their dicks came into contact.

But this wasn't for Aaron. This was Zaire's treat. So, Aaron detoured from Zaire's mouth, kissing, nibbling and licking his way down the column of his neck, along his collarbones, down his sternum, shifting the vest up under Zaire's armpits as he diverted briefly to Zaire's sweet little nubs and continued down his abs, finding the barest hint of a trail heading into the lacy thong.

As he licked across the waistband of the lilac fabric, Aaron glanced up at Zaire's face, knowing he would do everything in his power to keep this man.

Chapter Nine

He had died and gone to heaven. He must have because pleasure streamed through his whole body, tingling his extremities and leaving goosebumps along his skin. No one had ever made him feel the way Aaron did. Everything he did was to enhance Zaire's pleasure. Zaire could feel it.

As Aaron concentrated his attention on Zaire's lacy thong, Zaire gripped the sheets below him, wanting so much to touch his own body and Aaron's but knowing he hadn't been given permission. He had to endure. This was his reward, after all. Although, he couldn't understand why he was being rewarded when he'd been such a bitch earlier.

He wasn't going to complain.

As Aaron mouthed along his cock through the lace, it became even harder if it was possible, and Zaire moaned at the feel of its confinement. He needed to be free of the lace, regardless of how sexy it made him feel.

Aaron must have heard his thoughts because he lifted the front edge of the thong and allowed his cock to peek out of the top. Zaire breathed out his relief and sucked in air as Aaron's tongue lapped at the crown. He widened his legs at Aaron's insistence, rolling his head on the pillow as Aaron's hand fondled his balls, and a finger slipped under the thong, pulling it away from his crack.

A finger pressed against his hole, rubbing in circles around the muscles before pressing and retreating, never actually entering. Aaron lifted his head and swiped his finger along his own tongue. Zaire's eyebrows drew together in confusion until he saw the white fluid clinging to Aaron's finger. Aaron replaced the finger at Zaire's ass, Zaire's own precome being used as lube. It wouldn't be enough if he intended to have a cock in his ass, but a finger was fine, especially as Aaron sucked the head of his dick into his mouth, tonguing the underside as his hands continued to be busy.

Sweat was beading on Zaire's skin as he fought against his climax. He wanted to come more than ever, but his Daddy had not said he could. He wanted to be good for him, but it was becoming more difficult with each suck, with each finger press and with each tug on his balls.

"Daddy!"

Aaron lifted off his cock much to Zaire's disappointment, but it was only for four words to escape, "Come for me, sweetheart."

Zaire stared into those russet-brown eyes, twinkling in the fading light, and his body took over, clenching and releasing as he watched through half-lidded eyes as

Aaron swallowed every drop. Zaire's breath was non-existent, and his body curled in on itself.

Finally, his body slumped to the bed, and he closed his eyes.

Distantly, he heard Aaron moving around the room. He felt his thong being removed and a warm cloth sweeping over his body. He couldn't open his eyes to express his gratitude. He was exhausted.

Aaron slid his arms under Zaire's body and moved him to one side, pulling the covers over the top of him once he was free of them. Zaire wanted to speak to Aaron, but he was being pulled under by sleep.

HIS ALARM WOKE HIM, and Zaire flapped his hand around, trying to find his phone to turn it off. His muscles were heavy from sleep and relaxation, and he didn't want to move. But he had a job to do. Rubbing a hand over his face, he remembered the previous night and lifted his head quickly, glancing around for evidence Aaron was still there. It was a stupid thought because he knew Aaron had to work today as well, and he was sure Aaron would already be there as it was already seven on a Monday morning.

When no evidence was found, Zaire dropped his head back to the pillow and stared at the ceiling before he grinned. What a treat he'd been given. He hoped he'd be able to return the favour soon.

He swung his legs over the side of the bed, sitting

upright, and spotted a piece of paper and pen on the bedside table.

Zaire,

I've locked everything up and taken the spare key with me as I didn't want to post it back through your door in case someone managed to reach through and grab it. I'll give it back to you today. I would like for you to still work at the school, but it's your choice. If you decide to accept the offer, go and see Pamela for the paperwork and make sure you attend the staff meeting straight after work today. I'd like to introduce you to everyone.

Now, be a good boy. I made you a fruit salad for breakfast, which is in the fridge, along with a packed lunch for today. I'd like you to try and eat everything, please. You need your energy.

I'm sure I'll see you at work. I'm sorry if it makes things difficult for you. Make sure you tell me if anyone gives you grief about anything. And no, I'm not only saying that to you…I say that to all my staff.

A

x

ZAIRE SMILED at the kiss on the bottom of the note. He had been going back and forth about the position at Aaron's school, but if Aaron thought it would work, Zaire wanted to try. The job would give him a break from having to travel so far some days, he would get to know the children better than he would if he had only been there for a day or two, and he would get to work alongside some fantastic staff.

Mind made up, Zaire got ready for work.

A school day later showed Zaire he was right in choosing to work there. He'd been there for two weeks as a temp already but having agreed to a permanent position had staff coming by to see the new guy. News travelled fast.

When he finished grabbing all his things from the classroom, Zaire followed Uma to the staff room.

"We have these meetings once a week to go over different aspects of the school. Sometimes it's relevant to our class, other times it isn't, but there is always a bit of learning in there as well, so most of us try to attend regardless." Having been there for over ten years, Uma was a font of knowledge which Zaire would do well to learn from. Zaire had been in the school environment for as many years, but he didn't know the rules for this school. "Aaron has only been here a short time, but he has done so much for us already. I hope he plans on staying for the long term."

"Why would you think he wouldn't? He wasn't brought in as a temporary headteacher, was he?" Nerves roiled in Zaire's stomach at the thought Aaron wasn't staying around long term.

"Oh, no! He was brought in permanently, but you never know. Personal circumstances and all," Uma said quickly, diffusing Zaire's nerves. "Nobody knows what's going to happen in the future, do we?"

Zaire shook his head, knowing far better than she realised about the statement.

They entered the staff room, and Zaire's eyebrows rose when he saw it held a lot of people. A lot. It looked like the whole school was here, excluding temporary staff, that is, but it was a fair number of people. His gaze wandered around the people, trying to spot Aaron, whom he had not seen at all that day, but couldn't see him. He followed Uma to the far side of the room and sat down behind her as there were only a few chairs left. He could feel the heat of the sun through the windows on his back, and he closed his eyes and smiled at the warmth beginning to relax muscles he hadn't realised were tense. He had no idea how this was meeting was going to go. He only knew Aaron was planning on introducing him to the rest of the staff.

The door opened, and Pamela and another person came in, followed by Aaron with his head thrown back in laughter. Zaire's breath caught in his throat as he watched Aaron smile at the women and gesture for them to sit. Aaron's defined muscles were hidden from view under a navy-blue suit and white shirt, but Zaire knew what he looked like, and he salivated thinking about it. He couldn't keep his eyes off him, and Aaron's gaze surveyed the room, pausing with the corners of his mouth curling up when he arrived at Zaire, then carried on. Zaire's heart raced so fast, he was sure Uma would be able to hear it. He didn't expect any acknowledgement from Aaron, apart from being a new teaching assistant but seeing the secretive smile made Zaire's day.

"Good afternoon, everyone," Aaron said, taking a

seat at the front of the semi-circle of chairs. "I know you probably have questions about last week's meeting, so let's start with those."

For the next few minutes, Zaire listened as several staff members expressed their displeasure at some new procedures being put into place, but he noticed most of them were the older staff members. He surmised they were set in their ways and didn't like change, although it could be him stereotyping, and he could be completely wrong.

"Okay, so let's move on. I'd like to introduce two new members of staff: Amy and Zaire." Aaron pointed them both out, and Zaire held up his hand in greeting. "Amy will be working in Simon's class for the foreseeable future, and Zaire will be with Uma. I am in the process of sourcing one more permanent member of staff, but at the moment, I haven't found someone suitable."

Aaron spent a few minutes listening to staff who believed they needed extra staff before he continued talking. "Listening to your requests has brought me to my next announcement. My plan over the next few months is to spend a day in each class. When I'm there, I would like for you to treat me as a teaching assistant. That means you need to go about your job as you usually would and send me to do the things you need me to do." He chuckled after scanning the room. "I am not there to trip you up. I want to figure out what things would make your life easier, and I can't do that from my office."

The authority in Aaron's voice was arousing, and despite his surroundings, Zaire squirmed on his chair as his dick hardened. His gaze was riveted on the man at the front of the room. The man who took care of him and turned him on like no one had before. Zaire swore he could smell Aaron's scent from where he was, although he knew it was impossible. He swallowed hard as the gaze of the man himself locked with his for a few seconds before flitting away. Zaire inhaled slowly, jaw clenched against the need coursing through his body. He didn't think Aaron seemed as affected as he was, which was unfair. Zaire knew they weren't going to flaunt their relationship, but he could've acknowledged him in some way.

Zaire pursed his lips, withholding a smile. Maybe he could see if he affected Aaron as much as Aaron affected him. The next time Aaron's gaze slid to his, Zaire licked his lips, and Aaron's eyes widened. The next time, Zaire made a show of unbuttoning the top button of his shirt and caressing his neck. The following time, he ran his fingers along his mouth, his tongue flicking out briefly.

Aaron cleared his throat and clenched his jaw, and Zaire knew he was getting to him. He cast a glance around, seeing everyone else was facing away from him or hidden behind others, so he took a chance and slid his finger into his mouth and closed his eyes as he sucked.

"Right!" Aaron's voice boomed across the room, making Zaire jump and think he'd pushed Aaron too far. "I think that's it, so unless anyone has any questions, we'll leave it there."

Staff began mingling around, gathering their belongings as they chatted with the people close to them, the noise level steadily rising.

"Looks like you'll get to know Aaron a lot better," a

voice commented, and Zaire turned to see a guy he didn't know. The guy held out his hand. "I'm Simon. I teach Year Six."

Zaire slid his hand into Simon's, panic flooding his body as he wondered what Simon had seen. "Zaire. Nice to meet you. What do you mean?"

Simon's gaze slid to Aaron, and Zaire felt his stomach pinch when he watched Simon look Aaron up and down and lick his lips. "He's visiting the classes, isn't he? So, you'll get to know him better."

Zaire didn't know Simon at all, but he had the feeling there was an underlying meaning to his words which Zaire didn't understand. Simon's gaze was on Aaron, and Zaire narrowed his eyes, wondering if there was a past relationship between the two men. It certainly seemed that way. At least from Simon's behaviour. Zaire glanced over at Aaron, seeing him in conversation with another teacher.

"Yeah, I guess. I have to head out but nice to meet you, Simon," Zaire lied through his teeth as he gathered his belongings and, saying goodbye to Uma, left the room. He didn't know why it was bothering him so much. Both had pasts they had yet to discuss in detail. Having it thrown in his face, though? It hurt as much as Zena turning her back on him, which was a shock for Zaire. Aaron could've at least warned him Zaire would probably meet someone he'd been with from the school. It might not have hurt so much. He thought he meant something to Aaron. Maybe Zaire had made a mistake taking this job.

His heart wrenched at the thought of leaving the

school, especially as he had already made some friends there. It might be the best idea. He didn't think he could see Aaron every day and not remember what he thought they'd had.

He stuck his phone onto his magnetic holder in his car after dropping into the driver's seat and dialled Rod, flicking it to speakerphone. Clicking his seat belt into place, Zaire pulled out of the school car park and pointed the car towards home.

"Hey, Zaire! How's it going?"

"Yeah, good. Do you fancy going out tonight?" Zaire's tone was clipped, and he knew Rod would pick up on it.

"Sure?" Rod's voice was questioning, but Zaire couldn't talk about it without a few beers in him.

"Great. I'll be at our usual bar at…" he checked the clock, "six." His voice cracked on the last word, and he inhaled roughly, trying to keep his composure enough to get home.

"Alright. See you there."

Zaire hung up without answering, his throat thick with unshed tears. How could the relationship be over so quickly? He'd believed Aaron was different, that Zaire meant something to him, but he supposed he shouldn't believe anyone anymore. Hadn't he learned his lesson with the last few Daddy relationships?

Chapter Ten

AARON

Aaron couldn't believe Zaire's audacity. With every flick of his tongue or slide of his fingers, Zaire had Aaron hardening in his trousers…trousers that would show every inch. He ended the meeting without focusing on Zaire again and got distracted by several staff members wanting to ask questions. By the time he was free, Zaire had gone, but Simon was still present. Aaron inwardly rolled his eyes. Ever since Aaron had started, Simon had been insinuating they should get together, being the only gay guys in the school. Firstly, Simon was wrong; there were at least two other people in the school, they kept themselves to themselves, unlike Simon. Secondly, Simon was not Aaron's type, and he didn't seem to get the hints Aaron kept giving him.

"Hey, Aaron."

"Good afternoon, Simon." He refused to be brought further into a conversation unless he truly had no other option.

"So, you're going to be in my class at some point, are you?" Simon stepped close…too close for Aaron's liking.

He made a show of heading to his bag and hooking it on his shoulder. "Yes, I will be in every class over the next few months." And if Aaron had his way, Simon's would be one of the last.

"That's good to know. I'll make sure you feel welcome."

"Hopefully, you make all the staff in your class feel welcome," Aaron said, quirking an eyebrow.

"Of course!" Simon waved his hand, dismissing Aaron's concern. "The new guy seems nice."

The tone in Simon's voice caught Aaron's notice, and he shifted to face Simon, trying to show nonchalance. "Both new people are great. It's why I hired them. If there's nothing else, Simon, I have to go."

He bid goodbye. He wanted to get in contact with Zaire as soon as possible. He'd missed seeing him today. How he'd become so enamoured with the guy in such a short time, he'd never know. Grabbing his final things from his office, he exited the school and began the drive home, dialling Zaire on the journey. The phone rang but went to voicemail, so Aaron left a brief message, asking Zaire to call him when he had a minute. When he arrived home, he'd not received a call or message, so he sent Zaire a text as well.

Hi. I'm happy you decided to join the team. You'll do great. Would you like to come around for a late dinner? x

Hopefully, Zaire would get the message and accept. Aaron liked the idea of making some dinner for them both and pampering Zaire.

When he'd not received a message an hour later, Aaron tried calling again, to no avail. An hour after, he tried again. By this point, he was getting worried something had happened to Zaire. He had no other contact details for anyone in Zaire's life, so had no way of knowing if something happened to him.

He paced the living room, running his hands repeatedly through his hair and scratching his beard. When his phone rang, he dived for it, shoulders releasing when he saw it was Zaire.

"Zaire? Is everything okay?" He couldn't help the worried tone that escaped.

"Sorry, it's Rod, Zaire's friend."

"Is Zaire okay? Where is he? What's wrong?"

"Woah, slow down. Everything's fine. Or at least it would be if I didn't have a completely wasted Zaire in my company."

"He's drunk?" Aaron was surprised. Not that Zaire was drunk, but why was he drunk?

"Yep, and he needs looking after. I hear you're the person for the job." The humour in Rod's voice had Aaron relaxing.

"I am. Where are you?"

"In a taxi. The driver is patiently waiting for your address so I can bring Zaire to you."

Aaron gave Rod his address and hung up. He moved his pacing to the hallway as he waited for them to arrive. When he heard a car pull up, he threw the door open and stalked down the path. The taxi door opened, and Aaron quickly caught the body that almost fell out of the car.

"Fuh," Zaire laughed uncontrollably as he gripped Aaron's arm. "Hey, I know you." Zaire's words merged as his tongue fought to work properly.

Rod exited the taxi, asking him to wait for him to come back. "Sorry, he jumped out quicker than I could grab him."

"No problem. What caused this? I didn't think Zaire ever got like this," Aaron questioned as he helped Zaire up the path to the house.

"You caused this."

Aaron whipped his gaze to Rod's in confusion. "What do you mean I caused this? Everything has been fine between us." He continued into the house.

"Well, obviously not. You need to ask your past relationships to stop butting into your current relationships. That is if it is a past relationship."

"If what is a past relationship? You're making no sense." Aaron led an almost comatose Zaire to the sofa, laying him down and covering him with a blanket.

"According to Zaire, after he'd had a few drinks inside him, a guy cornered him at the meeting today, making insinuations. Zaire got upset you hadn't told him about your past with any staff, and it hurt him."

"You're not making sense, Rod. I've not had a relationship with anyone from scho—fuck! Simon." Aaron threaded his hands through his hair.

"He mentioned Simon, yes. You need to tell Zaire about the guy, and anyone else he might run into."

"He's got it wrong. You've got it wrong. Simon and I have never been in a relationship, never will be if I have anything to say about it. He's been flirting with me from the moment I started at the school. But I have never touched him."

"Then you need to explain to Zaire because he was completely broken up about it. Said he wasn't going to trust anyone, especially Daddies anymore. He can't go through life like that."

"I know. I will speak to him. I need to get him through tonight first." Aaron stared at Zaire. "He's going to feel like hell tomorrow." Aaron smiled. "And, although I will talk to him, he's going to hate his punishment for making me worry like that."

"It seems like he's in good hands. I better go; otherwise, I'll have to remortgage my house to pay for the taxi fare."

"Thanks, Rod, and here's my number in case you want to check up on him."

They parted ways, and Aaron locked up. Checking once more on Zaire, he pottered around, making sure he put plenty of water and painkillers in the bedroom, including two buckets—wash one, use one—some washcloths and a towel. Once he was certain he had everything he might need overnight, Aaron returned downstairs and hooked his arms under Zaire's back and knees before lifting him and carrying him to bed. There was going to be a harsh discussion and punishment the following day, but for now, he had to care for his boy. Both were going to be exhausted for school in the morning.

WHEN HIS ALARM blared through the silence, Aaron groaned and rolled over to turn it off. He'd barely had a couple of hours sleep. Zaire had been up throughout the night, alternating throwing up with sleeping, but Aaron couldn't sleep in case something happened to him. It was only when Zaire had finally seemed more settled Aaron had allowed himself to sink into the mattress next to Zaire.

Aaron's head pounded from lack of sleep, but he bet Zaire's head was worse. Glancing over his shoulder, he saw the object of his thoughts splayed out across the bed, snoring softly. A grin stole across Aaron's face, and he wished he could've taken a picture. Zaire looked so innocent. Aaron smirked when he thought about punishing Zaire that evening. It was going to be two-fold. After the display at the staff meeting, trying to get Aaron aroused while in the presence of other people, and the misunderstanding making Aaron worry something had happened to him, Zaire would have to put up with Aaron's decision on his punishment.

After setting the shower going, he returned for Zaire, picking him up and carrying his dead weight to the bathroom. Aaron had stripped him to his boxers the previous evening, so it was all he had to struggle to remove before walking into the shower, holding Zaire. Luckily, his shower was large enough for him to manoeuvre easily.

Zaire woke suddenly, clutching at Aaron's neck when the water touched his skin. "What the——"

"Shh. Calm down. Everything is okay," Aaron

crooned, holding Zaire tighter, so he didn't drop him during his squirming.

Zaire stared at Aaron, his eyes widening, Aaron assumed because Zaire hadn't realised he was at Aaron's house. "What...? When...?" Zaire shook his head and winced.

"Take it easy. You'll have a sore head this morning. Slow movements are best." Aaron lowered Zaire to his feet, holding tight to his waist until he was sure Zaire was steady. "You'll regret all the alcohol today."

Zaire's cheeks flushed as he inspected the floor. "Yes, definitely regretting it," he whispered.

"Let's get you cleaned up. You'll be sweating alcohol for a while, but we can get rid of some of it." Aaron reached for the soap and lathered his hands, running them all over Zaire's body with a pretended indifference. He ignored Zaire's hard cock—morning wood was morning wood regardless of how drunk the person was the previous evening—and focused on getting him clean. After he'd finished and rinsed Zaire, he noticed Zaire was gripping the tiles and breathing heavily through his mouth. "Are you feeling okay?"

Zaire shook his head slowly, exhaling deeply. "I need..." He inhaled again. "I need to sit down."

Aaron switched off the water and opened the shower door, holding Zaire's hand as he followed. He wrapped a towel around Zaire, not bothering to dry him, and guided him back to the bedroom, where he sat Zaire on the bed. He didn't have any clothes for Zaire, and he refused to let him wear what he was wearing yesterday, so he found a pair of joggers and a t-shirt that would bury

Zaire but would allow him cover as Aaron drove him home to change for work. It was the reason why Aaron had set his alarm so bloody early.

When he turned and saw Zaire studying the floor while wrapped in a large fluffy towel, Aaron thought he looked so young. There was an eight-year difference between them, but, at that moment, it felt like more.

"Zaire," he said when he stood in front of his boy. Zaire met his gaze, and Aaron's heart broke at the sorrow bleeding from them. He kneeled, resting his hands on Zaire's thighs. "I promise nothing has happened or ever will happen between Simon and me. You are the first person within the same work environment I have ever been close to. Please believe me. No matter what anyone else says, that is the truth." Aaron watched Zaire sit straighter, his lips tightening, so he continued, hoping to make Zaire understand, "Simon wants more. He has since I started working there, but I have rebuffed every comment and invitation he has offered. It's you I want, sweet boy. And I don't think you realise how much."

Tears cascaded down Zaire's cheeks, and Aaron cupped his face, reverently touching their lips together in a salty kiss.

"Ow," Zaire whispered. "Crying hurts my head."

Aaron chuckled. "I can imagine it does." He wiped away Zaire's tears. "Let's get you dressed so we can get you home."

They worked together to get Zaire into the larger clothes, laughing when they saw the result. Zaire looked like a kid playing dress-up in his parent's clothes. After a quick breakfast of toast, they drove towards Zaire's house, and Aaron dropped his bombshell.

"After work, you will return to my house. When you arrive, you will be punished for your behaviour."

He saw Zaire's head whipped in Aaron's direction from the corner of his eye, his gaze on the road ahead as it was. "What? Why do I get punished?"

Aaron quirked a brow. "Have you so conveniently forgotten your behaviour at the meeting yesterday?"

Zaire said nothing, just returned his gaze to his surroundings. Aaron thought he heard a muttered, "Shit," but he wasn't certain.

"Understand?"

"Yes," Zaire mumbled.

"Yes, what?"

Zaire sighed. "Yes, Daddy." Zaire linked his fingers in his lap, squeezing them together.

"Good boy." Aaron reached a hand over and placed it on Zaire's, rubbing his thumb against his fingers and, hopefully, soothing his worry. "Are you okay?"

Zaire moved his hand, threading their fingers together. "Yes, I'm okay. Apart from an awful headache, which is easing now the painkillers are kicking in. I expect today to be hell on earth, but I'll be fine."

"I know you will. You're strong. Just remember to drink plenty of water." Aaron had a thought. "Did you drive to the bar last night?"

"No, I drove home first and got a taxi. I knew it would be an…enthusiastic night." Zaire gave a half-smile.

Aaron squeezed his hand again and smiled at him.

"I'm glad you were sensible. You make me proud, sweetheart."

"Except when I'm an asshole," Zaire muttered.

"Stop! You don't ever call yourself that." Aaron's voice rose in the small area. "You are not an asshole and never will be. Certain people, yes. You, hell no. You made a bad choice. I agree. But it does not make you an asshole."

They were quiet for a while after his outburst, and he wondered whether he'd gone too far until Zaire spoke, "Thank you for believing in me. Although I remember someone else calling me an asshole before."

Aaron chuckled. "You told me to. I will believe in you always. Even when you don't believe in yourself. Especially then."

They lapsed into silence for the remainder of the journey. When they arrived, Aaron exited the car to help Zaire to his house but remained on the porch.

"You need to get ready, and you don't need me helping." He smirked. "We'd end up being late, and neither of us needs that."

"Okay, Daddy. Thank you for everything."

Aaron wrapped his hands around Zaire's back and kissed his forehead. "You're welcome. Remember what I said. Straight to my house after work." He pulled back and fixed a stare on Zaire until he nodded. "Good boy." He pressed another kiss to his lips and pulled away, waving over his shoulder when he reached his car.

Today was going to be a long day.

Chapter Eleven

ZAIRE

Regardless of what Aaron said, Zaire couldn't help but think of himself as an asshole. He hadn't even waited to get Aaron's side of the story from him before he thought the worst and put Aaron in the same category as the other Daddies Aaron had said treated Zaire wrongly. As he dressed for the day, he winced with every movement, his head complaining at him for his foolish antics. Rod had been a great listener, but maybe Zaire had told him too much about his relationship with Aaron. There was nothing he could do about it now, but he grabbed his phone and messaged him, apologising for being a crap friend before he hightailed it out of the door and to his car; otherwise, he would be late.

When he arrived at the school, he grabbed his bag and…shit, he'd forgotten to pack his lunch. He'd have to make do with whatever snacks he had in his bag. As he walked towards the school, he saw Aaron in his office on the telephone. He looked impeccable as always. A small smile graced his lips when he saw Aaron notice him and wave him in. Forehead creasing, Zaire headed straight towards the headteacher's office.

"Good morning, Pamela," he said.

"Morning, Zaire. Everything okay?" They fiddled with a few files on their table as they spoke.

"Yes, thanks. Aaron—Mr Brown—waved me in through the window. Not sure why."

"Okay, bear with me a sec." They scurried out of their chair, knocking quietly on the door and poked their head through. Lowered voices were heard, and they came back out, indicating for him to go in. "Yes, you're good. He's finished on the phone." They resumed their seat.

"Thanks." He headed through the open door, closing it when Aaron told him to. "Is everything okay?"

Aaron nodded with a smile. "Yeah. I have something for you." He pulled a white paper bag from under his desk and held it out. "I wasn't sure if you'd remember your lunch, so I got something for you from the deli when I got mine. If you have something, this can go in the fridge for tomorrow instead."

Zaire's throat narrowed, and he swallowed convulsively. He couldn't believe he was so lucky to have this man as his Daddy. He wanted nothing more than to go over and wrap his arms around Aaron and never let go. How he ever thought Aaron had been lying to him, he had no idea.

"Zaire?" Aaron came around the desk, and Zaire was worried he would do as he wanted, so he held out his hand palm forward. Aaron stopped, a frown on his face as he scanned Zaire from head to toe. "What's wrong?"

"I…You…God!" He rubbed a hand over his face and tried to regain his composure. After breathing deeply for a few moments, he managed to say, "Thank you so much." He waved his hand towards the bag in Aaron's hand. "For this. For everything you've given me so far. It's so much more than any other Daddy did. It seems completely unreal. I'm…" he broke off, not able to say anymore without bursting into tears.

"I understand. Take a few deep breaths, sweet boy," Aaron said in a low voice. "It can be overwhelming when you haven't had this before. If you want me to stop, I can, but I would like it if you could come to enjoy these little…gifts from me to you."

"Don't stop," he whispered.

Aaron smiled, but his mouth curled down when he looked out the window. "Take this and head to the staff toilets for a few minutes. I'll send a message to Uma that you'll be a few minutes late because I've asked you to do something. Once you feel able, head to work. Okay?" Zaire nodded. "Words, sweetheart."

"Yes…Daddy." The final word was mouthed rather than spoken.

"I really want to hug you right now, but I can't. I'm so sorry."

Zaire gazed at him, a smile gracing his face now he was settling again. The alcohol last night must have broken down some more of his walls because he wasn't usually so emotional. He took the bag Aaron passed him, grinned as best he could and sauntered out of the office to the toilets. Even being in Aaron's company had settled something inside him.

When he finally got to class, Uma sent him a worried gaze, and he knew nothing would get past her. It was a matter of time before she asked him if he was okay. Could he do this secret relationship? How was it even going to be possible?

Uma finally caught up to him at the children's break time, when one of the staff was covering while he helped Uma do some organising for the next part of the day.

"Is everything alright with you? You seem…out of sorts, today?"

Zaire laughed. "Is that your way of telling me I look like shit?"

Uma's eyes widened, then she chuckled. "No, although you do look a little worse for wear."

"Yeah, I had a long night last night. Too much alcohol was involved. I promise that is not my normal situation. I'm usually a lot more put together than this." He was worried she wouldn't want him in the class if he was deemed unreliable.

"Don't be silly. Of course, I know this isn't you. It's why I'm so worried. Is there anything I can help with?"

Zaire's heart softened. Uma was a generous and gentle soul. "No but thank you for the offer."

"Well, you know where I am if you need anything at all."

"Thank you."

The rest of the day was uneventful apart from when he opened his deli bag and saw a chicken salad sandwich, a small pot of pasta and two pieces of fruit along with an apple juice. Zaire had felt tears pricking again but refused to allow them free. Rod had replied to his message as well, telling him to stop being a jerk and talk to his Daddy. He'd rolled his eyes and didn't reply.

When he got in his car, he reminded himself to drive to Aaron's house, not his own, and when he finally pulled up, Aaron's car wasn't there. While he waited, he checked his phone, seeing another message from Rod.

You're all good, Zaire. What are friends for if you can't let the barriers go once in a while? Make sure you talk things through with Aaron. He seems like a nice guy. Let me know how you are when you get five.

Zaire replied as Aaron pulled into the driveway.

I'm good. I'm at Aaron's now. We briefly spoke this morning and things seem okay between us. I'll let you know if it changes. I'm not planning on being home tonight, so I'll message you again tomorrow. Thanks for everything last night. Especially taking me to Aaron's, even if it was because you didn't want to look after me, lol.

His phone buzzed again as he climbed out of his car, and he smiled at the middle finger salute Rod replied with.

"You look happy."

Zaire grinned up at Aaron. "Just messaging Rod. He's an idiot sometimes, but a lovable one."

"He seemed nice when I met him last night."

The reminder of the previous evening tensed Zaire's muscles, knowing what was going to happen when he entered Aaron's house, even if he didn't know the specifics.

"Come on in. Hang your stuff up and follow me to the kitchen."

Zaire did as asked without replying. When he entered the kitchen, Aaron was busy preparing some food and placed a plate with some fruit slices, a yoghurt and a glass of milk in front of Zaire.

"Eat up. I don't want you passing out from hunger if you can't last until dinner." Aaron chuckled as he said it.

Zaire ate his food, surprisingly hungry, though he didn't usually eat straight after work. When he finished, Aaron took the plate from him and rinsed it before coming back to sit next to Zaire.

"Alright. I don't usually delay punishments, but because of yesterday's events, I had to. Do you remember what you did yesterday that you need to be punished for?"

Zaire nodded and kept his gaze on his hands, which surrounded the chilled glass. "I was being naughty at the staff meeting."

"Yes. But I am also going to punish you for scaring the hell out of me last night. When I couldn't get hold of you, I was worried something had happened to you. No one would have thought to let me know if you'd been in an accident." Aaron took Zaire's hand. "You scared me, sweetheart."

Zaire had never thought about that. He wrapped his

other hand around Aaron's. "I'm so sorry, Daddy. I didn't think."

"No, you didn't. I know you were hurt, but you should have come to me with your questions. I'm here for you, no matter what you have to say. Even if it hurts me, I want you to tell me. I want to be able to make it better."

"I should have. I know now, but at the time, I was so upset and afraid I'd made a mistake."

"I understand. But you should have spoken to me about it. Even if I had told you what we had was a fling, wouldn't it have been better to know than to wonder?"

Zaire thought about it and realised Aaron was completely right. Despite the fact he would have to ask an uncomfortable question, Zaire would have known straight away, and none of this would have happened.

"I suppose I have a lot to learn about relationships."

"No. You have a lot to learn about our relationship. There is a difference. Our relationship will be different from any other relationship you have. That is one of the amazing things about having a Daddy and boy lifestyle."

Zaire said nothing. He couldn't disagree.

"Now, onto your punishment."

Zaire swallowed hard but didn't move his gaze away from Aaron's. "Yes, Daddy," he said solemnly.

"Go into the living room and sit on the chair in the corner, facing the wall. I expect you to stay there for thirty-five minutes. While you are there, you need to think about why you did what you did. I have my own ideas, but we'll discuss it afterwards."

"Yes, Daddy." Zaire stood and gave a small smile before heading to the living room. He didn't like the idea of sitting there alone for the next half an hour, but he would. He deserved it for what he'd put his Daddy through yesterday.

There was a wooden chair with arms, not particularly comfortable, and it faced the corner where there was nothing he could see except beige-coloured wallpaper. There was nothing to distract him from the time. And the time crawled.

He could do nothing but think, and it irked him something rotten. He liked being busy and getting things done, but here he couldn't do anything except fidget. Staring down at his shoes, Zaire thought about yesterday. He hated being a secret. It was that simple. He wanted a relationship he could shout to the rooftops about, not one he had to pretend didn't exist when he was at work but was full and bountiful when work finished. It wasn't fair he couldn't have it all.

Zaire frowned. How could they make it work? If he couldn't deal with it like it was, he either needed to find a new job, or he needed to leave Aaron. His pulse stuttered at the thought, and he knew there was no way he'd be able to leave Aaron. Even his stupidity of the night before didn't change the fact he was falling for his head-teacher. In fact, it exacerbated it. He reacted that way because he didn't want to lose Aaron and thought he had no choice. Now, though, he would fight for them. So, the best idea would be to find a new job. He hated letting Aaron and Uma down, but it was for the best.

"Zaire?"

Zaire jumped but didn't remove his gaze from the wall. His Daddy hadn't told him he could move, yet.

Aaron came around the front of the chair and crouched down.

"You've done so well, my precious boy. I'm so proud of you." Aaron rose and pressed his lips to Zaire's, licking across them to request entry, which Zaire would never deny. Aaron pulled away, leaving them both breathless, and lifted Zaire's hands to help him to his feet.

"Let's get changed and watch some TV before I have to go and make dinner."

Zaire smiled, and Aaron dressed him in what he called his comfort clothes—shorts, vest and robe—and he settled on the sofa to watch Tom and Jerry. He knew Aaron had left the room at one point but was too engrossed to wonder why.

"Time for dinner."

As soon as Aaron said it, Zaire could smell the spicy scent in the air, which he hadn't noticed before. Aaron led him to a chair at the kitchen table, pushing his chair in when he was seated. Zaire watched him as he pottered around, gathering plates and cutlery and adding finishing touches to the food before bringing over enchiladas.

"Mmm, smells delicious. Thank you, Daddy."

"You're very welcome, sweet boy." As they ate, Aaron brought up their topic for discussion. "So, did you think about what happened yesterday?"

Zaire nodded but didn't answer until he finished his mouthful. "I did. I don't want to be a secret. I don't like pretending I'm not yours." He wasn't touching on the Simon thing.

"That's what I thought, too. I think you were being bratty yesterday because you wanted my attention but were unable to have it because we're keeping things quiet. We need to figure out the best way to work together and be happy with the situation. Both of us happy with the situation."

"I can't see how we can without either telling people about us or me finding somewhere else to work." Zaire was silent for a moment. "I'm going to stay with the agency for a bit longer. See if I can find a job at another school nearby."

Aaron tilted his head. "Are you sure? I don't want you to have to leave somewhere you're happy to work. I know you've been looking for somewhere permanent. If you want to stay at this school, you're welcome to. Although a personal relationship is allowed within the school, we need to think about the bigger picture regarding parents and governors. It will prove tricky and will possibly test us, both as a relationship and as a boss and employee, but I think we are strong enough to handle it, don't you?" Aaron smiled at him.

"I would like to think we are. But it's for the best for me to find somewhere else. I'm sorry for leaving as soon as I agreed. I will stay at the school until you've found a replacement."

"It's not a problem. And thank you for staying to help. I will find someone as soon as I can. I think we should tell Pamela and Uma about our relationship; that way, each of us has someone who we can talk to if needed while I find a new teaching assistant. They are our friends, after all." Aaron smiled.

"Okay, Daddy." Zaire couldn't feel any effects of the alcohol anymore, yet he was shattered, but if he slept, he wouldn't get to see Aaron much. He wanted to spend as much time as possible with Aaron.

"Have you finished your dinner, sweetheart?"

"Yes, thank you." Zaire yawned.

"Let's get you ready for bed. You need your rest."

"But it's only six!"

"Well, I was going to suggest watching TV before bed, but I think maybe you need some more time in the time out chair." The tone was short and sharp.

Zaire ducked his head. "No! I hate that chair!"

"I think you're tired, Zaire, and you need sleep."

"I don't want to go to sleep yet! I want to spend more time with you."

"As sweet as that is, you need sleep," Aaron reiterated.

Zaire stood, scraping the chair back on the floor. "Fine. I'll go to bed, then." He stomped to the stairs, jogging up them and heading straight to the bed. Flopping down on the covers, he closed his eyes, all the fight leaving his body. Tears escaped from his eyes. He hated disappointing his Daddy, but he also hated not being able to be with him. He rolled to his side and gripped the pillow in his hands as his tears came. He felt the bed dip behind him and arms come around his waist.

"Let it all out, Zaire. I'm here for you, sweetheart. I'm not going anywhere."

Zaire twisted around and wrapped his whole body around Aaron's, face pressed into his chest as his tears soaked into Aaron's shirt. He had no idea how long it had been when he finally relaxed enough to think clearly. He took a deep breath.

"Sorry, Daddy," he whispered.

"It's okay, sweet boy. We will figure this all out. But we won't be able to do it when we're tired. We both need sleep, not just you. I didn't get much last night either. I thought if we both had an early night, we would feel better tomorrow and could think clearly about what to do. I should've explained it to you."

"It's okay."

"It's not okay. I want communication from you, but I also need to remember I need to communicate with you, too. It's not fair for me to expect you to behave in certain ways if I haven't explained how or why." They laid in silence for a few moments before Aaron moved. "We need to get ready for bed, or I'll be asleep like this." He chuckled.

Zaire smiled and sat upright. "I think sleep is a good idea."

Aaron stroked a hand over Zaire's head. "After some sleep, we'll be able to fight the whole world if we have to."

"We will, Daddy, but I hope we don't have to."

Chapter Twelve

AARON

Aaron had been correct when he'd told Zaire that Pamela and Uma wouldn't care about their relationship —not their Daddy and boy relationship, just that they were in one.

Zaire had spoken with the agency and agreed to stay on at the school until a replacement could be found. Aaron got right on it as soon as he'd set foot in the office that morning. He had several interviews set up for the following week.

When Friday finally rolled around, Zaire had asked if they could go to the club. Aaron wanted nothing more than to sit it out after the week he'd had, but he'd agreed. He didn't want Zaire getting the idea Aaron didn't want to be seen with him.

They planned to go to Infinity, and Zaire had invited Colin, who was still with Dave, and Rod, who was alone because his girlfriend was away with her friends, and Aaron had invited Nora, Geoff and Cord. It was turning into a get-together. Aaron was glad Zaire had suggested it because it would give their friends the chance to meet and mingle. There was one thing on Aaron's mind.

"Zaire?"

"Yes, Daddy."

"When we're out, what do you want to be? Do you want to be Zaire or my boy?"

Zaire tilted his head, and Aaron could see him working through his options. "Your boy, please, Daddy."

"You sure?"

Zaire nodded, a grin stretching across his face.

"In which case, I have something for you." Aaron's heart raced as he headed to his bag to fetch his newest acquisition. He'd been carrying it around for the last few days, not sure when or if to offer it. Lifting the box out, he twisted back to face Zaire. "You don't have to wear this, but I would very much like it if you did because you'd be seen to be mine."

Zaire's brow creased until Aaron opened the hand-sized box. Nestled inside was a beautiful, amber-coloured collar that matched Zaire's eyes. The eyes which widened as he stared. Zaire's hand reached forward, and his fingers brushed against the collar in an almost reverent action.

"If you don't like it, you don't have to w—"

"I love it, Daddy!" Joy spread across Zaire's face, his eyes sparkled, his cheeks flushed, and he did a happy dance on the spot. "Can I wear it now?" he asked, hope blossoming in his eyes.

"You can wear it whenever you want to," Aaron

answered, his heart expanding at the obvious excitement coming from Zaire.

"Please, Daddy! Now, please!" He clapped his hands together, and Aaron beamed.

He released it from the box and, placing the box on the top of the drawers, unfastened it before beckoning for Zaire, who came willingly. As Aaron fastened it around Zaire's throat, something inside him unclenched at the obvious ownership on Zaire's body. He felt like he had someone who he could share his life with. Someone who could help him as much as Aaron helped his boy. Once it was fastened, he ran his fingers across it and Zaire's skin.

"You look fantastic," Aaron breathed.

Zaire smiled, looking at him from underneath his lashes. "Will you help me choose what to wear, please, Daddy?"

"Of course, my boy. Do you have any ideas, or do you want me to choose for you completely?"

"Can you choose, please?"

"Of course. Go wait by the bed, and I'll be there in a few minutes."

Zaire sneakily lifted to his feet and planted a kiss on Aaron's lips before skipping off across the room. Aaron shook his head, smiling. He always felt so much lighter when Zaire was around. He made the world appear filled with brighter colours.

Deciding to choose a top for him first, he opened the wardrobe and rifled through the options. He came across a black halter-neck with a golden shimmery overlay, which he thought would look amazing with the collar. He checked out the options for Zaire's legs. There were skirts, dresses, trousers, shorts and probably other items Aaron had no idea about. He saw some white trousers and pulled them out, realising they were three-quarter length ones. They'd look great with the top and some heeled or flat shoes, depending on what Zaire wanted to walk in.

Heading over to Zaire, who stood at the foot of the bed, a dreamy gaze on his face as he stroked his collar, Aaron lay the clothes on the bed. Smiling at Zaire, he diverted to the drawers and opened the top, looking for nude-coloured underwear. He found a thong and plucked it out, hanging it from his finger as he pivoted towards Zaire once more. This time, Zaire's heated gaze was on Aaron.

Aaron wandered over to him, his gaze taking in every inch of Zaire that was exposed to him. Which was considerable as Zaire had finished in the shower and wore a small towel. As he stepped close enough to touch, he rested his fingertips on Zaire's chest, slowly skimming them lower as Aaron kneeled in front of him. They were going to be late meeting their friends.

His fingers slid over the growing bulge in the towel and down his calves to his feet, where Aaron tapped for Zaire to lift so Aaron could slide on the thong. When he lifted the thong up Zaire's legs, he made sure to skim his fingers over the skin along the way. As he reached the bottom edge of the towel, Aaron glanced up at Zaire and raised an eyebrow in an unsaid question. Zaire swallowed hard and opened his mouth as he exhaled in a rush before moving his hands to the knot in the towel. He undid it and dropped it to the floor next to them.

Unable to help himself, Aaron pressed a kiss to the erect cock right in front of him, and Zaire moaned. Aaron continued to lift the thong into place, leaving Zaire's cock poking out the top of the waistband but sliding his finger between his ass cheeks to ensure the back of it was in place. To do it, he had to get closer to Zaire's shaft, and Aaron lapped at the exposed head to the music of Zaire's harsh breathing.

"Fuck, Daddy! Please, don't leave me like this!" Zaire begged so beautifully.

Aaron brought one hand to the front and used one finger to pull Zaire's cock away from his stomach, giving Aaron more space. He took the head of Zaire's shaft into his mouth and lightly sucked, using his tongue on the underside. The hand that remained in Zaire's crack moved higher and pressed against his hole, eliciting a moan and a thrust forward and back, like Zaire couldn't decide which he wanted more.

As he hadn't used any lube, Aaron pulled his hand away and lifted it to Zaire's mouth, all the while suckling at his tip, playing with the tiny slit in the head and the extremely sensitive underside. Zaire's cock was now rock hard and barely constrained in the lacy thong. When he deemed his fingers wet enough, he removed them from Zaire's mouth and returned to his hole. Sliding more easily now, he pressed a little harder against the entrance to his passage. Aaron felt when Zaire relaxed because his finger slid past his muscle ring, and Zaire groaned.

"Oh god, please let me come." Zaire thrust between the two sensations, his rhythm faltering as he neared the precipice.

Not wanting this to be over quite yet, Aaron pulled away, and Zaire's legs wobbled. Aaron held Zaire's hips as Aaron stood, taking Zaire's mouth in a carnal, rough kiss and pushing him back onto the bed, all the while keeping their lips locked. Zaire spread his legs to allow Aaron room.

While bracing one hand beside Zaire's head, Aaron used his other to undo his jeans, pushing them down enough to free his cock. He grasped both shafts in his hand and stroked. They both groaned into the kiss as their hips thrust into his tight fist. Aaron's tongue mimicked the movement of his hips, and Zaire sucked on it, hurtling them towards the end.

Aaron pulled his mouth free, gasping for air. Gazing down at Zaire, he saw his pupils had blown wide enough to almost cover the amber colour of Zaire's eyes, his lips were ruby red and bruised, and his cheeks were flushed. Aaron tightened his grip, wanting to watch as Zaire flew. Zaire's mouth opened further, air audibly inhaled and exhaled as he reached for his climax. Zaire's back bowed, his nostrils flared, and Aaron told him to come.

"Fuck!" Zaire shouted as his release coated his stomach and chest, followed closely by Aaron's.

"God, yes! Fuck, Zaire!" Aaron growled as his climax roared through him, marking Zaire as his.

Aaron rolled to his back next to Zaire, breathing as if he'd run a marathon. Their hands threaded together as they lay there, regaining their equilibrium.

"I can't move," Zaire mumbled.

Chuckling, Aaron sat up. "You don't need to for the moment. Let me clean you up." He rose to shaky legs, locking his knees so he didn't fall back to the bed, even though it was where he wanted to be. Looking down at himself, he snorted.

"What, Daddy?"

Aaron glanced at Zaire. "I'm still fully dressed." He turned to show Zaire only his cock stuck out from his undone jeans, every other item of clothing was in place.

Zaire put a hand over his mouth as laughter danced in his eyes. "You look hot," he whispered.

Aaron leaned over the bed to move Zaire's hand and press a kiss to his lips. Their cocks slid against each other, and they groaned into the kiss before Aaron pulled away.

"I'll clean you up and get you dressed. We're going to be late as it is." Aaron grinned at Zaire, a lightness in him he had not felt for so long.

After cleaning Zaire up, Aaron pulled the lace over his cock.

"Are you not going to change the thong, Daddy?" Zaire's voice was shaky, and Aaron gazed up at him, seeing Zaire's frown.

He supposed some people didn't like wearing underwear they had come in, but neither of them had spilled anything on the lace. "No, sweet boy. I want you to remember what we did whenever you go to the bathroom and see this lacy thong. I promise you, they are clean, they…" Aaron leaned forward, pressing his nose into the fabric and inhaling, "smell like you and me," he finished on a growl.

As his gaze returned to Zaire, he saw his pupils dilate and knew they needed to get moving; otherwise, they would end up in bed again, and Aaron didn't want Zaire to miss out on his night out.

The clothes he'd picked for Zaire rested next to them, untouched by their previous actions. He helped Zaire stand and reached for the trousers, pulling them up his legs and over his ass before fastening them. They moulded to Zaire's thighs as if they were made especially for him. Aaron stood, grabbed the top and helped Zaire into it. As he thought, it highlighted the collar beautifully, and Aaron couldn't help but take Zaire in a long, deep kiss as his hands caressed the leather band.

"God, you're amazing, Zaire." He rested their foreheads together as he regained his breathing once more. "And you're dangerous." He chuckled and blew out a breath. "What shoes would you like to wear tonight?"

Zaire blinked at him a few times before seemingly shaking off his lust. "Um, I have some low wedge shoes which would work."

"Okay. Go grab them, and I'll help you."

In no time, Zaire was finally fully dressed, and they were on their way to the club—forty-five minutes late, but on their way, nonetheless.

As they entered the club, Aaron gripped Zaire's hand tight, not wanting to lose him amongst the Friday night crowds. They weaved their way around the bar, trying to find any of their friends and finally noticed Cord waving at them from a table near the back.

"What took you so long?" Cord yelled to be heard over the music.

Aaron glanced at Zaire, seeing a flush colour his cheeks. "We got waylaid."

"Yeah, you got laid, alright," Cord answered with a grin.

Aaron ignored him and pulled Zaire down onto one of the two spare seats at the large table they'd commandeered. Zaire introduced him to Rod and Colin again, and Aaron introduced Zaire to Nora and Geoff, who Zaire had not met properly yet. Once everyone knew everyone, Aaron waved down a waiter and ordered a round of drinks.

"So, how are things going?" Nora asked him, leaning past Cord to ask in a quieter voice.

Aaron grinned. "Really well."

"That's all you're going to give us?" Cord asked.

"Yep."

"You're an asshole."

"What more do you want? I'm not giving you a play by play of our activities." Aaron shook his head.

Nora laughed. "I see you have collared him, but have you hit the bump yet?"

Aaron glanced across at Zaire, seeing him in animated conversation with Rod, Colin and Dave, and focused back on Nora and Cord. "Yes. You know we had a bit of an issue on Monday, but with Rod's help, it got sorted quickly."

Nora raised her eyebrows. "You know that's not the bump I meant."

Clenching his jaw, Aaron grabbed his beer and took a long gulp. He knew exactly what she meant. In any new relationship, there seemed to be a general bump several days or weeks into it, where the boy debated whether he was with the right Daddy, or happy where he was, or something similar. Most other Daddies or Mummies he knew of had witnessed or experienced the same thing, just in different ways. He had hoped their differences on Monday was their 'bump,' but Nora made him reconsider. Zaire had taken everything so well, except for the Simon issue, but they got through it. He hoped Zaire would talk to him if he had any second thoughts about them.

Chapter Thirteen

ZAIRE

Aaron became quiet as the night wore on. Zaire wondered what had been said for him to retreat, but every time Zaire checked in with him, he'd smiled and said he was fine. Now, heading to Zaire's house in a taxi, Aaron was gripping Zaire's hand and staring out of the window as if all the answers of the world were out there.

Zaire had a fantastic night. He'd gotten to know Nora and Geoff, who were great, and Cord, who was a bit of an asshole, but he could imagine would be a wonderful Daddy to some boy. He'd been able to catch up with Colin, too. He was enjoying his time with Dave, and Zaire had double-checked he was happy, which he was. As for Rod, Zaire had hugged him to thank him for taking him back to Aaron on Monday. Although they had spoken throughout the week, Zaire hadn't seen him since and owed him a lot.

But his night had been overshadowed by Aaron's

silent behaviour. The only thing Zaire could think of was someone had said something to him, and it worried Zaire. He didn't want someone to warn Aaron away from him. He'd just found his Daddy; he didn't want to lose him again.

The worry had him resting his head on Aaron's shoulder and wrapping his free arm around Aaron's biceps, trying to get as close as he could without mounting him.

A hand came up and stroked his hair. "Are you okay, sweetheart?"

"Uh-huh," he answered. He wasn't sure how to explain what he was feeling, although he needed to try because they promised communication between them. It meant Aaron needed to talk, too. He kept silent until they got to his place. "Daddy?" he said when they were in the kitchen, Aaron grabbing some water.

"Yes, sweet boy." Aaron smiled across at him.

"You said we needed to talk to each other—to communicate."

"Yes?" Aaron said when Zaire didn't continue.

"What's wrong, Daddy? You've been quiet all night. Did I do something wrong?" He stood there, wringing his hands together, not wanting to bring it up but needing to all the same.

Aaron rubbed a hand over his mouth and beard before answering, "No, Zaire. You've done nothing wrong." He sighed, shoulder slumping. "It's…Come on, let's go sit for a minute. I'll explain what was said."

They moved to the sofa, and Aaron lifted his arm so

Zaire could snuggle up against him. Zaire took some comfort in the fact Aaron was not pushing him away, at least not physically.

"In many Daddy or Mummy relationships, there is a point when the boy or girl begins to doubt what they have together is true. We call it 'the bump.' Most bumps are minor, and everyone carries on as normal afterwards, but sometimes, the bump ends the relationship."

"And you're worried we haven't hit my bump yet?"

Aaron nodded. "Nora reminded me about it tonight, and it got me thinking. Monday was a bump, but I don't think it was one which could potentially make you reconsider what we have."

Zaire sat upright. "I don't think I'm going to have a bump, Daddy. I really don't. Monday made me realise I want you in my life. I want everything with you. No one has ever made me feel like you do. Haven't we already been through so many ups and downs?"

"Yes, we have. I want you to be happy, that's all. And if it ends up that I don't make you happy, I'll accept it, but I won't like it."

Zaire moved, straddling Aaron and bringing their faces closer together. "I can't predict the future, but as of this moment in time, I can honestly say I have never been happier." His hand trailed across his collar as he gave Aaron a beaming smile.

Aaron's melancholic expression lifted, and Zaire leaned in for a kiss, resting his hands against his Daddy's beard, feeling the scratchy texture tickle his palms. Their kiss was languid, and Zaire got lost in the sensations, his brain completely switching off from anything not related to the feel of Aaron beneath and around him.

As Zaire's arousal increased, he rocked his hips against Aaron, the friction barely there and not quite enough. Aaron gripped his waist, stilling his movements and pulling away from his mouth.

"Are you trying to take something you didn't ask for?" Aaron growled, his voice significantly deeper than usual.

Zaire's eyes widened as he flicked through his options. He could deny thrusting against Aaron and be guaranteed a punishment of some sort, and possibly not a good one, or he could admit it and possibly get a good punishment for being honest. The longer he stared at Aaron, the less sure he was of his best choice.

"Well?" Aaron prompted.

"Sorry, Daddy. I wanted some relief. I didn't think about what I was doing. I'm sorry." Zaire stared at Aaron's shirt as he waited for the verdict, hoping he had been apologetic enough to warrant some sort of reward.

"Okay, sweet boy, but remember in the future, you need to ask for what you want. As you were so impatient, we are heading to bed now, without any relief. For either of us."

"But—" Aaron's raised eyebrows halted his words, and Zaire bit his lip.

When Aaron pushed against Zaire and helped him stand, then followed suit, Zaire moped, keeping his gaze on the floor as he trailed behind his Daddy up the stairs. He was annoyed because all he wanted to do was feel Aaron sliding deep inside him and pounding him into the mattress. They'd been together for a while now, and they'd still not had sex. He had hoped to get Aaron aroused enough to finish the night off with a bang. Zaire had to go and ruin it by being impatient. He kept trying to remember that his Daddy knew best, but it was difficult. Even though he wanted someone to look after him, it was hard to let the reins go after being alone for so long.

"I don't think we need a shower before bed, but would you like one?" Aaron turned the bedside lights on, filling the room with a warm glow. Zaire loved that, even though it was Zaire's house, Aaron had made himself comfortable enough to take care of Zaire. Aaron didn't hesitate to do what he needed to do to make sure Zaire was looked after.

"I'm okay, thank you."

"Let's get you undressed. Are your feet sore from the shoes?" Aaron crouched down to undo the buckles and slip each shoe off Zaire's feet.

Zaire groaned and scrunched and flexed his toes into the carpet now they were out of their confines. "They are a little, but nothing I'm not used to."

Aaron helped Zaire remove his other clothing until he was stood naked in the middle of the room as Aaron chose something for him to wear. He pulled out a chemise Zaire rarely wore. It was light pink silk with thin straps and a lace detail across the chest. He glanced over at Zaire as if to gauge his reaction, but Zaire honestly didn't mind what he wore. Nodding his head, Aaron closed the drawer and stepped up to him.

"Arms up."

The material flowed down his skin, making him feel small and sexy, and he couldn't help but run his hands over the texture and sigh.

"You look gorgeous."

"Thank you, Daddy."

"You're welcome." He pressed a kiss to Zaire's lips. "Let's get this collar off."

Zaire's hand instantly went to the leather strap. "Can't I keep it on?" he asked, his heart racing.

"It's probably not a good idea. I don't want you to get a sore neck." Zaire pouted, his shoulders slumping. Aaron must have seen Zaire was upset because he added, "But how about if we take it off and put it right next to you on the bedside table so you can see it at any point and put it on straight away in the morning?"

Zaire mulled it over. He didn't want to take it off, but he knew Aaron was right. "Okay, Daddy."

The buckle came loose easily enough, and soon Zaire felt a loss he hadn't expected when Aaron first encased his neck in the warmed fabric. He'd truly felt like he belonged to Aaron when he was wearing it and, strangely, a little lost without it. He watched as Aaron walked over to the bedside table and placed it where he'd said he would. Zaire didn't like it, but at least it was within reach.

"Come to bed." Aaron held out his hand after flicking the cover back. Withholding his smile, Zaire sashayed over, a larger sway in his hips than he would usually make and made sure to brush against Aaron as he slid past him.

A chuckle met his ear as he climbed onto the soft, cool sheets, laying on his side so he could see the collar. It might seem silly to some that he was scared it would be taken away, but he'd never had one before. None of his previous Daddies had ever given him one. Whenever they had gone out to clubs or bars, they always kept him with them, and he hadn't been able to go and dance with his friends without them being there, too. The collar, although giving him a sense of being owned, also gave him more freedom as he was able to dance and go to the bathroom without anyone getting in his face because it proved he belonged to someone.

When he was tucked in, Aaron leaned down and pressed a kiss to his forehead. "Sleep, my sweet. I'm going to get undressed, and I'll be with you."

Zaire nodded, his blinking getting heavier, even though he tried to keep his eyes on his collar.

ZAIRE WOKE with his ass pressed against Aaron's groin, Aaron's deep breathing heating his neck and whispering past his ear. He wanted nothing more than to rub back against him, but his eyes snagged on his collar, and he remembered his Daddy's words from the previous night. Gritting his teeth against the need to move, he inhaled, hoping to calm himself.

"Daddy?" he whispered. When he received no answer, he lifted the hand Aaron had curved around Zaire's waist and pressed a kiss to his fingertips. "Daddy?" he said again, cuddling the hand against his chest, fighting against the urge to thrust his hips. He wasn't sure how much longer he could hold himself together.

"Hmm, good morning, sweetheart." Aaron's voice rumbled, husky and deep, into his back as his nose rubbed circles on Zaire's neck. He pressed a kiss to his spine. "Do you need something?"

"Please, Daddy. I've been so good. I woke you up to ask you instead of moving like I wanted to! Please can you make me come? I'm so hard," he whispered the last bit, a flush heating his cheeks at his admission.

"Oh, is my sweet boy needing his Daddy?"

"Yes, please!"

Aaron disentangled his hand from Zaire's grasp and smoothed it down Zaire's front using his fingertips, grazing across his silk-covered skin. Aaron trailed over Zaire's nubs, causing Zaire to buck his hips and gasp as a tingle was felt in his cock. An arm slid under Zaire's neck, and Aaron pulled Zaire back against him, wrapping an arm across his chest as his other hand continued its journey.

"Look at me, sweetheart."

Zaire rolled his head to the side and met Aaron's kiss in a fierce, hungry clash of lips and tongues. Zaire's eyes closed on a moan when Aaron's hand closed around his dick. Zaire rocked his hips back and forth into Aaron's hand and against the hard cock pressed against his crack. Needing a breath, Zaire twisted his head away, panting and gripping the sheets beneath him as his hips moved faster. He was so close.

Aaron pulled away, and Zaire whimpered as his rise to orgasm stuttered and dropped. He heard a scrape and a rustle, and Aaron was back. Zaire glanced over his shoulder and saw Aaron rolling on a condom and opening a tube to slick his cock and his fingers. Aaron threw the tube to the side, spooning Zaire once more, his arm sliding back under Zaire's neck as his lube-free fingers pushed against Zaire's upper thigh. Zaire moved his leg, opening him up to Aaron's questing fingers.

The first pass of the slicked fingers over his hole had Zaire's breath catching in his throat and arching his head backwards.

"I'm going to take care of my boy now," Aaron groaned into Zaire's ear as one finger pressed forward.

Zaire hitched his leg higher, giving Aaron more space to pump into his ass. "More, Daddy! I can take more!"

A second finger joined the first, Aaron taking him at his word. Zaire could feel Aaron's cock resting against his lower back while Aaron prepared him. As a third joined in, Zaire groaned, closing his eyes and felt: every slide of his fingers in his passage, every heated breath against his neck, every area of his body humming with arousal, and the press of Aaron's much larger cock against his hole. Zaire bore down, arching his ass to get closer, to get Aaron inside him quicker.

Aaron took it slow. Short, continual thrusts once he'd passed the tight ring of muscles had Zaire delirious. His eyes rolled back in his head, and Aaron's grip tightened against Zaire's leg as his hips pumped. Sweat coated them. The sound of their bodies coming together was loud in the quiet room, and Zaire loved every minute of it.

His eyes blinked open, gaze snagging on his collar,

and his orgasm flared closer. "Wait," he gasped, and Aaron immediately stopped, though didn't pull out.

"What's wrong, sweet boy?" Aaron panted, tension radiating through him.

"My collar."

Zaire felt a kiss press to his spine and, "Can you grab it?"

He reached forward, hooking it with the tips of his fingers and sliding it forward so he could grasp it. He held it up, and, carefully, Aaron took it from him, wrapping it around his neck and buckling it, all the while keeping their hips pressed together so Zaire could feel every inch of him inside him as his collar was fastened back where it should be.

Once it was done, Aaron held him close, kissing his shoulder. "It's perfect for you."

"You're perfect for me," he responded, turning his head for a kiss, which soon turned into a frenzy when Aaron's hips began to move once more.

The collar tugged at Zaire with every movement, with every swallow, and he loved the reminder of who he belonged to, and it increased his arousal. He was right on the precipice when Aaron canted his hips.

"Oh, fuck! Yes, Daddy! Can I come? Please! I'm so close." He rambled off more words, or maybe incoherent mumblings, he had no idea.

"God, you feel so fucking good. Yes, sweet boy. Come for me."

Aaron's hips pistoned inside him as Zaire's climax strained his body. His release dragged Daddy's name from his lips, and he felt nothing but pleasure flooding his system. He came back to himself to find Aaron, slowly pumping his hips.

"You with me, Zaire?" he asked.

"Yes, Daddy."

"Good. My turn."

Chapter Fourteen

AARON

Aaron rolled them so Zaire was almost on his stomach, and Aaron could brace his hands either side of Zaire's chest. One of Zaire's legs was bent, Aaron straddled his other. Once in a suitable position, Aaron withdrew slowly, both groaning, before he slammed his hips forward, Zaire hissing, probably because his sensitive cock brushed against the sheets below him. Aaron thrust repeatedly, watching Zaire watch him over his shoulder. Aaron's climax drew near, and he threw his head back and pressed his hips tightly against Zaire's ass as his orgasm rocked through him. He stayed that way for a few seconds until the tension released him, and he dropped his head to Zaire's shoulder.

"You okay, sweet boy?" Aaron asked.

"Perfect, Daddy."

"Yes, you are." Aaron lifted his head and smiled, leaning forward to kiss Zaire's lips and ending up groaning as his cock pressed further in again. Pulling back, Aaron withdrew and immediately felt bereft. He quickly cleaned them both up and snuggled Zaire back against him on the dry part of the bed with a kiss to the side of his neck, above the collar.

"You like the collar?" he asked, a hint of humour bleeding through his voice.

"Uh-huh. Love it," a sleepy voice answered.

"Sleep, sweetheart. We have all day."

Zaire's soft snores sounded several minutes later, and Aaron grinned. There was no way he'd be able to go back to sleep, even with the warm body next to him, but damn if he was going to move before he had to. The warnings Nora gave him last night were ringing in his ears; even though Zaire reassured him, Aaron couldn't drop the worry completely, but he needed to at least pack it away. Otherwise, he would be obsessing over it and would probably ruin their relationship instead.

With it being Saturday, they had nowhere to be, but after an hour or so, he became restless, so rather than wake Zaire with his fidgeting, he got up and pulled on some joggers. Heading to the kitchen to get some breakfast and a cup of tea, he thought about what to do today. Maybe Zaire would like a trip to the aquarium. It was something adults did as well as children, but if Zaire felt uncomfortable, they could leave. He made a note to ask when Zaire woke. Zaire had mentioned rock climbing, and while it was not Aaron's idea of a good time, he would happily take and watch Zaire. He wouldn't take part himself.

He sat with his toast and tea and grabbed the book

he'd already started. He'd not read as much since meeting Zaire, but he was soon lost in the world.

A hand sliding around his shoulders made him jump as engrossed in the fictional world as he was, and he flicked his gaze to Zaire's.

"Hi, Daddy."

"Hi, sweet boy. How are you feeling?" The chemise Zaire had worn last night was in place but with satin underwear and a long satin robe. "You look edible," he growled, feeling his cock perk up.

"Thank you."

Aaron slid his hand around the back of Zaire's neck —and collar—and dragged him into a hot and steamy kiss. Within seconds, he gentled it and nibbled at Zaire's bottom lip before letting go. "Would you like some breakfast?"

"It's okay. I can—" Zaire started, pausing when Aaron raised an eyebrow at him. "I would love breakfast, thank you. I'm sorry. I find it difficult to let go when we're at my house," Zaire admitted as he sat at the table.

Aaron rose and set the toaster going. "I understand, but I love taking care of you. Would you like butter or jam on your toast?" Aaron would bet Zaire wanted jam but would ask for butter.

As a blush tinted his cheeks, Zaire mumbled, "Jam, please."

Aaron beamed at him. "Good boy." He fetched the jam and some milk from the fridge, rummaging around to find a cup for Zaire to use. Finally, he grabbed a plastic tumbler and half-filled it. He wasn't sure if Zaire went little or just boy and didn't want to push things too far.

Usually, he would ask the boy, but he was afraid Zaire would reject everything out of principle, even though he'd had Daddies before. Aaron shook his head inwardly. Ever since Nora had mentioned the bump, he had been second-guessing everything. Although he knew his thoughts might be unfounded, he decided to test the waters with some items and watch Zaire's reactions instead of asking him.

The milk in a child's tumbler, the toast with jam cut into triangles, and an apple cut into slices were placed before Zaire as if he'd had them many times before. Aaron refilled his tea and sat back down as if nothing was amiss.

Out of the corner of his eye, he noticed Zaire hesitate and smile before ducking his head and picking up a slice of toast. When he'd finished his breakfast, Aaron gathered the plates and cup and took them to the sink, returning to Zaire and crouching in front of him.

"You did so well, my sweet boy. I thought we could visit the aquarium today. What do you think?"

Zaire's eyes lit up. "Really?"

Aaron nodded, heart content at giving Zaire what he enjoyed as well as what he needed. "Do you have any toys or colouring here?" He pushed a bit to see if Zaire would admit to wanting to do something.

Zaire stared at Aaron, biting his lip as he considered his answer. Minutely, his head nodded slowly.

Heart racing with the strength of the man seated in front of him, he smiled. "Would you like to play while I clean up?"

Zaire's gaze roamed his face, possibly searching for

any hint of disapproval or laughter, before he nodded again.

"Go on. I'll be there in a few minutes." Aaron rose, kissing Zaire's forehead. "Well done for telling the truth."

Zaire ducked his head and snuggled into Aaron, hiding his face in Aaron's chest. "I'm so used to hiding everything. It's difficult to open up after so long."

"I know, sweetheart, and I understand. I'm here to take care of you, to help you be who you want to be, to help us become who we want to be together. I won't make fun of you or be ashamed of you for what you want. You need to tell me, or I'll have to keep guessing."

"Okay, Daddy. I'll try."

"Go on. Go play."

Zaire stepped back and grinned, then pivoted and almost skipped out of the room. Aaron took a moment to lean back against the counter and digest that Zaire was his, at least for as long as Zaire wanted him. He was perfectly imperfect. A boy who needed a Daddy to help guide him. Breathing deeply to deny the sudden onset of happy tears, Aaron turned and washed their dishes before drying and putting them away. Once everything was back to normal, and he believed Zaire had enough time to relax, he grabbed his book and entered the living room.

He smiled when he saw Zaire laid on his stomach on the floor, surrounded by several Postman Pat houses, vehicles and characters. Currently, Zaire was conversing as two of the characters about some missing delivery, complete with voices. The sofa called to him, and he made his way over, making sure to become visible to

Zaire so he didn't make him jump. He noticed Zaire pause what he was doing and, when Aaron sat on the sofa and opened his book, went back to playing.

Aaron had no interest in the book at all, he flipped a few pages, allowing Zaire to believe he was reading, but he wasn't. He was watching his boy having fun and being so relaxed. Aaron desperately needed to help Zaire merge the two sides of his personality, but the question was, how?

There were almost three aspects to Zaire's personality: his work demeanour, his sexy clothes one, and his boy, although the sexy clothes and the boy seem to work seamlessly together. Zaire appeared to love wearing the clothes as a boy, too. Maybe Aaron could start by helping Zaire choose different clothes for work. There was certainly no need for him to wear suits. He could choose one of the three-quarter-length trousers or the rhinestone jeans Aaron had seen in there. Or even a lacy top instead of a shirt. It would take a lot more to get him to wear those items, and he wasn't sure if Zaire would fight him on it. Aaron would never make him feel uncomfortable, but there must be a way to help him. A phone call to Nora would be in his near future. Advice was needed from his best friend.

The clock showed it was time to get ready to go. "Time to tidy up, Zaire," he said quietly, not wanting to startle him.

Zaire looked at him, his stress-free face a balm to Aaron's soul. "Is it time for the aquarium, Daddy?"

"Yes, sweetheart. We need to have a shower, get dressed, and we can go."

"Yay!" Zaire scrambled to his knees and packed away the toys into a blue box Aaron had not noticed before, and when Zaire tidied the box into the cabinet, Aaron understood why. He had it hidden from view. "I'm ready, Daddy."

Aaron smiled. "Come on. Let's get cleaned up." He held out his hand for Zaire.

Thirty minutes later, Zaire stamped his foot and crossed his arms. "No, I'm not wearing that."

"Zaire. Is that how you talk to your Daddy?"

"I don't want to wear that top. It looks horrible on me," he whined.

Aaron frowned. "What do you mean it looks horrible. Why?"

"It makes me look skinny like it doesn't fit me properly, and I don't like it!" Zaire yelled the last part, and Aaron had enough.

He strode to the other side of the room and turned the armchair to face the wall. Having remembered Zaire had complained about this particular punishment before, Aaron decided it was the perfect time to show Zaire who was in charge again.

"Zaire? Sit down here. Now." He waited until Zaire stomped over and dropped himself into the chair, arms crossed. "I will not have you talk to me like that. You will stay here for thirty-five minutes, and when the time is over, you better have something to say to me."

"But—"

"Quiet!"

Zaire sighed, and Aaron went back to the wardrobe. He had no issue with Zaire not wanting to wear certain clothes. He could refuse to wear every item Aaron asked him to, but what Aaron wouldn't tolerate was being spoken to like that. There were better ways for Zaire to make his point. Aaron heard a snuffle from the armchair, and it broke his heart, but he refused to cave.

Aaron shuffled through the clothes that were hanging up, finding a strappy top similar to the halter-neck Zaire had worn the other night, but in white with a silver mesh over the top. He thought Zaire would look amazing in it. He chose some light blue skinny jeans and a white pair of ballet flats to complete the outer ensemble. He went to the underwear drawer and chose something fitting. Laying them all on the bed, he checked the time and sat against the headboard, not wanting to leave his boy alone.

When the time was up, Aaron rose and crouched in front of Zaire, witnessing the tear tracks left along his cheeks. "Good boy, Zaire."

Zaire threw his arms around Aaron's neck, knocking him backwards and onto his ass with a chuckle. "I'm so sorry, Daddy. I'm so sorry." Zaire repeated it over and over again as Aaron petted his hair and held him tight to calm him.

"It's okay, sweetheart. All done now." He murmured some more words until Zaire loosened his hold.

"I really am sorry, Daddy. I need to use my good words, not my bad ones."

"Exactly. But it's all over now. Let's get dressed. Come see what I've chosen, and if you don't like any of it, let me know calmly."

They rose and wandered over to the bed. Aaron

watched Zaire's expression, wanting to catch any unsure looks before they peaked.

"I love it."

Relief flowed through Aaron, and he helped his boy get dressed as he asked some questions about how Zaire wanted to play out the day.

"Do you want to be a boy when we're out or boyfriends?"

Zaire hesitated, biting his lip again. "I've never been a boy in public before. My previous Daddies only wanted it to be at home or clubs."

Once again, Aaron felt like he could throttle those irresponsible Daddies. It seemed Zaire's experiences were less than stellar. "We could always see how it goes. If you don't feel right, don't, but if it does, go for it. There's no right or wrong answer, Zaire."

"What do you want?"

Aaron measured his words, not wanting to push anything on Zaire. "I would like to be able to take care of you while we are out as well as at home."

"Alright. Can we try? And if I don't like it, then we stop?"

"Of course! Well done for trying, sweetheart. You're so brave. I'm so proud of you."

Zaire blushed and gave a big smile as Aaron helped him with his shoes.

"One more question. Do you want to keep your collar on in public?"

Zaire nodded before Aaron had even finished his sentence. "Yes, Daddy. Definitely."

"Right. I think we're ready to go."

THE RIDE to the aquarium was uneventful, although Zaire had found the website on his phone and got excited about all the different things he read about. The seahorses, starfish and turtles were the favourites going by how often Zaire mentioned them.

Aaron had to keep himself from chuckling the closer they walked to the place after parking the car because Zaire bounced on his feet and talked a mile a minute. At least, until Zaire saw the place. Aaron had honestly thought Zaire had been to the aquarium before, but when Aaron asked him, he'd said he hadn't. When they came upon the large building made from lots of windows, Zaire stopped and stared, mouth open. If it wasn't likely to spoil the moment, Aaron would've taken a photo. Instead, he pulled on Zaire's hand and, as pure unadulterated joy crossed Zaire's face, they entered.

"Oh my god," Zaire whispered, eyes round as he took in everything around him.

Aaron had been many times but tried to see it as though he hadn't. There was a reception area to the left, and to the right was a walkway, which, when followed, would take them to every area of the underwater haven. They would be able to cut in and out to different areas if they wanted to, but Aaron would try and keep Zaire on the winding route, so they didn't miss anything. From where they stood, they could see an enormous, floor-to-ceiling, cylindrical glass tube in the centre of the area, holding a multitude of rainbow-coloured fish.

"Let me go and pay, and we'll head on through, okay,

sweet boy," he murmured in Zaire's ear, receiving a distracted nod in return. He kept his eye on Zaire as he waited for his turn and joined him once more, Zaire wrapping his arm around Aaron's biceps. It appeared to be a favourite position for Zaire.

"Come on. The underwater beauty awaits."

Aaron couldn't remember a time when he had smiled so much at the genuine joy and exuberance of someone. Every little thing was magical for Zaire, and he was like a kid on Christmas morning. This was what Aaron had missed all these years. Taking care of Zaire was amazing, but Aaron also got to see Zaire's awe at experiencing something new…something Aaron had been able to give him. As he watched Zaire, his heart filled more. He knew there was no turning back for him. Not now.

Chapter Fifteen

ZAIRE

Zaire could not believe how amazing the aquarium was. He had always wanted to go but had never been inclined to go by himself. In some ways, he wished he had gone before because he hadn't realised what he was missing, but in other ways, he was glad because he'd been able to share it with Aaron.

They'd taken a few selfies of themselves in front of different exhibits. It had been a fantastic day, and although they were on their way home, Zaire had loved every tiring minute of it.

He rolled his head on the headrest towards Aaron, watching as he concentrated on the road ahead. "Did you have a good day, Daddy?"

Aaron spared a glance at him and grinned. "I had a wonderful time, Zaire. We'll have to go back again sometime."

Zaire beamed. "Really? I'd love to go back. The seahorses are so small, I never realised that. And as for their babies, they are so cute," he said in a high, squeaky voice, then giggled. Actually, fucking, giggled. That thought had Aaron snorting and shaking his head.

"What's so funny?"

Zaire sighed, smiling out the window as he thought about the day. "I realised how happy I am. I didn't feel strange when I called you Daddy, and I was able to ignore any weird looks being sent our way. It was nice not to have to worry about anything because I knew you were there to take care of me."

"Yes, I was, and I will continue to if you'll allow me."

Zaire bit his lip. "I'd love that."

BY FRIDAY MORNING, Zaire was so calm and content, he didn't even mind getting up early to get ready for work. He'd stayed at Aaron's the previous night, but they'd grabbed some clothes from Zaire's house on the way back from rock climbing, or rather, Aaron had grabbed the clothes. His weekend had been unbelievable: the aquarium on Saturday and rock climbing on Sunday. Zaire's perfect weekend. He'd spent the majority of the time as a boy, letting Aaron do whatever he needed to do to look after Zaire, and he'd spent time watching TV and relaxing with his toys. At several points, Aaron had joined him on the carpet and raced cars around the track or helped build a castle to protect the people from an evil dragon. It had been wonderful. The working week had been a normal week at Aaron's school. It was his last day there because Aaron had found a replacement for him, and although he was sad, he knew he was making the right choice. He didn't want to confuse the lines of their relationship: Daddy and boy, or boss and employee.

"Zaire? Time for breakfast!" Aaron called from the kitchen.

Zaire grinned and raced down the stairs, tightening his robe around his waist as he went and stopped by his chair. "Pancakes!"

Aaron laughed. "Yes, sweet boy. You deserve a good breakfast before work this morning." He checked his watch. "We will have to leave soon, so make sure you eat up, and I'll help you get ready."

"Yes, Daddy." Zaire sat and drizzled some syrup onto his bite-sized pancakes and proceeded to inhale them.

"Woah, slow down there, buddy. You'll make yourself sick." Aaron rested his hand on Zaire's wrist.

Zaire swallowed what was in his mouth before answering, "I thought we were in a rush?"

Chuckling, Aaron replied, "Not that much of a rush! Take your time. I have coffee to drink." He held up his cup. "Don't forget your milk, too."

Zaire gave a closed mouth smile, which no doubt looked like a chipmunk from the food he had stuffed in it, but he didn't care. He felt…carefree. Like he could conquer the world.

After washing his face in the bathroom to get rid of the syrup, Zaire joined a hesitant Aaron in the bedroom.

"I have chosen some clothes, but they're not what you usually wear. Please talk to me—properly—about any issues you have with them." Aaron raised his eyebrow, and Zaire understood his meaning.

Seeing what was spread out before him had Zaire's heart racing. There was a slimline version of the tailored trousers he usually wore, and a cream shirt with lace at the shoulders. He could see Aaron had tried to keep things close to what Zaire usually wore, but now they had a gentler look. There would be no doubt in anyone's mind at work that he liked to wear what he knew they would call feminine clothing. He wasn't sure if he could do it. Memories of his father's words flitted through his head, girl, pussy, weak. He'd avoided receiving those comments by separating himself, and only visiting places he knew would be accepting of what he wore. Anywhere else, he was 'normal.'

"I…I don't know if…" He cleared his throat, staring at the bed.

Aaron wrapped his arms around him from behind. "You can say no, Zaire. I never want to make you feel uncomfortable. But I would like to try and find a happy medium between your work and home lives." Aaron pressed several kisses against the side of his face and neck.

In his mind's eye, Zaire could see how the outfit would look on him, and he realised he wanted to try. It surprised him how much he wanted it. He didn't know if he could, though.

"Can I take a change of clothes with me?" he whispered.

The arms holding him tightened briefly. "Of course, you can. You tell me what you need, and I will make it happen, sweet boy."

Zaire exhaled heavily. "Okay. Let's try this."

Aaron spun him around and pressed their lips together in a quick kiss. "You are so brave. Don't let anyone tell you any different. You deserve the chance to be who you are, Zaire. And I would love to be able to help you get there."

His hands gripped the back of Aaron's shirt as he pressed his cheek against his chest until he remembered they needed to be quick. "Oh, we'll be late!" He pulled away and undid the belt of the robe.

"We're okay, sweetheart. Don't worry."

As Aaron dressed him, Zaire became concerned about the reaction to his clothing, not only from staff but from the children as well. When he mentioned it to Aaron, he simply said, "Tell the children the truth. You like wearing them because they make you feel happy." And if that didn't sum up Zaire's feelings about the matter, nothing did.

He felt tears prick at his eyes, but he refused to let them fall. They were happy tears, but he knew he would worry Aaron. Finally dressed, Zaire stood in front of the mirror and studied himself. He looked good. It seemed strange seeing himself in the clothes but no makeup. He usually wore makeup when he was wearing—what he was now calling—his home clothes, but he felt it was a step too far at that moment.

"Time to go, sweetheart!"

Zaire picked up the bag with his change of clothes and padded down the stairs. He was surprised to find Aaron stood at the bottom, holding a box out. He tilted his head and frowned. "What's this?"

"A gift."

Zaire grinned and placed his bag on the floor. He lifted the lid of the box and moved the tissue paper aside, revealing a beautiful pair of black leather ankle boots with a small heel.

"I knew you didn't have any work shoes to go with your outfit, so I found these. I hope you like them." Aaron's voice sounded unsure, and Zaire stared at him, incredulous.

"I love them! But when…?" He shook his head, returning his gaze to the boots.

"I bought them online and got a quick delivery. I had hoped you'd agree to the clothes I set out for you but didn't want to presume. These would've kept until you were able to take that step." Aaron cleared his throat. "I chose some with only a small heel because I know you are sometimes on the floor with the children and rushing around. I didn't want you to chance falling in higher ones."

"They are perfect, Daddy. Thank you so much!" Zaire took the box from Aaron's hands, placed it down and twined his arms around Aaron's neck. "Thank you," he said sincerely and pressed his lips against Aaron's.

The kiss was bittersweet. Zaire tried to show everything he was feeling in the kiss because he knew he couldn't say the words yet. When the kiss ended, Zaire pulled away and, with a grin, plonked himself on the stairs and slid on his new boots. He knew they might pinch a bit by the end of the day, but he didn't care.

"Come on, my boy. Let's go slay some dragons." With a wink, Aaron opened the front door of his home, and Zaire walked through.

"OH MY GOD! YOU LOOK..." Zaire waited for Uma to finish what she was saying, but his heart raced, and his cheeks flooded with heat. "amazing!" She came to him and embraced him tightly. "I knew there was something inside of you that you kept locked away. I hoped one day you'd have the courage to fly, and I'm thinking Aaron had something to do with this change."

Zaire breathed deeply, flooding his body with much-needed oxygen. "He did."

"Well, I love it. The outfit suits you, and, apart from looking a little pale, you seem lighter."

Grinning, he said, "I feel it, too. I never realised how much holding back was weighing on me. I'm a nervous wreck," he held out his hands to show how much they were shaking, "but I need to do this."

"I agree. You can't live your life hiding, Zaire. What's the point if you do? Be who you want to be, not who you're told to be."

Zaire leaned in and hugged Uma again, pulling away when the next staff member entered, the butterflies starting all over again. When nothing was said, and no snide comments were made, he relaxed once more. He wasn't naïve enough to believe everyone would be as accommodating, but so far, so good.

It was when assembly arrived, he encountered problems.

"What are you wearing?" A voice sneered from behind where he was sat at the side of the big hall.

Zaire glanced over his shoulder, already feeling heat

bleed into his cheeks and his muscles clenching with a tension he had hoped would stay gone. Simon was sat, looking him up and down as if he were dog shit on his shoe. Zaire's gaze flicked to the children looking at them with interest from the floor next to them. There was no way they couldn't have heard what Simon had said. He gave them a small smile, turned back towards the front where another teacher was telling a story and swallowed hard, beating back the threat of tears.

"You look like a girl. Is that what you are now? Aaron will hardly go for you if that's what you're trying for."

Zaire ignored the comment, concentrating on the children and the words being spoken from in front of him, not behind. He saw Uma, looking over at him, and she mouthed, "You okay?" to which he nodded and tried for a half-smile. He had no idea whether he managed it or not. Probably not, given the look she returned him.

He stood for their physical activity session, wriggling around and making the kids laugh as they joined in with him.

"God, you're even wearing girly shoes. Jesus Christ," the same voice continued when he returned to sitting.

Zaire honestly didn't know if he could keep the clothes on after Simon's comments. Everyone he worked with in Uma's classroom and all the children had loved what he wore. The children were amazing and had asked lots of questions. Even though what he wore was not feminine, there was a definite softer vibe going on, and the children saw it. He'd done exactly what Aaron had told him to do and explained that the clothes made him feel good about himself and happy, so why shouldn't he wear them? They'd accepted it. One child had even come up to him and whispered, "I want to be a princess when I grow up," and Zaire had hugged him and told him he could be whatever he wanted to be.

When faced with adults, it was a different matter. They were already so set in their ways and beliefs, he knew there was no way he would be able to change their minds about certain things. His choice of clothing one of them. Others had their own stereotypes firmly planted in their heads, and nothing Zaire said would ever change them. He didn't want to in some respects. What he did want was for people to stop thinking it was okay for them to force their opinions on others, especially children. How many times had he heard the phrase, 'Do unto others as you would have them do unto you?"

Unfortunately, it didn't apply to a lot of people.

As he stood and adjusted his top, getting ready to lead the pupils back to the classroom, Simon's parting comment hurt.

"People like you should not be allowed in schools. I don't need to dress like that to get men."

Zaire bit his lip hard enough to hurt, trying to stem the tears threatening. He would not give in to them when the students were looking to him for guidance. He smiled through his pain, inhaling through his nose and took them back for playtime. His sister's voice aimed at their mother floated through his head, "You're choosing this prissy fag over me and Dad?" As soon as the children were occupied outside with their supervisor, Zaire returned to the classroom.

"Are you okay, Zaire?" Uma came over and draped

an arm around his shoulder, rubbing the top of his arm repeatedly in a calming gesture.

"Not really. I need to go and change," he muttered, twisting away from her.

"Why?"

"I can't...do this," he said, throat thick, gesturing to down his body. "I'll be back in a few minutes."

"Zaire, wait!" Uma called after him, but Zaire left the room.

He hustled towards the staff room, wanting to avoid others as much as possible. He refused to break down in front of people he worked with. The closer he got to Aaron's office, which he had to pass to reach the staff room, the easier it was to discern voices.

"—children think, eh? What about the parents when the children go home talking about it? You will have the phone ringing off the hook about this."

"It is none of your concern, Simon." Aaron's voice was tense, and if Zaire was not mistaken, angry.

"What do you mean it's none of my concern. I'm thinking about school. The whole picture. You might want to change things around here, Aaron, but some things will not be accepted."

"I will change things in this school, and you have no choice but to go along with it. For instance, this animosity you have for Zaire is not about how he is dressed, is it?"

Zaire had been about to scamper past the open door but froze with the words Aaron spoke.

"I see how you watch him. You could do so much better."

"You mean you? No, thank you, Simon. I have told you before. I'm not interested."

There was silence for several tense minutes, and Zaire was ready to flee in case one or the other exited the office.

"How can you let him in this school dressed like that! He looks like a girl!"

"No, he doesn't. He looks like a boy. My boy. So, back the fuck off and get out!"

Chapter Sixteen

AARON

With those words, Aaron flung his hand out, indicating the door. He was fuming. He couldn't remember the last time he had been so angry as he was at that moment. Everything inside and out was vibrating with a wave of fury so strong, he could taste it.

Simon glared at him and marched over to the door, flinging it wide so it banged against the wall loudly and stopped. Standing in the doorway was Zaire, and Aaron had no doubt he had heard enough to be ready to run.

"Zaire? Come here, please." Aaron's voice brooked no argument, although he could see Zaire wanting to. Zaire remained stubbornly where he was, gaze flicking from Aaron to Simon and back again. "Simon, leave. Now! You've done enough today, I think. We will be taking this further."

"You bet your ass I'll be taking this further. Enjoy the time with your girlfriend," he sneered as he slunk past Zaire.

"Zaire!"

Zaire's pained gaze met his, and Aaron wanted to soften towards him, but it was not what Zaire needed right now.

"In my office. Now."

Zaire shuffled forward until he was a step across the doorway, and Aaron withheld a chuckle at the show of obedience versus Zaire's need to run.

"Shut the door and come stand in front of me."

The door clicked shut, the sound loud in the silence. Zaire stepped closer to Aaron, but there was too much space as far as Aaron was concerned.

"Here," he said, pointing to the floor right in front of him. Zaire trailed closer until they were almost toe to toe, and Zaire had to lift his head to look at Aaron. "His words mean nothing. Do you understand?"

Zaire swallowed, his Adam's apple bobbing quickly, but he didn't reply.

"His words mean nothing. Do you understand me?" Aaron reiterated, this time with a raised eyebrow.

Zaire licked his lips, and his nostrils flared. "Yes," he uttered.

"I didn't hear you."

"Yes," Zaire said louder, though Aaron could hear the tremor.

"How did your colleagues react this morning when you entered the classroom?" Aaron made sure to keep their gazes locked. He didn't want to lose Zaire's focus.

"Um…everyone was nice."

"Did anyone say anything horrible to you?"

Zaire shook his head.

"Are you close to those people in your class?"

Zaire nodded. Aaron would allow him the non-vocal answers for the moment.

"If you had to spend time with the people in your class or Simon, who would you choose?"

Zaire's eyebrows lifted, creasing his forehead. "What? My class, of course."

"Why are you letting the words of a man you do not want anything to do with affect how you feel about yourself? Or how you think other people feel about you? You already have the evidence from your class colleagues. And I can't imagine the children saying anything mean to you."

Zaire shook his head, a small smile playing around his mouth. "No, they had a lot of questions, like you said they would, but they were so accepting of it."

"Those are the people whose minds we need to focus on changing. The children. This world needs to grow up believing in themselves, believing they can be whoever they want to be and be accepted. And I believe we need to start with the children here, at this age. Teach them what is unusual, out of the ordinary and make them believe it is 'normal.' I want it so very much." Aaron's passion bled into his words. He hated that people didn't consider others. He wanted a world that was free of prejudice, free of hate, free for everyone. He knew it was a pipe dream, but if he could change even one child's view, he would be happy.

"Thank you."

"Thank you, what?"

Zaire smiled and looked at him from under his lashes. "Thank you, Daddy."

"Better." He wrapped his arms around Zaire's waist and pulled him closer, not caring they could be viewed from the school car park. "Were you coming to see me?"

"Huh?" Zaire's brows drew together.

"You were outside my office. Did you need me?"

Zaire focused on Aaron's shirt. "No. I was coming… to get changed," he admitted softly.

Aaron pressed a finger under Zaire's chin until their eyes met. "And now?"

"Now, I need to get back to the children."

"Good boy."

Aaron closed the remaining distance between their mouths and tasted coffee and Zaire. He wanted nothing more than to take it further than the exploration of Zaire's mouth he had managed before a knock at his door sounded. He pulled away, breathing heavily.

"Yes?" he called.

"Mr Brown, Uma asked me to locate Zaire, but I can't find him. She's worried," Pamela answered through the door.

"You can come in, Pamela."

Zaire moved to pull away, but Aaron tightened his grip on him, restricting the space he could move.

Pamela opened the door, stopping, eyes wide. "Ah, I see." They smirked. "You could have told me you knew where he was." They rested a hand on their cocked hip.

"But I wouldn't be able to revel in his blush, would I?" Zaire pushed away, but Aaron pressed a kiss to his forehead first and allowed him space to leave. "Oh, and Zaire?" He waited until Zaire faced him. "Be a good boy and come see me if you have any more issues, okay?"

"Yes, I will." Zaire turned to leave, but once more, Aaron stopped him, needing the words, despite their audience.

"Yes, what?" he growled.

Zaire's gaze flicked to Pamela, who was standing there silently, then back to him. "Yes, Daddy," he whispered as he turned and fled.

"That wasn't nice," Pamela noted.

"He needed to say it. We both needed him to say it in front of someone at work who cares about us." Aaron hadn't realised how much that was true until he said it out loud. He and Pamela had many discussions in the past about their aligned kinks when Pamela had inadvertently seen something Aaron had been looking at.

"I'm glad I was able to help."

"I need your help again now."

"What's up, boss?"

Aaron chuckled at their response. "I want to know everything about Simon. Simon has been put on my shit list after talking crap about Zaire." At their raised brows, he added, "I would be like this had he said it about anyone."

"I know. I've never heard you swear before."

"Not loud enough for you to hear anyway." He laughed. "Simon is denying Zaire the right to wear what he wants. He wants Zaire out of the school to stop him—and I quote—looking like a girl. I want his head on a platter, Pamela. Nobody is allowed to stop someone from being what they want to be in my school." His voice rose at the end of his sentence, his anger returning tenfold.

"Firstly, calm down. Secondly, I will see to it. Thirdly, speak to Uma. Safety in numbers. Until we have something on Simon other than 'he said, he said,' we need to be careful. You do not want to be sued for wrongful dismissal."

Aaron inhaled deeply, resting his hands on his hips as he stared outside. Pamela was right. He needed to be careful; otherwise, Simon would be staying, and Aaron would be out instead of the reverse.

"Thank you, Pamela."

"Just doing my job," they replied as they exited, closing the door behind them.

Aaron settled himself behind his desk, determined to get some work done before any more distractions happened.

When the clock rolled around to three o'clock, Aaron left his office and headed towards Zaire's class. He would not allow Simon to corner Zaire at any point, and it would give him the chance to have a quick word with Uma.

He entered the class as the children were lining up by the door to be collected. A few children called, "Good-bye, Mr Brown!" to which he replied with a wave and a smile. At his name, he saw Zaire glance up, blush and return to cleaning up. He headed over to Uma's desk and sat on her chair, waiting while she saw the children to their parents.

"Can I help you, Mr Brown?" Uma asked with a twinkle in her eye.

"Actually, yes," he replied, vacating her chair, indicating for her to sit and seeing her eyebrows rise at his serious tone as opposed to her joking one.

"What's wrong?"

He leaned his hip against her desk, keeping an eye on Zaire as he answered, voice low, "Simon is causing issues. I'm handling it at the moment, but I need your help to keep an eye on Zaire. I do not want it escalating more than what it is now."

"And what is it now?"

"Simon has made his thoughts clear on what he believes is needed at this school, and what is not."

"Asshole," she cursed.

"I'm going to speak to the governors and get their backing, but I want Simon gone. I do not want his words hurting any of my staff."

"Okay. Not a problem."

"Thank you. And I'm pinching your helper." He grinned as he pushed away from the desk. "Zaire? Come on. I need you." In more ways than one.

"But I need..." he trailed off when he saw Aaron's face.

"It's okay, Zaire. We're almost done. And besides, you came in early today," Uma backed Aaron up.

"If you're sure." Zaire looked anything but, though he dropped the toys he held into a box and straightened. "Have a good weekend, Uma."

"You, too. Both of you," she replied.

Aaron left the room with Zaire on his heels after Zaire collected his bag and coat.

"I need to nip to my office to grab some things, and we can head home."

"Okay."

Aaron wanted to get Zaire home so he could spoil him rotten. After the day Zaire had endured, Aaron wanted nothing more than to pamper the hell out of him. And it was exactly what he planned to do.

When they arrived at Aaron's house, he helped Zaire out of the car and held open the door for him. Helping him out of his coat and shoes, Aaron grasped his hand and led him up the stairs to the bedroom. Letting his eyes do the talking, Aaron stripped Zaire and himself, walked him to the bathroom and switched on the water. As he let it warm, he cupped Zaire's jaw, pressing little kisses from his forehead, down his nose and to his lips before sipping from his full lips. Once Zaire had relaxed into him, he pulled Zaire back into the shower and proceeded to wash every inch of his body, paying special attention to the hard to reach places.

Zaire's whimpers were music to his ears, and Aaron dropped to his knees. Taking Zaire's cock in his hand, Aaron aimed it towards his mouth and sucked the head.

"Oh my god!" Zaire's hand came to the back of Aaron's head, resting against it.

Aaron rubbed his tongue along the underside and around, seeking any precome he could find. He lowered his head, taking the shaft further into his mouth, hollowing his cheeks to create suction as he bobbed up and down. The hand against his head gripped tighter as

Aaron's ministrations became more focused on getting Zaire off rather than soothing him.

"Daddy!" Zaire called as his body tensed, and he shot his release down Aaron's throat.

The blowjob had been quick and dirty, but the aim was to help Zaire relax, which Aaron believed he had managed because when he stood, Zaire rested back against him like a wet noodle. Aaron proceeded to wash Zaire's cock once more, switched the shower off and dried him before picking him up and carrying him to the bed where he laid him down.

Zaire's eyes were closed, but Aaron knew he wasn't asleep. "I'll be back in a minute, sweet boy."

The whimper Zaire made when Aaron stepped away made him want to wrap himself around Zaire in the bed, but he had other plans. He grabbed some joggers from his bag and slid them on, ignoring his half-hard cock and stepped to the drawer of underwear and gorgeous things Zaire—and Aaron—loved so much. He picked out a silk vest and shorts combo and Zaire's favourite robe before stalking back to the bed. Zaire was lying on his back, but his breathing was more even than it had been.

"I'm here, sweetheart," he whispered. He pressed his hand gently against the bed next to Zaire's ankle, advertising where exactly he was so he didn't make Zaire jump and moved his hand to Zaire's shin. "I'm going to help you get dressed now."

The shorts were hooked over Zaire's feet and skimmed up his legs with minimum movement required from Zaire, but Aaron needed him to lift his hips. Zaire mumbled something which Aaron didn't catch but lifted, and Aaron slid them into place, running his hand across the front of them—and Zaire's spent cock.

"Let's sit you up, now." Aaron's slipped one arm underneath Zaire's back, helping him to a sitting position. Zaire's eyes were open but unfocused, the kind of look you get when you want to go to sleep but have to wake up. "Lift your arms." Zaire followed Aaron's instructions slowly. The vest was settled into place, and Aaron crouched in front of him. "We'll put your robe on, and you can go and play for a bit while I make dinner. How does that sound?"

Zaire gave a dozy smile and nodded. "Great, Daddy."

When Aaron had settled Zaire in the living room with his Postman Pat toys and cars, he hesitated by the door to the kitchen, looking back at the boy who had changed everything. In such a short time, Zaire had become everything to him. He didn't want this to be a short-term relationship. He was in it for the long-haul, and his need to keep Zaire safe was growing by the second, especially with what happened with Simon that day.

As Zaire sped the cars around the toy town, Aaron's mind was on their next steps—his next steps. Unless he could get more evidence of Simon's discrimination, there was nothing he could do about him without a possible lawsuit being drawn up against him. And Aaron knew he would get hammered in that situation because he had no proof of Simon's wrongdoings. He would take care of Zaire tonight, and they would have a discussion in the morning about the plans going forward. He would have to brace himself for Simon's behaviour to devolve more before he could do anything about it.

Zaire glanced over his shoulder and smiled at Aaron, and his heart soared. There was not much he could do about his need to look after Zaire—he was head over heels in love with him.

Chapter Seventeen

ZAIRE

After Aaron had tucked them into bed the night before and wrapped his arms around him, Zaire had lost himself to the oblivion of sleep. His weekend had, once again, been wonderful. Zaire hadn't a care in the world while Aaron had been looking after him. He played with his cars until dinner, which had been homemade macaroni cheese—his favourite—and they settled onto the sofa to watch Top Cat, while Aaron had read. When it had been bedtime, Aaron had led him up the stairs, kissed him hungrily and covered him before sliding in behind him. Zaire had never felt so relaxed, pampered and safe as he had at that moment.

When he woke that morning and realised it was Monday, he worried. He would be visiting a different school that day as his contract with Aaron's school had finished. He was trying to decide whether to continue becoming who he wanted to or stay as he had been for years. He stared at his toast as he chewed what was in his mouth. Aaron finished making his own breakfast and came to sit next to him.

"Are you okay, Zaire?" his Daddy asked.

Zaire took note of his emotions and answered, "I'm nervous. I'm going back and forth about what to wear." He rushed on when Aaron opened his mouth to say something, "I don't want Simon to win by changing who I am, but it's so easy to push myself back in the box, Daddy," he whispered.

"I know, sweetheart. I know. I will support you however you want to do this, but I don't want Simon to dull your shine. And Friday? You shone so brightly because you were true to yourself." Aaron covered his hand with his own and squeezed. "I will support you no matter what you decide to do."

"Thank you, Daddy."

"Finish your breakfast, then we can make all the diffi-cult decisions, alright?"

Zaire nodded because he'd taken a bite of toast. Aaron grinned at him and dug into his food.

Several minutes later, he stood in the centre of his bedroom, wringing his hands in indecision. Aaron stood in front of him, waiting for the answer to his question of what he was going to wear.

"I…"

Aaron rubbed his hands on Zaire's shoulders, calming him. "Whatever you decide," he reminded.

Zaire filled his lungs and blurted, "I want to wear my clothes, not my work clothes."

The smile that crossed Aaron's face made all the uncertainty worthwhile. Aaron leaned down and pressed a kiss to his lips then stalked to the wardrobe. "I know exactly what you could wear today if you want to. I saw it the other day when I was looking through them."

Zaire's heart was in his throat so he couldn't reply, but he smiled when Aaron looked over his shoulder at him, probably checking he hadn't run out of the room, screaming.

Aaron returned with something purple, and Zaire knew exactly what top it was. He bit his lip in a nervous tick. He knew he would wear it; it was one of his favourites. Aaron pottered around collecting items for a moment until he stood before Zaire once more.

"You okay?"

Zaire nodded, swallowing hard, but beginning to feel more certain about his decision.

"Let's get you ready."

Aaron helped dress him as he usually did, and it helped to centre Zaire even more. Once everything was in place, apart from his shoes, Zaire turned to the mirror. He wore black skinny trousers, ending above his ankle, and a mid-thigh length purple jumper that was also three-quarter sleeved. Zaire tilted his head, approving of the choice, but something was missing. He stepped to his drawers, chose a thin black belt and cinched it around his waist.

Zaire watched as Aaron stood behind him. His hands skimmed from Zaire's shoulders down his arms to link their fingers together. "You look gorgeous," Aaron growled in his ear, nibbling on his lobe. Zaire moved his head to the side as he rested it against Aaron's shoulder, and Aaron kissed down his exposed column. "If it wouldn't be a step too far, I would be marking you here, right now." Aaron licked at the area where his neck met his shoulder, and Zaire shivered. "Come on, my gorgeous boy. Let's show the world who you really are."

Nerves fluttered in his stomach with the words, but Zaire nodded in determination.

By lunchtime, Zaire's stomach was in knots. No one had said anything to him, but he had been getting a few side looks from staff and parents alike. He had to keep reminding himself this was what he wanted, what Aaron believed he was capable of, what he needed to become a whole person; otherwise, he would've changed into something different. Zaire believed in Aaron and that he would help him through this uncertain time. But Zaire also needed to grow a backbone—or rather re-grow his backbone. He never used to be unsure and nervous, but he also never used to merge the two halves of his life. He needed to regain his equilibrium and bring his confidence back. To do that, he needed to make peace with who he was becoming at work.

He loved that he was able to be himself more now, and it was helping him. It was the whispered comments he couldn't hear and couldn't fight against because he didn't know what they were saying. After finishing the pasta salad Aaron had made for him, he stalked to the kettle and made himself a drink. He only had a couple of hours left, and he would be picking Aaron up from the school. Aaron had wanted Zaire to be there as soon as he had finished.

When he parked the car in the staff car park, as Aaron had told him to, even though he was no longer working there, he got out and leaned against the side of the car, waving to some of the children as they left with their parents.

"Jesus Christ! Did you lose your brain cells along with your masculine clothes? You're not a staff member anymore. Move your car."

Simon's angry voice skated down Zaire's spine, and he clenched his jaw and fists, though didn't respond.

"Have you nothing to say?"

Zaire inhaled shakily. He had plenty to say, but he couldn't say it. Simon wouldn't listen anyway like Zaire's dad didn't.

"You're looking more and more like a girl every time I see you." Simon chortled, while Zaire closed his eyes. "You won't be able to hold onto Aaron looking like you do. He wants someone masculine; otherwise, he wouldn't be gay, you stupid hussy."

"Enough!"

Uma's voice startled Zaire, and he looked over Simon's shoulder to see several staff members, male and female, standing there. Simon turned, too, and Zaire saw when he paled at the audience.

"Either change your behaviour, Simon, or you'll be out. Zaire can dress and look however he wants to and will have the unwavering support of this school and many people in it. You and I had a conversation several months ago if you remember, and I told you to your face I was not interested. You have no say in who I have a relationship with. If you don't like it, leave."

Aaron's voice had Zaire swinging around to see him standing several steps to the side, an angry expression on his face. Zaire's heart raced at the number of people who had his back. He had never believed anyone would support his choices, but this show of people was almost more than his emotions could take. He swallowed hard against the tears, hoping they would stay locked away until he was in private.

"Fine. You will have my resignation on your desk tomorrow." Simon sneered at Zaire, looking him up and down, then pushed past him, stopping to the side of Aaron. "You'll regret choosing this…bitch," he growled, glaring at Zaire.

"Enough! Remove yourself from the property immediately. I do not need your resignation because you are fired with immediate effect. John, Ruth, please go with him and ensure he takes only what is his and leaves the property without issue."

Zaire knew what that meant. Aaron was concerned Simon would do something on his way out and wanted to reduce the chances of it. When the three had left, Zaire sagged back against the car, breathing hard.

"Are you okay, Zaire?" Uma's soft voice brought his gaze up to her concerned one, and he nodded. "I'm so glad I was near when he started."

"I wondered how you happened to be there."

"When I heard him yell at you, I got the attention of a few other people to make sure there were witnesses to whatever he did."

"I didn't do anything for him to say that. I—"

"Don't you dare blame yourself for what happened here."

Zaire flinched at the whip of Aaron's voice. He gazed

over at Aaron, seeing him standing where he had been, clenching his fists. Zaire couldn't think of anything to answer with.

"That man—and I use the term very loosely—deserved everything he got. You are in no way to blame for anything that happened. Do you understand me?"

"Yes."

"Yes, what?"

Zaire's eyes widened as he knew what Aaron wanted. He glanced around, seeing people moving away from them now the drama was over.

"Well?"

Returning his gaze to Aaron, he saw barely leashed anger vibrating through his Daddy, and he could do nothing more than obey. Zaire shuffled over and wrapped his arms around Aaron's waist. "Yes, Daddy."

As close as he was to Aaron, he felt the shiver that went through him and arms enclosed him in a too-tight hug, but Zaire wouldn't complain. If Aaron needed this, Zaire would let him have it.

"God, I'm so sorry you had to deal with that asshole. But I'm so proud of you. Standing strong and not talking back to him, not denying who you are?" Aaron tilted Zaire's head back and cupped his jaw, pressing his lips against his in a brief kiss. "You are such a brave boy. My boy." He hesitated, searching Zaire's face for something he must have found because he pressed another kiss to his lips and rested their foreheads together, whispering, "I love you, Zaire."

Tears overflowed, and he burrowed his face into his Daddy's neck. "I love you, too, Daddy. So much."

They stood there for a few moments before Aaron pulled away. "Let's go grab my things, and we can go home." Aaron held out his hand with a smile.

Zaire grinned and linked their fingers together.

ZAIRE DROPPED into the booth seat, four days later, with a huge sigh of relief. That week had been easier once he became a bit more confident in himself, but the school environment hadn't been completely welcoming. Several members of staff ignored him when he spoke unless there was no other option, but most of them were welcoming and didn't say a word about his clothing choices.

"Long day, huh?" Nora commented.

Zaire lifted his head from the back of the seat and half-smiled at her. "Long week." He chuckled half-heartedly.

"I know what that feels like," she replied.

"When does Geoff get back?"

She sighed. "In three days. God, I miss him when he's gone."

Geoff occasionally worked away from home, and it was one of the reasons they had come out tonight. Aaron had said Nora was moping and needed cheering up, so they had changed their plans of a night in to take her out instead. Zaire was tired, but he was determined to help Aaron distract her.

"He'll be home before you know it," Cord said, squeezing her shoulder.

"Do you like to dance?" Zaire asked her.

"Yeah."

"Come on." He slipped out of the booth and held out his hand. "Let's dance."

Zaire had no idea how long they had been dancing before he needed to sit down. They returned to the booth, seeing Rod and Delia had joined their group. Aaron slid out of his seat and let Zaire sit next to Delia, pulling out a stool to sit on instead and passed Zaire a bottle of water. Zaire grinned at him and drank half of it in one go.

"Thank you, Daddy."

"You're welcome."

"Zaire?" Rod's voice interrupted their mutual staring contest. "We have something to tell you. Two things, actually."

Zaire twisted in his seat to face his friend. "What's that?"

Rod looked at Delia and wrapped an arm around her shoulder, pulling her close. "Delia's pregnant."

"Oh my god! That's great news, guys!" He leaned forward and pulled them both into a hug.

"That's not all."

Zaire pulled back, narrowing his gaze. "It's not twins, is it? Because it would serve you right," he joked.

Delia laughed and punched his arm. "No, asshole."

"We got engaged, too," Rod said.

"Wow, you two have been busy." Zaire hugged them again and pulled back. "I'm so happy for you!"

"Congratulations to you both," Aaron said, holding out his hand. Rod shook it and thanked him.

Zaire knew he didn't want kids for himself, but he knew he'd be the best uncle in the world to them. He looked at Aaron, knowing he would spoil the kid rotten.

They spent the next few hours dancing, drinking, celebrating and commiserating in equal measures until Aaron declared it was time for them to go home. Zaire was secretly grateful for the news because he was shattered and wanted to sleep. As Aaron draped his jacket around Zaire's shoulders and snuggled him close, Zaire let out a contented sigh.

"See you guys soon," Aaron said, and Zaire waved at the table's occupants.

He woke when the car door opening made him jump.

"Sorry, I was trying to be quiet."

Zaire rubbed his eyes and realised they were at Aaron's house, which felt more like home than his own did. "It's okay. Sorry, I must've been tired."

"You're still tired. I'm taking you inside to bed, my sweet boy." Aaron helped Zaire out of the car and into the house, removing Zaire's shoes and coat for him. "Come on." They climbed the stairs, and Aaron led them to the bedroom. After quickly stripping Zaire and slipping a teddy over his head, Aaron pulled back the covers and tucked Zaire in. Sliding in behind, he spooned Zaire and rested a hand over his waist.

"Daddy?"

"Yes, sweetheart?"

"Can we go to the zoo tomorrow?"

"We'll see.

"Daddy?"

"Yes?"

"Can we find a cuddly toy for Rod and Delia's baby, too?"

"I don't see why not. Get some sleep."

"Daddy?"

Aaron chuckled, the exhale warm on the back of Zaire's neck. "Yes, Zaire?"

"I love you." Zaire threaded their fingers together and pulled Aaron's hand as close as he could.

"Love you, too, sweet boy."

Five Months Later

AARON

Aaron watched Zaire as he stood at the front of the assembly, reading the afternoon story to all the children. He was a natural and had everyone's attention, including staff. Zaire made the story come alive by using different voices and, occasionally, props. It made the children ask for him more often than not when they had the choice of narrator.

Zaire was now fully employed with the school after a long discussion between Aaron and the governors, who agreed Zaire could work there as long as any decisions needing to be made, which affected Zaire in any way, would be done jointly with the deputy headteacher. They wanted to ensure they couldn't be pointed at for favouritism. As soon as permission had been granted, Zaire had left the agency and joined the school full time one month ago, doing what he loved in Uma's class.

When Zaire finished the story, the children cheered, and he took a bow, his face beaming. Aaron strode up to the front and slid an arm around his shoulder, squeezing. "You're amazing," he whispered in Zaire's ear before turning to the children. "Wasn't that great?" The children responded with a loud affirmative. "Well, we can't do any better than that, so we are going to finish there. Please wait until your class teacher is ready before you stand. Good afternoon, children."

"Good afternoon, Mr Brown. Good afternoon, teachers."

Aaron realised he still had his arm around Zaire, and he removed it, though he didn't want to. "Are you okay?"

"Yep," Zaire confirmed with a grin.

"Any plans for this afternoon?" Aaron asked. They had not seen each other because Zaire had been at his mum's house over the weekend and had driven straight to school from her house that morning.

"Nope."

"Would you like to come round? I have a surprise for you." He didn't need to offer the enticement, but he did anyway.

"I'll be there. As always."

"Good. Don't take too long. You have a key. Use it if I'm not back before you."

"Yes," he looked around and whispered, "Daddy."

"Good boy."

With a wink, Aaron pivoted and left Zaire there. If he hadn't, he wouldn't have let him go back to the classroom and do his job. He would've taken him to his office and done things that would have gotten him fired. Two days and three nights without him was too long. Once in his office, he set to work, getting some paperwork finished. He needed something to take his mind off his boy.

Zaire's car was present when he arrived home, and he called for him when he entered the house. Quick footsteps sounded, and soon he was engulfed in his boy's arms as Zaire jumped up against him. Aaron laughed and wrapped an arm around his waist and under his hips as he walked further into the house.

"I missed you, sweet boy." He kissed him as he had wanted to do all day, demanding entry to Zaire's mouth and exploring the warm, wet area. Their tongues duelled as they fought to get closer to each other. Aaron turned and pressed Zaire against a wall, not wanting to hurt either of them by continuing to walk when he had his eyes closed from the pleasure of Zaire's mouth. Their hips thrust, their hardening cocks sliding together. Zaire's hands were in Aaron's hair, holding tight as moans left him.

They finally pulled away, gasping for air, and Aaron nuzzled his nose along Zaire's jaw and neck until he reached his favourite place. His teeth gained purchase on the area between his neck and shoulder, and he sucked—hard—marking Zaire where his skin was exposed with the off-the-shoulder jumper.

Zaire groaned, and his hips thrust harder against Aaron. "Daddy! Please. I need you."

Knowing his boy as he did now, Aaron reached a hand down and undid his trousers, pushing the fabric out of the way and slipping his hand between the satin and skin, gripping his cock.

"Oh! Daddy! Please!"

"I know, sweet boy. I've got you." Aaron pumped his hand, stroking up and down and twisting at the top, all the while kissing Zaire and muffling his moans and groans. Zaire's hips increased in speed, and Aaron knew he would not last much longer. He tightened his grip and kissed up to Zaire's ear. "Come for Daddy."

"Ah! Oh, fuck! I'm…" Zaire's cock released over Aaron's hand and no doubt over both their clothes, but he didn't care. All he cared about was the blissed-out look on Zaire's face as he regained his breathing.

Aaron brought his hand up and licked off the come from his fingers, watching Zaire's eyes dilate further at his actions. Once his hand was clean, he rested his hand under Zaire's ass and lifted him away from the wall. He carried him up the stairs to the bedroom and dropped him on the bed to Zaire's laughter.

Aaron stripped everything off and watched as Zaire got with the programme and did the same. When they were both naked, Aaron crawled over Zaire and took his mouth. His cock ached painfully and needed relief in the only place he could get it—with Zaire. Pulling away briefly to grab the lube, he slicked himself and settled between Zaire's legs. They had done away with condoms a couple of months earlier and nothing felt better than being bare inside Zaire.

He pressed his cock against Zaire's hole and surged forward, and as he seated himself fully inside his boy, he leaned down and kissed him reverently. Zaire began wriggling underneath him, indicating he was ready for more, and Aaron withdrew and thrust, groaning with the feel of Zaire's inner warmth. After being so long without him—three days was a long time to him—he knew they wouldn't last long, so he didn't mess around. His hips pistoned as Zaire wrapped his legs around Aaron's back, and Aaron slid his arms around Zaire's back. They were as close as they could be, and the position must have been right because Zaire whimpered and gripped Aaron's neck tightly.

"Fuck, my sweet, sweet boy. I'm there. Ah!" Aaron's hips stuttered, and before he released, he felt Zaire tense and a flood of warmth between them as Zaire's ass clenched on his cock. "Fuck!"

They stayed there for several breath-heaving moments before Aaron pulled back after a quick kiss. He stood and fetched a cloth from the bathroom, cleaning them both and settling next to Zaire to pull him into a hug.

"God, I missed you."

"I missed you, too, Daddy."

"How was it?"

Zaire was quiet for a moment, and Aaron allowed him time to collect his thoughts. "It was embarrassing as hell but also cathartic. At least we don't need to hide from her now."

Zaire had visited his mother so he could explain their relationship to her. As he said, he hadn't wanted to be someone different when we were with her, so he'd wanted to tell her everything their relationship involved. Aaron had been surprised but overwhelmingly proud of how far Zaire had come since they'd met.

"How did she take it?" Aaron brushed his fingers through Zaire's hair.

"It took a bit of explaining, hence the embarrassment, but she understood by the end. She doesn't understand why we need it, but she understands we do."

"That's all we need her to. Nobody needs to understand us; just accept us. I'm glad you'll be able to be yourself when you see her."

Chuckling, Zaire said, "Are we really talking about my mother when we are naked on your bed and after doing what we did?"

Aaron laughed, then sobered. "Our."

"What?"

"Our bed." Zaire lifted his head to look at Aaron, a question in his eyes. "I'd like you to move in if you want to."

A brilliant smile crossed his face, and he moved, straddling Aaron and resting his hands either side of his head. "Really, Daddy? Really?"

The child-like excitement was contagious, and Aaron grinned as he slid his hands up Zaire's back. "Really. Truly. Honestly."

"Yes, please, Daddy." Zaire pressed kisses all over his face. "Yes, yes, yes!"

"I'll take it as a yes, shall I?" Aaron laughed.

"Hell, yes!"

Aaron stilled Zaire's movements and locked gazes. "I love you, sweet boy."

"I love you, Daddy."

ZAIRE

ZAIRE THOUGHT back to the conversation he'd had with his mother. It had been one of the most embarrassing moments of Zaire's life, but it needed to happen. His mother had been such an important person in Zaire's life, and now Zaire was embracing both sides of himself, he wanted to ensure he could do so in his mother's company, too.

After the initial explanation and question session about what their kind of relationship was, his mother had agreed, although she didn't understand it, she would never turn him away from it. She made him laugh throughout the weekend with small questions here and there, but she'd hit the nail on the head with one of them.

"Do you think the need to be…free from responsibility has come about because of what happened with your dad?"

Zaire thought about her words and realised the truth to them. "Yes. Whenever my thoughts head in the direction of what happened and what he did, I find myself getting stressed and wanting to hide away from everything. Being a boy helps me to let go of everything for a short time and forget what happened. It allows my brain a chance to recover, rest and rejuvenate, so I can think like a grown-up again."

"I'm so sorry for everything that happened with him. I tried to shield you from it as best as I could. But when he got worse, I did the only thing I knew would work."

Zaire and his mother had a complete heart to heart, and everything was finally settled. He felt much better about the situation, and it was made even better by the arrival of Car. His brother, whom he hadn't seen in around a year, had turned up out of the blue—at least to Zaire, his mother had known—and they'd had a fantastic weekend of reconnecting.

He would have loved to have involved Zena, but he didn't think she would ever forgive him for what she saw as being his fault—breaking up their parents. He may try reconnecting at some point but not right now.

Next weekend, he was taking Aaron to see his mother, and he was excited about it.

Almost as excited as he had been when Aaron had announced he could start at the school again if he wanted to. He'd jumped at the chance as soon as Aaron had explained the rules behind it. Uma had been happy to see him, and Zaire happy to be back with the children again.

Now, he lived as a whole person rather than hiding part of him away. Or at least he was trying. He dressed how he wanted, although he had realised skirts were not the best thing to wear when he would be up and down climbing frames and playing with the kids. He stuck to trousers from then on. He'd even begun wearing natural makeup. There had been some upset about what he wore, to begin with, and some parents had made complaints, but Aaron had arranged a parent's evening so it could be addressed. In his usual straightforward way, he had explained, in no uncertain terms, what was expected of the parents of the school. Questions were asked and answered, and from that moment, no issues were raised.

Occasionally, his old fears came to the forefront when

they were going somewhere new, but Aaron was always there with him in that situation. He never left Zaire to face it alone.

Zaire would never be able to tell Aaron how much he appreciated everything Aaron had done for him. He had literally changed Zaire's life for the better in every perceivable way.

Aaron loved him, and he loved Aaron. What more could he ask for?

HAVE YOU READ THE DADDY/LITTLE book from the Crush series? Love Scene is Book 8 but can be read as a standalone. Eric introduces Samuel to the lifestyle, but there are struggles ahead.

Sign up to my newsletter to get a free Crush prequel short story, Love Conquers and a serial newsletter story every month.

I am Elouise East but feel free to call me Elli. I write sweet and steamy connections in gay romance. I also touch on taboo stories under the name Elouise R East.

Books that tell the stories where friendship and family are the focal point - be it blood family or chosen - is very important to me. That's why I include a variety of personalities, talents, ages, situations and abilities as I believe a story needs, or a character needs. I want my characters to be real, to be relatable, to be free to have whatever views they tell me they have. And trust me, most of the time, I do not have *any* say in the matter!

My characters come to life on the page for me as well as my readers. Their stories unfold in front of me, and I have very little input into how they want to be shown. Just like real life, the lives of my characters change with every choice, every interaction and every conversation. And I wouldn't have it any other way.

I write books that are emotionally realistic, even if liberties are taken with other aspects of my stories. I don't know any other way to write. It comes from deep inside.

Who am I? A single parent to two children who make life worth living. An avid reader who still devours every book she can get her hands on. A student of learning about any subject that takes her fancy. An author of books she would read herself. And a romantic at heart who loves anything cheesy.

Who's in?

———

Stalk me here… ;-)

Website
https://elouiseeast.com/

Newsletter
https://elouiseeast.com/newsletter

All links
https://linktr.ee/elouiseeastauthor

Out of the Frying Pan

Smokescreen

<u>JUST A LITTLE CRUSH</u>

He's Behind You

A Special Love

Three Thirds

<u>DARK & DIVERGENT</u>

Forbidden Temptation

Too Many Secrets

When Fantasies Collide

<u>STANDALONE</u>

Treehouse Whispers

Star-Crossed

Protecting the Thief

Sizzling Chauffeur